SUPER-
HEROES
NEED PR

ALL SUPER-HEROES NEED PR

ELIZABETH STEPHENS

Montlake

Published by Montlake, Seattle

www.apub.com

Amazon, the Amazon logo, and Montlake are trademarks of Amazon.com, Inc., or its affiliates.

EU product safety contact:
Amazon Media EU S. à r.l.
38, avenue John F. Kennedy, L-1855 Luxembourg
amazonpublishing-gpsr@amazon.com

ISBN-13: 9781662523397 (paperback)
ISBN-13: 9781662523403 (digital)

Cover design and illustration by Elizabeth Turner Stokes

Printed in the United States of America

To an eleven-year-old Elizabeth, who wrote her first sci-fi saga on a busted-up computer the size of a planet, for never giving up and bringing me here. I owe you everything.

This book is also dedicated to you, as the child you once were, with big, big dreams.

HEADLINES

Villains Network, championed by the Marduk, launches attack against SDD naval vessel but is met head-on by Champions Taranis and the Olympian. Though the vessel was breached, nothing was reported stolen.

After months of deliberation, Deimos accepts the VNA's bid to become the world's next supervillain, tilting the balance. Villains: 17. Heroes: 16. Amid global concern, Champions Coalition president Mr. Singkham says, "Good will always prevail."

In a surprise bid speculated to be worth over $10 million, Champions counter the VNA for relatively unknown free agent the Pyro.

Champions hire small marketing firm The Riot Creative for the Pyro's rebrand. Will it be zero to hero? Or a wasted effort?

Chapter One

Vanessa

I shuffle the papers in front of me, arranging them until they're perfectly fanned across the conference room table, the headline of each newspaper now visible. My gaze snags on the headline from the *London Champions Daily*, the third largest newspaper globally and the single largest newspaper whose content is exclusively dedicated to the Forty-Eight.

> Taranis, master of lightning, saves pediatric surgeon
> from collapsing at hospital, states, "Some heroes wear
> white coats, not capes."

I push the newspapers out of place so I can see the full picture dominating the space below the headline. I sigh, wishing that *he* was the clay I had to work with. A knight clad in a baby blue so pale it appears white, contrasting against his light-brown skin and accentuating his smile. It's a smile that Margerie would—and has—called *panty-dropping* and that every single person on earth has universally concluded belongs to the most attractive man who ever lived. Except, well, he isn't a *man* exactly.

I think about how effortlessly and elegantly he smiles for the camera. Six foot something. Perfect fade with a trademark lightning bolt shaved behind his right ear. Big purple eyes—not blue, not aqua, but bright violet—that have been on the cover of almost every magazine ever made—that could afford him, anyway. Scary likable. I've met a few folks from Selkie Global, the media firm that manages his PR, and though they've always been tight-lipped about what it's like working with him, I imagine it's a dream. One that I definitely won't have a chance to take part in because he's not the one I'm here to see.

I rearrange the papers so that the *London Champions Daily* is third down instead of right there on top, laughing at me. Because the truth is that I'm the teeniest bit grateful he's *not* the client I'm coming to meet. Taranis is perfect. *Too* perfect. And just so . . . *pretty*. I don't do well with men, pretty ones in particular. I haven't dated a guy seriously since college, and I haven't dated a guy who looks like Taranis *ever*. Men make me nervous. Actually, everything makes me nervous, but guys who look like that? Terrifying.

"Aren't you scared?" I jolt at the sound of Margerie's voice, and she snorts out a laugh that she not at all convincingly disguises as a cough. My chief marketing officer and emotional support person leans into my shoulder and gives the back of my arm a pinch. "What were you daydreaming about?"

"How you move like a ninja in those shoes." I scowl, glaring down at her feet. She's almost six inches taller than I am without heels and chooses to wear stilettos every day to work. These are baby-pink satin and look more expensive than all the shoes in my closet combined. "You'd give any of the Forty-Eight a run for their money in those—literally."

She laughs a little harder, voice more muffled as she covers the bottom half of her face with her notebook. She glances to the glass wall of the conference room, evidently trying not to be overheard by the members of the Champions of Earth Coalition standing on the other side of the glass. The staff are waiting in the hallway—lining the hallway—like a royal congregation welcoming a king. I try to refocus on the feel of the newspaper under my fingertips instead of my next breath, which fails to arrive as promised.

There's so much on the line here—literally, possibly, the fate of the entire world—and somehow me and my small firm are the team that nabbed the short-term contract to convince this mysterious holdout to become a good guy.

A hero.

I shrivel at the thought. "Stop." Margerie's hand comes down on the newspaper stack like the blade of a guillotine on my intrusive thoughts. "Don't panic. We got this."

I nod, but the words I mean to repeat get stuck in my throat. I can't *not* think about the newspaper lying right there on top. Two weeks old—an eternity ago in the eyes of the press—but not wrong . . .

> The Riot Creative is set to be the smallest firm to work with one of the Forty-Eight. Supernatural Defense Department chair says that this shows Mr. Singkham and the Champions "aren't serious" about Pyro acquisition.

After weeks of assessment, my team arrived at the same conclusion. Though we'll be paid for our work on the proposal we put together, there's a strong chance we'll be leaving this office today without anything more than that. Margerie keeps reminding me that to have made it this far is already a success—that we have other clients, that our team is highly skilled, that I formed a company capable of taking on a contract like this in only seven years. Even if there's blowback from this and the Pyro becomes a villain, as we all suspect he will, we're a PR firm specializing in crisis communications. We can recover. And if we don't—if the world burns tomorrow and my company collapses with the rubble—we'll all still be fine. My team is highly skilled, capable of finding new work, and I . . . I could start a new company, but . . .

I don't want to do any of that. I don't want my team to leave me. My social anxiety made hiring people hard enough that I resisted for the first two years, working myself into the ground trying to do everything by myself, until two things happened in the same month: my family staged an intervention and a client fired me. So, after a lot of work with my therapist, I managed to open my mind up to the idea of hiring staff. And I lucked out. I found Margerie.

My core team has been with me for four years now, Margerie for five. I know they'll eventually look for new jobs, take their next steps, form families, move out of Sundale, do normal people things, but my hope is that maybe, just maybe, if we can nail this short-term contract and successfully convince the Pyro to become a hero in the next three months, I can get them the long-term contract. This sexy, massive *ten-year* contract to cover the Pyro's PR for the duration of his contract with the Champions would take us to places I couldn't have ever dreamed of when I started The Riot Creative; my team will all want to stay and I won't have to change anything.

"Hey." Margerie's voice has gone all soft, and I look up at her, and she looks down at me, her perfect eyebrows drawn over a perfect nose. "What did I say?" She says each word carefully, speaking to me like I'm about to have a panic attack.

I am about to have a panic attack. It wouldn't be the first time. I inhale deeply and think how annoyed my therapist would be with me. Not only have I not been doing my breathing exercises, I've stopped breathing altogether.

"We got this," I repeat, knowing that it's not just my fear of abandonment that'll fuel me today. Looking up at Margerie, the truth is that I like my team. The fight for this contract feels like a fight for them in a way that no contract has ever felt before, based on the size, scope, and notoriety of this contract alone. All I can do now is hope and pray the Pyro turns out to be a decent, nice person—well, superbeing—and maybe, maybe, just *maybe* . . . a hero.

Margerie frowns. "Make me believe it."

"We got this?"

Margerie sighs. "We've gone over this. It's worth the risks. The bad stuff is just speculation. All we know for *facts* is that the Pyro is a free agent. The VNA placed a bid. The COE placed another bid. We don't know the amounts, but we know they're attractive enough for him to consider working with the heroes despite the fact that he's never worked with anyone on anything before and doesn't seem to really give a shit about . . . well, anything," she huffs. "That's why we got the bid," she says, trying to be reassuring.

"That's why we got the bid," I repeat, taking another breath in and holding it for five seconds before releasing it between us. "He's not special."

"He's not special."

"We're not special."

"We're fucking great." She grins. "There's a reason we got this contract."

I nod, my lips thinning and my shoulders rolling back. "There's a reason we got this contract."

"We're great."

"*You're* great."

She rolls her eyes, a little blush dotting the tops of her cheeks. Humble, Margerie dislikes receiving compliments almost as much as I do. I know that she's uncomfortable anytime articles mention her as the face of the company—not because she's a trans woman, which is often the source of a lot of mind-numbingly dumb controversy, but because she actually is the nicest person I've ever had the pleasure of knowing and wants me to take credit for some of my ideas when I'd rather not take credit for any of them.

I like the anonymity of being behind the scenes, even if I did found The Riot Creative. It's a bit of an irony, my brother Charlie once pointed out, that I hate being in the public eye even though I run a public-facing media company. But marketing and branding are about so much more than PR. I've always liked the creativity of it, the problem-solving side of it, and I like making good people and products shine.

Though I suppose the Pyro doesn't need much help in the shine department, considering the terrifying scope of his powers . . . I shudder.

"We wouldn't be here if it weren't for you, Madame President." Margerie grips my shoulder and rubs the center of my back through my basic navy blazer. "And I promise we've prepared everything as best we can. We just need to make it through today, like we've practiced. Then you can go back to being the mysterious genius behind the most successful boutique marketing firm in all of North America, and I can go back to taking credit for all of your genius."

She winks. I snort out a short laugh.

She and I both glance at the team scattered about the room, getting all the packets and snacks laid out and fretting over the projector for the thousandth time, and I can't help the swell of pride I feel watching them, the comfort I feel with them. I take another breath, hold it, and sigh. "I know no one thinks this is real, but I think we can get this contract."

"That's the spirit." She beams. "If today goes well—which it will— we'll get the extended long-term contract to manage the Pyro's PR, which will feed our children's children's children. So don't go doubting us now, after all we did to get here."

I nudge her hip with mine. "You don't even want kids."

"Damn straight. But that doesn't mean I don't want to use my kids' kids' kids' money to buy a yacht and retire at thirty-eight."

"If you retire at thirty-eight, I will knife you."

Margerie's laugh booms through the room, loud enough to turn heads. It wrenches an unwilling, choked laugh out of me, and several other members of my team start laughing too, even though they have no idea what we're talking about. Margerie's laugh has that effect.

"Come on, let's go reorganize the packets for the thirtieth time while we wait for his late ass to show up."

"Let me check the presentation again . . ."

"No . . . you already did that four hundred times over coffee this morning. Let's do the packets. Also, you never answered my question."

"What question?"

"Whether or not you're scared."

"Of him? Of meeting one of the Forty-Eight?" I ask, genuinely confused.

She rolls her eyes, and her perfect mermaid waves shift elegantly around her shoulders; she's the spitting image of Ariel. I have long, voluminous curls that are the same length as Margerie's but lack all the civility of hers. "Of course."

I blink again, still unsure if we're speaking the same language. A small spike of embarrassment I don't usually feel around Margerie shoots up the back of my neck as I try to make sense of what she's said. "Oh. No?"

"No?" She smiles and follows me as I make a second round around the table, pushing packets around and carefully making sure everything is even and equidistant. Pen, packet, pencil—it's all in a perfect line, all thirteen places around the table. I force myself to stop when Margerie suggests that the breakfast spread could use a little sprucing. "So you're really not scared? Not even a little bit?"

"What would I have to be scared about?"

"I've never met one of the Forty-Eight in person, and I know you haven't either. And it's not like we're meeting Taranis either," she says, jerking her thumb over her shoulder toward the papers on the table and the most prominent recent *London Champions* headline. "This guy is kind of supposed to be the worst."

"Not the *worst*, just . . . unknown . . ."

"Idle."

"Allegedly . . ."

"And when he does get involved, it's to blow up shit that's kind of important."

"Never without cause."

"Yes, it's *because* he's the worst. He blew up the historic Old Sundale Bank."

"He was only twenty-one . . ."

"He still blew it up!"

"While there was a robbery in progress . . ."

"Everybody knows there's no money in that place. The robbers were morons . . ."

"And *robbers*. What they were doing was illegal . . ."

Margerie's raspy whisper rises up into a high squeak when she says, "He lit them on fire!"

I . . . hesitate, snapping on gloves as I prepare to rearrange the croissants for the second time. I long to throw out three of them that are smushed or broken, but I force myself to move on to the fruit tray. "Well, I guess that's true."

Margerie coughs to cover her laugh. "Okay, I'm officially a bad person. I should not be laughing at that." She looks up at the projector as the screen saver changes slides to a different historic landing spot—this one is Pele's. She landed in Hawaii, fitting given that she can control lava with nothing more than her mind.

She was the fourth member of the forty-eight superbeings who crash-landed on Earth as children. With no memory of where they came from but with extraordinary gifts, the Forty-Eight were welcomed by humanity with surprising civility. After the initial arrival, they were placed within host families under the care of the SDD, the Supernatural Defense Department. They were studied, but overall an attempt was made to integrate them into our world.

It worked . . . for the most part. But when the kids started to get older, some of them showed troubling signs. Some became . . . destructive. The Meinad was then officially termed a *villain*—a young boy who clawed apart his host parents. He went on to join with the Marduk, whose power over thunder was used to wreak havoc on the city in which they lived—not far from Sundale, actually.

Together, only in their early teens, the two of them formed what's now known as the VNA, the Villains Network of America. They have branches all over the world now, with seventeen supervillains contracted to cause chaos. They rob, steal, and take contracts to kill. They are indiscriminate in the kinds of mayhem they engage in. But why?

No one really knows. In a historic interview two years ago that my team would have done terrible things to be a part of, the Marduk was asked why he had formed the VNA and what its purpose was, and he'd just smiled at the camera, all cavalier and beautiful, and said, "I'm looking for something."

"What?" the journalist had followed up.

"You'll know when I find it."

The landscape on the projector screen changes to Sundale's very own Memory Park, where Taranis landed. The Champions of Earth Coalition was formed as a counter to the villains soon after the Marduk and the Meinad teamed up. That's where capitalism came in, with the COE paying forty-eight members to join the heroes team. In his midteens, Taranis became the first to sign up. Some of the Forty-Eight have remained holdouts all this time, like the Pyro, but . . .

"He's here," I say, clenched, eyes catching on the glass. People have started stirring. There's some commotion outside. Jeremy and Dan are doing a power-suit sprint over to us—an event I decide should most definitely be entered as an Olympic discipline. They're both huge comic book nerds, and meeting one of the Forty-Eight has been on their collective bucket list for years.

"You still want me to lead the presentation, Madame President?" Margerie whispers in my ear.

"Of course."

"You sure?" She huffs quietly, "This is our biggest bid, and nobody knows his feelings on trans women yet."

My nerves are disrupted by what she's just said. I blink up at her. "Nobody said anything to you, did they?" If they did, I was fully ready to take a page out of the Pyro's notebook and set the building on fire.

Margerie gives me a flat look. "No, *Mom*. Nobody's been anything but nice and professional."

"Good." This wasn't always the case. A Black woman–founded corporate consulting firm with a white trans woman CMO wasn't always met with open arms. Don't even mention the fact that the rest of the C-suite's members were either minorities, queer, or both. A couple times, we'd even won blind bids and still been denied the contract, the client preferring to go with someone who had the kind of *face* they wanted to represent their firm.

"Then we go as planned."

"You, our mysterious brain? Me, the face?"

"That sounds like the plot of a horror movie."

Margerie laughs as we're separated by Dan's and Jeremy's jostling bodies. Dan grabs my shoulders and shakes me.

"He's here!" His voice is a squeal. He's older than I am by a couple years, but right now he sounds like he's six instead of that plus thirty. Dan grabs my arm too hard, pinching me above the elbow until I make a sound. "Sorry, sorry!" he whisper-shouts.

"Shush! And don't bruise her damn arm." Jeremy pushes me from behind, tugging down on the short cap sleeves of my white button-up. I paired it with navy pants that I think make my butt look gigantic and accentuate the pouch below my belly button, but Dan and Jeremy and Margerie said it looked good, even if they did try to convince me to wear the lavender two-piece—*lavender*. Maybe Margerie can pull off pastels, but I like the dark colors. They help me blend in to the wallpaper better.

"Would y'all stop it?" Margerie hisses.

Dan and Jeremy don't stop it, and soon my entire team is crowded near the swinging glass double doors. I'm somewhere in the middle, Garrison on my left, Jem up in front of me, Vanya at my back.

"Y'all, assume the position! Not this position!" Margerie quickly shoves everyone back. "Not you!" She grabs my shoulder and wrenches me forward just as Mr. Singkham's assistant comes bustling down the hall.

She opens the door and looks at me. "Ms. Theriot, the Pyro has just arrived. While we clear him with security, Mr. Singkham will be arriving shortly to greet you. When the Pyro comes up, your team can begin your presentation."

She must see something on my face because she pauses as she shuts the door and adds, "Nothing to worry about, Ms. Theriot. The same proposal you provided us is sure to wow him as well." She beams, her face lighting up.

That was a written proposal—a written *proposal.*

"Thank you, Mrs. Morales," Margerie says, while I stand just in front of her in a position a Valkyrie would take in front of her army . . . except I feel like a lamb next up at the slaughter.

Mrs. Morales gives Margerie a warm smile and a nod and gives me a confused look that I'm a little used to. *Is she okay?* No. No, I'm not okay. I'm about to have explosive diarrh—

"He's here!" Jeremy speaks in an even higher pitch than Dan had.

"False alarm, Jer," Dan says, pushing Jeremy away from the door so he can pull it open for the COE president, Mr. Singkham, or . . . wait, should I call him Kun Prasit? Mrs. Morales referred to him as Kun Prasit in several emails. I looked it up—it's an honorific in Thailand—but as an American who hasn't had much chance to travel and doesn't have a whole lot of Thai friends (*try friends, full stop*), I'm not sure how to address him in person. Holy moly. I'm going to botch the first words I ever say to him in person.

There's no time to debate it with the team. There's no way to grab Margerie and thrust her in front of me either. Because, to my horror, he's there in the flesh, his dark hair elegantly arrayed, his finely tailored suit making me feel like I'm meeting the president of a country, not the president of a coalition, an intragovernmental agency with all the power of the world's top leading economies and ten times the revenue of the NFL.

He enters the room, and his eyes settle immediately on me. "Ms. Theriot," he says, his French pronunciation of my name making me realize that not only do I not have a title for him, I don't even know how to pronounce his title—either version. "It's a pleasure to have you here. Thank you so much for waiting. It would seem that our guest has finally decided to grace us with his presence." He gives a light, warm chuckle and a little shake of his head and I stare at him, petrified enough to keep from collecting all the packets, tossing them up into the air, and running out of the room screaming.

"And this is your team," Mr. Singkham prompts when I say nothing, gesturing to my staff. I nod. His smile starts to waver.

My jaw starts to work, and when I still come up with nothing, Margerie smoothly intervenes. "Mr. Singkham, I'm Margerie Gates. Thank you so much for accepting our bid. Our team has the utmost confidence we'll be able to build a brand the Pyro—and your team— will be proud to represent and that, at the end of this first probationary month, should he accept, the Pyro will want to stick around." She gives him a wink. A *wink!* How does she make it look casual and not awkward? I can't wrap my head around it. Anytime I practice winking at myself in the mirror, I look like I'm broken.

Mr. Singkham's eyes crinkle at the corners, and he takes her hand, giving her an almost scarily manicured smile. "I appreciate your team's confidence, as well as your proposal."

"Our CEO can be credited with the bulk of the brilliance," Margerie says, tossing the puck back to me. Is that the expression? Can you toss a puck? Pass one maybe, but toss? That would be more like a softball. But I'm pretty sure you lob a softball . . .

I realize that Margerie's chucked the ball directly at my head, and Mr. Singkham's attention has returned to me along with it. The regular thing to do right now would be to say something.

I choke, body flushing with heat. I put on deodorant this morning, but I'm suddenly regretting not having worn black everything. "It was a team effort."

Mr. Singkham smiles more fully. Margerie directs his attention away from me and introduces the team, Dan and Jeremy, COO and CFO of the company respectively. They all shake hands while I shift to the side, hoping to lob the baton back to Margerie standing at the front of the room. Too bad it's a boomerang.

"And of course, you've already spoken with our CEO and founder, Ms. Vanessa Theriot. And apologies, but I must confirm: should we refer to you as Kun Prasit or Mr. Singkham? And another apology if I'm pronouncing those incorrectly. Growing up in Wisconsin helps very little when it comes to my prowess in phonetics." Her smile is bright. As is Mr. Singkham's as he then confirms that he's adapted to the American style of salutation since working in this country for over a decade. Mr. Singkham is fine.

I'm both grateful and a little humiliated when his attention turns to Margerie more fully. "Our potential client is being escorted up now by my team. How would you like my staff and I arranged? We will be six, including the Pyro."

I edge back, using Margerie's outstretched arm for cover as she gestures toward the conference room table and says, "Yes, please come on in. We'll have you here at the head of the table. Our CEO will be positioned at this end. Dan, Jeremy, and I will occupy two seats as we'll take turns standing as we conduct the presentation, though our other staff members will be positioned at that back table to take notes. If you have a reporter of your own who you'd like to take notes, we can put them here at this additional spare table . . ."

As Mr. Singkham's attention turns toward the back of the room and the small table in question, I try to use the opportunity to make it to my seat, except Jeremy's there and I run into his shoulder face-first. "You okay, boss?" he mouths to me, grabbing me by the shoulders.

Embarrassed, I step back, but my short heel plunges into Dan's foot. He curses. I turn and open my mouth to mutter a quick apology, but another voice cuts through first.

"What's wrong with you?" The voice is deep, acidic, and frighteningly calm as it claims the attention of every person in the room. Margerie stops talking midsentence. I look up toward the door. Shadowed slightly by Mr. Singkham's frame is a much, much larger individual whose presence feels like a storm.

He looks like he just came *in* from a storm. His black hair hangs long and evidently untrimmed down to his chin, brushing the stretched collar of his shirt in the back. His beard is just as uncared for, thick and rough. His T-shirt is black and has a hole over the stomach the size of a softball and large enough to reveal . . . uhh . . . abs . . . or, more accurately, a *ripped* abdomen.

His sweatpants have holes over both knees and one on the thigh that I'm grateful isn't three inches higher up. His boots are so badly scuffed, I don't think the sole is attached to the shoe because it flaps when he shifts his position, taking a half step back as if struck by shock. And I realize as my gaze travels back up from his feet to his face that he might be. Because his full red lips are tight and his thick black eyebrows are drawn together, the expression on his face excoriating. He's glaring right at me.

Right.

At.

Me.

And his eyes are *glowing*.

Air that tastes of chicory fear and saccharine embarrassment slams into me as I watch his lips whisper words that feel meant for me alone: *"What are you?"*

My left knee buckles, and I swoon—*swoon*—like some Victorian-era maiden with her corset tied too tight to breathe. I start to fall. The unfamiliar male who looks like he just came in from a bar brawl lunges, pushing past Mr. Singkham and causing the older man to stumble directly into Garrison, who's holding a cup of coffee. It goes flying.

Jem screams, "Not my hair!" Mrs. Morales drops the stack of papers she's holding. Jeremy surges to try to stop *something*, slips on the papers, and falls over backward. Dan tries to catch him. They both collide with the rolling chairs, which scatter. Margerie releases a loud "Ooph!" As a chair hits her in the knee, she topples over and Vanya opens her arms to catch her, but Vanya is half Margerie's size, and they both go down onto the hardwood. The entire crowd has dispersed into chaos around me, which means there's nothing to stop the Pyro from reaching me.

He arrives in front of me in the time it takes for me to blink and catches my arm. His hand is a shade of brown darker than mine. Huge, it envelops my elbow, holding me upright and keeping me from falling. We're the only two at this point who aren't leaning against a wall or table or scattered like bowling pins across the floor. And he doesn't seem to notice.

He's too busy invading my space, staring at me in a way that makes my toes actually curl. His eyes are blazing white until spots of pink start to flutter through them, and my mouth is hanging open in dumbfounded shock. I can't get past his pink-and-white eyes ringed in heavy black lashes, looking like fireworks. Staring into them directly is like staring at the sun during an eclipse. I feel . . . woozy.

I waver on my feet, and the Pyro drags me to the left. He pushes me in front of him so I'm forced to walk backward. My ankle rolls, and my arms windmill to catch myself. The Pyro curses.

"Clumsy," he hisses and grabs my waist. He lifts me up and plonks my ass down on the edge of the table, then slams his hands down onto the sleek charcoal-gray tabletop on either side.

"You . . ." he snarls, and a deep rumbling fills the air with what can only be described as vibrations. Chills shoot through my body as the overwhelming sense that something impossible—or at least deeply improbable—is happening and that I'm not prepared for it. I am just a simple human, with deep insecurities underpinned by a whole heap of anxieties, who happens to be good—really good—at marketing. I'm not meant for supernatural shit.

I sit up straight. I feel like I've been tased. He steps back like he felt it too. Someone shouts behind the eclipse of his body, "Earthquake!" which is my thought, too, until he shakes his head so subtly I think I might be the only one who sees it.

His eyes flare bright white, and when he clenches his jaw and the little vein across his forehead pulses and the muscle twitches beneath his left eye, I finally understand the intensity he's throwing at me like a javelin. I can finally put a name to it.

Hate.

This man—male—hates me, even though I've never met him before in my life. And then, as Mr. Singkham and Margerie attempt to restore order and Jeremy approaches the Pyro from the side, the Pyro acts.

He lashes out, his arm moving with shocking speed as he grabs Jeremy by the front of his button-up. He drags Jeremy in close. He does all this without ever once looking away from my face with those eyes that were once white and are now flickering with pinks and faint oranges.

He points at my face in a way that spells trouble. My parted lips flounder, working but saying nothing. It wouldn't matter, anyway. I don't think I could say anything to stop these trains from colliding, my career the innocent bystander tied to the tracks between them.

"I want her gone."

Chapter Two

VANESSA

"It wasn't that bad," Margerie insists for the four hundredth time since arriving at Bah Bah Black Bar. It's already packed, the bar area more so than the restaurant side, so we head there, Dan and Jeremy crowding after Margerie and me, Garrison and Vanya pushing ahead of us, Jem leading the charge. We snag a high top, the last one available, and Jeremy immediately orders a round of red wine for everyone.

"Red wine?" Vanya asks as she slides onto the stool between Margerie and me. She's fresh out of her master's program, a Russian woman who majored in Arabic. Immediately afterward, she realized she didn't want to become a career diplomat, as she'd always envisioned, and was desperate for a job, and I wasn't stupid enough to let her slip through my fingers when her résumé landed on my desk. She's a genius, and if we'd landed that COE contract, I'd have had enough to give her a significant pay raise. Combined with my incessant prayers, I'd have stood a good chance of her not getting poached. Now I'll be lucky if any of them last the week. For the thousandth time, I flush, embarrassment making me choke.

I think the sheer overwhelming force of my embarrassment is the reason I'm here at this bar to begin with. I *never* go to bars. Never ever never. Too big a chance for strangers to try to talk to me—but after the day I've had?

The waiter slides a glass of dark-red liquid in front of me and I sniffle once into my glass before taking a sip. And then a bigger sip. "Tastes good," I mumble. There's a lipstick stain on the rim, but I don't even bother sending it back. I just wipe it off and keep going. *That's* how far gone I am already, and I've only had a few sips. I'm surprised I didn't break down in the bathroom, but I think the strange feeling in the pit of my stomach kept me from it. Shock, probably.

Meeting one of the Forty-Eight turned out to be just as traumatic as I imagined it might be. Maybe Elena is right. Maybe there is something off about them and they should never have come here. Or maybe the problem wasn't with him. Maybe it was *me?*

"That's because it's a day red," Jeremy answers as if that means something.

"Day red?" Vanya smirks, then her expression switches to something more appreciative as she brings the glass against her glossy red lips. "Wow. That's delicious."

"Strong." Jem makes a face and whispers something under her breath in Amharic. She's head of my legal team and the most impossible-to-please woman I've ever met. She's only been working for me for six months, way overqualified and way beyond our budget, but she's amazing. If she doesn't turn in her resignation Monday, I'll have to make a sacrifice to whatever god takes sacrifices and has a special affinity for legal.

"I know. Fabulous, isn't it?" Dan adds, releasing a sigh as he sips happily, his hand on Jeremy's thigh under the table.

"What makes it a day red?" Jem says, hailing a waiter and ordering a margarita instead. Mezcal. Top shelf.

Jeremy loops his arm over the back of Dan's high stool and makes a reproachful sound as he toasts his glass of day red in Jem's direction. She hisses at him, actually hisses, like a cat. He laughs, actually laughs—like we weren't fired only an hour ago!—and says, "It's an easy-drinking red wine, dry but with fruity forward notes, that's served chilled and cures any and all instances of did-that-meeting-really-just-happen and I-can't-believe-what-an-asshole-the-Pyro-turned-out-to-be. Womp womp. What a disappointment."

"Meeting your childhood heroes always is," Jem says.

"Or your childhood villains?" Vanya adds, making Margerie and Jem laugh despite her cynicism. "What did you even expect from him? He gets a perfectly adequate subsidy from the SDD, doesn't need to work, gets to sit around on his butt all day and do nothing if he feels like it."

She shrugs and drains the rest of her glass in one swallow, then flips back her blond hair. Her bright-red lipstick screams confidence, and I envy her in this moment, how flippantly she seems to be able to shrug off such a brutal and unwarranted rejection. But then again, she didn't feel the full force of his ire like I did—ire and whatever *else* that was.

Jeremy huffs. "I don't know. I expected *something* else. More. The other Champions go out and save people from burning buildings, act where the police and emergency workers are too slow or in places they can't access. Fight the villains. And even if he was a villain, I thought he'd be more . . . like . . . I don't know! Cool, I guess."

"He was pretty hot, though," Dan adds, winning him an elbow to the ribs from his partner.

Jeremy smiles, his cheeks turning pink. "Okay, yeah. He was, kinda. In a rugged, unwashed mountain man kinda way."

"Are you all insane? He was rude, a scoundrel. I didn't like him one bit," Jem says.

"Is that a line from *The Mummy?*" I mumble.

Jem winks at me. "Of course. But I'm serious. Did you see his clothes? They had holes all over them, and he looks like he hasn't shaved his beard in three weeks." Her perfectly coiffed curls bounce around her cheeks as she shakes her head in disgust. "He was exactly as expected. Boring and full of himself—as all the Forty-Eight are. I'm glad we didn't get the contract. We've gotten dozens of other proposals that Jeremy and

I have been weeding through since our bid was accepted by the COE and the press had a field day dogging us—good proposals. I'm excited to get back to the office and have a look. What do you say?"

I realize she's talking to me and wrinkle my nose, drain my day red, and then roll my shoulders back. "You're right." *But you didn't feel what I felt. Not the energy. Not the humiliation.* "You're right. I just hope you all aren't too disappointed . . ."

A collective groan goes up from the team members gathered around me. Embarrassed, I look away and find the waiter, order another round, and distract myself with day red when the waiter returns with full, fresh glasses.

"It's not like we had real hope of convincing him to the good side. Chances are he's working with the VNA anyway," Dan adds.

Nodding all around helps ease my humiliation. "Probably," I whisper.

"And after how he treated you, we wouldn't want to work with him anyway," Margerie adds.

"Well . . ." Dan starts.

I feel my cheeks heat and watch as Vanya and Dan exchange a few words in Arabic. I can tell Vanya is admonishing him in her standard Arabic mixed with the Egyptian she learned studying abroad, while Dan replies in his Syrian dialect. She rolls her eyes at whatever he says, but I don't want to hear the translation. I just want the day to be over.

Jeremy—who's been learning Arabic for Dan, his partner—asks Vanya, "Did you just call him an ass?"

"Yes. I told him he has a red ass, like a baboon."

Everyone laughs at that—except me. "I just . . . don't know what I did so wrong," I say, my voice a little slurred. Very slurred? I'm not totally sure. How many glasses have I had now? The waiter keeps coming back with more. How long has it been since we got here?

I glance at my wristwatch, but my wrist is bare because I've never worn a watch in my entire life. We've been here an hour so far? Maybe fifteen minutes? My team shushes me with docile platitudes, Margerie and Garrison leaning in from either side to give me one-armed hugs. I shrug them off and try to shrug out of my jacket, but I'm not wearing a jacket. Was I wearing one when I started the day? Such a hopeful girl I was back then. Back before I fell and the entire room fell apart around me.

"You didn't do anything wrong."

"You guys haven't even let me talk about me falling," I all but wail. "That was an insane domino effect."

"Because it wasn't a big deal," Margerie says, squeezing me tighter and trying to shush me at the same time.

"I don't even know what you're talking about," Garrison adds, but he's hiding his smile in his glass, and when I elbow him in the ribs, he chokes and red wine dribbles down his chin and onto his tie.

Even though Garrison moved from Tokyo three years ago, he hasn't adapted to the more relaxed corporate culture of our office. I don't mind what anybody wears, so long as they are actually serious when they say that losing the contract won't cause them to run shrieking from our offices Monday morning.

"I think even Mrs. Morales ended up on the floor," Jem grumbles. "You got coffee in my hair," she accuses.

She and Jeremy start bickering back and forth while my head continues to swim. I think I . . . drank too much. Not wanting to be seen completely plastered in front of my team, I excuse myself and make it to the bathroom. Hiccuping on my way back, I come to a stop, debating . . .

What's the worse option?

Be seen completely sloshed by all my team members I just made a total idiot of myself in front of earlier today? Or take a chance at potentially having to talk to someone I don't know at the bar as I get a water?

I glance at the daylight streaming in all the way at the other end of the bar. *I can do this,* I think, taking a deep breath and veering away from the restaurant area into the bar. Spring has sprung early this year.

It's only barely April, but I still haven't needed a proper coat for two weeks now. That also means the darkest evenings are behind us.

Someone bumps into me from behind. They apologize at the same time I do, and I quickly duck and make my way forward, squeezing myself through a crowd made up of folks off work early on a Friday until I finally reach the bar's sleek black concrete countertop.

Call it luck of the day red, but as soon as my fingers touch down onto the bar, the couple sitting to my right slides off their stools. With a meek smile, I quickly take one of them at the same time that a my age-ish man takes the other. Our eyes meet as we take our seats, and he winks at me. I force my face to form a small, awkward smile, which he returns in a much more natural way.

He's got brown hair and perfectly clear white skin with a blush in his cheeks that would make most women envious. He's wearing a badge of some kind clipped between two of the buttons of his shirt. I don't get a good look at it, distracted and startled when he asks me what I'm drinking.

"I, uh, um—it's day red." I flush. "But I was going to get a wa—"

"Day red?" He smirks at me, cutting me off, his blue eyes bright.

"I . . ." I swallow hard, nervous that I might be sweating again. "My friends got the first round—" The first three—four? Good grief. "I'm not sure what it's called."

I feel a blush rush to my cheeks as his gaze drops to my outfit. I'm wearing my clothes from the meeting. They're all rumpled now. His gaze lingers on my legs, and I get that uncomfortable feeling that he's judging me and place my hands awkwardly over my knees.

The bartender fortunately interrupts us then, and my stool neighbor orders me a glass of merlot—not day red, sadly, and not a water, even more tragically—and himself a rum and Coke. Then he sticks out his hand. I take it automatically, unsure of how to get myself out of this, and let him shake my arm like it's jelly while he says, "I'm Jeremy."

"Jeremy? That's funny. My coworker's name is Jeremy. He's right over there in the restaurant area."

Jeremy—new Jeremy—looks over my shoulder, trying to root him out. His eyebrows furrow a little. The bartender slides our drinks across the table. "Your coworker waiting on you?" I don't know why he says the word with such sudden hostility.

"Uhh . . . they might be?" I want to get back to them, but the heat in my face and chest has melted me to my seat. My stomach is a bundle of nerves. This is why I should have chosen the awkwardness of being drunk around my colleagues. At least I know them. Now I have to somehow get myself out of this. Panic!

My brain fires in every direction, anxiety making my stomach lurch, but I focus on my breath, on counting up to three, and then ten, and then finally on his next question.

"You're with a group?" I feel like he's accusing me of something, and I wrinkle my nose.

"Yeah, I should, uhh . . . probably get back," I say brittlely.

But he perks up. "I didn't get your name."

"Vanessa. Sorry." I wince as I apologize again.

"No worries. You okay to stay and chat? At least until you finish your day red?"

I shuffle on my stool and give him a tight, nervous nod. Jeremy smiles and swivels on his seat until his knees point toward me. "What do you do, Miss Vanessa?" I notice him glance at my left hand and feel my fingers tingle. I'm not wearing any jewelry at all, so there's nothing to mistake there for a wedding ring.

"Marketing." My voice is soft. I'd meant for it to be louder. I drink my merlot even though I shouldn't. The world is tilting sideways, and my words are coming out syrupier than they should. I should get back to my coworkers, but he's already bought me a wine . . . and I don't know how to extract myself from this. You'd think with five brothers I might have developed a better sense of men in general, but they might have actually been a hindrance given how obnoxiously overprotective they are of me.

I love them for it deeply.

"Marketing?" He leans in closer. "Like an associate or an intern or something like that?"

I nod quickly and drink more of my wine. "Yes." And then I clear my throat, eager to divert his focus anywhere but toward me. "What do you do?"

He points at his name tag, a confusing action. He seems proud to be wearing his name badge at happy hour, pointing at it like I've asked him for his name and he's forgotten but is proud at least to have written it down.

QNTEQ is what it reads, though I have no idea how to pronounce it. I smile and say, "Wow. Sounds fancy." I wrinkle my nose, hoping I don't sound too dismissive, but I don't want to pronounce it wrong, and I'm guessing by the way he shows off his badge so proudly that he assumes I should be excited about Centech? Cue-en-tech? Q-and-tech?

"I like to think so." He seems satisfied by my reaction and slides his hand across the bar closer to mine. "You know, you're really cute." My eyes widen. I feel totally unprepared for this level of flirtation and wonder if I've misheard him through the haze of day red. His hand edges a little closer, fingers brushing mine, and I jerk, lifting my glass too forcefully and sloshing red wine over the lip of the glass and onto my shirt.

"Ohmigosh, I'm so sorry. I've really had too much . . . day red . . ." I scramble for a napkin, but I haven't released my glass and end up spilling more of it onto the bar counter. He chuckles, and with the ease of someone to which everything in life comes easily, he reaches behind the bar and grabs a wad of napkins from a holder.

"Oh, thanks," I say, stuttering wildly, but he doesn't hand them to me and instead moves them toward my chest where red wine seeps through my shirt over my bra.

"It's all right," he says in a deeper voice than he'd been using. "I can tell you're shy." I'm shocked stiff, stunned in disbelief and far, far too gone to stop this train smash. I just watch, my jaw hinged open as this strange man reaches for my *boob*—my *actual* breast—and says, "I like shy girls . . ."

He touches my chest—the upper curve of my boob where the bones of my chest soften out into full D cups—and the glass I'd been drunkenly wielding like a baton tumbles toward the floor. I watch it happen in slow motion, breath gathering in my mouth as I wait for everyone in the bar to turn at the sound of smashing glass and see me sitting here, white shirt covered in red, a random guy who can't remember his own name and has to keep it written down on his lapel pawing at me in a way that would have made all five of my brothers smash chairs and beat their chests.

But my brothers aren't here, and even though I manage multimillion-dollar advertising budgets for some of the country's biggest brands, I suddenly can't remember a damn thing my therapist has been telling me the past two years I've been seeing her to tackle situations like this.

I can even hear that boundaries song they make little kids learn playing on a broken loop in my head. Because being touched without permission, and by a stranger no less? It's triggering something deeper than that. As if my social anxiety is just the Band-Aid covering wounds too deep to stitch. And trust me, I've tried, but every time I do, I end up bleeding all over the place.

Stop crying, and get up off the floor. I didn't even hit you that hard. You're such a little shit, Vanessa.

"*Vanessa.*" The word washes over me in a whispered hush. No breeze off the sea ever felt so lovely or so warm. The strange thing is, I'm not sure the word was said aloud. My ears cock, but all I hear are the sounds from the bar. But that breeze? That decadent rush of heat followed by cool? My spine arches as I suck in a breath, and my whole body sways toward it. I open my eyes . . . and would have jumped out of my own skin if I weren't attached to it.

The Pyro is standing there. Right there. Head lowered, nose only a foot away from mine. He's staring into my eyes, and as I register their pretty shape, I notice the same miraculous thing I did earlier when he had me in a position not utterly unlike this one, seated on the tabletop in that boardroom.

"Pink." It takes me a moment to realize the word belongs to me.

The Pyro has the same medium-dark-brown skin and jet-black hair I recognize from every photo of him ever taken, the same full lips, pretty mouth, high cheekbones decorated by thick scruff rolling down a brutal jaw, but his eyes . . . There's no doubting it this time. His eyes are a deep, striated pink. Fuchsia toward his pupils, darker and wine colored on the outsides.

I open my mouth and . . . burp. The cold hand of humiliation is valiantly trying to creep up my spine, but it's having a hard time getting past that lingering warmth. It doesn't seem squashable, not even when the Pyro's lips flatten and a muscle underneath his left eye twitches.

And that's when it finally hits me, what's so off about his expression and demeanor and hard-cut countenance: he's *pissed*.

He slams the glass—my glass—down onto the bar top beside me, bracketing me within the cage of his arms and chest. My back presses against the bar top as I try to make space between us, and my strange, treacherous body doesn't know what to do with the closeness. I flounder and repeat, "Your eyes are pink."

"I fucking know that. Why was that dead man groping your chest?"

"Dead . . . dead man?" I glance to my left where Jeremy was sitting a second before, only to find the barstool empty and Jeremy motionless on the floor. The people who were standing behind us have cleared out a small space, but not a soul has reached out to help him.

"Is he . . ." I gasp, horror flooding my veins. I reach up, touch my mouth, and whisper through the gaps between my fingers, "Did you kill him?"

"No. Why was he touching you?" He fires his words like bullets, and I'm struck by every one.

I reach for a shield, but my hands come up empty, so I carry on. "I . . . spilled."

"You wanted his hands on you? You know him?"

"I . . ." I shake my head in a very small gesture.

The Pyro curses and makes a lunging gesture toward the motionless man on the floor that almost makes me fall off my stool. His hand shoots out. He catches my elbow.

I hiccup. "D-don't . . ." I start, wanting to tell him not to hurt the guy on the floor any more than he has already, but his eyes have narrowed even further. He lets me go like touching me pains him, flexing his hands as he draws them back toward his pockets, and my voice trails off.

"You pissed?" he hisses.

It takes me way too long to understand the question. I point at him first, then at me. "You . . . *you're* pissed," I answer, distracted when two random guys, also wearing name tags with the same Q symbol printed on them in huge block letters, scuttle forward and grab Jeremy by the arms. They drag him away, throwing cautious and curious glances back at the Pyro while Jeremy's hair collects the red wine I spilled all over the floor. I wonder if those men recognize the Pyro. For the sake of whoever lands his PR contract later, I certainly hope they don't—and for my sake, I pray. I do not want to be caught on camera beside him, especially in my current not-so-sober state.

"I meant, are you drunk?" Though he's speaking at a normal volume and the room is loud, he feels louder. His cheek ticks, and that vein in his forehead is standing out. I realize too late that every single part of him is impossibly tightly clenched . . . and he's a dangerous male. No, he's a male capable of incredible violence. And I'm just . . .

Drunk. "Yes." I hiccup, as if to accentuate the point. I could have told him I'm tipsy or not *that* drunk really, because if I'm being honest, I have been drunker than this a few times before.

The first time, my brother David added vodka to the house orange juice, trying to get back at my other brother Vinny for some reason nobody can remember now. I'd been fourteen and hadn't had alcohol before, and I just thought the OJ was off. Unfortunately, I threw up all over Vinny, so David's revenge plan sort of worked. Fortunately, I hadn't yet made it out of the house.

The memory triggers my gag reflex, and my stomach clenches with force. I meet and hold the Pyro's stare with a boldness that's only fueled by a desperation to keep the vomit *down*.

The Pyro looks down, his nostrils flaring for a moment, then, just as quickly, he wrenches back like he senses what's about to happen. I burp again and slap my palm over my mouth. The Pyro glares at me.

"You let him call you an intern." Orange blazes in his pink irises so brightly, it expels light onto his cheeks.

The taste of wine crawls up the back of my throat, and I fight it *down*. I nod. I don't need to explain to this supernatural maniac that I can create pivot tables with conditional formatting encompassing decades of data in just a few minutes just as easily as I can illustrate short animated videos for ads but can't tell a guy at a bar no.

He makes that same rumbling sound he did four hours ago, right before he kicked my sorry ass out of the building, and this time I know I'm not imagining it. I can see movement past his impossibly broad shoulders. People are starting to stare and point at him, sure, but also at *me*. My stomach clenches. No no no no no no no. This can't be happening . . .

He doesn't seem to realize how close we are to doom because he doesn't back up. He doesn't even cast a cursory glance over his shoulder. His intensity is just as brutal and fixed to me as it was earlier. "Why aren't you with your people? Why are you over here by yourself?"

I reach up and hold my left temple. My adrenaline is peaking. I need some air.

"Hey." His voice is hard as brick and so is his hand as it shackles my upper arm. I cringe away from the violent touch, extracting myself from it while my stomach completes another revolution around a dark sun. "Hey." He lets me go immediately, and when he speaks next, his voice is a little softer than it was. "Did he hurt you?"

I shake my head. "I have . . . anxiety," I say simply, hoping that's enough. I certainly have no intention of giving him my full medical history here or ever. I just need him to give me grace, and I'm shocked as hell when he does.

"Fuck." He takes a step away from me and curses under his breath twice more in quick succession. "I'm sorry, okay?"

The words are such a shock, I get a pang in the left side of my neck with how fast I whip my head up to look at him. His expression hasn't changed *much*. He's still glaring at me like I stole his ice cream, only now there's a crease between his thick eyebrows, he's got his arms crossed over his chest, and his eyes are white instead of pink or orange.

"Okay?" he repeats more angrily this time.

"Oh . . . kay."

"I need you to get the fuck out of here." He points at the exit, not that I can see it through the sudden mass of people who are staring. Some have their phones out, and I can see little beams of light shining our way.

Oh no. No, please no.

I'm shaking my head, but he doesn't understand. I'm not telling him no. I'd love to get the fuck out of here. I'm just trying to shake away what's to come, but the burning in the pit of my stomach increases with every click of a phone camera. With every shrill laugh from the bar patrons. With every whisper.

"No?" he hisses.

I manage to glance back up at him but not past his neck. His throat works like he wants to say more but doesn't. He doesn't move out of my way either. I feel myself starting to sag. My adrenaline is dipping. My stomach is pitching. A wave of heat overwhelms me, followed by a dangerous cool.

"I don't feel well."

Instead of immediately making fun of me, the Pyro inhales sharply. His hands move from his pockets to my chin, and he tilts my face up with his fingers. All of them touch me at the same time. My stomach rolls. Nerves blitz me. Uh oh. Mayday, Mayday, Mayday. And then I blink and register the anger in his eyes, and I try to jerk back, but he doesn't let me. His left hand circles the back of my neck while his right hand very, very gently moves over my forehead, back through my hair.

"Shit, you're hot. Grab your things. I'm taking you to a hospital."

"No." My voice is firm. Firmer than it should be. My stomach is soft. Softer than it should be. "I'm fine."

His eyes narrow and he stops touching my face, but his hand on the back of my neck never moves. It's so warm. "You're piss drunk, and your skin's fucking on fire. I'm taking you."

"I . . ."

"Don't be stupid." *You're so fucking stupid, Vanessa.*

I flinch as if struck, but when I try to back away from him, my spine hits the bar. I have to push his hand off my neck with my own palm, and I immediately break out in cold sweat. *Stupid, stupid, stupid.*

"*You* need to leave," I wheeze, the world starting to close in, the lights starting to dim. My body is on fire, but it has nothing to do with the booze—well, it has less to do with the booze than it does with the knowledge that my photo is being taken alongside one of the most famous people on the planet and is likely to end up all over the internet. I don't want to be seen. And not only is the Pyro *seeing* me, he's making me visible to everybody.

"Excuse me?"

"You and I . . . we don't . . . d-don't work together, Mr. Casteel." Mr. Casteel. I'm proud of myself for remembering that he actually has a name and for actually using it, because I can see as I use it that he visibly stiffens. With that small confidence, I manage to lift my gaze to his.

"And?" His jaw is clenched; I can tell even beneath the beard. It's an attractive look for him, this mountain man, warlord, king of the wildlings thing he has going on. It makes him look volatile and dangerous, which is why it's a look I'd have rather admired from afar. A very far.

"I'm not being paid to have to talk to you." Mr. Casteel doesn't move much, but his nostrils flare again, and this time *smoke* curls out of them. Smoke. He still doesn't speak, so I slur, "I need space."

"I'm not leaving you here." He takes an abrupt step to close some of the distance between us, and I can't help the way I lower my head and lift my arm, a trained response. Old habits die hard.

The moment catches around me, swirling winds from a past life tickling the wine cooling on my clothes and making the hairs on the back of my neck stand on end. I hear the clack of thunder, the bolt of a door, the creak of my trailer's musty floorboards, but when I breathe in . . . all I smell is smoke, a bonfire after a blaze when only the embers lie lonely. And then I'm pulled back into the present by the curl of warm fingers around my raised left wrist.

I open my eyes as Mr. Casteel coaxes my arm away from my face. His eyes are narrowed but blazing the brightest white, so white that the light they cast chases away the darkness under his brow. His mouth has an angry set, but when the line of our gazes clash, he blinks. Mr. Casteel swallows once, twice, a third time, and wipes his free hand, the one that's not lightly draped over my palm, on his sweatpants.

He leans in toward me without moving his feet and gives my hand a firm squeeze. "I may be many terrible things, Vanessa," he whispers, and his voice is rougher, like he swallowed nails dipped in whiskey and gasoline. "But I would never do that."

And the strange thing is that the tension releases from the tops of my shoulders and eases down the rest of my back before dissolving at my feet. I bask in the feeling and then immediately hate myself for it—for wanting to believe.

"Words without actions are meaningless, Mr. Casteel," I whisper and then hiccup. "And today, your actions did enough."

His expression shutters even though the light in his eyes continues to beam, maybe even a little more brightly. "Roland," he says suddenly, and the tension in his forehead releases like a rubber band snapped. His whole demeanor changes in a way that I find alarming.

I open my mouth to ask him if he's okay, but the pit of knots in my belly chooses that moment to finally release. My stomach heaves, and this time I can't stop the inevitable. I hiccup, and the burn in the back of my throat gets hotter. I flail my hands, trying to gesture for him to back up, which of course causes him to do the opposite . . . just in time for me to projectile vomit . . .

All over him.

The force is enough to propel me out of my chair, but a heavy arm blocks my fall, and the pressure of that arm on my stomach causes me to throw up another belly full of day red all over his gray sweatpants. Did I say gray? No, not anymore. Now it looks like he's been dipped in a vat of my blood.

As he holds me in his arms like a bedraggled damsel, his hoodie looking like it's been dipped in my insides, I can't help but wonder if maybe it's not such a terrible thing that we didn't win his contract. After all, with the photos that will come out of this evening, he really will look every bit the villain that I know he is in his heart.

There's a pause, and then a woman's shriek marks the final fall of the axe over my throat. "Oh my God, it's the Pyro! She just threw up on the Pyro!" *What a lovely headsman,* I think as I stare up into the Pyro's shocked pink eyes before I finally, thankfully, pass the fuck out.

Chapter Three

VANESSA

Where am I? There are people shouting. "Jesus Christ, who the fuck are you . . ."

"*Who the fuck am I? Who the fuck are you?*"

"*I'm gonna fucking . . .*"

I must be dreaming because the voices sound familiar. A murmured response is followed immediately by, "*Brother? She . . . Margerie said I should bring her here. She lives with you?*"

Another murmured response is drowned out by a louder voice that shouts, "*What the fuck did you do?*"

"*Jesus Christ . . .*"

"*Hand her over and get the fuck out of here, asshole.*" Is that the sound of a shotgun being racked?

"*Jesus Christ . . .*"

"*Where's Elena?*"

"*Jesus Christ . . .*"

"*Don't you curse in this house, boy! And don't you dare fire that gun!*"

"*Where's Elena?*"

"*Jesus Christ . . .*"

"Stop saying Jesus fucking Christ!"

I'm cold, then I'm hot, then I'm cold again, then I'm nice and dry and toasty warm, and people are bringing me things to drink, and right at the point that I think I might throw up again, consciousness eludes me.

Chapter Four

VANESSA

My brothers are pissed. Not quite as pissed as the Pyro was when I met him or when I threw up on him yesterday, but pissed enough. Last time I saw them this pissed off collectively was when I told them that I was moving out of our parents' house to live on my own in the big bad city, despite the fact that I was twenty-one years old and already out of college, and all of them but Luca and Emmanuel, who were still in school at the time, had moved out already. They've treated me like I was thirteen from the moment that I moved in with them when I was thirteen, and over the last twenty-one years, I haven't aged at all in their eyes. Though . . . right now . . . maybe I can sort of see why.

The CEO spine I sometimes manage to cobble together from all the roughshod bricks of my personality is nowhere to be found. It's crumbled the fuck apart. I slink down in my seat at the dining table, my back curled into a C shape, my eyes hardly visible over the edge of the table. In the smallest voice I've ever even heard, I squeak, "Sorry."

I hiccup and burp, and Emmanuel shakes his head at me. "Jesus Christ."

Elena, our mom—their bio mom and my adopted one—slaps him upside the head. "Otros cinco dólares en el tarro."

"*Cinco?* Since when is the going rate for cursing five bucks?" Emmanuel grumbles, but he pulls money out of his wallet anyway.

"Inflation," Elena responds, pointing to the jar on top of the refrigerator marked with a skull and crossbones and stuffed full of dollars.

"I've got twenty. Anybody break a twenty?" Nobody pays him any attention. My other four brothers are all still busy glaring at me while my dad prepares breakfast and Elena makes coffee.

"So you, uhh . . . *all* are here?" My stomach pinches uneasily as I choke down another bite of tamale. Elena swears by her tamales as a hangover cure, but right now I'm eyeing my dad standing at the stove, hoping against all hope he'll finish making blueberry waffles before I have to choke down another mouthful. Elena's tamales are legendary for their experimental and, more often than not, horrifying flavors.

She might be Mexican, born and raised, but she's lived in Sundale for the past fifteen years. A former nurse, she's gotten really into the health-food movement in the last couple years. Her best friend, Tina— my brothers', my dad's, and *my* archnemesis—owns a fancy natural food and wellness store and has been encouraging Elena on her journey. *Enabling* her, may be a more accurate word for it.

This tamale recipe is undoubtedly Tina's and is among the more outlandish that I've had the misfortune of sampling. An unholy union of corn, quinoa, and hempseed with black bean, kale, and pineapple filling. *Pineapple.* The sweetness of the pineapple does not complement the salt of the black beans, and—did she even cook the kale at all? Big chunks of it float around in my mouth like the stiff pieces of construction paper from some kid's unfinished art project.

My dad stands at the stove glaring at me. He doesn't break my gaze as he flips over a single egg with the speed of a man who sees his hungover daughter is suffering and fully intends to make her pay. And pay I do as I take another bite of tamale. I'm paying dearly.

Elena returns to the table and passes me a cup of coffee. Emmanuel gets up and goes to the swear-word jar on top of the fridge that's permanently stuffed full of cash and starts rummaging through it, trying to find change. Luca, David, and Charles all glare at me with a glare that makes them look eerily similar, even though Luca and Charles take after our dad, who's Black, and David, like our other brothers, is Elena's spitting image.

Vincent's stare is the least harsh, but that's only because he's half-distracted by his phone—new girlfriend would be my first guess. Work, my second. He's a commercial airline pilot but, on his off days, sometimes takes tourists sightseeing by helicopter. Vinny has a stake in the helicopter sightseeing company Vantage Point, and it's doing really well.

I swallow hard and try a new tack. "You have a flight today, Vinny?"

"No, Vanny." He sets his phone face down on the table and gives me a glare twice as harsh as the rest of theirs combined. So much for solidarity. "Talk."

"I went out drinking." I make a stupid gesture with my hands like I'm trying out for cheer squad. In my haste to redirect it, I reach for my coffee. "After the workday I had, I got a little drunk."

"A little drunk?" Vinny scoffs.

"How's, um . . . the waffles . . ."

"The waffles will be ready when the waffles are ready," my dad answers. "Sunday breakfast is sacred and can't be rushed."

I hadn't forgotten that my brothers all piled into my parents' house every Sunday for breakfast, but I had forgotten that this week's brunch had been moved to Saturday because of Luca's lacrosse game tomorrow. Despite the fact that both Mani and David were in serious relationships, it was rare that any of us missed this. I'd already planned not to attend—and given them three weeks' notice—because of my meeting with the COE.

I'd been expecting to need to use the weekend to get started on our work for the short-term contract, but that had been voided, our fee was still unpaid, we'd taken on fewer clients in preparation for the COE work, which would have been our largest contract to date, both in cost and prestige, and it's now unlikely we'd get any more work again *ever*, given the fact that my face is currently plastered all over the internet.

My brothers had, bless their hearts, at least had the decency to turn the TV off and take my phone away from me.

I turn to Luca. "So, are you ready for your game tomorrow? Last one of the season and all?"

"Vanny." Luca might be younger than I am by thirteen years, but he's just as stern as Charles, who at thirty-seven is the oldest. "Answer the question."

"I forget the question."

"Then start from the beginning," Charles says. Not Charlie—Charles. "How the fuck did you end up being *flown* by a fucking supervillain home from a bar drunk as a skunk and sick as a dog?"

"Dios mío." Elena makes a sign of the cross over her chest, as she does every time someone mentions one of the world's seventeen supervillains—*eighteen now*. I shudder. *Don't think about it. Don't think about how I might have cost the world everything by simply . . . doing what? Existing?*

A fleeting and unfamiliar anger flits over me as I think about how rude Mr. Casteel was to me. And how strange my reaction to him had been. Maybe it's how everyone reacts to him—that intoxicating smell, the intensity acting so bizarrely as a lure rather than a repellant—but regardless, I don't like it. It makes me . . . want to know him.

Not that Elena would ever stand for that. She was pissed when I told her that my company wanted to bid on the contract. She made the sign of the cross over her chest, just like she does now—just like she does anytime anyone mentions any one of the Forty-Eight *aliens*.

Me? I pitied them, knowing what it's like to be alone as a child. After all, they arrived here twenty-two years ago when they were children with no memories of where they came from. Given up by some parents somewhere, they must have been scared, especially when they were rounded up, poked, and prodded. Some, like the Pyro, were kept for years in governmental facilities—agencies that later became one single entity known as the SDD, the Supernatural Defense Department—before public outcry forced the agency to release all of them and place them with loving host families.

Elena was among the few who quietly thought that they should still be locked up somewhere, that they were dangerous, and I'd always thought it was a poor moral failing on her part to think so . . . but after meeting the Pyro, I'm feeling a little less generous toward alienkind and am starting to wonder if Elena was right after all.

I turn to her for help. "It wasn't that bad. I just had too much day red." I push out my bottom lip and watch Elena's face soften. She comes around the table to me and reaches for my shoulder, but before she can touch me, Charlie swats the back of her hand.

"Don't you dare. And you . . ." He points at my nose. "The lip thing's not gonna work this time. You can make your eyes as big as you want." He slaps his palm down onto the table, rattling his orange juice glass, bringing back memories that make my stomach revolt.

Elena turns her concerned stare into a glare and thrusts the coffee pot in her other hand in my face threateningly. "You are good, Vanny. Gracias, Charlie, for setting me straight." She mutters something in Spanish under her breath that I don't quite catch. Embarrassingly, my Spanish is okay but still not fluent. I've never been good at languages, and I don't really know why. No, I know why. I don't practice. I'm too scared to say something wrong and sound dumb. *You're such a stupid little girl, Vanessa.*

My brothers all laugh lightly at whatever she said, and I feel my face heat. I sip gratefully from my yellow coffee mug, handmade by Mani in his university wheel-thrown ceramics class. Elena loves it. She has artwork all over the house from all her sons. Mine, too, though I didn't really make any art worth putting up until later in high school. Coloring just reminded me of childhood therapy. I didn't really like doing it in my free time so much.

"Go on, Van," my dad says, clomping over from the stove, a steaming skillet in hand. He dishes out eggs onto everyone's plate but mine, and when I look up into his eyes, he's got one eyebrow lifted.

"Are you holding my breakfast hostage?"

"You already have breakfast. And you're not eating near enough to soak up all that wine. It was wine, right? The poor man—alien—was covered in it." Elena tsks. She also makes the sign of the cross as she settles into her seat at the other side of the dining table. Her gaze moves to me. They're all staring, and I can't help it, my lips quirk in a little contented sigh.

Everything here is familiar, and I feel at ease in ways I'm not used to. I can tease here; I can be teased and know it won't hurt. I can tell them about falling and causing a ripple effect that took out the whole boardroom and about new Jeremy—though I withhold the bit about my boobs—and I can tell them how I was caught, on camera, projectile vomiting onto the Pyro and how that footage has been circulating freely all over the internet in a sickening spiral that's taken all the top headlines.

The Forty-Eight are rarely caught in anything but heroic or villainous circumstances, and if they are, they're always looking dashing and elegant, walking down city sidewalks to collect coffee or doing other mundane tasks that prove they're *really* just people too. Too pretty to touch, to be one of us, but not too godlike that they can't be among us. Because they are, by whatever twist of fate, here with all their smoky smells and burning pink eyes and soft promises. *I wouldn't do that.*

I tell them about all of it—except that. I don't tell them about the soft moments. Those . . . feel like mine, and I'm strangely loath to share them. They feel too dreamlike. And like a dream, I don't want to voice it and have anyone tell me it wasn't real.

I sigh. "And then I actually passed out. I didn't know he . . . um . . . brought me home until Luca told me this morning." The thought that *I* flew with a super—uh—person is insanity. I can't wrap a shred of a thought around it, so I don't even stop to try.

"Oh mi niña . . . corazóncita . . . mi amor . . ." Elena murmurs sweet things under her breath and shoves away from the crowded circular kitchen table. She comes to me and wraps her arms around me. She gives me a hug that I feel all the way through my soul. She kisses the side of my head and crouches next to my chair. "You must have been so upset to be treated like that. You are so professional, and that creature doesn't sound like he has an ounce of decency in his bones." Her cheeks flare pink, and her dark bangs bristle against her eyebrows when she scrunches up her nose.

I can't help but grin. Elena's sincerity makes me feel so seen . . . and exposed. I want to retreat, but I don't at the same time. And then my dad comes over and gives me a squeeze on the shoulder, and when my dad swats Luca on the arm, he reluctantly leans across the arm of his seat and one-arm hugs me, and then my other brothers reach across the table, except for Charles, who continues glaring.

"None of that explains the wine."

Vinny and my dad both groan. Elena's jaw drops in shock. "Have a heart, Charlito."

"No me llames Charlito." He points at her and then at me. "And you still owe us an explanation for why you got drunk enough to let a fucking asshole *carry you home*." He punctuates each word by reaching into his wallet and pulling out three five-dollar bills.

"You only owe two," my dad, William, says.

Charles grunts. "Bank one for later. I'm gonna need it."

"He wasn't . . ." I swallow hard, meeting Charlie's gaze tentatively. Charlie returns my hesitancy with a glare that's unflinching.

He has dark eyes and a dark complexion the exact same shade as my dad's with only slightly looser curls. Elena always jokes that God played a cruel trick on her, making her carry a baby that turned out to be the spitting image of his father and without a shred of her. She also jokes that he must have heard her complaints because her next three sons all took after her with lighter brown skin, darker hair, and waves instead of outright curls. Luca looks the most like both of them with skin somewhere in between and dark, glossy curls.

I . . . don't look like any of them. Of course, that's only if you look closely, which most people don't. Most people see my brown skin, my mass of loose, puffy curls, and the same brown eyes we all share—except for David, whose eyes came out hazel—and just assume I'm Elena and William's. Nobody ever corrects them.

But if you look for just a second longer, you'll notice my skin isn't the same shade of brown. It's milkier, less golden caramel. I wash out in the winter and look like a ghoul in all our Christmas photos compared to the rest of my family, who all remain a vibrant, rich brown three sixty-five.

My hair is finer—not thin, to be sure, but I don't have the thick strands Elena's genes gave the boys. My hair is a lighter brown than any of theirs, mousy and kind of boring, if you ask me, which is why I keep it layered and colored so that it's highlighted all the way through. It hangs around my shoulders, long and insanely poofy unless I twist it or put in a roller set before bed, which I rarely do. I kind of like the poof. Like disappearing into a big shrub, it helps me hide a little better. Well, I *usually* like the poof. But right now, I can see the way it sticks straight out of the side of my head in my peripheries, whacking my family members in the face every time they dare come too close to love on me.

"Wasn't what?" Vinny prompts, seeming to have softened toward me again. He's drumming fingers on the back of his phone.

"He wasn't . . . an asshole to you guys, was he?"

My brothers all scoff. My dad grumbles something as he bites into his eggs. Waffles have been served and so has bacon—some of which has even made it onto my plate. I greedily abandon my tamale derivative and devour the fat and bread, that good southern cooking churning in my stomach, probably twice as likely to make me purge as the tamale.

"He was an asshole," my dad finally grunts loudly enough to be understood.

I blink, shocked to hear my dad curse. "What?"

"You heard me," he grunts.

"También debes cinco dólares," Elena huffs.

"What did he do?" I speak on top of her, surprise morphing into nervousness as I wait.

"First off," Luca butts in, speaking louder than my other brothers, though all of them try to speak first. "He landed in our driveway like he owned the goddamn place . . ."

"My driveway—" Dad interjects.

"Ahem?" Elena coughs theatrically into her fist.

My dad sinks into his seat a little bit. "Our driveway."

She gives him an even more pointed look.

"Elena's driveway."

I smile. My brothers all smirk.

"Point is, he landed in the driveway, walked right up to the door—didn't even knock—and the asshole *melted* the doorknob."

"He melted it?"

Luca nods, but it's Vinny who says, "I was still up—jet-lagged from Greece—watching TV on the couch in the living room when the door opened and a stranger fucking walked in carrying my baby sister's body like a corpse."

Vinny frowns, and I understand now why he's more reluctant than the others to offer sympathy. That vision must have been . . . not so nice. If it had been him, I can't imagine how I'd have felt. He exhales deeply and cards his fingers back through his long hair, pulling out the hair tie and letting his man bun fall loose over the shaved sides of his head. He might be the only guy in the universe that can pull off the look, in my opinion, though when Elena first saw it, she about had a heart attack.

Vinny snarls, "I obviously got up and freaked the fuck out, and the bastard—even though he broke and entered—demanded to know who the fuck I was and wouldn't hand you over, even after I told him I was your brother. Woke Luca up. He came in with his goddamn lacrosse stick—"

"Which he burned to shreds! Literally vaped it on the spot! The bastard owes me a new lacrosse stick!" Luca slaps his palm on the table, and my dad slaps him upside the head.

"To be fair, you did whack him in the back with it . . ." David adds.

"He was trying to steal our baby sister!"

"I'm older than you," I grumble.

Charles is thirty-seven, Vinny's thirty-five, I'm thirty-four, with David right behind me at thirty-three, and then there's a huge gap in which Elena was done having kids before an accidental Emmanuel, who's now twenty-five, came along. Not wanting him to be "alone," as she puts it, she had one more kid, Luca, who's now twenty-one and about to graduate from undergrad.

Luca stabs David in the ribs with his elbow while Elena brings the swear jar from off the top of the fridge and slams it down in the center of the kitchen table. Charles is glowering at me, like *I'm* the problem. "He took you back outside and would have flown off with you if Mom hadn't woken up and seen him holding you and screamed bloody murder."

"And even after he came inside and put you on the couch, he still hit me," Luca sputters, showing me the back of his head. I can't see anything through his curls, but I still feel my heart lurch.

"He *hit* you?" I choke on my mouthful of coffee.

"He took my whole face in his hand, and he shoved me all the way into the bookcase. All the way across the room!" Luca should be outraged, but once his expression breaks, he can't keep the grin off his face. "I didn't know he'd be that strong. He barely touched me. Did you see it, Vin?"

Vinny's mouth twitches. He nods. "It was fucking insane. I can't believe you haven't posted about it." He glances at his phone.

Luca sinks into his seat sheepishly.

Vinny raises his eyebrow. "You did? How many views?"

"Five hundred K. Nobody believes me, though. They want to see him on the house cam, and nobody believes we don't have one."

"Don't need companies spying on us," my dad grumbles. "A good old-fashioned gate'll do the trick."

"Not if the intruder can fly!" Luca chuffs.

"That's what the shotgun is for."

"Did dad tell you he almost shot him?" Emmanuel snorts.

"Dad! You can't shoot one of the Forty-Eight!" I squeak.

William shrugs. "Nobody comes into my house and threatens my little girl."

I'm not sure how it's possible to feel so much love, so much shame, and so much terror in equal doses, but the combination is too much. While the rest of my family might be chuckling and reliving the adventure, tears prick the backs of my eyes. I also feel like I could faint all over again.

"I . . . I'm so sorry, everybody. I didn't want anybody to get hurt." My throat constricts.

"Hey," Charles says. "It's not your fault. The drinking is," he says, pointing his fork angrily at me. "But everything that happened after is on him."

"You could have gotten hurt. He's *dangerous*."

"We had it handled," David insists, and that gets everybody talking simultaneously, including me.

"You slept through the whole damn thing," Mani shouts.

"No lo tenías *handled*," Elena says at the same time.

I all but screech, "He shoved Luca into a wall!"

"It didn't hurt. I could have still taken him." Luca's cackling. Emmanuel, seated beside him, tries to shove him off his stool.

"Querida, todo está bien ahora. Todo el mundo está bien y sano." Another sign of the cross before she switches to English. "It's good that we don't ever have to see that terrible creature again."

"And if he so much as sets foot on my porch, I'm gonna blow his damn head off." My father bangs his fist on the table.

The doorbell rings.

Ding ding.

It happens like we're in a movie. The laugh track rolls as we quiet and stare around at each other like we're about to be invaded by enemy combatants. We all hunker down and, the children we still are, look to our parents. On my right, coffee frozen halfway to his mouth, David says, "You expecting somebody?"

"¿Durante el desayuno?" Elena's eyebrows pull together, and she slaps her linen napkin down onto the table. She starts to stand, prepared to go to war, but my dad puts his hand on her arm and pushes back from the table. A heavyset guy who's six two to my mamá's five four, he certainly *looks* more intimidating that Elena does—but that's only if you haven't met Elena and disturbed her family brunch.

"I'll get it," he says, sparing whoever's life is on the other side of that front door. Or, well . . . that's what I thought until . . .

"Papá!" Luca, Mani, and I all shriek—because as my burly teddy bear of a father leaves the kitchen, he grabs his shotgun, which just so happens to be casually lying on the window seat, nestled between Elena's brightly colored pillows.

"Sit down," he grunts, and so we sit and remain seated, mouths open wide enough to catch flies. We're all completely quiet, straining to hear the sound of my dad undoing the locks and the new door creaking on an old frame. Some light murmuring . . . but it doesn't sound hostile . . . before my dad returns.

"Shit, Vanessa." My dad hooks his thumb over his shoulder, his dorky purple T-shirt with wolves howling at a faraway moon presenting an odd contrast to the shotgun hanging limp in his right hand. "You didn't tell us you knew the president of Cambodia."

"Oh shit," I whisper.

"Vanny!" Elena shouts, more surprised, I think, than anything. I never curse.

"You know the *president of Cambodia*?" Luca's mouth hangs open.

I stand up from my seat in an awkward tangle of limbs, and David has to lean over and grab my arm to keep me from face-planting. I mumble a quick thanks, swat Luca on the back of the head as I round the table, and dust off my clothing. Who am I kidding? I'm wearing my goddamn pajamas. The ones from Tía Luisa with Mickey Mouse's face printed on the bottoms and Minnie Mouse's demented face handsewn on the front of the long-sleeve T-shirt. The ears stick out and flop around where my boobs are.

I could have changed. I have plenty of old clothes here from college, but when Elena came into my room this morning and took a flyswatter to my forehead until I got up and got downstairs in time for breakfast, I wasn't exactly thinking of how I'd be presenting myself to potential clients—least of all the one who'd just fired me.

My stomach lurches up into my throat as I stagger over to the window seat, and my brothers immediately crowd in behind me, throwing pillows and elbows to make space at the glass.

"Shit, that really is the president!" Mani hisses.

"Mani!" Elena shouts. "¡Cinco dólares, por favor!"

"He's not the president of Cambodia. He's Thai, and he's the president of the COE." My heart joins my stomach up in my mouth, barely contained by my rattling teeth as I peel the curtains back and see the massive car sitting there in my parents' driveway. "How did they get past the gate?" I glance over my shoulder to see my dad standing there, gun on his shoulder. He shrugs it.

"I opened it. Should I not have?"

"Shit," I whisper.

"Vanny!" Elena cries out.

"I'll pay her fees," Charlie grunts, grabbing the back of my pajama shirt and dragging me away from the window. "Vanny, you wanna talk to him or you want us to run him off?"

"President or not, we can take him," David helpfully shouts.

"Fuck yeah! I got another lacrosse stick!" Luca interjects.

Meanwhile, behind me I hear Elena say, "I'm going to be able to buy a yacht with this money before we finish breakfast . . ."

"What are you waiting for, hermanita?" Mani pokes me in the ribs, making me buckle. "Go talk to him!"

"Did he seem p—angry?" I ask my dad as I push through the wall of my brothers and head to the entryway, wiping my sweaty palms on my pj's.

Dad shakes his head and gives me a shrug with his shotgun-wielding shoulder. He follows me to the door. "Nope."

I grunt. My dad is not a man of many words and has the emotional depth of a cucumber, which is why I'm so surprised when he gives me a kiss on the cheek and a pat on the head before he opens the door for me. "You got this, sweetheart. Whatever it is."

I smile up at him, and suddenly my stupid outfit and my bacon-scented hair don't feel so important. I take a breath, this one deeper than the last one was, less shaky, and remember: What's the worst Mr. Singkham can do to me? Fire me again?

I step out onto the low porch, a surprisingly warm breeze rolling in from the driveway where Mr. Singkham stands in front of a parked black SUV. He steps away from it when he sees me and, to his credit, masks his momentary shock at my presentation with a bright smile and a small wave. I pretend not to notice the way he completes a quick scan of my outfit before returning his gaze to my face, his expression one of utmost professionalism.

I don't bother with my favorite nervous gesture: trying to smooth down my clothing. If I do, it'll just make Minnie's ears flop around at best and, at worst, draw more attention to the fact that I'm not wearing a bra. Instead, I actually manage to use the few parts of my brain that weren't obliterated by day red the day before to focus on my breathing techniques. Five counts in, five-count hold, five-count release. I manage two cycles before Mr. Singkham and I come close enough to shake hands, though we don't.

"Mr. Singkham, I wasn't expecting you," I say stupidly, my voice a little hoarse. Of course I wasn't expecting him. I'm in my Minnie pajamas!

Mr. Singkham glances over my shoulder, and I know he's looking at the kitchen window where my brothers are eavesdropping. David claims he can read lips—he can't—but I don't doubt they'll all be clustered there trying their best. My lips twitch. I don't mind them watching, really. I'm braver with them there.

My trust in them wasn't instantaneous. When I moved into the house, I was terrified. My caseworker hadn't cared that I was a thirteen-year-old girl alone in a house with four boys, two of whom were older than me. It took me almost six weeks before I realized that they might not be interested in hurting me—they mostly ignored me—and three months after that to be sure of it.

Charlie was already in high school, Mani was just four, and Luca hadn't been born yet, but Vinny, David, and I were at the same middle school. I didn't have any friends, but a group of nice girls started inviting me to lunch. They didn't make me talk or ask me personal questions. They didn't make fun of my hair or the fact that I was a foster kid. They just . . . let me be and included me.

I felt really stupid for not realizing that Vinny was dating one of the girls' older sisters and had set the whole thing up. And a few weeks after that, I realized that they weren't just uninterested in harming me; they actually maybe even wanted to help me.

A group of basketball players took turns asking me to the winter dance as a joke, and Vinny and David beat the crap out of them, and Charlie beat up one of the guys' older brothers. They all got suspended for three days. And then I knew that they weren't just interested in helping me as a pity case, but maybe even *liked* me, when Elena and William didn't punish them for getting suspended. Instead, they pulled me out of school on their suspension days and took the whole family on a trip to Florida to celebrate.

And finally, I realized they might even *love* me when, two months later, Elena quietly sat me down and offered me adoption paperwork. She gave me every assurance in the world that they'd do their best to do right by me but that she wouldn't dare try to pressure me into it, that I could remain a foster and they would try to find me a family I liked better, if it came to that.

That was the same moment that I realized I might have even loved them back.

Staring at Mr. Singkham now, I let the overwhelming presence of my family hold me up like a buttress and cross my arms tightly over my chest. I inhale and exhale with slow, measured breaths.

"Ms. Theriot, I offer my deepest apologies for bothering you on a Saturday."

I wait, unsure if this is the type of sentence that requires a response. When he doesn't say more but watches me expectantly, I stutter, "I, um . . . yes?"

He exhales roughly, the wind tousling his perfect hair. It looks less gelled today than it did yesterday, and even though he's wearing a tie, it's a little off, the tail sticking out longer than the front bit. Is Mr. Singkham . . . disheveled? "Thank you for coming outside to speak with me. What I'm about to share with you is in the utmost confidence. In that vein, I must request that any camera system your family might have here be disengaged."

I jerk my thumb back toward the house. "My dad—he, uh, has a shotgun."

The dusting of Mr. Singkham's eyebrows rise, causing creases in his otherwise flawless forehead. "Pardon me?"

"Sorry, I meant that he has a shotgun instead of a security system. He doesn't use cameras."

"Oh. Well then." Mr. Singkham glances back at my house again. "That's excellent," he says, but very unconvincingly, closing the distance between us another half step. The air is sticky with summer's approaching warmth. I focus on that feeling, on the strange reminder it brings of the Pyro—of Mr. Casteel—and the way he'd felt just like this approaching me in the boardroom and then at the bar, like the promise of summer . . . before dropping winter's axe over my head.

I know my body language isn't inviting when he glances down at my crossed arms, my slippered feet angled away from him, and stops his advance. He swallows. *Swallows.* Like he's . . . nervous. Oh no.

"Wh-what happened?" I gasp.

"Happened? Oh, you misunderstand, Ms. Theriot. I don't come here today to rehash any of the unpleasantness from Friday—yesterday," he blurts, as if having lost track of time. "Frankly, I come on a much . . . friendlier mission than that."

Friendly? I don't dare say the word aloud. I just keep my head cocked and my face twisted up as I try desperately to understand what the fuck is going on. My brain is still sluggish, using fingernails and sheer grit to claw its way up a mountain of coherency. Is he . . . speaking English right now?

Mr. Singkham licks his lips, checks his tie, and when he looks at me next, his shoulders sag . . . he just looks defeated. "Ms. Theriot, the nature of my request is, frankly, an embarrassing one, and no matter its outcome, I must ask that nothing I say to you here be shared outside of my confidence." It's a bold ask. The day red has long since drained from my system, which means I'm not nearly drunk enough to ignore the profoundly inappropriate nature of his request. Anything that we previously discussed was protected by the NDAs in our previous—now voided—contract, but he and I have no more contracts left between us. My team and I left his offices yesterday with hands empty and tails tucked.

"If this is a contractual question," I say, swallowing hard, "I'm going to have to ask us to move this meeting to my offices where Jem—where my legal team can review . . ."

He takes a step toward me and places a hand over the lapel of his royal-blue suit. I counter by taking a step back and don't miss the way his front teeth bite together. Nerves sweep my body. The tension is unbearable. "This is extremely uncomfortable, Ms. Theriot, but the concerns I have with . . . I don't mean to put you in an uncomfortable position, but I came to speak not with The Riot Creative but with *you. Personally.*"

I frown. *Me?* I point at my chest.

Mr. Singkham nods. "Mr. Casteel has come to me with an unusual proposal."

I feel my facial muscles perform cartwheels and backflips, a circus all unto their own. "He's . . . reconsidering working with the COE?"

"Do I have your word, Ms. Theriot? That you will not broadcast what I say next?" He glances shiftily to the side.

I really hate to agree, but I also recognize that there *isn't* a contract between us. He can ask me not to say anything, but he can't bind me to it, which means right now he's not actually asking for my confidence. He's asking for my trust. Nerves and a profound sense of curiosity combine to form my next sentence. Just a word: "Yes."

"Then I will begin by offering my deepest apologies. His behavior and that of my team was not representative of our values at the COE. And, with that in mind, I must ask if you would now, at present, be open to reconsidering your working relationship with the COE and Mr. Casteel."

"I don't . . . understand. He told me to leave the room and then berated me at the bar when he ran into me."

"He didn't run into you, Ms. Theriot. He followed you there. It had been his intention to put this proposition to you directly, it would seem, but when that didn't . . . work out," he says, floundering, "he came to me."

"Came . . . to you? When?" The sky is overcast today, but it's still overly bright, making me feel like I'm squinting against an eclipse as I stare up at Mr. Singkham, trying to piece together the puzzle of his words. And every piece is an edge. There are no corners. All understanding I thought I'd successfully mined for has dispersed in the wind like the seeds of a dandelion.

"The middle of the night, directly after leaving your family home. He demanded that I put together a new contract. It's what my team has been working on all morning. He wanted to incorporate your ideas—all of your ideas—into the contract. He wanted them *guaranteed*."

"Our ideas?" I feel like a parrot, repeating every third thing he's saying while forgetting the other two.

"Ms. Theriot, Mr. Casteel woke me up at two forty-five this morning at my own home to declare that he was accepting the COE contract with the added amendments to include *all* of your long-term proposal ideas *and* to ensure that you remain on the project for the entirety of the ten-year duration. I was dressed not entirely dissimilarly to how you are dressed now, though I do wish my pajamas had a bit more flare." He smiles a little, glancing down at my Minnie Mouse ears.

"That's . . . that's . . . I'm sorry, Mr. Singkham, but if I may be so blunt—that's insane."

He laughs, and I feel my own cheeks twitch in a smile as he says, "Yes. My thoughts precisely. But he made his position clear. He wants you to work with him for the next ten years. In return, he'll become a hero, he'll don the cape, he'll accept the Lois Lane clause, as you outlined in your design portfolio—he'll even trim his beard and trade his sweatpants for spandex."

I shake my head, feeling flattered, feeling nauseous, and feeling . . . suspicious too. Something about this isn't right. "But I . . . I'm nothing without my team. I mean, I'm head of a firm. If his expectation is to hire me without The Riot Creative, then that won't work."

"No, of course not. His push was more to guarantee that you would be on his contract as part of The Riot Creative's acceptance of the long-term bid. That you would be his case manager, his agent, and that any other one-on-one line items that should come out of your rebrand packet will be handled by you *personally*."

"Personally . . ." I start, needing serious clarification on that, but he doesn't let me interrupt and raises his tone just slightly enough to speak over me.

"And if you can agree to this contractually, I can ensure that your firm will neither fold nor falter while you hold a contract with the COE. We will do whatever we can to support The Riot Creative, whether it be with expanded office space, direct seconding of our staff to your team while you scale—your team is currently twenty-two full-time staff, correct?"

I nod, flustered by the abrupt direction the conversation has taken. "Uh, yes. Yes, twenty-two."

"And you lack an in-house design department?"

"We have three graphic designers, but they work in digital and 2D media. The mock-ups we did of the uniform, for example, those we had to have a clothing designer consult on."

Mr. Singkham nods, and there's something different in his demeanor. Something more relaxed, like . . . he knows he's got me even though I haven't come to that conclusion yet. Though . . . haven't I? He had me the moment he stepped out of his car.

"Most of the Champions have marketing teams of at least forty, though some of the larger brands like Taranis's are nearly a hundred."

"A hundred?" I almost choke.

"He has over a hundred brand endorsements and brings in a lot of money for the COE. If I told you how much . . ." He lets his voice trail off to an awkward chuckle, and I do something I never do: I try to make a joke.

"You'd have to kill me?"

He stares into my eyes, blinks, and the laugh that then bursts out of him makes me physically jump. He laughs for a good thirty seconds, almost scarily, before coming toward me, wiping tears from his eyes. He clasps my right hand in both of his, and as he blinks and nods, he looks older, reminding me of my granddad. My bio grandpa. And it's probably, possibly, because I'm thinking of that old man, that kind man who once came to see me before his daughter threw him out—the one who died two years later, before I ever really got to meet him—that I soften. And maybe it's that softness that causes my vision to blur.

Because when he says, "Wonderful. I hope this means you'll consider signing on with us, despite our rocky start?" I agree.

I agree even though I have this strange, unpleasant feeling in the back of my mind that I'm missing something.

"That's wonderful," he says, finally releasing my hand.

"I . . . I'll need time to talk to my team and work out a new proposal . . ."

"Your team can have the week to work out a new proposal for the long-term contract for The Riot Creative, but I cannot leave your driveway without a yes from you *personally*. And without a signature." He pulls a paper and a pen out of his inner jacket pocket and hands me the crude sketch of an offer so hastily drafted it has typos—*typos*—but I still get the gist. Ten-year gig working for the Pyro, he becomes a Champion in exchange. The Pyro accepts all of the PR and marketing ideas outlined in the initial presentation my team put together, so long as I *personally* manage the one-on-one tasks.

I know the presentation by heart. I wrote most of it myself. I came up with half of the ideas—mostly at three a.m., sitting upright in bed, typing haphazard notes that I was really excited about on my phone. There *aren't* any one-on-one tasks. Everything is a team effort, even managing his social media. "A single well-curated social media account is the work of three people . . ." I hear myself mumble as I skim the brief, shoddy contract.

Mr. Singkham shrugs casually. Far, far too casually. "And you'll have assistance with that, of course."

"But . . . then what am I doing that's not with my team?"

"Some of the other ideas in your presentation were what I believe Mr. Casteel was referring to. Liaising with the COE, for example, acting as his representative with brands. That kind of thing—though, of course, I am not the expert." He gives me a smile that should feel reassuring but doesn't.

I nod and continue reading aloud. "Salary and details to be fixed at a later date?" I say, frowning as I read the words.

"The Pyro's PR budget is $180 million, Ms. Theriot. That's salaries and ad spend. Your hardware budget and office space rentals are included under a different line item. I trust that from that pot, you'll be able to carve out a nice salary for yourself as both head of his PR management *and* his personal representative, no?"

One hundred and what? I think I black out for a moment. That's . . . huge. Huge. The largest ad budget I've ever worked on was $2 million. One hundred and eighty . . . I shake my head, trying to snap out of it, and when I come to, that icy cold feeling of suspicion licks at my heels even as I take the pen he holds toward me.

I can't help but look at Mr. Singkham's signature in the blank space below the crude contract. Harsh scribbles. What surprises me is the signature below that. Large but neat, Mr. Casteel's signature takes up more than its fair share of space, but it's beautiful really. Making a decision that would have had my first boss, a wonderful South African woman who taught me everything I know about marketing and running a business today, sobbing into a handkerchief, I sign below Mr. Casteel's name. *Roland Casteel.* My mind flashes to last night. He told me to call him Roland—or did I drunkenly hallucinate that?

"He's, um . . . I have some social anxiety, Mr. Singkham." And PTSD. Mild to moderate PTSD is how past doctors have classified it, but nothing about the way I feel when confronted with violence feels mild or moderate to me. "If Mr. Casteel is serious about this, he's going to have to learn to work with me too."

"Mr. Casteel has been made aware that his attitude in our last business meeting won't be tolerated. I would like to have your team back in the office Wednesday to sign the final papers for the official contract between our two companies. The Pyro will be but a cool ember when you meet with him then, Ms. Theriot. He has assured me."

I watch him tuck the papers I just signed away in his inside jacket pocket and whisper, "No."

"No?"

I blink. "Sorry. Wednesday works for our team, Mr. Singkham. I was just already thinking ahead of myself to the name."

"The name? His name? The Pyro?"

"Yes. Along with his gruff attitude, that's the first thing my team and I would like to get rid of."

"What name did you have in mind?" He smiles broadly, looking far too much like the cat who caught the canary, making that tension in my stomach tighten.

As I explain to him some of the ideas my team and I came up with, I can all but feel that paper burning a hole through his pocket, mocking me. I'm missing something.

But I know my proposal, and I read the contract; I negotiate contracts in my sleep. It can't be anything serious—that really affects me. And that's what I tell myself, and my parents and my brothers when I go back inside after Mr. Singkham leaves, and they pop a bottle of bubbly to celebrate me—even if Vinny and Charlie and, well, all of them are still holding a deep, deep grudge against the Pyro for the events of the previous evening.

That's what I repeat to myself as I make my way back to my town house in the city, crawl into my bed, and stare at the ceiling.

But the one question that wakes me up three hours later, shivering with cold sweat? The one that I realize only now I should have demanded Mr. Singkham answer on the spot in my parents' driveway?

From the first moment he saw me, Mr. Casteel acted like I shat in his soup and ripped the heads off his dolls—like we'd been two members of rival families in a lifetime that came before—and now he wants to work with me closely for a decade?

Nuh-uh. No way. This is a dumb, dumb idea. Because if my team was sure that he was a villain deep in his heart, then I just signed on to *personally* do the bad guy's PR.

The amount of expletives I shout into my pillow as I try and fail to fall asleep are enough to overflow Elena's jar.

All I can do now is pray that my stomach settles, that my team was wrong, and that our meeting this week with Mr. Casteel the *Champion* goes smoothly.

Chapter Five

Vanessa

I've never been in a more tense meeting in all my life, and I'm including the last time I was in this exact room. It's so tense, I'd call it painful. The last meeting had been painful, but this is pain of an entirely new and considerably less pleasant variety.

I shuffle in my seat, wanting to toss the rolling chair back and run. I'd prepared for this, been so prepared. But I couldn't have prepared for *this*.

My team and I strategized every possible scenario as we worked and reworked plan after plan and cobbled together clause after clause to finally complete a contract. We worked through Sunday and late into the night Monday and Tuesday before finally getting something together that we were happy with and that we could present today. I was thrilled with my team's work and wished I could reward them with a few extra days off, but we would have to hit the ground running; our first press release would be tomorrow, and there we'd announce Mr. Casteel's new name—the $180 million brand.

"One foot in front of the other." That's what Margerie said to me at the end of our first team meeting Sunday morning, in a very different tone than the one she'd arrived with when she'd all but shouted, "Emergency PR overhaul to redirect the narrative?" and stumbled into our small office, prepared to throw down to help clean up the mess I'd made—literally and figuratively—when I threw up all over our newest client.

Even though it was only April, Margerie showed up on Sunday in a summer dress and heels and sunglasses that made her look like a celebrity trying to remain anonymous. She was the last person to arrive to our small office. The shock on her face seeing my entire twenty-two-person team stuffed into our not-quite-big-enough conference room was priceless.

"Not quite," I answered with a grimace. "I actually called you all here to let you know that Mr. Casteel changed his mind."

"Changed his mind?" Margerie looked around, taking a seat on a high stool against the wall next to Melody, one of two legal associates working under Jem. "On what?"

"Everything." I swallowed hard. I was dressed in an oversize button-up with leggings underneath. Some unfortunate combination of still hungover but trying to be professional. "He wants to join the Champions, and he wants our team on the long-term contract." The cheers that went up after that only happened after a long moment of utter astonishment as I explained to them what had happened in my driveway yesterday morning.

"I need the comms team to get started on a campaign to explain the, um . . . the situation at the bar. I need the legal team to start drafting long-term contract amendments based on the generic contract Mr. Singkham sent us. This is the same base contract the large brands are using to work with the other Champions, so we need this tailored to our client and our work.

"I need ops to start looking into what hiring might need to look like for the next six weeks, because we'll need to scale up but not so quickly that we can't manage our work and onboarding simultaneously. Mr. Singkham mentioned potentially contracting space and seconding staff from the COE offices themselves since our space here isn't big enough. Dan, can you oversee that? And lastly, I need to see Jem and Margerie privately."

As my team dispersed in a frenzied panic, I spent the next half hour going over the nauseatingly sparse countersigned contract copy Mr. Singkham had sent me. Neither Jem nor Margerie was particularly pleased.

"You signed this?" Jem said, holding up the sheet of printer paper. "This looks like a four-year-old put it together. It's not even an original."

"We'll get an original Monday."

Margerie huffed. "This seems sketchy."

Yes. Yes, it did. "We know the proposal. There wasn't anything in there for one person to do."

"There were a few things in there one person *might* be seen as being potentially capable of doing alone."

"What Margerie is so inelegantly saying is that he's not a PR expert, and some of the ideas listed in the proposal were vague," Jem said. "They could be interpreted to be jobs for a single individual."

"Like what?" I counter, giving Jem a flat look.

"Social media management, to start."

"That's clearly a multiperson job. It's listed in the description as needing a graphic designer, plus I already raised that with Mr. Singkham, and he said he understood . . ."

"What about the personal assistant or the Lois Lane clause? Either of those could be interpreted, based on language, as being the responsibility of one person."

"Even if he wanted a fake girlfriend to spruce up his brand, it clearly said in the proposal that this was a public speaking gig—someone to pose with him in photos and to make most of his speeches for him since he's basically an asshole." I hissed out that last part, face flaming as I tried to defend myself. "But the job requires another someone to actually write the speeches and yet another someone to liaise with journalists and media agencies, not to mention the someone who would be managing her or their joint social media pages. Lois Lane was just the fancy name we gave the speaker of this house—because, unlike his name suggests, we don't want it set on fire!"

Margerie laughed while Jem narrowed her eyes and slammed one angry finger down on the single-page contract. "What about the PA position? His personal assistant? *Personal. Assistant?*"

My face reddened. My stomach churned. "I . . ."

"Jesus Christ, don't tell me you signed a contract to be a PA for ten years," Margerie wheezed.

Oh my God. It was what I had missed, I was sure of it. Panicking, I babbled, "Let me make a call."

Mr. Singkham answered on the first ring, and he was strangely . . . reassuring, promising me that having a PA was one amendment to the contract the Pyro wouldn't mind striking or delegating to someone else.

I left the call pleased but still confused because there wasn't anything else we could find. What did he want me to personally work with him on? I planned to ask him at some point during our Wednesday meeting and expel the sick feeling in my belly once and for all, but now, seated in the room across the table from the world's newest Champion, the butterflies in my stomach transform . . . balloon, grow *teeth*.

No, maybe I won't ask him today. Not today. Not tomorrow. Not ten years from tomorrow. Not if he keeps doing what he's doing, which is the same thing he's been doing since my team and I showed up and filed into the boardroom to find him already seated at the table.

He's staring right at me.

Right.

At.

Me.

His pink eyes bore into my skull like a damn drill. I can all but hear the shrill sound of the bit as it pummels through drywall to reach the brain stud behind it. Dark pink around the edges of the iris, his eyes bleed lighter and lighter pink the longer he stares.

"Ms. Theriot came up with the idea." Margerie's voice is like a cattle prod to the side.

I jerk and look up in time to see Mr. Singkham grinning huge from the head of the table. "The Wyvern. I like it." He raps his fist on the tabletop twice. "What do you think, Mr. Casteel?"

Mr. Casteel tilts his head to the side and blinks. "Say it," he says to me. It could only be to me because he hasn't looked at anyone else since we walked into the room. At first I thought my hair was dancing or that I had boogers in my nose, but I didn't find anything wrong the three times I excused myself to take a look at my face in the bathroom mirror.

"The Wyvern?" I repeat, trying to sound strong. My throat is dry. I glance at the water pitcher in the center of the table but don't dare reach for it.

"The Wyvern," he repeats, and though quiet, nearly gentle, the way his voice wraps around me gives me chills. "What is that, Vanessa?" At the sound of my name in his voice, paired with the flare of white light from his irises, I shiver fully.

"It's a mythical dragon."

"A dragon?"

I nod quickly and even more quickly sputter out, "We thought the other fire names, like Pyro, were too obvious. Most of the heroes—Ch-Champions," I correct on a slight stutter, using the preferred moniker, "have drawn on names from fantasy and mythology. We ran through lists of fantasy creatures and mythological gods who can wield fire before settling on the Wyvern. More subtle than a dragon, it tested best with our focus groups, both those who knew and those who didn't know what a wyvern is." My voice fizzles out, and we're left in silence.

"And it was your idea?"

I glance again at my water glass on the table, needing a sip because it feels like I've been sucking on cotton balls all afternoon, but the pressure of eyes on my face is too much. I don't move. Can't.

"It was a team effort."

His expression turns severe then, and he drums his nails into the top of his packet. His nails look well trimmed, but they still mottle the glossy surface of the pack, digging shallow little trenches on each touch. "Was it, Vanessa?"

Vanessa, you're such a fucking disgrace.

I shake my head, feeling reprimanded, feeling scorched. "My team came up with many ideas. I happened to come up with that one, yes."

"Hm," he says, and he goes back to searching my face as if it were a riddle he remembered the answer to once but with time has forgotten. He watches me with frustration and fascination in equal measure, making me feel like a bug beneath a microscope.

Silence prevails. I hate it a lot. His arms cross over his black T-shirt—hole-free this time—and hoodie, and I pray that he threw the gray sweat suit he was wearing last time I saw him in the trash—no, that he used his powers to incinerate it—because it needs to be gone from this earth.

I shuffle my feet against the bag I brought with me. I cough into my fist. Mr. Casteel raises a black eyebrow and glances to the glass of water in front of me. In a panic move, I reach for it, and as I feared I would, I fumble the glass. Condensation glosses the exterior, and my clammy hand slips. It falls, spilling, winding idle rivers toward Mr. Casteel and threatening the small projector box along the way.

I gasp, frantically lurch up, hit my thighs on the underside of the table, grunt at the shocking pain that slices through my knees, and, grimacing, still force myself to stand. I reach for the black napkins fanned so elegantly down the center of the conference table, but I'm not tall enough to reach them. Not that it would have mattered. Roland's hand is already there, pushing the napkins on the table within my reach away.

"Sit."

I sit. Like a damn dog. Heat suffuses my cheeks, but it's nothing compared to the heat that suddenly emanates from Roland. He's standing in front of his chair, the wad of napkins completely soaked and doing absolutely nothing for the flood I've started. He's abandoned them anyway and is staring down at the water, his eyes glancing over it almost absently, every other second flicking back to me. I don't know where to look because, as much hold as those pink eyes have on me, I can't help but be amazed by the fact that the water on the table is *evaporating.*

When the table's slate surface is entirely dry, the wet napkins go up in a small, angry blaze. Roland sits down insouciantly, but before he does, he pushes his full, untouched glass of water across the conference table until it's right in front of me and grunts, "You okay?"

I nod jerkily, though it's a lie. No, I'm not fine. No part of me is fine. He's supposed to be mean and combative, frustrating and confrontational. He's not supposed to be . . . *nice.* He's not supposed to use his powers to *help me.*

He squints at me, and his eyes fade from the palest shade of pink to a darker fuchsia color. "Wanna hear you say it. Use your words."

I heat unexpectedly and hope that the color doesn't pinch my cheeks. "I'm o-okay." I clear my throat. "Mr. Casteel. Thank you."

Silence simmers and sputters, the oil too hot not to burn. His eyes are changing color again, but their focus is unwavering. "A wyvern breathes fire. I don't just breathe fire," Mr. Casteel finally says, voice softer than it has a right to be.

I shrink down in my chair even farther when his eyes blaze a bright orange before settling back to their normal color. And then fire suddenly erupts on the tips of his eyelashes like little sparklers, and I jump. It spreads across his cheekbones before disappearing as it hits the collar of his hoodie and then shooting across the backs of his hands and off the crests of his fingernails in a shower of tiny sparks.

"I *am* fire. I generate it through every pore."

I jump, jolt, and shiver. I swallow hard. "We, um . . . knew that . . . but we couldn't find another creature to more aptly describe your abilities." We did . . . but it wasn't a good name for a Champion.

The devil and his demons, after all, could generate a fire like that according to some of their depictions throughout history. Luckily for us, our rebranding efforts were strictly secular, and luckily for Mr. Casteel, he has neither claws nor fangs nor horns. Luckily for all of us, because I don't know what I'd do if a more monstrous Mr. Casteel were here staring at me like that.

Abruptly, Roland rolls his chair forward. He opens the packet to the correct page, the one with the images of wyverns on it from various mythologies, without looking down. "I like it."

I swallow hard and glance up at Margerie, who's leading the presentation from the front of the room and staring down at Roland like he's grown three heads. I clear my throat.

She looks at me and shakes out of it, then says, "That's very good to hear, Mr. Casteel. Now, if you'll turn to the next page of your packet, we can look more at some of the design prototypes we've come up with so far . . ."

A few more minutes pass, questions are asked and answered, and then Margerie makes space for Jeremy to come to the front of the room to discuss the contract. "After we go through the details, our legal team will finalize anything that needs correcting in the terms, and when we come back from the break, Vanya will talk to us all about tomorrow's press conference."

Roland's still looking at me, and if I had to bet whether he heard anything Jeremy said, I'd bet ten to one against. He glances at my hands and then at my water glass. I still haven't picked it up. I'm too nervous.

He looks . . . angrier than he did a second before and huffs, "Let's do this quickly. I'm ready for lunch."

Jeremy wraps up at warp speed, and as the two teams break for lunch and everybody disperses, I remain seated. If I thought I could get away with it, I'd have grabbed a sandwich and eaten it sitting on the toilet in the women's bathroom, but lunch isn't sandwiches—it's sushi—and trying to juggle soy sauce, wasabi, and chopsticks on my lap in the bathroom doesn't sound particularly appealing.

Also unfortunate? The moment the group breaks for lunch and gets up from the table, Roland stands and starts to come around the conference table. He all but runs Garrison over in his effort to steal his seat, the one directly to my right. He drops into it, his knees pointed toward me, and stunned silly as I am, when he grabs the underside of my chair and swivels me to face him, I don't do anything but let him.

His thighs move to bracket the outsides of my knees, and he cocks his chin at my feet. "What are you hiding under the table?"

"Oh! I, um . . ." Flounder. "This is for you. A, uh . . . hoodie to replace what I . . ." threw up on. " . . . ruined. I bought you pants, too, because I, um . . . well . . ." I make a frantic hand gesture while my body cooks to a simmering boil. "I didn't get shoes, though I would like to. I don't know your size. If you could tell me your size, that would be helpful."

I kick the bags under the table inelegantly toward him, the crinkle paper crunching inside as I do. I've been using work as a distraction from thinking about the images splattered across social media like blood from the jugular, but right now, hearing that paper crinkling . . . thinking about his sweats and what I did to the old ones on Friday . . . those pictures start to batter their way in. The moat is dry, the drawbridge is lowered, and when I lift my gaze and catch his profile—because for once he isn't staring straight at me but is giving the bags some apathetic consideration—I can see those shaky cell phone photos and videos clearly.

"You look like a Black Fay Wray," Jem said when I caught her scrolling socials Sunday evening before we all dragged ourselves out of the office to bed. Jem was the only one who still seemed alert despite the fact we'd been working for ten hours straight.

"Jem! Close that shit," Jeremy chided her, and she had the indecency to look incensed.

"What? She looks gorgeous draped over his arms like that. A proper Ann Darrow to his King Kong, don't you think? The 1933 version, of course." She's a monster movie fanatic and does not discriminate against a film's age—or its quality. She really fits all of those typical second-generation Ethiopian, Mezcal-slinging, monster-loving, shrewd lawyer stereotypes.

Jeremy slammed his hand down on Jem's computer, but the damage was done. When I later looked up the movie poster that Jem had been talking about, I almost passed out. Because it wasn't the fact that I was draped like a beach towel between Roland's strong arms, or the fact that his sweats were covered in splotchy patches of throw up; it was the way he was looking at my face. He'd had and held an expression all the way through the bar, up until the point that he curled me into his chest and rocketed into the sky, caught by so many different camera angles. He looked . . . not angry. Very, very not angry. I swallow hard. He almost looked . . . intrigued.

"There are two of them." He turns back to face me, but I don't let his pink eyes hook me or reel me in.

"I . . . yeah." I tuck my hair behind my ear and smile abruptly down at the boxes for reasons fully passing understanding. There's just something strange about the question. It's the kind of question I'd ask, so boldly random. "I got two different size sweat sets. Large and extra-large. I wasn't sure what would fit you best. They're navy blue and charcoal, though. I couldn't find light gray to replace the ones I threw up on." It's a lie. I found gray. There were tons of gray. But humiliation prevented me from buying the identical shade; if I ever even see him in light-gray anything ever again, there's a strong chance I'll simply perish.

"The receipts are in there too. I bought them at that store in Sundale—Westwood—in case you want to exchange them. The address is on the receipt in case you don't know where it is. Also I, um . . . I'm not sure how to say this, but I . . ." I choke, wondering why he still hasn't taken the bags yet. "My brothers . . . I don't think you . . . If we're going to be working together in the long term . . ." Does he hate the sweats? He hasn't even looked at them yet. "I just wanted to say . . . fighting them . . . it wasn't . . ." I can't take this anymore. "Do you not like the sweatpants?"

He grunts. "Your brothers fought me first."

"Right, but . . ."

"I won't do it again."

Air punches out of me in a shallow burst. "Oh, okay, thanks. I . . . the pants . . ."

"They're fine."

"Oh . . ." Fine. I feel my cheeks heat anew. I tuck my hair behind my ear and then immediately untuck it, wanting to make the shrub of my hair large enough to disappear behind. "And I, um . . . Margerie and I could have gotten a cab, you didn't need to fly with me. It . . . that's . . . I didn't agree . . ."

"She wouldn't give me your home address. Only your family's." His gaze blazes *orange* this time, and his softness is gone. Back is the monster I met in the boardroom. I jump at the sudden severity of his tone. "And I wasn't about to send two drunk women in a cab home alone at night."

I try to keep my shoulders rolled back, try to push my toes into the floor and get some space between us, but his knees clamp around mine, holding me in place. "Jeremy and Dan could have taken us."

"I wasn't about to let your drunk ass take a cab with two men I don't know."

"*I* know them . . ." I start, but he leans in toward me, grabs the arms of my chair, and yanks me in until my knees meet the edge of his seat.

He lowers his head and speaks very quietly, his voice taking on the cadence of faraway thunder. "And I know that this is really fu—really new," he says, censoring himself for inexplicable reasons, "but you're going to have to get used to talking to me if you're going to go through with this contract for the long term."

I inhale, hold it, and then . . . nothing. The breath doesn't come out. I shake my head, feeling slightly incensed. "I . . . you . . ." I can't get anything I want to say out, and I feel like a freaking fool.

You're such a dumb little slut, Vanessa.

"I . . . you are going to have to learn to be less . . ." I wave at him frantically, trying to get my point across, because there are no words to accurately summarize how he's being right now. No one has *ever* been like this to me before.

"Less what?"

"Less *intense*."

Brow furrowed, he starts to stand and, fully towering over me, offers me his hand. He exhales, and I realize he'd been holding his breath too. I wonder . . . why.

"I'll try." He nods once, and my gaze swims over his extended forearm, shrouded in pilled black fabric. He needs a makeover, and . . . he agreed to one, I guess. All because I agreed to work with him. I don't understand it, and yet I tentatively take this peace offering for what it is—at least, for what I *hope* he means for it to be—the flimsiest of olive branches.

I say, "I'll try, too, Mr. Casteel. But like I told you at the bar, and as you can probably tell, I'm not really the one who usually does the talking in these meetings."

His hand is big and warm and dry and fully envelops mine. It feels so personal, having my hand held like this. I actually . . . can't remember the last time anyone held my hand, and I don't free my fingers as quickly as I should. That said, he also doesn't release me but applies an even greater pressure.

As he continues to hold my hand and stare at me, his lips tilt down into an uncomfortable grimace. "You never have to talk to anybody in this building—or anywhere else—ever again, Vanessa, but I expect my wife to talk to me and, when she does, to call me Roland, not Mr. Casteel."

"Your wife?" I glance around, feeling deeply uncomfortable holding his hand like this knowing he has a wife. How did that not come up in our research? "You have a wife?"

He freezes. "Yes. *You.* Or did you not understand the terms of our deal?"

My jaw unhinges, and my eyes flutter, and my knees go weak, and Mr. Casteel curses as he lunges to catch me.

And as I faint for the second time in that same boardroom, truly giving the classic Fay Wray a run for her money, I think back on that mockingly simple contract laughing at me from Mr. Singkham's fancy suit jacket pocket and the feeling I'd had that I had missed something. Because it would seem that I had missed something big.

Chapter Six

VANESSA

"This is so inappropriate," I squeeze out in a tiny, tinny tone, one that Mr. Casteel—*Roland*—immediately talks over.

"This is what I wanted. I thought that was really fuck—really clear." He shoots me a side-eye from where he's seated in the uncomfortable leather chair neighboring mine. Up on the thirtieth floor now in Mr. Singkham's private office, Mr. Singkham sits across the table from us. Jem sits on my right on a leather ottoman from the equally unpleasant-looking leather sectional against the far wall, a laptop open on her knees, an angry expression pulling her small features into the center of her face, making her look like she's about to explode.

Meanwhile, I've been reduced to a puddle of melted knees. All I can do is watch Mr. Singkham and hope that he can resolve this reasonably . . .

"Mr. Casteel, the COE was under the impression that, per your written request, Ms. Theriot was to come on board as your manager—"

"You're a liar, Prasit. I was really fucking clear." He leans back in his seat, and both of his clenched fists erupt in flame as he grips the leather. It instantly singes, the brown turning black.

Mr. Singkham squirms. He makes a farting sound whenever he moves, which I wish would cut the tension but doesn't. He glances at

Jem as if paranoid, which he has every right to be, adjusts his tie, and clears his throat. "Can we speak off the record?"

"No," Jem barks.

"Jem," I hiss and nod. "Yes, I think this all is probably just a big misunderstanding."

"In a sense," Mr. Singkham says at the same time Mr. Casteel says, "I told you what I wanted. You're begging me to light this goddamn building on fire . . ."

"There's no need for theatrics, Mr. Casteel. We did speak, Ms. Theriot and I, and she agreed to your conditions. She asked not to have her skills utilized in the capacity of your PA and further stipulated which of the tasks we might have seen as being managed by one individual, but Ms. Theriot, you did not mention your opposition to the Lois Lane clause . . ."

"But . . ." I say breathily.

Mr. Singkham speaks over me. "And Mr. Casteel, while Ms. Theriot may take on the role of Lois Lane, the proposal clearly lists this as a superficial PR position, posing as your girlfriend to help boost your PR image and make you more relatable, sure, but moreover this is a public speaking role. Did you not read the brief? Because while the COE may be in the business of building heroes, we are not in the business of mail-order brides."

Mr. Casteel doesn't respond. Instead, the fire in his fists goes out, but not the one in his eyes, which are a bright orange; I can literally see the illusion of flames dancing where pupils and irises should be. He glances at me, and something small happens then. Something . . . that *wounds* me.

A dusting of deep pink strokes the tops of his brilliant brown cheeks.

He's *embarrassed.*

I understand embarrassment. I understand its sick, crushing weight, and I feel it bleeding from his skin like a fatal wound, and I slip and slide around in it. I'm going to drown in it.

I clutch the arms of my seat and picture Ann Darrow in the arms of an embarrassed King Kong. I cringe. He doesn't get embarrassed. Superman doesn't get embarrassed. The Pyro—the Wyvern—doesn't get embarrassed. He's a hero. And I can't be the one responsible for bringing him down like this.

He opens his mouth, and though smoke curls out into the space between us, no words follow it.

Meanwhile, I'm clenched together so tightly that I burst. "I . . . what . . . maybe we can . . . I can . . . I'LL TAKE THE LOIS LANE CONTRACT." My voice is way louder than I mean for it to be, and the entire room falls silent. I clear my throat and wrestle my tone down until it's barely above a whisper. "We'll just . . . I just . . . don't want to do the public speaking . . ."

"You don't have to," Mr. Casteel says at the same time Jem balks, "That's the main role of Lois Lane as we wrote her. Plus, you'll have to move in together eventually, or no one in the public eye will believe y'all are—or were ever—really dating. You're really okay with that?"

Oh my God, no. I'm not. I'm definitely not. Though I have no idea what I'm going to say next, I open my mouth to speak but am spared from it when the sirens start blaring and the bright red-and-white emergency lights start to flash.

Two storm troopers dressed all in white—COE security—burst into Mr. Singkham's offices, the heavy wood door slamming against the wall as they enter. "Emergency protocol. There's VNA incoming."

I stand and reach for Jem. She's still seated on the ottoman, and her laptop slides off her lap and onto the floor when I grab hold of her wrist and start to pull and—*BAM*. The outer windows explode inward.

I somehow manage to keep my feet as my arms move to shield my head and face. I hear a deafening rumble so loud I almost can't hear COE security shouting, "Thirtieth floor! Thirtieth floor! President's nest, I repeat, we are under attack in the president's nest!"

I have no idea who they're talking to, but when the whoosh of the blast finally settles, I glance over my shoulder to find that the place where the windows once were is now open, revealing the Sundale skyline—with no barriers to prevent us from meeting it.

Nothing but Mr. Casteel. Roland. *The Wyvern.*

The Wyvern has squared off against the void, broad shoulders looking expansive enough to keep us from falling thirty stories. "It's the Marduk. He was my VNA contact," he shouts over his shoulder, glancing around the room. "I'll handle this. You!" He points at the storm trooper closing in on my left. "Get her out of here. I'll be back in a second."

And in less than a tenth of that, he bullets out of the window in a blaze of flame, leaving a trail of ash behind him as his hoodie and sweatshirt entirely burn away. He plunges into the sky, hurtling toward a small object that I would have thought was a bird at this distance.

If I'd had half a mind—and had actually passed the practical in my war journalism course—I might have thought about pulling out my phone camera, but I don't. I just stare in absolute terror and bewilderment as the Forty-Eight with the power over flame and the one with the power over thunder and wind battle a football field's length from where I stand swaying toward a long, *long* drop.

"Let's go!" The storm trooper shouts at me. "Ms. Tsegaye, Ms. Theriot! Come on!" He gestures for us with a huge sweep of his arm, but I hesitate, reaching instead for Jem and her outstretched hand. Before I can touch her, a huge burst of light draws my attention up to the massive blaze lighting up the sky and then—*BOOM*.

I hear the sound before I feel the harsh slice of the wind cut through my clothes and hair and across my face. I'm tossed up off my feet, and my shoulder slams into the storm trooper's armor-clad chest. I shout, he grunts, and then I moan again when Jem slams into my back and all three of us go flying. Somehow avoiding collision with the chairs or the desk, we land on a soft area rug in a tangle of limbs.

I blink and plant my hands beneath me only to grab Jem's calf instead of finding the floor. She isn't moving, but when I look up, I see she's awake. The storm trooper is lying face down with Jem's head on his back. Her face has little scratches all over it, and there's glass reflecting in her black, curly hair. When I lift my head, I can hear glass tinkling in mine too.

"Holy shit, close your eyes!" Jem screeches a second before another gust of wind hurls into us, slamming us against the wall.

"Ooph," I groan, Jem's knee hitting my spine and driving the air clean out of me. My eyes open on instinct only to see the massive chair Roland had been sitting in tipping onto its side legs and threatening to fall directly onto us.

"Jem!" I manage to squeal.

I lift my arms, and a gruff groan sounds from behind me as the storm trooper suddenly shoves my outstretched arms aside and grabs the chair before it lands. He hurls it to the side with my and Jem's help, but the joint movement sends us toppling over one another all over again. I land on his leg just in time to be distracted by another burst of cataclysmic orange—this time from farther away. I brace for the responding windstorm, but it never comes. I take a breath . . . and then a deeper breath.

My heart is pounding as I watch, stunned and speechless, as the Wyvern and the one he'd been fighting break apart. The two grains of rice hovering in the sky separate, one getting smaller and smaller, one getting larger until the Wyvern comes back into focus. He lands hard on the glossy wooden floor of Mr. Singkham's office, fully freaking naked except for one slightly singed piece of elastic slung low on his hips, holding up a fluttering tag of black fabric.

It's not hiding much. I gulp and refocus on his face. His cheeks are pink as he stalks across the floor, glancing around only once before coming directly to me. He shoves the storm trooper's torso off my legs and untangles me from Jem's grasp, pulling me up into a seat.

"Fuck," he grits under his breath, his eyes molten pits, his front teeth bared and mean. "I mean, fuck," he says again as his fingers move over my hair, trying to pluck glass bits free.

I shake my head again and again, answering a question he hasn't asked me.

"You hurt?" he says the same time that I blurt, "You look good."

"What?"

"What?" Realizing what I just said, I quickly blurt out, "I mean you look healthy. No. Fit. I mean . . . you don't look injured even though . . ." I point lamely at the missing wall. "The battle . . ." My voice trails off.

He cocks his head. "I'm not," he says, and that's when I see it: high in his cheeks, just a peppering of pink. "Are you okay? Did you hit your head?"

"I'll do it," I say instead of focusing on my mortification.

"What?"

"The Lois Lane contract. I'll do it for two years."

His cheek ticks, and a feathering of fire fans over it, the world's most insane highlighter, making me jump. He continues to pin me with his gaze, even as emergency personnel swarm the space and medical checks out Jem and Mr. Singkham, who was knocked behind his desk. Meanwhile, Roland ignores it all and keeps his focus trained on me.

"So, deal?" I hold out my hand.

He glares at it. "Five years."

I blink in shock. "Two," I repeat.

"Ten."

"Three."

"Fifteen."

My jaw drops. "Four."

"Fine." He grabs my hand, then pulls me to my feet so roughly, I tumble against his naked body. I cook from the inside out as he ducks his head, lips moving within striking distance of mine as he says in a low voice that tastes like smoke and chimes with victory. "Then get a room ready for me. I'm moving in with my *girlfriend* tomorrow."

Chapter Seven

Roland

There are only two truths I'm sure of in this moment: I'm stupid obsessed with Vanessa fucking Theriot, and I'm absolutely going to kill something.

I weigh the two realities, calculating how my obsession will be affected by the murders I'm about to enact, and unfortunately, I don't much care for the math. I need to keep them alive, keep them alive, keep them alive. Don't kill the reporters. *Not in public, anyway. They need to look like accidents.* So I spiral, imagining a host of deaths, each one clandestine and utterly spectacular.

Standing on a raised platform, a sea of reporters staring up at me, I can handle. What I'm struggling to swallow are the nerves emanating from the woman standing to my left. She isn't speaking yet, but she has agreed to, and she's a nervous fucking wreck. We stand side by side watching the Margerie woman field questions from reporters like she's dodging bullets—impressive—but Vanessa's on next.

Vanessa. My girlfriend.

My cheeks heat at the thought and then, when I glance down at her, heat some more. Even if they are making her uncomfortable, the reporters have to live. Vanessa likes her job. I can't fuck this up for her.

I clench my teeth so hard, I wonder how my jaw doesn't crack, and of course Vanessa takes that moment to look up at me and meet my gaze, her pretty dark-chocolate eyes widening. I watch her pupils shrink and bite back a curse at the wild fear that flashes across her face. I've put fear in her eyes before, regardless of whether I meant to do it, and I do not like it. I need to get my shit together.

But I can't.

Because—and see exhibits A and B—I'm obsessed with Vanessa fucking Theriot, and because she's literally shaking next to me, I'm going to kill something.

Everything.

I force a smile to reassure her that I'm not pissed with her, but I can tell it doesn't work when she quickly snaps her focus forward to Margerie, who continues fielding reporters' questions about the COE's newest *Champion*—the Wyvern. Me.

The reporters want to know about the contract's worth (obscene) and how this affects the balance between good guys and bad (I'm the tipping vote, making the two sides even). I know that the COE bought me simply so the villains couldn't have me, which pissed the villains the fuck off if the Marduk's assault on the COE headquarters is any indication. Money didn't have anything to do with why I took the contract, though.

I glance again at Vanessa and watch her shuffle her note cards in a way that keeps my fists flexing. I have to fight the desire to rip those stupid cards out of her hand and get her the fuck out of here.

Never thought twice about a human before I walked into that conference room and saw her standing there, looking so surprised to see me, it was as if she and I had already met. I literally never gave two shits about any of them. Didn't care when I was with the SDD morons at their facilities. Didn't care when they put me with a host family who tried to get me to celebrate Christmas. I don't read their letters now. I've never sent a response. I've spent my entire life—that of it that I can remember, anyway—bored and unable to escape the feeling that I'm waiting for something . . .

I think I might have found it. And I'm not letting her go until I'm sure.

They call me *hero* now, but I'm a bad fucking dude. I want to kidnap her. If she hadn't agreed to let me move in with her, I might have had to.

Because there's something about those cards and that perfectly neat, tiny handwriting and the way she wears her hair big enough to disappear into that gives me a fucking headache and fills my whole chest with this hollow ringing sound, a gong in an empty temple. I don't know what to do with the feeling—haven't known since I laid eyes on her. Freaked out, I'd tried to get rid of her. Hadn't set us off on the right foot exactly, so right now I just shuffle mine and try to keep it together.

My fingers tap against my thigh, feeling the cold weight of my brand-spanking-new COE cell phone in my new sweats. I stick my hands into my pockets, feeling like a jackass as I'm caught off guard again, this time by an unfamiliar bout of self-awareness.

I knew I should have dressed up for this when I woke up this morning, but I didn't even know where to start. I've never dressed up for anything before in my life. And now I'm out here in sweats representing my girlfriend and her business—her company, a company that's worth millions and that she *owns*—like a goddamn slob.

Fuck.

I haven't shaved. Didn't cut my hair. Meanwhile, hers is all glittery in the sunny day, big curls like clouds around her soft, slightly rounded cheeks, hiding her too-small ears, two clips on either side of her part. Lavender. Like her shirt. It's a simple lavender button-up sweater paired with light-blue jeans. I don't know which of them officially dressed her, but it was a ludicrous fucking choice.

It makes her look *young*. I know she's got to be over thirty, running her own firm and all, but she looks twelve, and I'm gonna look like a goddamn pervert standing next to her, staring down at her note cards, which are way too close to her tits. It's gonna look like I'm staring down her shirt in the photos. It's modest, but still, she's got . . . her tits, they're . . . proportional, I mean. They're not so small that it would look like I was staring past them, is all that I mean. That's all.

Fuck this, maybe I should just kidnap her, I think, rubbing my jaw.

She stiffens suddenly, and I flinch, worried I mighta said the thought out loud. When I look up though, I see Margerie gesturing for Vanessa to approach the podium studded with a dozen different microphones and swathed in plexiglass. *Bulletproof* plexiglass.

Vanessa leaves my side, and I glance out at the crowd, eyes narrowing, gaze assessing every single fucking person and then expanding out toward the security perimeter the COE has set up. The gong in my chest is ringing again softly, just enough to grab my attention and make me want to grab her and wrench her back against me.

I don't know what it is, but when I first saw her, every instinct in my body told me to do one thing: protect her. I feel that again now.

I can feel fire in my mouth and smoke wafting from my nostrils as I take a step, but Margerie, damn the woman, deftly veers away from where she'd been headed. She hooks my elbow and gives it a menacing squeeze as she passes in front of me to take the space Vanessa just vacated. She makes a face that's frankly terrifying, lips peeling back from her teeth like she's going to lurch forward and take a bite out of my cheek.

"What are you doing?" she hisses, spinning around with a smile on her face. She lets go of my arm after giving it a final bruising pinch. A threat.

"This is fucked," I say, keeping my teeth clenched.

She smiles brightly and speaks to me in a closed-mouth grimace. "We've barely started. You can't ruin this yet."

"She's scared. Pull her."

"She's tough. Don't cut the legs out from under her."

Heat burns through me, hot and impulsive, but her words have their intended effect and keep me grounded. I scan the skies one more time before returning my attention to Vanessa as she reaches the podium, using a small step stool to put her in the right place at the mics that Margerie hadn't needed to use with her heels and her height.

I don't *think* the Marduk would be up for an attack two days in a row, not in the shape I left him. I managed to burn him badly from ankle to groin. I wanted to take his cock for being such a pain in my ass, but the bastard managed to throw me off before he took off. He'll heal fast—all of us Forty-Eight heal faster than humans—but we don't heal *instantly*. I don't doubt he'll be thinking of me over the next week every time he goes to take a piss.

The unofficial head of the VNA, the Marduk is a big blond bastard with a thick beard and gruesome tattoos inked from his neck to his wrists—his kills. He's got over twenty of 'em. Never bothered me before, but now, if I see him again within a hundred yards of Vanessa, I'm gonna rip those tatted arms off and beat him to death with 'em.

I hadn't expected him to seek revenge after I rejected their bid—at least, not so quickly. Granted, I'd all but signed on the dotted line agreeing to join them and had also *maybe* even agreed to entertain the COE proposal only as a means of gathering intel on the COE headquarters—more specifically, how to break in. When I contacted the Marduk to let him know I was out and that I wouldn't give him jack shit about what I'd learned, he was a *little* put out.

Yeah, I guess I should have expected the hit.

And that my response to it would be violent. I don't like things touching her. Only me. And only with consent. I didn't like the way it felt when she recoiled from me. I liked the way it felt when she swooned toward me after the Marduk attack, seated on Mr. Singkham's desk. Whether she was aware she'd done it or not, I wanted her to do it again.

I rake my hand over my face roughly and then drag it back through my hair. For fuck's sake, what's happening to me?

The gong in my chest is gonging, Margerie is glaring, I'm glowering right back, COE security is circling, drones are buzzing overhead, the reporters are champing at the fucking bit to ask their questions, and Vanessa, goddammit, is making me see red.

She has a tiny little Band-Aid on her forehead—clear so reporters won't be able to pick it up easily in photographs—as well as two on her neck and six on her arms and hands. Her fingers are fumbling the cards in front of her, and I tense as she drops one and it's immediately swept away in a turbulent breeze.

"Fuck," I hiss.

"Fuck," Margerie repeats through clenched teeth. Margerie yanks at my wrist, and I can feel the bite of her hold briefly before she moves ahead of me and picks up the two—now four—cards Vanessa let fall.

"You got this," I hear her whisper to Vanessa, too low for human ears to hear. What I *don't* hear is Vanessa's response. She just stares at Margerie like she's about to beg the taller woman to grab her around the waist and whisk her out of there.

Margerie can't do that, but I can—already would have, if Margerie hadn't returned to me with a look on her face and hissed, "Give her a chance."

Give her a chance. I rub my chest where it aches, not soothed at all when Vanessa speaks into the microphone in a voice that's way too loud at first. "Hello. I'm . . . sorry. Sorry. I, um . . . I am Vanessa Theriot. I know many of you may have seen me in the video . . . oh no. That's not the right one."

She flips through her cards, searching for whatever she's searching for, all that neat little handwriting utterly worthless in the face of her fumbling. I've seen this woman's proposals. Heard how she talks to her team. Her competence makes me wanna perform hara-kiri because I know I'm not worthy and then shove my organs back into the slit of my stomach just to perform the ritual all over again knowing that I'm the reason she's in this position. I forced her to be here.

She said no to the proposal. But then she changed her mind. I still don't know what happened to make her agree. It wasn't the Marduk attack; she said she'd take on the Lois Lane contract before that, when I was busy being an asshole. Why'd she agree? I've been a dick. And she's been a clumsy, perfect little thing.

Fire shimmers across the backs of my hands. I roll out my wrists and force calm.

"Come on," Margerie hisses beside me.

"I'm ending this," I say, louder this time.

"Wait—" Margerie grabs the back of my hoodie as I take a step.

Vanessa must hear the commotion because she turns and takes a sideways shuffle that has the edge of her foot tipping off the step stool—a small, easily corrected mistake that she resolves by flinging the cards out of her hands like they're covered in snakes. They hit the glass barrier, some hit the ground, and one gets picked up by the wind and tossed into the sea of reporters, who all reach out to try to grab it.

"I'm sorry," she whispers. The microphone makes that terrible squeaking sound, and I grimace. "I'm a little nervous." Her words get her a responding chuckle from the crowd, but she doesn't laugh, and it no longer feels so much like they're laughing with her but at her. Her hands clutch the top of the podium, her forearms bracketing the mic. The wind pushes her hair in front of her face, and she doesn't bother to brush it back.

"I, um . . . I was a little nervous on Friday, too, in case it wasn't clear in the photos." She gives an awkward little chuckle, but this time no one laughs with her. A journalist in the front shoots her hand into the air, taking advantage of Vanessa's pause. *Give her a fucking minute.* These reporters are goddamn cannibals.

"I, um . . ." Vanessa clearly spots the journalist. Her arm waving in the air encourages several other journalists to raise their hands too. Vanessa's stutter gets worse. "My company's s-small, and I was pretty sure we wouldn't—shouldn't—even be considered for the bid with Roland's and my r-r-r . . ." She's not gonna be able to get through the word. She tucks her hair behind her ear. Her fingers fumble over the podium as she searches for the nearest note card. She fumbles that too.

"Are you trying to say *relationship?*" the journalist who shot her hand up into the air first shouts without prompting.

Beside me, Margerie lurches forward half an inch. Her bottom jaw juts out, and she's baring her teeth again, and I take that as the final signal I need.

"All right, enough," I hiss. Margerie grabs my arm, but this time I shake her off, look her dead in the eye, and say evenly, "I got this." I can hear the rapid increase of drones' tempos as they whoosh closer, frenzied by my sudden movement as I halve the distance to Vanessa.

"Are you suggesting that you and the Pyro are in a relationship?" a reporter shouts.

Vanessa makes a soft sound that guts me and nods.

"And that's why you threw up on him?" another journalist stupidly blurts.

"I . . . no . . . of course not . . ."

Vanessa doesn't hear or see me coming, so she doesn't step off the step stool as I reach it and bracket her arms with my own, lining her back with the front of my body. I slam one fist onto the edge of the podium and let it erupt in flame as I point at the last journalist who spoke.

"Don't ask my girl stupid fucking questions."

I field question after question, shooting reporters down and getting them off her back while she rigidly stands there, refusing to lean even one inch of her back against me. And when it's all over and we're back in the safety of a quiet conference room in the COE building, Vanessa turns to me and looks up at me with those big doe eyes, a single note card still nervously clenched in her right fist.

She says, "Thank you, Roland." I feel the fabric of my being shift. And that's it. It's decided. She's mine.

I'm gonna grab her, steal her, take her away so nobody can fucking find her again . . .

No. That's what a madman would do. My hands flinch and react toward her in menacing, kidnappery pulses that she doesn't seem to notice, and I know that if I stay here another second, she's going to make a villain out of me. So I do the only thing I can do to avoid committing a crime as everything within me says to *snatch*. *Kidnap kidnap kidnap.*

I take a step back, get the fuck away from her, and take to the sky.

Chapter Eight

VANESSA

Don't ask my girl stupid fucking questions.

My eyes open. It's dark in my room, but I can't sleep. Haven't been able to sleep since the press conference last week and the media frenzy that followed, even though I'm absolutely exhausted. I understand now why Mr. Singkham said that there were teams of a hundred plus *just* working on the comms, PR, and marketing for some of his Champions.

Of course we'd prepped, but we couldn't have prepared for him. For *that.*

You don't talk to her, you talk to me.

In a single afternoon, the Wyvern had played a role and built a persona for himself that we had hoped to build over the next several months.

She's shy. I see any of you hounding her on the streets, I'll melt the cameras to your hands and light your underwear on fire.

He'd made threats even more violent and imaginative over the next seven minutes and sixteen seconds that he'd taken question after question.

So you don't think it's nepotistic for Ms. Theriot's company to win a PR contract for the COE despite the nature of your relationship?

The bid was blind, and she won it before we met, without me having seen it or her. After I asked her on a date the first time, Mr. Singkham made us sign a whole bunch of shit to be sure whatever happens with us doesn't affect the company. Nessa's a good fucking girl and smarter than the lot of you combined. She got here on her brains, not on her back, and if any of you ever suggest anything like that again ever, I'll tear out your spines. Nessa. He called me Nessa.

And is the nature of your relationship sexual?

Not that it's any of y'all's fucking business, but no, it ain't. Not yet. Not yet. I shudder where I lie in bed, replaying those words over and over. I know it's part of the brand, the package, but he sounded so damn serious. He can't be serious. And yet, the warmth that spreads across my thighs and between them is. *You ask another personal question like that, I'll light that microphone you're holding on fire and shove it up your ass.*

The more violent his declarations got, the more rabid the reporters became. When he finally did what he'd promised and turned all the raised microphones into mini torches, the reporters present all laughed, right after they'd screamed.

I'd been really worried, but Margerie hadn't been when we'd gotten offstage. She'd been scrolling my accounts and assured me that the press conference had swayed public opinion on the Wyvern already but warned me not to check the accounts personally, reminding me what I usually reminded all my clients—that people could be mean.

And like my typical client, I didn't listen. I wanted to see.

The comments were insane. People—mostly women, but people across the gender spectrum too—had gone absolutely feral every time he'd threatened a reporter for me. The top comment on the seven-second clip Margerie posted from that day read, *"Any good ducking girls in the building?"* It already had twenty-four *thousand* likes.

Nobody was talking about the wine incident anymore. All anyone was talking about was me. Analyzing how we looked together. How I looked at him. How he looked at me.

She's shy.

"Awwwww." That was the top comment on the clip Margerie posted to his official page. He already had 180,000 followers. I had half that many. And yeah. Margerie was right to tell me not to go through the comments. Because while most of them were loving the Wyvern's love story with the shy, awkward Blerd, a lot of people were also loving trashing me. It didn't matter that the Wyvern had shown up unshaven in sweatpants with dirty hair or that I'd spent two hours getting ready that morning. I was still too short, too tall, too skinny, too fat, too uptight, too, too, too . . . ugly . . . for him.

And after the conference, I wanted to talk to him, but all I'd managed to do was get a weakly uttered thanks out. He'd responded by glaring at me and then leaving.

You're just an ugly little shit, Vanessa. I can hear her voice in my head, a constant reminder of a life I don't seem to be able to leave behind.

I remember being a kid when the Forty-Eight fell and discovering that they'd all lost memories of their childhoods. How jealous I'd been.

I move my phone to the nightstand and close my eyes. I do my breathing exercises even though I've been doing them on repeat already and my chest is starting to hurt. I know I can't control what people say about me. I know it's stupid to try. But *maybe* I could afford to lose a few pounds. I grab my stomach fat under my belly button and squeeze. I could go for a run tomorrow morning.

You take too much after your deadbeat daddy. No man's ever going to find you pretty.

I roll onto my side and reach for my phone, set a new alarm and close my eyes purposefully.

I can still see the notifications blipping with cruel taunts and jeers, so I squeeze my body into a tiny ball and force my thoughts in another direction. It's easy once I give myself permission.

You stupid little—

—Nessa. A warm syrup paints up and down my spine. *Nessa's a good fucking girl.*

He stood up for me. I know logically that I can't trust him. Actions speak louder than words, and so far his actions and words have been a nail bomb where each nail is either outright angry or almost nice.

He caught me when I fell in the boardroom, then told me to get lost. He took me to my parents' house when I couldn't stand, then beat up my brothers. He fired me, then bound me to a contract that will keep us close for years. He told me he'd move in with me but didn't.

I don't understand, and yet . . .

You don't talk to her, you talk to me.

I exhale into my pillow, close my eyes, and dream.

Chapter Nine

VANESSA

"Vanessa! Vanessa!"

"Vanessa, over here!"

"Is it true you're already on the outs with the Wyvern?"

Yes, I think bitterly, though I don't bother answering the two journalists following me.

I keep jogging—not because I feel pressured by social media comments but because these past three weeks when I've set out to *walk* from my town house to the COE headquarters, I've been approached by journalists. Mobbed. I've found that keeping up a good pace can help deter them.

And in the past three weeks, I've barely talked to the Wyvern. He's been dutifully reporting to all the meetings, letting designers poke and prod at him to fit him for his uniform. The COE wants photos taken at the end of the month with him and the other local Champions. He's unenthusiastically agreed to all of it.

He still hasn't moved in with me.

And while I'm not *upset* he hasn't, it's just left me feeling off-kilter. Like I did something wrong. I know my performance at the press conference was pitiful. Maybe he's having buyer's remorse.

No man'll ever love you like I do, Vanessa. Tell 'em, sweetheart.

Without us, you'll be alone forever!

The last things the people who gave birth to me said before they were taken away by the cops. They were wrong. I realized that after meeting the Theriots. I've known that every day since.

But . . . that little part of my brain still stuck in a past life worries about my inability to talk to men. What if . . . I never find a partner? I'll still have my family. I'll still have my work. But it might be nice, maybe, to one day be able to come home to someone. Ideally someone reliable, who'll be in my corner no matter what.

Who'll say things like, *I see any of you hounding her on the streets, I'll melt the cameras to your hands and light your underwear on fire,* without flying off immediately afterward. Maybe a human man who also won't mind me being fake girlfriend to a superhero with a surly attitude and only two pairs of sweatpants.

Yeah, right.

The reporter with the floppy blond hair struggles to keep pace with me as I near Memory Park. "Is it true?" he huffs as we pass the glittery bronze statue of Taranis at the park entrance.

It's Taranis as a little boy. This is where he fell. Sundale's own hometown hero, he was the first member of the Forty-Eight I ever saw in person. It had been in a parade. I'd been thirteen and he'd been somewhere around there, presumably. Smiling around at the crowd, he'd had lightning bolts dancing on the ends of his fingertips and occasionally would make the lights lining the parade flare and die and dance in different colors. He's back on top of the headlines now, even if he was displaced by the Wyvern for a few minutes.

"Is it true that you can't please him sexually and that's why he's cheating on you with the Olympian?" I stumble, almost fall, but catch myself and pull ahead a little bit faster. I'm not used to jogging quite this fast, but that's a really stupid question, and I want to get away from it. Not the first part—because that could definitely be true, as inexperienced as I am, but the second part is one of the greater reaches

I've heard in a while, and I have no desire to piss off the Olympian's PR team.

I pass the kiddie pool to my right and lose the reporters in a crowd of strollers. Their questions keep up with me, though.

I *did* accept the Lois Lane contract. Even if it was insanity that compelled me to, I should actually *do* the job I signed up for. If he doesn't want to see me anymore, that's fine, but we do need to be seen in public. It's a fake relationship, but if we can't even get our picture taken over coffee, all those little fake pieces are going to crumble.

I huff, annoyed. I can be a better Lois Lane than that. I just need him to buck up, get over whatever it is that he doesn't like about me, and match my Lois to a halfway passable Clark.

Clark. Ha. Who am I kidding? He's more of a Kylo than a Clark.

Maybe I'll make Margerie yell at him, I think with a smile as I jog through the skate park feeling light, already going over what I'll say to him—what I'll try to say to him—next time I see him.

You're such a chicken shit, Vanessa . . .

No.

You ever suggest anything like that again ever, I'll tear out your spines . . .

"Vanessa! Over here! Is it true the Wyvern isn't really . . ." The reporter jumps out at me from behind the half-pipe, and *clumsy* doesn't even begin to describe my response.

My feet leave the ground as I fall, arms cartwheeling, and I can feel my mouth open in a silent yet dramatic wail. My phone, which is strapped to my left wrist in its handy jogging holster, hits the ground first, the loud cracking sound making me wince before my torso hits the ground on top of it. My chin hits the pavement last, knocking my thoughts loose. A bright pain flashes through my mouth and a much milder one through my chest.

"Ow . . ." Aware that I should get up, move, and that they're probably, most definitely still filming, doesn't help propel me to my feet at all. On the contrary. I'm grounded. My left arm is stuck, and my legs are tangled, and the sun brushes my face and is soothing in a way that has me tearing up.

I blink in the sight of pavement and people shouting. "Hey!" "The fuck?" "Those guys with the cameras knocked that lady over!" Kids' voices. Low and warbly and prepubescent and adolescent and almost grown and all the things in between.

Fingers nudge my right shoulder against the ground, and I wince, disliking that I'm being touched by strangers until I hear a little voice squeak, "Hey, miss, you okay?"

"Dude, give her some space!"

I roll onto my back to find a little girl and a little boy looking up at me. No, looking down at me. I'm down, they're up. Whatev . . . "Ooph."

"You don't look so good," the little girl says, her head cocked, her long black braided pigtails swaying with the movement.

The slightly older boy gasps. "Oh, cool! It's her! That's the Wyvern's girlfriend!"

A chorus of gasps go around, and I nearly laugh. I let the kids in front of me offer me their hands and pull me up into a seated position. I wait a few seconds for the adrenaline to settle to make sure I haven't injured myself worse than suspected. Feeling shaken but otherwise okay, I nod. "Yuh, I dam." Wait. What did I just say?

"Ohh! Where's he now?" The little girl's round brown face beams with excitement.

"He's not going to light us on fire, is he?" The boy, who could be her older brother with how similar their skin tones and face shapes are, is already looking up at the sky, and I laugh.

"Doh, doh, dot at all. Dank you for help . . . me." Something's off. My mouth feels like hell and I can taste blood.

"Yeah, don't worry, lady. We ran those guys off!" I glance up at the new voice that's spoken to see a boy, maybe thirteen, with an awesome naturally red Afro pointing down the path where the reporters are being blocked by a small armada of kids wielding bicycles, scooters, and skateboards. The reporters try to intimidate the kids into letting them through, shouting louder and brandishing their badges—that is, until someone throws a gigantic compostable cup down onto them from the top of the half-pipe.

The kids all burst out laughing as blue goes everywhere, soaking the reporters' shirts and cameras, and I can't help but bark out a laugh with them that makes all the bones in my chest ache. I cover my sore mouth with my hand and wince again. My chin hurts, too, I realize, and my head is spinning a little. I should probably get a lift out of here but know that I can't as soon as I remember the shattered phone on my wrist.

"Hey, do you haff a phone?" I slur like a clever drunk, just able to be understood.

Three kids offer me theirs. I take the first, and since I don't know any numbers but my parents' and I'm definitely not calling them to pick me up out here in a pile of children feeling like a child myself, I call the generic number for the COE. After giving them my employee code with increasingly slurred speech—not because I have a concussion but because I most definitely bit my tongue—I'm eventually patched through to Tor, head of the Wyvern team's operations, who promises to send me security and a car.

Feeling a little embarrassed they're sending security, I don't have another choice but to wait. As I do, most of the kids resume skating. Some still loiter around, though, including the boy and the girl who sit on the ground peppering me with questions about the Wyvern until help arrives.

And not from the direction it's supposed to.

But from the sky.

A superbeing touches down in the center of the jogging path wearing navy sweatpants and a navy hoodie—that I gave him. I don't know why, but my lower lip quivers a little bit when he looks at me, his gaze scanning my body from the top of my ponytail to the toes of my sneakers. His eyebrows are pulled together, his countenance intense.

I cover my mouth with my hand, the bright pain on the left side of my tongue making me feel silly because I sound like a cartoon character as I say, "Whab a-ou doing-ere?"

Roland arrives in front of me in a blur of movement, and as he drops to one knee between the two kids, surrounding me with the sheer mass of him, smoke curls from his nostrils. *Smoke.* "I don-think I'll ebber get ova that," I whisper.

He jerks back. "What?"

"De smoke," I answer sheepishly.

He jerks back even more. "You dying?"

I burst out laughing so hard it sends pain splintering across my chest. "Ow. Don't make me laugh." The kids on his either side are laughing too.

"What happened?"

"Just some stupid reporters," the little girl says. "But don't worry, Mr. Wyvern. We scared them off!"

He looks at the kids on either side of him and then at the mob of children slowly forming around him before glaring back into my eyes. "Wanna hear you're okay. Use your words, Nessa."

Nessa. I don't know when he decided I needed a nickname, but I like it. Maybe I'm overreacting. Maybe he doesn't want to ditch me as his fake girlfriend.

"Do you wanna getta coffee wibbme?"

"What? Now?"

I nod.

"Did you hit your head? How badly are you hurt? Did you see her hit her head?" He asks the kids, voice sounding a little strained.

I reach forward and grab his sleeve and smile and say, "No, no. I'm fine. Weally. I mean . . . as giwlfwend an-boofren. Fake. Fo-work. We should . . ."

"Jesus Christ. You're trying to plan a work appearance for the two of us right now? Am I getting that right?" He's right. I am. "Have you lost your damn mind?" I think he may be right about that too.

"It's adrenaline!" the little boy shouts. "My daddy works as an EMT, and he says that people talk a lot after they're in accidents. She's been talking a lot so far."

"That right?"

"Uh huh." Both the little girl and boy nod in unison.

"Nessa, Nessa," Roland says, shaking his head, and I hear the sound again, the same one I heard before, back in the COE building. A rumbling. And I'm oddly comforted by it.

"Y-y-yeah?" I stutter.

"Shush."

I laugh choppily and feel my bottom jaw chatter against my upper teeth. I cover my mouth with my hands as soon as I register the blood taste. "Ow." I wince.

Roland stands up and hands the little boy a phone. "I want you to write down your name and the name of every kid here who helped my girl today, okay? When you're finished, come back to me. Don't forget to write your own."

"Okay. Do you, um . . . is it okay if we get a picture after?" The little boy is about to burst excited goo out of his eyeballs.

Roland grins, just a little, just with one corner of his mouth. "Yeah, kid, you can have a picture, but why don't you meet me here tomorrow, same time? Today I gotta take care of my girl."

"Okay, okay, yeah. I can do that! Can Toni come too?" he says, gesturing to the little girl.

"Course. Tell all your friends to come. I'll skate with you too."

"Cool!" He sprints off, the little girl screaming for him to wait as his friends start to gather around and he starts to type a frantic note in the Wyvern's cell phone while Roland turns back to me. I try to cover my mouth with my hand as Roland looks me over so probingly. He's blinking slowly, and his lips are slightly parted, his jaw slack.

"Nessa," I watch him mouth, though he doesn't say the word loud enough for me to think I'm meant to respond to it. Then he clears his throat and adds more audibly, "Lower your hand, baby. Don't hide from me."

"Sowwy, Rol-Rollo." Wait . . . did he just call me . . . *baby?* Maybe I did hit my head harder than I thought.

His eyebrows knit together, and heat gusts out of him in a burst. "You get the names of the reporters?" he says as he looks at my face.

I shake my head. "It doesn't . . . feew . . . thad bad. And tey didn't push me or anyfen," I garble. "I feww. Fell. I fell."

He hisses, gaze tracking over my face, lingering over my mouth and chin, before moving down to my forearms and knees. "Shoulda been there," I think he mutters under his breath, but he speaks too softly.

"Whad?"

He reaches for my sneakered feet and exhales abruptly. "Can you move?"

I nod, confident that I haven't broken anything, at least.

"You in shock?"

I shrug. All I can think about is repeating my speech about coffee because I don't think he was listening the first time I said it. "No?"

He nods more slowly, his nostrils flaring and smoke curling between us. It smells absolutely divine, and I find myself leaning in toward that magical scent. Not like burning skin or hair but like a bonfire on a big summer's night. Weighty with the expectation of sunrise and full with the promise of home. I blink quickly and am so distracted it takes me a few seconds to understand his next question.

"Is it okay for me to touch you?"

It takes me too long to answer. My swollen tongue has lodged itself in my throat. I'm wrenched back into a bitter past, one full of skinned knees, bit tongues, twisted ankles, broken limbs, and worse. Nobody ever asked me that when I was growing up, not when I was living with those things that not even a dictionary could correctly identify as parents, and not after the system picked me up. This is so . . . minor . . . compared to all that. I don't know how to respond, what to say, how to be.

"Tank yup, Rollo," is all I can think to say, so I say it, stupidly. *Stupid* . . . No. I don't feel stupid for this. Looking at him now, I don't feel stupid for anything.

His gaze has glazed a little bit, and he looks a little uncertain. My knees scrunch into my chest, the skin pulling, pulling, unlike his brow, which is softening, softening . . . He edges away. Not a lot, but a little. Enough for me to feel a relief I didn't know I needed pull all the way through my soul.

"Sorry," I say. "I mean yesh. You can tou-ouch me, Roll-lo."

He gives me a final skeptical look, which fills me with another wave of relief—more like calm—and I clear up any indecision he might still have by reaching for him first. Shoot. My palms are all bloody and scraped up. I hesitate, turning my hand over so I can see the carnage. It really isn't too bad, and I know I've definitely had worse.

Roland—Rollo now, according to my swollen tongue—reaches to close the distance between us, aiming to touch my arm with his hand, but I pull back again, more slowly this time, and manage to find my voice. "I dun want to ruin your clodes again." I brandish my palm at him as a warning.

His expression turns from concern to incredulity to flat boredom. "You'll buy me another set."

I don't bother reminding him that his paycheck triples mine and my entire company's combined but instead feel an awkward smile coming on. I'm sure I look gruesome with blood seeping out from between my teeth, so I give him a closed-lip smile instead.

He rolls his eyes, and his warm hand slides around my outer forearm. I snort a little laugh as he pulls me into him, the force enough to send my buttery limbs sprawling in every direction. He doesn't make a sound, though, doesn't make fun of me. He just gathers me up against his chest, which is a freaking radiator against my side. It makes me smile.

"Something funny or you just losing your mind?" He's sitting cross-legged, my feet between his legs, my butt perched up on one of his thighs, his left arm wrapped around my back. He's as warm as a blisteringly hot summer day.

I smile and blurt, "Rollo, you . . . you're hot."

"You coming on to me?"

Mortification hits me, but I have the strangest sense that he's not *upset* by what I've said. His face doesn't hold one single hint of a smile, but he doesn't seem angry. Well, he seems a little angry. He always seems a little angry. Right now, he seems angry at my hands.

"That's no wh-I meant," I say in a small voice, my tongue starting to really hurt.

"I know." He huffs through his nostrils and gives his head a short shake, focusing entirely too hard on the scratches on my hands. "Not too deep. Your knees look salvageable too. But your ankle's a little swollen. This hurt?" He presses on a spot on my left leg right above my sneaker, and I recoil from his touch.

"Ouch."

"Sorry," he hisses. He glances at my face and looks away quickly, then glances back. His eyes are still glowing but differently than they had been. Just a ring of white around the pupil. "You sound funny. Open your mouth."

I comply without hesitation, responding easily to the authority in his tone. He seems surprised by my easy acquiescence but quickly refocuses on my lips and teeth and tongue. He shakes his head and glances past me. The kids are in a riot, all shouting the spelling of their names at the same time.

"Tell him my phone number too! If he needs a buddy, I'm his guy!" I hear a boy shout.

"I bi m'tongue," I offer on a laugh.

He exhales smoke through his nostrils again, and I grin. His gaze flashes bright pink-white. "I can fucking see that."

I shrug. "Ith okay. Coffee?"

Rollo rolls his eyes and moves to stand without releasing me. The little boy and his sister return not a second later. "I got all the names!"

"Hey, I helped," she adds.

"Good work, you two. Now remember what I said, okay? Meet me here tomorrow. I'll bring presents for all of you, and we can skate and take as many pictures as you want, okay?"

The kids start cheering, and that little cheeky grin Roland wears slowly morphs into a full-on smile. I blink three times to make sure I'm not seeing things. By the hammer of Thor, his smile is spectacular.

He looks at me, that smile tragically disintegrating into concern, and, on a smoke-laced breath, huffs, "I'm gonna fly now. You got any objections to that?"

"COE shecurity ith coming . . ."

"They aren't. I'm your security. Now tell me, you afraid of heights?"

"Yeth."

He hesitates. "I won't let you fall."

"Oh—okay."

His eyes widen slightly, as if surprised by my answer. "You trust me?"

Not as far as I can throw him, which is not at all. "I thon't think you'll let me fwall."

He looks away from me quickly and I can't interpret the expression that crosses his face, but I can feel his hands tighten around my body. "Fine," he says. Then, with no prompting at all, "Good."

"Where we . . . going?" My eyes widen. I'm not sure how I feel about flying again. But I still know that I'd be hard-pressed to walk on out of here and, if what he said about COE security is true, I don't really have a backup option, unless I want one of these kids to try to jerry-rig a skateboard gurney and haul me out. That would make for an interesting photo op.

"To get coffee," he deadpans.

I can't tell if he's joking. He must not be. Coffee was, after all, my last suggestion. "Tank you, Rol—" I can't get the word off my tongue and try again. "Thank you, Roll-oh."

He nods once after a short hesitation. And then he rises to his full height with me still in his grip, and keeps on rising. I squeak and grab hold of his shoulders as the ground gets smaller and smaller and the screaming kids turn to little grains of sand below. My stomach flutters, full to bursting.

"I got you," he whispers in my ear, and it's too easy to believe him as we fly off into the early morning light amid a chorus of children screeching in delight, chanting the name that I gave him. *"The Wyvern, the Wyvern, the Wyvern!"*

Chapter Ten

ROLAND

Thank you, Rollo.

My chest feels funny. Okay, cry me a goddamn river. My chest has felt funny for the past month, but right now, back at the COE, I feel it again, changed. Less like a subtle ringing and more like an itch I can't scratch, concentrated in the place where her breath dampened my T-shirt, right in the divot between my left shoulder and pectoral. She burrowed there deeply as she braced against the cold.

She flew well. Well, better than last time. She was more relaxed in my grasp than I expected her to be, up until she started shivering halfway through the ride. I tried to stay low so she wouldn't totally freeze in her T-shirt and shorts, but it didn't help. So I then opted for speed as I carried her to the COE's private hospital here in the center of the COE compound.

The COE campus is a sort of fortress. A single thirty-story tower sits in the middle of a ring of five lower buildings. Five massive glass balls, they look like the forgotten golf balls of giants, and through four of the glass domes you can see the dark green of tropical plants. In the fifth, the unique roof reflects the buildings and the blue of the sky, airplanes, clouds, and birds that pass overhead, while absorbing the glint of the sun. It was strange watching myself, Vanessa in my arms, as

I touched down. I really did look . . . like a hero. I wasn't sure how to feel about it. All I knew was that I liked the way Vanessa looked at me.

She's trying not to look at me now while I make no effort to disguise the fact that I'm staring at her from where I'm standing against the wall. The room is a good size medical suite with a white tiled floor and bile-colored wallpaper.

She's sitting up on the bed, drinking cranberry juice out of a little box, covered in Band-Aids, her hair looking . . . My lip twitch doesn't go unnoticed, not even by the woman who's doing everything within her power to *not* stare back at me.

"What?" she says, a tilt of her head that makes me want to weep. Every single thing she does affects me. My cock is . . . being a fucking dick. My chest is itching. I scratch at it.

"You still mad at me?"

She pouts. When she realized toward the end of our flight that I had every intention of taking her to the doctor, she'd protested—albeit feebly. She was shaking so badly, I could barely understand her blathering, largely centered around coffee. I plan to get coffee with her after she's been cleared, if she still wants that. How could I not? *She* asked *me*. Yeah, she'd been in shock. Yeah, her adrenaline had been spiking like crazy. Yeah, she'd been hurt, too, but . . . I'd still take it.

"Yes."

"Dr. Larsen's okay. She's gonna let us out of here soon. Then we can get your coffee."

"Yeah?"

I nod. "Yeah."

"You want . . . to get coffee? For the photo op, I mean?"

"Yeah, baby." Her cheeks get bright red when I call her that, which makes me want to call her baby a thousand times over. I smirk and, when I glance at her hair again, smile outright.

"What?" she says in a higher pitch this time.

"You, uh . . ." I lift my chin. "We're gonna have to get you a swim cap for next time."

It takes her a couple seconds to understand what I'm talking about. When she does, her blush spreads. She pats her hair down, but it doesn't help. Buffeted about during our flight, her hair now sticks out in every direction.

"I . . ." Her words die. They often do. I didn't understand it at first, and then I had Mr. Singkham give me her file. Well, I stole the file because he's old-school and likes hard copies too. Everything I read pissed me off, until I got to the bit about her finally getting adopted. The Theriot family was only meant to foster her. Not sure how they even got the gig considering they'd stopped fostering a few years earlier, shortly after they had their first biological child. But they did, and when she landed in their laps, they had six months with her before they filed the adoption paperwork. Her file got a lot thinner after that.

I get why she doesn't like to be touched now, and I'm pissed at myself for having been so forward with her. I get why she doesn't like to be yelled at and why she doesn't respond well to anger. I'm gonna work on it. Just need her to have a little patience. *I* just need to have a little patience.

"Yeah?" I lift an eyebrow and wait. *Patience.* I mine for it with everything I've got.

She looks all over my face; like an explosion, I can feel her everywhere at once. And then she refocuses on my eyes, gaze flitting between them. I wonder what color they are now. My guess is white. My eyes had never changed to that color before we met.

She licks away the droplet of cranberry juice clinging to her bottom lip, and then she asks me the last thing I expect. "There's going to be a next time?"

My bones lock up, and I struggle to breathe through the fire that pools in my abdomen. Is she . . . flirting with me?

I went through a phase as an almost twenty-year-old in college when I leaned into the whole Forty-Eight thing and actually went to bars and out in public and let people try to talk to me. Women flirted with me so obviously, there wasn't any mistaking their interest. It was fucking boring. And though that phase was short and I haven't revisited it since, I would have thought that the lessons I learned then would have lingered, but right now . . . I'm not sure if she's flirting with me intentionally or if I'm just being a prick.

I feel my face heat and look away from her, nodding absently at the ugly wallpaper. "Probably. Given your track record." I'd meant them as a joke, but my words sound harsh.

She doesn't respond.

Fucking hell. I look back at her and see a full-body shiver come over her again. "You cold?" My eyebrows knot.

She shakes her head, then nods, then shakes her head again and sucks down the rest of her cranberry juice, the tiny straw making gurgling sounds as she finishes the box. "I think it's still the shock. I haven't been that clumsy in a while."

"Mr. Singkham's boardroom begs to differ."

Her jaw drops. "You are such a jerk!" She throws her cranberry juice box at me, and it falls far short.

I laugh. The gong is clanging again. The itching is worse. I inhale and exhale and try to forget the strange terror I felt when I saw her lying on the park pathway covered in blood, an angry mob surrounding her. It took me a couple seconds to realize the mob was made up of kids who were being pretty fucking rad and stepping up in her defense. A few of them showed me pictures and videos of the reporters who had harassed her. I've got them memorized. It won't be hard to find them, and when I do, I'll incinerate at least a couple of their organs.

They won't die right away. It'll be slow. Painful. So many doctors wondering how this could have happened. They'll write medical reports and scientific papers about it, and most importantly of all, nothing like that's ever gonna happen to her again because I'm not gonna let her out of my sight. Enough. *Kidnap kidnap kidn*—no. I've got a better idea than that.

"Gonna move my stuff in tomorrow."

Her eyes get bright, but at the same time, she freezes. "I . . . you are?"

I think about asking her if that's all right with her, but the coward in me won't. "Yeah."

"Okay. There's just . . . I . . . there's just one thing."

"Whatever it is, it's fine."

"Okay, but I should tell you . . ."

"Ms. Theriot—Vanessa, can I call you Vanessa?" Dr. Larsen busts into the room. I'm familiar enough with her to be comfortable with her looking Nessa over. She's been my doc the past month, making me do stupid physicals but making the stupid a little less annoying by being a weirdo. She's an older white woman with graying blond hair that looks as crazy as Nessa's does now, even without having been buffeted about by the wind.

"Um, yes. Vanessa's great. Thanks, Dr.—"

"You can call me Emily. I'm happy to say that you don't have a concussion. Your scans came back clean. You don't have any fractures either, but that is a pretty bad sprain you have in your ankle, and I'm going to give you a note requiring you to work from home for the next week." My chest is tingling. I'm starting to like this doctor.

"Stay off your feet. This is a grade 2 sprain, not a minor one that would improve with a little stretching and rest. I'll give you a wrap you need to wear consistently for two weeks. Even if you're feeling better, don't take off the wrap." She shakes a structured black wrap at Vanessa, and I smirk at the angry look that crosses Nessa's face.

"I can't be off my feet for that long."

"Well, then, I think my surgeons may have a little extra time. Let's cut it off and get you an implant, and you can sprint on out of here with your new bionic leg. What do you think?"

Vanessa frowns, her brow sinking low. I cover my mouth, but my ensuing laughter is mixed with the strange reverberations of my lungs and chest. In the past month, I've heard myself audibly release what sounds like low thunder or a cat's purr for the first time in my life—at least, in my living memory.

Dr. Larsen must hear it, too, because she turns around and gives me a look I know well. "Is that *you*?"

"Yeah."

She scratches her bangs, and they stand up away from her forehead. "You didn't tell me you had this ability in our first meeting."

"I didn't know I had it in our first meeting."

"You didn't tell me about this ability in our last meeting either."

To that I just shrug rather than lie outright. Dr. Larsen comes over to me and places her stethoscope on my chest. The sound dies.

"Is he okay?" Vanessa says, doing what Dr. Larsen just expressly told her *not* to do by trying to edge off the bed and place her feet on the floor. She looks concerned, but my irritation with her burns hotter.

"Don't move. Get back in bed," I snap.

She freezes with a large-eyed stare and, strangely, without protest, obeys. Dr. Larsen gives a good nod to Nessa over her shoulder, but it's clear she's distracted. "You're making the sound again," she tells me right before she presses the whole side of her face against my sternum and holds my arms when I try to back away. "This is incredible. What muscles are you activating to make this sound?" she asks.

I shake my head and frown, feeling uncomfortable telling her that this is Nessa's doing in front of Nessa herself. "I'm not aware when I'm about to make the sound and don't know how I'm making it."

"You've made it your whole life? There's nothing about it in the reports."

"No. It's a recent thing."

"Like your eyes? Did the two start around the same time, about a month ago?"

"Goodbye, Emily. Is Vanessa free to go?" I say, pushing past her with some force to reach Vanessa's bedside. I take the brace, shove it in the pocket of my hoodie, and then slip my arms around her while she stares up at me with pinched eyebrows. "I'm gonna lift you now."

"I can walk."

"No, you can't. Or did you lose your hearing in the fall?" I pick her up and hold her firmly against my chest. I like the weight of her there. It feels right. I notice, much to my surprise, that the sound of the rumbling in my chest is getting louder.

Nessa scowls up at me. "I need to go to the office to get my things."

"Someone will bring them to you."

"What about coffee?" Her voice dips.

I look down at her and hate my body's physiological response to having her up against me like this. She's injured, but somehow that just makes the sensation worse. She's softness and vulnerability all laid bare, and I just want to do dark and terrible things.

I grunt and head to the door, ignoring my blood pumping and my chest burning and Dr. Larsen entirely. "We'll make a stop. See ya, Doc."

"Don't think you're getting out of this scot-free. I'm scheduling you an appointment for tomorrow!"

"Make it next week. I've got a date tomorrow with a bunch of kids in a skate park!"

Chapter Eleven

VANESSA

I don't know if it's the lingering shock of my fall this morning or the fact that he actually took me to a coffee shop afterward, but I'm feeling like my entire universe was tipped on its side and all the sanity that it once held has fallen out and scattered like marbles under furniture.

He carries me up the stone steps to my front door, and nervousness washes over me. "I can't believe you'd never been to a coffee shop before," I say, trying to ignore the feeling of his hand clenched around my thighs and the other around my back, palm pressed between my arm and my side, fingers shifting over the side of my sports bra. I haven't had a second to worry if I'm stinky or anything like that up until now.

"Nope."

"What have you been doing this whole . . . time if not . . . ooph!" I drop my phone, and he somehow ducks, still holding me, and catches it. I look at his face. It's awfully close to mine. I open my mouth to say something, anything to break the tension, but all words run screaming out of my brain.

He smiles. He's been doing that a lot. Smiling so, so softly at me. I'm struggling to reconcile the male I first met in the conference room, who later yelled at me in a bar and who fled from me after the press conference, with this stranger. "Waiting."

My stomach . . . I hiccup. And then immediately clap my hand over my mouth. "I'm not going to puke, I promise," I say quickly, and the Wyvern—the freaking Wyvern—tips his head back and laughs. He laughs riotously as he pulls my key from *his* pocket, though I have no idea how he stole it from mine—somewhere in the air? Sometime in the doctor's office?

My antique red door swings inward, and I freeze up as he invades my town house, too many confusing thoughts smashing into me from different directions.

I've been working to de-modernize a lot of parts of my 1800s home with Elena's help, but my brothers think some of it is really stupid. What if Roland agrees?

Also, what did he mean by "waiting"?

Why is he being so nice to me?

And was he serious about moving in? What's he gonna do when he finds out . . .

"I liked it though," he says, glancing around my entryway and then heading to the right. My door closes behind him, and I jump at the realization that we're alone. It's also noon, and I haven't started working yet at all. "What was the thing you made me order?"

"A vanilla Viennese. It's my favorite."

He smirks and sets me down on the sofa before taking a seat on my giant, round ottoman, first pulling it closer. It's dark-pink velvet. It matches his eyes. He leans forward onto his elbows, and I twist to the side to face him, curling my good leg under me and keeping my swollen ankle outstretched. "It was good," he says.

"Seriously, though, how have you not been to a coffee shop?" I say, trying to keep any sort of judgment out of my tone.

He tilts his head to the side. "You read my file, right?"

I nod.

"Then you'll know I was with the SDD for a few years and with a host family from ages they suspect were somewhere around eleven to sixteen. They were nice enough, but the host family they placed me with lived in the middle of nowhere. The SDD thought it best to keep us placed outside of cities. They said it was to give us free rein to exercise our powers, which they encouraged, but I think it's so that if shit went south while we experimented, we stood less chance of hurting others."

I nod along as he speaks, my mouth feeling so, so dry. My fingers curl into my palms. I'd really like to be back in the coffee shop. Alone with him, staring at me like this, I'm overwhelmed. I've never . . . had a guy in my house before . . . like this.

And then the tension between us shoots up a thousand degrees as he says, "Didn't have a coffee shop in unincorporated Sundale backcountry."

I stiffen, and the subtle ache across my chest burns cold. "You lived out in the boonies?"

He nods and then tips his head to the side, and he says the last thing I want him to. "Yeah. Not too far from you. Different time though. You'd already moved out by the time I arrived."

Hell freezes over, and I do too. All those warm fuzzy feelings from the day die as quickly as they bloomed. My heart just about stops. I reach up to catch it, as if afraid it's about to tumble straight out of my throat.

"What?" he says, and I see on his face a genuine confusion that absolutely terrifies me. Because he has no idea why I might be upset by what he's said. Because he's *not* a hero. He has no concept of right and wrong.

"Did you run a background check on me?" I say in a frustratingly high tone when I'd meant to sound strong.

"No." He sits up and massages the uneven beard on his chin. "I stole your file from Singkham's office. Not a big deal. Why do you look like you just saw a ghost?"

Because I am seeing ghosts. I can't meet his gaze, feel my whole body start to retreat and cringe away.

"Nessa, what—"

"You had no right to do that."

He balks. "I had every right. I needed to know who I was gonna be living with and working with the most . . ."

"You had absolutely no right to look at that. Those files—my childhood—" What childhood? "That time in my life is private."

"You saw my damn files. Stop freaking the fuck out."

"No, I didn't. The COE doesn't share your personal files with us. Only the relevant pieces of information that pertain to the job. This is a job."

"You're my girlfriend."

"Your *fake* girlfriend."

Smoke is coming out of his nose now in swooping curls, every bit dragonesque. "You're a hypocrite."

"What?" I say, voice barely above a gasp.

"A control freak. Lack of control in your early childhood has led you to want to control the world around you. That's what your therapist wrote, right?"

I wince like I got slapped. He read my therapist's notes? Jesus . . . "I'd like you to leave, please." My voice is cold. The pain meds and the shock are gone, giving ground for another monster. I've never felt rage like this before. I want to *hurt* something.

Roland's expression flattens. His eyes flicker orange momentarily. "No. I live here now."

I scoff, my eyes getting hot. "And you're going to sit here and lecture me about control? After you barge into my house and into my life? Make me sign some insane contract? Call me your wife?"

His face turns deep red, a red that makes my heart hammer and hurt. But I'm feeling destructive, bent out of shape, and it's because of that that I blurt out a question I'd been scared to ask since I saw him touch down in the skate park earlier. "How did you even know where I was today?"

He doesn't answer. He just gives me a hard look, one I can't help but wither beneath. His jaw is set, and his eyes are orange and angry. He has a temper. His knee is bouncing, and he's looking like he's going to lunge at me.

"Did you follow me?" I say, my voice shaky but no less loud. I don't know what's come over me, but for maybe the first time in my life, I don't feel like backing down.

He jerks, leaning in toward me, knees pressed to the edge of the couch. "I didn't see anything in that file that made me think any less of you, Nessa."

"That's not the point," I say, running my hands back through my hair, roughly rumpling it. "The point is that you had no right to see it at all. That part of me is over. I don't go back there ever. That's why I don't even tell people I do trust about it. Because they might bring it up in casual conversation and take me places I don't want to go. Not all of us are so lucky that we get to have our earliest memories scrubbed."

"How the hell do you get close to anybody if you never open up?" He's leaning in even closer.

And now I'm leaning in even closer. "Maybe I don't."

My face heats. Embarrassment is a little like a shield you don't want to hold on to. It helps mask the terrors that lurk beneath. Helps make it easier to concentrate on something outward like perception, rather than go to the dark places within where light doesn't reach.

"Maybe I don't want to, Mr. Casteel. If what you found in my file is why you're suddenly being nice to me or following me around or doing whatever it is that you're doing, then stop. I don't need a boyfriend, not even a fake one, and definitely not a pity one. I have family. I have friends. This may be a foreign concept to you, but I actually have people who look out for me."

My gaze flicks to his, and the rumbling of his chest abruptly cuts. I know I've gone too far. Fuck. "I . . ." I start.

"You're being a bitch."

"You're being an asshole." I glance at his mouth. It's so close to mine, I could close the distance between us with a breath.

I lean in. His hand moves to cover the side of my face, his thumb rubbing roughly over my cheek. The hysteria monster has taken on a new shape, this one just as unfamiliar. My mouth moves toward his in an awkward jerk, but he holds me back, licks his lips, and seemingly finds sanity and restraint.

"You don't get to back outta this."

I'm breathing hard. So is he. I shake my head, looking down at my lap in humiliation as I realize what I'd been about to do—and moreover, the fact that he was the one to pull back. "I don't even know what this is, Mr. Casteel."

"Fuck you, Nessa, and fuck that. You may be my *fake* girlfriend, but you're still *mine*. And I look after what's mine." After a few seconds in which the tension hums with its own tune, he stands and pulls some things from his pocket. He sets the pill bottle from the doc on the ottoman, then squeezes the instant ice pack and drops it onto my ankle.

Without another word, he heads to the front door, which I hear creak open even though I keep my hands trained on my lap. "I better not see you at work tomorrow, Ms. Theriot." He closes the door softly behind him, and I realize, staring blankly into space for the next few minutes, that this is the first time I've ever yelled at anybody and the first time I've ever had anybody yell at me back as an adult.

I smile and laugh into my hand before catching the sound in my palm. My eyes flare with heat as I think back on our conversation with both wonder and horror, and I'm crying as confusion grips me with an iron fist and shakes me around for good measure.

He didn't coddle me like most people do. He wasn't nice. He certainly wasn't honorable. He called me a bitch because he believed I was strong enough to take it, or maybe because he's just an asshole.

But I called him an asshole and berated him like that because he wronged me, yes, but also because at no point in our shouting match did I feel unsafe, did I hear my subconscious mind whispering to me in the voice of my mother.

I felt safe enough to shout at somebody, I think, guffawing audibly.

The novelty of the moment is too big, too much, too new . . . so I do the only thing that makes sense in that moment. I schedule a therapy appointment and, while I wait, grab my laptop, settle into the couch with an ice pack, lunch, and determination, and bury myself in work.

Chapter Twelve

VANESSA

"Oh em gee!" She actually spells the acronym out. "Are you there?"

"What?" I say, unsurprised at how groggy I sound. After working all day and a late-night therapy appointment that made me feel considerably worse than I had expected it would, I stayed up way too late crafting emails to Roland Casteel that flirted with the line between apology and additional beratement.

I currently have a three-page masterpiece, cut down from the twelve-page dissertation I initially wrote, idling in my drafts folder. I don't plan to send it without drinking a bottle of wine in its entirety first. Unfortunately, it's midday now and a little too early for wine, considering I spent the entire morning working and am only just getting breakfast.

"At the skate park in Memorial! Some kids are filming your boy! Apparently he had the COE accounting department up all night setting up a school savings account for each of the kids who helped you out yesterday and put ten grand into each of them! The kids' parents got notice this morning, and some of them even came to the skate park *crying* with how grateful they are! Please tell me you're there. This photo op cannot be left to the videography skills of a horde of excited preadults!"

Putting Margerie on speakerphone, I hop over to the vintage burnt-orange corduroy-covered stools pushed in underneath the breakfast bar next to the window with bright-yellow trim. I take one and sit. "Is it on social media?"

"What? It's everywhere. And now he's skating with them! You didn't tell me he could skateboard. That wasn't in his file anywhere." I wince thinking of files, their paper wings filling my stomach. "Whoa. Look at him go."

"Is he live?"

"Yeah, a few times. I reposted a few of the lives to his account. Check them out."

Pulling out my work cell—grateful I have one given that my personal was damaged beyond repair in my fall—I'm already there, tracking the live footage back to their various sources. I see excited faces pressing in on the camera in between flashes of parents holding up their phones, showing the education savings accounts with $10,000 balances.

"Margerie, there must have been over twenty kids he collected names from . . . and he hasn't even cleared his second paycheck with the COE yet. They pay the Champions in installments. That might have been his *entire* first check."

"Oh em gee. My ovaries," she coos.

I snort. "How is he paying his rent?"

"Is he? I thought he was living with you."

Guilt kicks me in the skull, and I clear my throat. "No. No. He, uh . . . hasn't come by yet."

"That so?" she says, sounding appropriately suspicious.

The camera for the live footage I'm watching now pans back up the half-pipe. The Wyvern is standing on a skateboard that's actually his size—bigger than average—which makes me wonder if he actually had one or if he bought a new one for the occasion.

As the camera swivels around, I don't miss the flash of a brown face I saw yesterday with hair down to her low back, a boy who looks just like her with his arm protectively looped over her shoulders. He's pointing up at the Wyvern, and I smile, so glad that they both made it back to see him. The little boy was so excited.

"You ready?" he asks the crowd. They all screech and cheer.

The Wyvern drops into the half-pipe easily, and as he comes up the other side, he takes off into the air in a blaze. The kids lose their minds. The camerawork leaves a lot to be desired, and I snort and realize that I'm such a chump, and I've got snot in my nose and burning in my eyes. I switch out of the video and scroll. Even in his normal feed, all the videos of him were taken by children under fifteen years old.

"He skated with them for almost an hour. Looks like he just left. And you weren't there?" Margerie says, making me jolt when I realize she's still on the line.

"He didn't tell me he was going."

"Funny, because when I saw him in the office this morning, he said it was your idea, you planned the whole thing, and the only reason you weren't going was because of your foot."

I gape down at the phone. "That's entrapment."

She laughs. My doorbell rings, and I hobble over to it. I have a vague suspicion of who it might be, but that doesn't at all soothe the pattering of my heart as I wonder if it might be him . . . No. Memorial Park isn't that close. He couldn't have gotten here yet. Why would he even want to come here after what I said to him? I don't even want to see him after what he said to me. But . . .

I pull the door open to see Margerie standing there holding a tray of four coffees and an enormous handled paper bag. "You two need to get your story straight."

I feel a blush on my cheeks. "What are you . . ."

"Why are you standing up? Your boyfriend warned me you'd be trying to move around on that ankle. It's the size of a bowling ball, Vanessa. Go sit down. I'll bring you all the cinnamon rolls your heart desires, just sit. Shoo!" She shoves me into the house and back onto the living room couch, where I have essentially been living for the past twenty-four hours.

"I should probably shower," I say on a yawn. "Also, he's my fake boyfriend."

"That's what he said you'd say. Trouble in paradise?"

"You could say that."

She gives me a once-over. I'm pretty sure that's a Chanel logo on her tweed suit jacket. She's paired it with jeans and literally looks like a runway model. Her sunglasses are pushed up onto her head, and she gives a big sniff in my direction. "You smell fine. Besides, we have work to do. Did you see the email from Mr. Singkham?"

"Yeah." The COE is planning to send the Wyvern on his first mission. In two weeks, the forest rangers are planning to do controlled burns over twenty-one acres in Vermont. The US Forest Service has asked the COE for the Wyvern's help. They think he can help spread the fire, but his powers are also in controlling flame. He can put them out after and ensure they don't spread beyond the designated boundaries. It's a great idea.

"I should be healed enough by then to be able to be on-site with him," I say, just as my front door opens and Garrison and Vanya come in carrying what looks like an entire office's worth of supplies. Garrison trips over a loose cable, and Vanya tries to catch his arm, but the box of pens she'd been carrying goes flying, and pens go shooting out like throwing stars.

"Oh my gosh, are y'all okay?"

Garrison and Vanya are laughing, so I take that as a good sign. Margerie starts off toward them, and together they get things upright. "Are you sure you want to go?" Margerie says as she and the marketing team completely take over my dining room table. It's an open-plan space, more or less, and I can see through the wide archway from my living room to the dining room easily. Past that is the kitchen.

"I'm not the best photographer, but as the, um . . . Lois Lane, it would be good to show support."

"We'll have an on-site photographer with you," Margerie says. "No worries."

"You found one?"

"We poached Monika," Vanya squeals from the dining table.

"You did not!" I gasp, doing my best to sound incensed, though inside I'm elated. "What did you have to pay her for her to leave Vayne?" Vayne is an online journal that we've had run-ins with in the past. Its CEO is a sexist pig, but unfortunately it's one of the largest online news outlets and the most consumed e-journal by Gen Z and millennials.

"Ask Jeremy," Margerie says. "But she's coming on next week."

"We're never going to get placement with Vayne again. You know that, right?" I'm still grinning. My team is amazing. Monika is one of the best reporters in our industry.

With a background in war journalism, she's deeply underutilized at Vayne. Working with our team, tagging along on the Wyvern's missions, she'll get the best of both worlds. It's a good move for her too.

"Luckily for us, we work with the COE now. Vayne has a contract with them for a minimum number of placements a month," Garrison adds, opening up his laptop.

I kick my feet, giddy. "Yeee!"

The other two laugh, but Margerie comes over and slaps me with my own ice pack. "This isn't even cold anymore," she huffs. "We'll book your flights with Monika and the Wyvern then, if you're planning on going to Vermont."

"Does he want me to go?" I say, feeling strangely exposed as Margerie returns from the kitchen with an ice pack that's as chilly as her expression.

"What? You two have a fight or something?" Her voice is casual. Too casual.

I shrug, wincing when she drops the ice onto my leg. "I'm not a good Lois."

"He's not a good Clark. You know, you don't have to go, but I will say . . ."

"Don't be shy, Margie. Just tell her." Garrison is grinning over at me, the natural curve of his cheeks turning his eyes into crescent moons.

He looks as giddy as I feel about our newest team member, and that makes me decidedly nervous.

"What?"

"Somebody's got a crush on you," Garrison says, making his voice go up and down in a way I definitely don't enjoy.

Vanya throws a pen at him. It hits him in the chest. "What are you, five?"

Margerie is laughing and shaking her head as she resumes her seat at the table with them. She opens her computer, all of her actions way, way too casual. *Way* too casual. Way, way, *way* too . . . "The Wyvern was in a piss-poor mood at the office this morning, but he did come in early. At seven." Margerie yawns.

"What did he want?" I stammer, annoyed that she's being so vague and keeping me in suspense.

"He wanted to talk to us about the reporters responsible for your fall yesterday . . ."

"We had to tell him that it wasn't okay to melt people's organs," Garrison adds. "Did you know he could do that?"

Vanya shrugs, staring at her screen. "Sounds cool. I'd have given him the go-ahead."

"Luckily for the reporters, the rest of us talked some sense into him. He *was* pissed though," Margerie says, looking at me quickly, then away.

"So . . ." I should be doing work or at least eating the breakfast burrito Margerie brought, but my laptop is still sitting open, screen black, on the ottoman, the burrito still wrapped sitting beside it. I reach for the coffee, still hot, and wrap my hands around it. I hold it under my lips as I lean back into the pillows stacked on the arm of the couch behind me. It's not a Viennese, is the thing I notice on my first sip.

"At the end of the meeting, before he left to meet with design, he asked the women at the table what they liked from their partners when they'd fucked up," Vanya says. "We told him we like melted organs as a sign of affection. Ideally wrapped in black bows . . ."

"We *told* him that there wasn't a one-size-fits-all approach, but that if he messed up with a woman, he should try talking to her about it," Margerie adds. I sip on my coffee hurriedly, because when Margerie looks at me, she sees straight through me. "And if the woman in question isn't exactly a talker, then he could try a nice gesture."

"I told him diamonds. Or a car. Can't go wrong with shiny stuff." I snort at Garrison's response and shake my head.

"I'm not sure all stuff is fixable." I'm not sure *I'm* fixable. I reach for the burrito, though it's difficult not to grab the cinnamon roll first. I know the cinnamon roll won't be as good as the ones my dad makes, but a cinnamon roll's a cinnamon roll. I'll take it. Unfortunately, Elena's voice is in the back of my head reminding me that, between the two, the burrito is the only one with some substance. Ugh.

"What did he do?" Garrison says out of the blue after we've been working in near quiet—as quiet as my team of bickering creatives gets—for another half an hour or so.

I debate whether or not to tell them—or rather, what. "He . . . read my file. Redacted information. My therapy notes. Everything."

A small silence simmers across my staff before Garrison breaks it. "Gonna take a lot of diamonds then, huh?"

"Where did he get the file?" Vanya asks.

"He stole it."

"Shit."

"That's not cool."

"For fuck's sake. Is he a stalker or what?" Vanya says, leaning back from her computer as my employees all talk over each other.

"Maybe." I shrug.

"Well, I hope you let him have it," Garrison adds.

I nod, smiling. "I did."

"Good."

And then Margerie's voice, too quietly, too . . . openly . . . says, "You did?"

I look up, and her expression is thoughtful. I feel myself blush as I nod. "We got into a bit of a screaming match."

"He yelled at you?" Vanya shouts at the same time that Margerie says softly, "You . . . yelled at him?"

I nod.

"What a fucker," Vanya continues.

"Agreed," Garrison says. Margerie, meanwhile, says nothing. She just smiles softly at me before turning back to her computer screen while Garrison continues, "Good thing he's not moving in with you then, huh?"

I frown. "Last I heard, he was supposed to be moving in today."

"He told the COE he changed his mind, but they'd already packed up or sold his stuff for him. I think tonight he's staying in a hotel while they get him a new apartment."

I swallow hard and then shove down the guilt I feel and nod. "It's probably for the best. Moving in here would have been a tight squeeze."

"It's a twenty-five-hundred-square-foot town house. How would it have been tight?" Vanya says on a dry laugh. Her bluntness and dark humor are my two favorite aspects of her personality, but not right now.

"Well, I never really planned on having a roommate, so when I redid the rooms, I didn't set up a guest room. I tried telling him a couple times, but I kept getting interrupted. There's only one bed in my house."

"Oh shit. Sounds like the start of a porno."

"Garrison!" Margerie scoffs. "That's your boss!"

"Sorry. Did I say that out loud?" He actually has red in his cheeks, even though his smile shows no contrition at all.

Vanya throws three pens at him at once and a balled-up sheet of paper she'd been scribbling notes on. "Men are imbeciles. Correction—males are imbeciles. Whatever he said when he was yelling," Vanya says, waggling a pen threateningly in my direction this time, "don't forgive him right away. Make him suffer."

"He's my client, people, not my boyfriend!" I remind them shrilly.

They all smile and chuckle, sharing laughs that I wish didn't feel so incriminating. Vanya just shrugs, seemingly unaware of how her words turn my stomach into a dreidel, and says glibly, "He sort of is."

I snort and don't answer. I just simmer in my blush as I go back to my coffee and my laptop, feeling strangely warm despite the ice on my ankle, and content despite the heaviness in my heart. I should talk to him . . .

I open my drafts folder and read the start of my email twice before deciding I'd rather throw myself down stairs than send this off. I'm going to have to talk to him in *person*. Ugh. I scroll through my contacts and land on his name. Roland Casteel. But I don't dare place a call or send a text. The problem is that I've never yelled at a man—male . . . er, superbeing—before, and while my therapist and I agreed that this could be seen as a small measure of success for me, we didn't talk about how to proceed. And I don't think I'm up for another eleven p.m. emergency appointment . . .

"Time to go. Ms. Boss Lady needs rest, and so do we," Margerie says. I sit up abruptly, absorbed as I'd been in my laptop for the past . . . *five* hours? Good grief. "We've been working too hard these past weeks. Five p.m. is closing time. Go, go, go!"

"But it's just getting good," Vanya says, pointing up at my TV from the armchair she's relocated to, her laptop on her lap, a beer in her raised hand. I glance up at the snowy mountain scene and the news reporter covering the catastrophe. "They sent Pele in, but she's making a damn mess trying to use her laser sight as well as actual lava to get the people out of the snowdrift."

"Shit, I'm seeing it here," Garrison says, pointing at something I can't see on his laptop. "She just caved the area FEMA carved out, trapping thirty-some odd members of their team."

"Chyort . . ." Vanya curses in Russian, her native tongue, before grabbing the remote and flipping through channels, finally landing on *48 Today*, which specializes in coverage of the Forty-Eight.

". . . incredible to see. The scene here in Whitestone Pass is absolutely unbelievable. Lightning struck the peak of Whitestone during a blizzard that raged overnight. The blizzard came on too quickly for the majority of guests to evacuate. While several of the hotels and ski lodges have been able to communicate to FEMA and the local police departments that their guests are all accounted for and safe, three hotels near the mountain's peak have lost electricity and connectivity. FEMA and local law enforcement had been working to dig them out, but that's not where our current concern lies.

"At seven fifteen this morning, the self-service cabin rental management company Northwest Luxury Cabins reported that forty-two guests inside of thirteen cabins have been out of contact since the storm hit and that sixteen individuals, who reportedly rented out the largest cabin on-site, were actually outdoors at the time of the avalanche. They are believed to be trapped beneath the snow directly, most fearing them dead . . ."

Shaky footage shows rescue teams attempting to bore holes into the snow to reach a cabin. A man dressed in a massive red coat and labeled on-screen as an executive from the rental management company shouts over the sound of the storm raging around them. "We think that this group of university students was outside trying to evacuate. They must have left too late and gotten lost in the snow. There's a chance they're trapped in their cars. All we know is that one of the girls, a Ms. Mallory Zhu, has an SOS app on her phone, and it hasn't stopped pinging local police since ten fifteen. The GPS on her Find My iPhone app hasn't moved either."

Another interviewee, this one from FEMA: "We just can't get to them."

And then the reporter flashes back onto the screen—a woman dressed in a dark-blue puffer coat that makes her blond hair stand out like a torch against the darkness of the world surrounding her. It's supposed to be two, the time zone making it only three hours earlier there, but it looks like night.

Wind is whipping her hair about, and there's still snow falling in harsh droves all around her, forcing her to shout. "The FEMA team was met with another challenge. FEMA enlisted the help of world-renowned Forty-Eight Champion Pele, named for the Hawaiian lava goddess . . ."

"She's an ancestral deity," Margerie corrects.

". . . who attempted to use her laser sight to carve a pathway through the snow. The cave that the FEMA team had already dug out collapsed, sealing thirty-six members of the rescue team within. Twelve have been dug out so far, but there's very little hope for the remaining . . ."

I cringe. "That's terrible."

"Not a good look for the Forty-Eight, either," Margerie says with a grimace. "We'll need to put out a press statement."

I nod. "I'll work on a draft and send it to y'all in an hour." Margerie opens her mouth to try to stop me; I can feel it. I jerk my thumb toward the door. "I'm not tired."

She frowns. "Well, I'm ordering you dinner at least."

"No, don't. My brothers are coming over tonight. They called for a mandatory movie night. They're pissed I didn't tell them about my ankle." I wave my phone at her by way of explanation, and, begrudgingly, Margerie sighs and leaves, dragging Vanya and Garrison with her. I turn off the TV.

I work on the press release draft and have just sent off some notes to Margerie, Vanya, and Garrison when the doorbell rings and my brothers flood my house, street tacos in tow. My stomach rumbles and my mouth waters as my brothers grunt and rage and annoy the crap out of me about my ankle—like they haven't all broken bones before or been in even worse accidents. Vinny was in a helicopter that malfunctioned once and had to be in the hospital for a week, but my brothers didn't react half so dramatically as they do to my little swollen foot.

"So, what'll it be, Vanny?" Charles says after tacos have been devoured and dishes have been put away. He plops down onto the other end of the couch and moves my feet into his lap. He hands me a bowl of Elena's homemade dulce de leche ice cream, made with actual dairy this time; she must really feel sorry for me tonight.

My brothers scatter around the living room, each moving like a synchronized swimmer to his respective station. Only Luca shakes things up, taking the armchair instead of the window seat since Vinny isn't here but is flying to Europe.

"Yeah, what'll it be? Some stupid show about baking or a true crime thriller?"

"I'm a girl. Sue me." I stick my tongue out at him. "But it's fine. Y'all can pick tonight," I insist, a little tired of being babied.

Luca and David don't hesitate before launching themselves at the bookcase, where they proceed to knock three of my neatly arranged figurines of Miyazaki characters onto the floor in their battle to the death over the remote. David wins. Luca skulks off with a scowl.

Charles and Mani argue over whether or not a new blockbuster sci-fi movie that just released is better than the original movie while I add snide remarks about how sexist the book is and how none of them should ever read it—not that they ever would. Vinny's the only one who ever reads anyway, and that's only because he flies so much.

I sit smiling as I check my emails, looking for an update from Margerie on whether the press release was sent to outlets for tomorrow's papers or posted in part on our socials. I'm annoyed she hasn't responded yet. I know she's not a machine, but . . . she kind of is. More than annoyed, I'm actually kind of worried.

I scroll over to text her when I get a surprising call. I clear my throat and make wild hand gestures at my brothers to turn off the volume as I answer. "Mr. Singkham."

"That the president of Cambodia again?" Luca shouts.

I gesture angrily at him, and David throws a navy-blue velvet pillow at him. Luca laughs and throws a pillow back, almost knocking David's ice cream out of his hands. Charlie's not helping at all but sitting beside me laughing.

"Mr. Singkham?" I say, surprisingly out of breath.

"Yes, did I catch you at a bad time, Vanessa?"

"No. Not at all. Just wrapping up dinner." I hold my finger to my mouth to encourage my brothers to shush the hell up, which they more or less do.

"Sorry to call you after hours again, but I wanted to let you know that the Wyvern has been deployed to Washington state to assist in the extraction of the trapped skiers and now the emergency rescue team."

Shock. I sit up bolt straight and set down my bowl of ice cream before it topples onto my rug. "They requested him directly and think he can help?" My heart is pounding. Oh my gosh, this is huge . . . and dangerous.

"I . . . was apprehensive to send him. His gifts aren't in the realm of ice and water at all, and I worried that sending him could result in more collapse, like with Pele. We don't need another firestorm—figuratively or literally." I'm nodding along, but I freeze when Mr. Singkham clears his throat and says, "But the Wyvern assured me he could extract them easily. He volunteered. It was so out of character for him, I didn't really feel I could say no. I just got off of the phone with FEMA, who got approval from the president." The president of the United freaking States? Oh my gosh!

"I wanted to let you know we're sending his handlers—COE security trained to support him in these types of situations. They are boarding the plane now and should be in Washington in five hours, weather permitting. Is there any essential person you'd like to include on board . . ."

He's barely finished speaking when I blurt, "Yes! Can we send our photographer?" I explain Monika's qualifications and get Mr. Singkham's verbal approval.

"She'll have to sign liability forms . . ."

"She'll happily do so from the plane. She'll be there in thirty minutes. Can you wait that long?"

"Not a moment longer."

He hangs up, and I'm on the phone with Monika in the next second. My brothers have changed the channel to the news coverage of the accident. It looks like they've managed to get six more of the emergency workers out of the snow, but there are still eighteen more trapped. No news has broken yet about the Wyvern's arrival. We know before anyone—a fact that Luca is freaking out and trying to text all his friends about.

"Can you take his phone away from him? Please? Thanks, David and Mani. Monika? Yes, sorry, Monika, hello. This is Vanessa Theriot from The Riot Creative. Yes. Yes, so excited to be working with you, too, on Monday, except I have a small question. How would you like to start working for us four days early?" I explain what I need from her and get her on the flight in thirty minutes' time. I call Margerie, and my team goes absolutely bananas when they realize what the Wyvern is doing. Margerie is back at my house forty minutes after that.

"Whoa. There's dude in here."

"We can make space," Charlie says, lifting my legs like they're a blanket and giving Margerie a funny look.

Margerie returns the stare with one of her own but shakes her head. "Tempting, but this is a work call. Good thing we left all this set up." She gestures to the dining room table.

"Did you let the rest of the team know?" I ask her.

She nods as she takes her seat at the dining table. "They know, but I am trying to convince them to sleep and not watch the TV so, after we work all night, they can take over in the morning. You want me to start with a few graphics or the press release?"

"I've already got a few words written. Let me finish what I've got in the next few minutes, and I can send it to you. We might be able to get this out in the next hour."

"Boys, let me know as soon as the news breaks that he's on-site, and I'll start hitting socials hard," Margerie says.

"Monika won't be there for a few more hours."

"You got Monika on-site?" Margerie asks, wide-eyed.

I nod, feeling excitement bubble. "She got on the flight with COE security."

Margerie pumps her fist. "Score!"

It takes another hour before Luca jumps out of his chair. "It's happening! Can I post now?"

"Shush!" Margerie, my brothers, and I all yell.

"Breaking news!" the *48 Today* reporter all but shouts. It's a new reporter this time. A man, and he's clearly freaking out. "We have just learned that a new Champion is going to attempt to extract the remaining emergency personnel and civilians. As the world's newest Champion, we can only ask ourselves if he will be up for the task or if this will be another dumpster fire, so to speak. I've got word that the Wyvern is here. He's . . ."

The reporter lifts his hand to his ear, his dark skin reflecting the light from the camera while the world behind him has turned to pitch. "It . . . it seems like, even though the Wyvern has only just arrived, he's already saved a life. I repeat, the Wyvern has already saved a human life!"

Margerie just about falls out of my dining room chair in her haste to scramble back into the living room. She shoves Charlie's arm, which he happily lifts, along with my legs. She slides between us, dressed in the same outfit she left my house in earlier, only she's shed the jacket. The Margerie equivalent of a corporate suit loosening their tie.

"Holy shit. We need Monika's eyes. Where are the eyes?!" Her fingers are flying over her phone. My fingers are flying over my keyboard. I send off the press release and grab my phone and toss it to Luca.

"Luca, take our picture. Are all of you okay being online?"

"Hey, I want to be in the pic," Luca complains as he snaps a few shots anyway.

"I'll credit you as the photographer," I say as he hands the phone back. It didn't take much staging. All of us in the room look utterly enrapt, the light from the TV reflecting off our faces, off my cheeks. Luca did a good job. He got my ankle brace and all of my brothers and Margerie on-screen. He took another picture, too, this one from the back, so you can see the TV and the breaking news banner shifting across it. *The Wyvern saves life in avalanche.*

"There!" Margerie shouts, bouncing in her seat, shaking my legs with every move. She's pointing at the screen, one hand on Charlie's knee. His expression is . . . cute. He looks shocked but maybe even a little smitten too.

Charlie knows Margerie; they've met before. He was surprised when I told him she was a trans woman, but it didn't change the way he looked at her. Not one bit. Charlie's a catch. All my brothers are. Charlie's just . . . picky. But if Margerie's what he wants, well . . . despite what I might have told the Wyvern last time I saw him, I love love. I just . . . love it for other people.

"Oh my gosh, are you looking, Vanessa?" She bounces in her seat again and whips her head to look at Charlie. She stills, then looks down at her hand on his leg, an awkward and loud laugh bursting out of her. "Oh my gosh. Sorry, Charlie. I'm just excited."

"No problem. You can put your hand wherever you want."

"Eww! Charles Benedict Theriot, I am sitting right here!" I shout, my head thrown back in laughter while my brothers all throw couch pillows at him.

Margerie elbows him in the side and removes her hand from his leg to point back at the screen. "Seriously, y'all. Look!"

". . . where the Wyvern," the reporter says, placing emphasis on Roland's *Champion* name in a way that sends electricity shooting through to the tips of my toes, "has managed to rescue eight of the eighteen trapped workers in minutes. Let's take a look. Our cameraman has been granted permission to get closer, and you can see here . . ." An image appears on the screen, blurry and a little distorted by the snow and the darkness, but the outline of his back is clear. He's . . . he's not wearing a shirt.

"Isn't it freezing?" Mani says.

David slaps him upside the head. "He's made out of fire, moron," he says in Spanish, loud and slow enough that I actually understand him. "Isn't that right, Vanny?" He switches to English when he speaks to me.

I nod but can't respond. My fingers are pressed to my lips, and I'm sweating. "I hope he'll be okay . . ."

"He's clearly okay. He's crushing it!" Margerie's legs are bouncing. Charlie reaches over to her and holds one down.

"You're gonna knock my beer outta my hand bouncing like that."

"Sorry," she says, and I might be too distracted by the sight of the Wyvern's bare body surrounded by mountains of snow and red-clad emergency workers, but I swear I see her blush in the light of the TV.

The camera pans over the hole in the snow that a shirtless Wyvern is disappearing into. He's gone for so long, I start to feel feverish. "The mountain is stable . . . The snow seems to hold, unlike it did when Pele attempted to use her laser sight to burn her way through. Instead, the Wyvern appears to be melting the snow with his steps. Everywhere he touches, snow turns to liquid, but not so much to risk a cave collapse. Gradually, he's able to work his way through and—look! Now he's returned, and he's carrying . . ."

The Wyvern returns into focus, trudging up the mountain in a way that doesn't look easy. On the contrary, he's making it look hard, grunting with every step, but he doesn't stop. He's wearing boxers only, whereas before he'd been in sweatpants. That's the first thing I notice, I'm ashamed to admit, but when I manage to unhook my gaze from his body, I see what he's carrying. *Bodies.*

His hair hangs in his face, which is pointed at the ground as he stomps barefoot through the snow. You can't see his expression as he lowers four people onto the ground, two from each shoulder, but you can hear his labored breath.

I have my hands clasped to either side of my face. "Priceless," Luca says. "Can I post this?" He shows me the phone, but Margerie steals it away. "That's too good for your account. Let me post it on the Wyvern's official one."

"No way," Luca starts to argue.

"I'll pay you for it," Margerie says, already sending the photo to me. Then she proceeds to toss Luca his phone back and steal my phone right out of my lap.

"How much?" Luca asks.

"A thousand."

"A thousand? Shit, that's a good deal."

"Never take the first offer, idiota," David grunts. He's a lawyer, so that makes a lot of sense.

"Fine, make it ten."

"Ten? You're crazy," Margerie says, fingers flying over my phone like a madwoman. "I'll do five, though."

"Score!" Luca throws himself back into his seat, looking as smug as a house cat while I stare transfixed at the screen, having a hard time remembering that I'm supposed to be working.

"They're alive, Vanny. Look," Mani says from across the room, where he and David are sharing a love seat.

As the reporter catalogs the survivors' injuries and cameras zoom in on the blue-tinted faces of four, then eight, then twelve groaning, moaning, writhing emergency workers, the medical staff on-site report that everyone is alive. And the Wyvern keeps going until all eighteen emergency personnel are pulled out alive.

I whisper, "He wasn't supposed to go on his first tour for two more weeks. That was when the COE gave him approval . . . FEMA's recommendation was not to send anyone else in until after the storm. They thought it could lead to more casualties, especially with what happened to Pele. And he's a Forty-Eight. The liability . . ."

"Well, looks like your boy said fuck off to liability." Luca laughs. He claps his hands and points at the screen. "You know, I hate to even fucking say this, Vanny, but I'm starting to like your boyfriend."

Fake boyfriend, I open my mouth to correct, but I don't . . .

We must watch the Wyvern uncover people for most of the night. The live coverage flickers in and out as the storm gets worse. I can't help worrying that he isn't wearing a coat, and several times I fight the compulsion to call him. I have his cell phone number, but I've never used it. I don't even know if *he* has *my* number.

He's been working for hours, first rescuing the FEMA staff before moving on to the ones they were originally trying to help. "And here we have it, the Wyvern has made it deep enough into the snowbank; he's found the cars. It . . . we're hearing reports that there was another collapse . . ."

I don't breathe for the hour it takes the FEMA workers to excavate the tunnel the Wyvern disappeared into as it collapsed once and then a second time.

Margerie is panicking. She's gotten up from the couch and is pacing behind it. "Monika's there," I say as soon as the text hits my phone, making me realize we've been sitting here glued to the screen for six hours.

My brothers are still here; David had to go home to his girlfriend, but Emmanuel is still in the love seat looking like he's gonna pass out, and Luca is still riveted to the screen, fielding message after message of his own because all his friends know that his sister is dating the Wyvern, and not one of them knows it's not the real thing. He releases a boisterous laugh every once in a while that startles the rest of us.

Charlie comes back in from the kitchen with sandwiches and a pot of coffee, the saint. He glances at Margerie as he pours her a mug—black with sugar, how she takes it. He dumps half a cup of cream into mine, and I take it with a weak thanks.

The images that start to blast my phone are from Monika. I email them as quickly as I can to Margerie for her to assess the best, which ones we'll keep for official COE press, which ones we'll post, and which one's we'll sell to other outlets. I understand the price tag they put on Monika's contract very quickly. Because the pictures she gets of the Wyvern are absolutely fucking incredible.

She captures the moment the FEMA employees clear the snow and the Wyvern's face first emerges. He's clearing the tunnel he's created from his side too. And behind him, he's dragging the door of a car on a thick chain. There are *eight* people clinging to it. And Monika captures it.

Rollo looks like he's in pain as he hands over the people. He doesn't stop to check any of their vitals but returns to the darkness. And Monika, the cheeky and talented woman, manages to evade security, who are too busy scrambling with the survivors, and follows him.

Monika Neumann. An ex–war journalist who was born in Seoul and raised in Germany before moving to the States and pursuing a career that's made her famous, particularly because of the fearlessness she displays right here. She follows Rollo past the point of no return. She sees the warning, BEWARE YE WHO ENTER HERE, spits into her fist, and smears her palm all over the signage.

She heads into the dark, snapping photos as she goes. She opts for pictures instead of video, and it's clear why. The Wyvern is *glowing*, emitting just enough light to see by. She wouldn't be able to use her night vision—he's moving too fast to use night mode—so she follows and takes pictures, her flash every so often reflecting off his back, but more often than not, she takes photos in the dark just like that. And each of them is spectacular.

She captures the moment he finds the first car, the one he previously emptied, and follows him as he digs deeper into the snow, melting it and pushing it aside like a heavy curtain with his hands. He heads in one direction, like he knows exactly where he's going, and soon enough, a second car appears. Monika hangs back here.

The photos that come through are sensational. Margerie's already on the phone with news outlets, and soon, in a crazy twist, I start to see Monika's photos appearing on the screen in front of me, moments after they first hit my phone.

"This is incredible material, coming from The Riot Creative's war journalist, Monika Neumann. For those who don't know, The Riot

Creative's founder and CEO is the Wyvern's partner, Vanessa Theriot. I am told that she is watching our coverage live, as I speak . . ."

"Oh shit, that's us! I took that pic!" Luca points at the screen, startling Mani so badly, he knocks his water glass off the table. It hits the ground, blessedly empty, but Mani's alert now and staring at his own face on the TV. "Shit, I needed more than five grand for that," Luca says.

"Too late," Margerie quips.

My face is hotter than the sun as the image Margerie just posted on the Wyvern's official page hits the TV. My face looks huge and frightened and hopeful. My brothers look appropriately impressed. Margerie looks concentrated and concerned. And then the image switches to the one I posted, from the back, showing the screen with the reporter we're still watching. And then, in a strange twist of time, all that falls away, and the reporter is speaking once more, showing images of the Wyvern coming up the dark, scary shaft as they're sent by Monika.

"Monika Neumann is one of the best in the business, if I may say so myself, though I'm being told FEMA staff aren't particularly pleased, and there may be fines for The Riot Creative after all this is over, and . . . oh. I'm just getting word that we're getting footage from *inside* the car. This is incredible stuff, people . . . I certainly hope that you all at home are holding on to your chairs—including Vanessa, who must undoubtedly be feeling strong emotion for her boyfriend. Hang in there, sweetheart. It looks like the Wyvern is about to make another rescue . . ."

"Sweetheart?" Margerie makes a gagging sound. I don't love it either, but I'm too stunned watching the scene unfold.

A very shaky phone camera is transmitting to a social media live stream—good grief. The news report has captured the footage and is broadcasting it far and wide. Heart messages and crying emojis clutter the screen as they crop up. I see darkness and then the flash of light and then hear the Wyvern's voice before I see him.

"That girl alive?"

"We . . . don't know . . . She got hit hard . . . by the snow." The female voice speaking is shaky. She's shivering that badly. "We dragged her in . . ."

The Wyvern looks at the one speaking, just above the camera. His chest starts to glow, flames licking up and down his chest and abdomen before disappearing. They come in easy waves like surf on the shore. He keeps it up as he looks around, his face hardening. "Are you alone?"

"Nobody's been . . . they . . . I don't know." She starts to cry.

"You're doing great, kid," he says in a low voice. "Can you move at all?"

"I don't know."

"Don't move then." The camera goes dark as the fire on his chest goes out and he reaches for the girl holding the phone. There's shuffling fabric and a muffled voice—Roland's—asking, "How many in the car?"

"Seven."

"Seven. Is that including you? What's your name?"

"M-M-Mallory Zh-Zhu. And y-yeah."

"Did somebody leave the car?"

"Br-Brian Hughes. He's the b-best climber. T-t-tried to g-get help."

The Wyvern makes a gruff sound and turns. The camera flashes back out and I catch a glimpse of a woman with dark hair crouching in the absolutely terrifying snow tunnel. She's got a flashlight in her hand that blinds the camera for a moment before she points it at the wall.

There's grunting, and the Wyvern keeps moving, passing Monika in the death corridor. A few moments later, a few more pictures hit my screen.

The Wyvern is carrying so many bodies, he's almost unrecognizable as a human—or, I guess, as the being that he is. I can hear the sounds of his struggle with each step he takes, transmitted through the TV. Meanwhile, I pass on the images to Margerie, who hisses at what she sees. "Jesus Christ, this guy is a beast."

"I wanna see." Luca dives across the room to look over Margerie's shoulder at the computer screen.

The news coverage finally pans back to the world beyond the hell that had swallowed the Wyvern up, and we see him emerging from the snow, carrying so many people, I can't count them all. He collapses as he drops the last one to the ground, landing on one knee, and I make a sound that's even higher than a squeak. My phone is buzzing, but I don't reach for it. I can't. My bones are all shaking. I think I'm trembling as badly as the girl he pulled out of the car.

"He's gonna be okay," Charles says at my side.

I nod, wanting to believe him so badly.

There's so much shuffling and commotion happening, it takes some time before the Wyvern is standing again. There are medical personnel swarming him, but he waves them off and staggers back toward the opening in the ground.

"What are you doing?" a doctor shouts. A Black woman with tight ringlets. She grabs his arm. "You need to rest. Your heart rate . . ."

"Gotta go back. Left one kid."

He disappears, and this time FEMA stops Monika from following as their workers enter the tunnels the Wyvern has excavated to put up supports and bolsters to prevent the cave from collapsing again. While I'm grateful for the additional security they're providing him, it means we're just left to watch coverage of the injured as they're cared for and assessed and loaded into the emergency medical helicopters. Many of them are in critical condition. One . . . a young man . . . isn't breathing.

It takes an hour for the medics on-site to pronounce the boy dead. Still the Wyvern hasn't returned. The sky outside is starting to lighten. My brothers stand up to leave. "I'll drive Mani," Luca says, giving his older brother a heavy clap on the shoulder, startling him awake.

"And I'll take this one back to her place." Charlie scoops Margerie up off her dining room chair. I hadn't realized she was completely passed out, draped over her laptop. I'd stopped fielding photos and checking our social accounts. Monika isn't sending many photos through now anyway. She's getting pictures of the young kids lying on long gurneys, but I'm not going to post any of those. I don't want any of them to see the light of day. They're so tragic. The kids are eighteen to twenty—college age—but they look like babies, their skin all blue, their teeth all chattering. *And Roland saved them.*

"Thanks, Charlie."

Charlie stops behind the couch while Margerie grumbles sleepily in his grip. "Put me down," she says.

He just chuckles and shushes her. "Go to sleep. I'll get you home once you give me your address."

She mumbles that too. "Sleep, Vanessa," she slurs.

"Sleep, Vanny," my brothers all repeat in turn. Emmanuel stumbles over to me, rubbing his eyes. He leans down and kisses the top of my head. "He's gonna be all right, Vanny. Don't worry. You'll see him soon."

I shouldn't want to, but I do. I have the strangest pinching in my chest—it resembles guilt—that makes me think he might, just maybe, be doing this because of me. And if he gets hurt, I'm not going to . . . I just . . . can't even think about that. So, ignoring the advice from my siblings and Margerie, I stay awake and stare at the screen like I'm stuck in *A Clockwork Orange*, until . . .

"And wait—I'm hearing that we might have some movement from below." The female reporter is back, looking somewhat well rested; that makes one of us. The camera pans to the mouth of the tunnel where rescue workers are moving in and out until, finally, the reporter cries out, "And here he is! The Wyvern has returned, and he's not alone! He's successfully saved the last student skier trapped between the vehicles. The young man had been trying to get help and had gotten lost along the way. His friends, those well enough to speak to us earlier, stated that he was the best equipped among them to survive this, and thanks to the Wyvern, the world's newest Champion, it appears that he has."

Roland staggers up into the mouth of the tunnel, bolstered on both sides by FEMA rescuers, and there's lightness enough in the sky now to see just how rough he looks. He's got scrapes all over his skin; he's got deep, dark purple bruises under his eyes. His eyes are blazing orange, and he's carrying, with what looks like great difficulty, a young skier dressed in thick, thick clothing. He's only a couple inches shorter than the Wyvern and, in so much clothing, looks nearly as broad. He's falling all over the Wyvern's arms, but his head is bobbing. He tries to look up and manages to look directly into the camera before FEMA medical staff swarm him and the Wyvern too.

The camera pans back to the reporter. Her cheeks are flushed. "In all my years, this is one of the greatest acts of heroism I've ever seen. The COE was absolutely right in its choice to enlist the Wyvern to the Champions. Even now, his body appears to be close to giving out after a night of saving lives through the use of hard muscle, grit, and incredible power, but he's insisting on going back in to help excavate some of the hotels and cabins. FEMA staff is working tirelessly on that front, having already excavated and evacuated the largest hotel while the Wyvern was at work. I believe FEMA as well as his team may be encouraging him to rest . . .

"Yes, it appears the Wyvern will rest for a few hours, but he will stay on-site and help evacuation teams over the course of the next day to ensure all hotel and rental guests are able to safely evacuate. Wow. This is truly something. I certainly hope all of you at home understand the condition the Wyvern is in and the fact that he is not immortal. He is suffering, but he's determined to stay to help. Now, let's speak to FEMA's medical director about the state of the boy who was just brought in . . ."

I stay and watch for a few more hours before finally shutting the blinds and laying my head on my pillow. I send off a few additional instructions to the relief team, but they don't need it. Margerie had already sent them a thorough brief before she passed out on my table. Charlie texts me to let me know she got home okay. I'm grateful. I stare at the text and then exit out of Charlie's messages. I go to draft a new one.

Please take a break. I stare at it as I find Roland's contact. He's listed in my phone as a client. Roland Casteel, COE.

I can't help but think about what he said. *How the hell do you get close to anybody if you never open up?*

And what I said. *Maybe I don't.* I wince. I haven't forgotten what he called me. Or what I called him. I hope he didn't mean it. But I don't know that I didn't. He was an asshole. A control freak. A jerk.

But I'm not sure I was any better.

I was scared. Am scared. *I don't need a boyfriend, not even a fake one.*

That's true . . . but . . . do I *want* one? Fake or . . . not?

I delete the message and type another. I hit send before I can chicken out . . . and immediately regret it. It was too forward, too much, not at all in consideration of our past fight. It was weird and stalkery—exactly what I accused him of. It was just . . . too much.

But I don't unsend it. I don't edit it either. Instead, I panic about it until my phone slips from my fingers and I slip into dreams of snow and heat.

Chapter Thirteen

ROLAND

My whole damn body is a bruise. I've been working for almost two goddamn days straight, and after the first hour, I'd already started to regret this shit. I waded further into regret with every additional step I took into the snow piles. Hauling that shit with my arms was intense goddamn work, even with my powers helping. I couldn't burn through with full intensity. I had to go slow to make sure the walls and roof of the tunnel I cleared stayed intact. Once, I tried to move faster, burning rather than hauling, and that shit backfired right quick. Thank fuck the FEMA workers later managed to bracket the tunnels and keep them up. Fighting my way out of the snow with weaker human bodies to protect sucked.

I can't say I didn't *care* I had saved people. I did care. I do. But none of their thanks, none of the congratulations I got from the people in red running all around me, none of it meant anything compared to the text I got from her.

You're my hero.

My heart is in my mouth. No. It's somewhere else, but that's not something I want to focus on in front of all these people. There's a space blanket on my shoulders that's really fucking stupid considering I am heat incarnate, but I guess they feel like they gotta help me by more than just staring at me while two people work on stitching me up.

I got cut up on the cars. My hands are burning but not anywhere near as badly as the pinging in my chest. That itchy spot I felt when she breathed on me, *trusting and needing me,* hurts. I can't stay here.

"What? Sir?" The FEMA medical staff member is looking up at me confused as hell. He's stitching up my knee while his colleague stitches a gash in my shoulder. I've got scratches all over my face, bandages covering most of them by now. My hair and beard are completely mangled, but none of that's gonna stop me from getting the fuck out of here.

"I gotta get back." I stand up. The medical staff falls away from me, landing on their asses even though I haven't touched them.

"We're not finished!" The guy on the ground points at my thigh, and I see that there's a needle dangling from my leg. I take a step. My right knee gives out. Shit.

Several people rush forward to catch me, and I feel embarrassed, but damn, I'm fucking exhausted. "Need a plane." I'm not gonna be able to fly out of here.

"We're planning on one . . ." My COE handler is on-site, along with two COE security guards and a journalist from Vanessa's agency. She's a damn beast. She slept when I did—only four hours, maybe fewer than that—and she's been up ever since. Her face looks haggard and insane, brown skin drained of almost all color. Her lips are blue-tinted, and I've seen her a few times putting her camera down and dipping her fingers in warm water. She doesn't wear gloves. Can't imagine how cold she is. She's still on me now, never too far. I look at her and give her a tip of my chin. "Let's go."

She nods without hesitating, and I notice her waver on her feet as she rises to stand up fully.

I look to my handler, a middle-aged Black guy who's built like a tank. When I first saw him, I thought he was one of the security guards until I realized he wasn't wearing white or carrying a big gun. His was smaller and buckled to his belt. "Get us out of here."

"Where should we take you?" He's already on the phone. I appreciate that.

"Back . . ." To my girl. *She doesn't want to see me.* I had them put a hold on moving my shit, the little of it that there is from my empty-ass apartment. But now, standing here shaky as I am, I don't want to go back to that. I don't want to go to a generic hotel either. "Take me to my girl. Anybody asks, tell them I did this for her."

Chapter Fourteen

Vanessa

It's Saturday evening. I've ordered takeout—again—and even though my foot's already feeling a lot better, I'm still trying to keep up with the doctor's suggestion and not do too much. So I've only been doing what I do best: working. The news cycle has been mental. It's been so hard to keep up with. And worse, a lot of news outlets want to hear from *me*, Vanessa the Wyvern's girlfriend, not Ms. Theriot, head of The Riot Creative. I've had to issue statements, but they've been strange to issue—especially from behind the safety of my own computer and especially because they all come from a place of absolute truth.

He's my hero, and I'm so proud of him. I hope the world is too.

When my doorbell rings, I answer it on a wobbly leg and thank the man who hands the food over. Luckily, he doesn't seem to recognize me in the slightest, despite the fact that Luca's pictures of me have been plastered all over the place. Outlets have homed in on them, coupling pictures of my nervous, hopeful face with images of Roland looking like a snow god emerging from the mountain. He recovered all the kids and all the trapped medical staff. Five are in critical condition. Two . . . didn't make it. Sixteen more had significant injuries but are already out of intensive care or out of the hospital, and the rest made it out with bumps and scrapes and nightmares that I'm sure will haunt them for a while. But it's thanks to Roland that they made it out at all.

I did it for her. That's what media outlets are reporting he said to FEMA staff, but nobody caught it on camera, and I . . . definitely don't believe it. It's been hours since his plane left Washington. He was helicoptered off-site this morning after almost two days of helping people nonstop. It was . . . insane. I've been glued to the TV this whole time—and to my phone, since Monika is also a nutjob and is clearly already in need of a raise. The photographs we've sold so far have almost paid her entire salary for the *year*. It's . . . crazy.

Half finished with my sushi, I get distracted by some of the latest pictures Monika sent through. The last one before she signed off shows the Wyvern trying to sleep in the helicopter to the airport. Oh my god, he looks untamed, positively feral.

He's covered in bloody scrapes and scratches, bruises that have already begun purpling. His head is lolling uncomfortably on his neck, making me wish I could reach through the still frame and hold up his head against the metal backing behind him. He just looks so exhausted. I feel so guilty. I glance down at my phone for about the billionth time since I texted him last night, wishing I hadn't sent it. But he's seen it. It's too late to take it back.

And he didn't answer.

The doorbell rings, and I swallow my next bite of sushi and wash it down with sparkling water. I'm dragging a little bit from too little sleep and too much adrenaline and worry pumping through my veins at present, but I tell myself it's nothing compared to what Roland's been going through or what Monika's feeling after using a strength bordering on supernatural to keep up with him. And she's supposedly human. I don't believe it.

Thinking it's Elena coming to check on me, as she's been threatening to do for the past three days—forget the fact that she already *did* come by this morning—I stagger up to my cherry-red painted front door without bothering to look at what I'm wearing. If I'd taken an extra second to put on a sweater, or a bra, I might have avoided what happened next.

And if I'd taken an extra second to put on that sweater, I might have avoided what happened next . . . and regretted it.

I wrench the door open wide without checking the peephole to find Roland on my front step, leaning heavily against my doorframe. His lips are slightly parted as if he's about to speak, but he looks almost as shocked as I feel to see him standing here, which is strange; *he* came to *me*. And then I recognize that he's not actually looking at me but at my chest. My thin-strapped tank top is white, and even though it's baggy, it's almost see-through, and my nipples instantly perk at the first whiff I get of his scent.

"Rol—oh . . ." I gasp. I take a half step back on my brace-wrapped leg.

His gaze lifts back to my face. He takes a half step to counter mine, and before I can do or say or think anything more, Rollo's stepping fully into my space—so close that his still bare scratch- and scrape- and suture-covered abdomen brushes my chest.

I look up at the same time that he dips down. His fingers are so, so soft against my chin and cheek. They flutter; the same hands that wrenched bodies out of the snow with brutality and ferocity, they flutter now. Almost . . . trembling. And I no longer remember that we're in a fight when his lips alight on mine so, so softly.

They're warm and dry and full beyond belief. He tastes like he smells, like a bonfire. The scratch of his beard on my face is rough, but I still feel myself lifting my bandaged leg while leaning forward onto the ball of my good foot and then onto my tiptoes. But just as my tongue leaves the safety of my lips to taste him . . . just a little taste . . . he retreats.

He clears his throat, and I fall forward like an idiot and catch myself on his pecs and abdomen before I can place any weight on my bum foot. My fingers scrape over his rough stitches, and I struggle to prop myself back up. "Ohh. Sorry, Rollo. I didn't . . . I'm sorry." Embarrassment sweeps my chest, and if I were a lighter shade of brown, the heat there would no doubt be visible.

Rollo's hands are gentle as they cradle my waist and push me up. He leans back down and kisses my temple, and then, as if he isn't even paying attention, like he's caught in the dream, he wraps his arms around my shoulders and pulls me into his chest. I stumble again, straight into his heat, and as he holds me, I don't have a choice—not because he's so much stronger than I am but because I can feel just how badly he *needs* this—I hug him back. I wrap my arms around his middle and squeeze as hard as I can until he releases a muffled grunt.

"I'm sorry," I say, feeling nearly dizzy with emotion. "Are you all right?"

"No." He chuckles. His hands are on my jaw and neck again. He's cuffing my neck gently, but it feels . . . good. I can't help the weight that suddenly falls into my lower abdomen . . . and then lower than that. "But I feel better after that."

I give him a little swat to his stomach, not enough to hurt him but enough for him to release me. My cheeks pinch with the restraint it takes me to withhold my grin. "You, um . . ."

"I know I shouldn't have come by, but I didn't want to crash at a hotel. Can I . . ."

"Of course. I mean, yes. You can crash here for as long as you want." *You can move in, if you want.* It's on the tip of my tongue to say it, but I know better than that. We need to talk.

"Thank you, Nessa." *Nessa.* "Your guest room upstairs?"

"Um . . . yeah, that's the thing." He starts into my house, closing the door at his back, and I chase him up the stairs as he starts to stomp up them without me. Well, not *chase* so much as hobble behind him.

"What's the thing?" he says, pausing halfway up. "And you're not supposed to be on your feet." He grunts, looking upset.

I can't believe he's still only in his boxer shorts. I can see medical equipment dangling off his legs. Oh my gosh. "You're still hurt!"

"Yeah. I'd like to sleep. I'll find a bedroom. Stay down here unless you're coming to bed too."

"I wasn't . . . planning on it yet. And I can sleep in the living room. No worries."

"No. Not interested in that arrangement. You give a holler when you want to come upstairs, and I'll carry you."

I frown, pouting as he moves up another step, and I quickly switch underneath his arm so that I'm standing on the stair above him. It puts us nearly at eye level. It's so intense. I'm never eye level with him, and this is a level of . . . closeness I'm not sure I'm ready for . . . I just needed to stop him and explain.

"I'm not going to wake you up. Not after everything you did."

"After everything I did for *you*." His eyes are light pink, white around the pupil, but the longer he stares at me, the lighter his pupils get too. "I'm sorry, Nessa. I am a fucking asshole. I didn't think about your stuff . . . Didn't mean to call you what I did."

I inhale deeply, startled by the abrupt change in conversation but grateful he brought it up. When I exhale, I taste relief. "Me either."

We stand there for another few seconds, uncomfortable ones, but not because I'm still upset. I have the strange desire to reach out and touch him. I manage to restrain myself at the last second, remembering that downstairs he was the one to pull away. Awkwardly, I turn to the side and cock my thumb over my shoulder instead.

"Let me, um . . . show you the bed." I cannot believe how dirty that sounded and wince. He chuckles. While mortification blankets me, I bite my bottom lip and immediately turn and limp up the next step, only for my feet to be swept in the next second. "You've got to be kidding me. You can barely walk! Put me down."

"Not until we get to the top." He doesn't set me down then either. Instead, he moves to the left, down the short hall to my room. To the right should have been the other bedroom, but I turned it into a library à la *Beauty and the Beast*—or Hannibal Lecter's. There's a third bedroom up here that's my office. He peeks inside before moving to the door at the end of the hall.

He steps into my bedroom and only then sets me down. He does a slow turn, only one revolution, taking in the built-in bookcase surrounding my bed, my wide, curved windows that overlook the street below, the reading nook and benches covered in funky, colorful pillows. This is my private little sanctuary. Nobody's ever been in here before.

"This your room?" he says, glancing past me as if the guest bedroom he expected to find will suddenly make its presence known.

I nod. "That's what I was trying to tell you before. I . . . um . . . Well, I never have guests over, so I got rid of my guest room. I only have the one bed. But like I said, I'll sleep downstairs. It's no biggie."

His eyebrows are high on his forehead, making him look like a cartoon character. His mouth opens and closes like a fish. His eyes are big, and the way he holds himself, this big brute of a male covered in war wounds . . . he looks so vulnerable.

"I promise. It's not a big deal."

"Nessa," he says in a rough, rough timbre, speaking the moment I start to turn back toward the door. "Not a chance. We're sharing the bed."

"Oh . . . I . . . no."

"It's a king, not a big deal. I swear I'm not gonna try to . . . make a move or anything."

Oh my gosh, this is so . . . not *cool!* "Oh, I, um . . . it's not . . ."

"I know you're upset with me, but I'm hurting and need sleep. You look like you need sleep too. You haven't been staying up watching my feeds, have you?"

I don't try to lie. I just shake my head. "I'm not . . . I've never . . ."

"I know you're still pissed at me. I swear to God, I'm not gonna try anything. I'm too tired for that."

I'm embarrassed that he thinks that I think he's a pervert, so embarrassed that I fail to control my volume when I shout, "I've never done that before."

He waits for me to say more. I don't. I just shift my weight between my feet, forcing him to finally blurt, "What?"

"Slept with a guy. Like, overnight. I'm not a virgin, but I'm . . . I've just never done the sleeping part." It feels too intimate. Too vulnerable. An exchange of far, far too much trust.

I hear him coming closer. Feel his heat. The backs of his fingers graze my cheek. He whispers, "Look at me."

I struggle to comply. He doesn't really give me a choice. I wrap my arms around myself, feeling so exposed, and finally dare to meet his eyes. His brows are drawn, his expression one of absolute consternation. He isn't giving me anything, not ceding any ground.

"I'm not gonna do anything you don't want to, but we both need sleep. Couch won't do. If you don't want me here, I don't mind getting a hotel."

I bite my bottom lip. I'm too scared for this . . . It's a big step . . . for me . . . and we're not . . . anything. He's my *fake* boyfriend, and after our last conversation, I wasn't sure he'd even want to keep up with the charade. I wasn't sure I'd want to either. And now . . .

"We could try it . . . just once," I whisper.

He rubs his jaw. "Yeah?"

I nod.

He grins, one eyebrow lifted, then surprises me when his tone turns harsh. "On one condition."

"Wh-what?"

"That you never mention another man to me again."

I get the chills. His voice is laden with threat. "It was only one guy two times," I whisper, but he cuts me off by pressing the rough pad of his thumb to my lips.

He leans in close, and I can feel the vibrations of his chest as he growls, "Then he'll only die twice." He gives my chin a little pinch. "Come."

"Wait," I say, stumbling after him as I try to put myself back together in the absence of his touch. "I have a condition too."

He smirks. "And what's that?"

"I know you're exhausted, but I'm sorry, you've got to shower and take out the needles dangling off of your legs first."

Rollo scowls, but he begrudgingly turns toward the bathroom. "Fine. I shower. You get ready for bed. I'm going down hard, and you're coming with me." He disappears into the bathroom without waiting for my answer.

I get him a towel and a fresh toothbrush, but I don't have any men's clothes. My brothers have never stayed the night, and I don't have, uh . . . gentlemen callers. I loiter in my library, skimming the titles of books like I don't know them all by heart. I wait until I hear the shower turn off and then wait a little longer. I have no idea what he'll do, but he doesn't shout at me to ask me to get him anything to wear, so I have to assume he's found an appropriate solution. Maybe he's just rewearing his boxers?

. . . Or maybe he's just in my bed buck-ass naked.

I stare down at the bed—my bed—and the *alien* spread out all over it. I have a king bed because I'm a diva, but he still takes up so much of it. The blankets that were perfectly made are now totally rumpled, like he's been sleeping for forty hours even though he must have only just passed out. He's got one leg straight, covered in blanket, and one hooked at the knee, spread across the middle of my bed, totally naked and exposed up to the groin, which is only just barely covered by a flimsy corner of one thin sheet.

"Don't bite," he says, making me jump. "Can feel you having a nervous breakdown, and it's distracting. Get your ass over here and sleep."

I snort but still find myself turning off the hall light, padding across my bedroom, and sitting down on the edge of the bed. I'm wearing my pajamas to make up for his lack, but it still feels like I'm naked when I lie on my back and stare up at the ceiling in the dark. It's so dark in my room, thanks to my blackout curtains, that it makes his presence feel even more menacing. He's so warm. His heat snakes across the sheets, and . . .

I squeak as his hand circles my upper arm and pulls. He drags me over the bed, and, ass-naked as he is, he cups my body with his, lining us up big spoon to little spoon. His body smells like my shampoo, and like smoke and like . . . him.

"Relax." His fingers press firmly into the nape of my neck, massaging down the muscles of my shoulders, down my outer arm. He's got the blankets drawn up over us both, and as his hand reaches my hand, he laces our fingers together. I find a strange ease in him being close. Feeling him, I don't have to worry about what he's doing on his half of the bed. Ironic, since this isn't exactly what I'd call *not doing anything*, a promise he made that I'm not so sure he plans to keep . . . or if I want him to.

Chapter Fifteen

VANESSA

Is he . . . dead?

He's been asleep for almost fifteen hours. He woke up once to go to the bathroom. I could hear him thumping around while I sat next door in my office, typing out an email to my C-suite team that was as close to angry as I got. How could they have scheduled Monday for his official Champions photo shoot? He isn't even fully healed!

Just a few minutes ago, I heard him moving around again. It's almost nine in the morning, and we went to bed at six last night. I can't decide if I should wake him or not. Ordinarily I'd say no, but he must be hungry. After hitting send, I head downstairs as carefully as I'm able and return with energy bars and a couple bottles of water. I debate knocking but then decide that it is *my* bedroom and I'm not going to walk on eggshells in my own private space. I do that in public spaces enough already.

I push open the door, make it to the bed, and set down my items, and while I had every noble intention of sneaking back out so long as he isn't awake—which he definitely isn't—I don't. *Pervert.* Instead, I'm a bit . . . enchanted.

My gaze passes over the alien in my bed, twisted like a snake among my rumpled sheets. Lying on his stomach, he's taking up almost all of the king bed. His arms are out to the sides, his legs just like they were last night when he first collapsed onto my mattress—one straight, one hooked at the knee. His back rises and falls so slowly, and it's so *pretty*, even covered in scratches. He's got a larger one over his left shoulder blade that took some stitching, but otherwise, the rest are scrapes that already look more healed than they did yesterday. Not that I was ogling him or anything . . .

Not that I was noticing how the brown of his skin is so . . . so . . . robust. Like he's got a light on within. I huff-chuckle. I suppose he does. Maybe a dragon was the wrong symbol for him. Maybe we should have called him Ra like the ancient Egyptian sun god. We could have given him a falcon for a logo or a sun crest. Too bad a second rebrand isn't in the stars for us, not with how he's dominating the headlines. Not even Taranis's recent work repowering a New Orleans power grid during a catastrophic storm could take top billing over the Wyvern's recent heroics. The news cycle will eventually cycle him out, but for now the Wyvern, my *boyfriend*, is all anybody wants to talk about, and if I do my job right, it'll stay that way for a few more weeks. My *fake* boyfriend.

I frown a little and take a step away from the bed. I debate covering him up better with the blankets, but it's pointless. He stole the covers all night anyway—not that I needed them. He was wrapped around me like a snake with a score. I'm not going to be able to wear my flannel pajamas tonight if he plans on the same arrangement. My cheeks burn at the thought. It had been my first time sleeping all night through with a guy. I didn't think I'd be able to—had always told myself it'd be too annoying to sleep beside someone else—but it was easy. Better than easy. It was nice.

The floor creaks under my feet, and he releases a heavy sigh. I freeze, not wanting to be caught peeping. *Pervert.* As luck would have it, his eyes stay closed as he kicks one knee up and rolls onto his back. His knee flops open. His elbows are spread wide, his right arm cocked up, his left hand draped over his stomach. The blanket is barely—barely—covering his . . . um . . . equipment. I can see his chest and

his ribbed abdomen and his tree-trunk thighs and his arms, and he's
. . . my goodness, he's a good-looking guy. And with his beard and hair
long and scratches covering most of him, he looks like some marauding
Viking berserk who stormed the castle and plans to stay a while.

I cover my mouth with my hand, worried that I'm drooling. What
am I? A dog salivating over a bone? *Pervert.* I'm leaving, I swear . . . only
I'm not. I'm still staring. *Pervert!* And now I'm getting closer to him
because I start to notice something funny on his left pec. I thought I'd
noticed a scratch last night, deeper than the others, but now that I'm
able to focus on it uninterrupted by, well . . . him being awake—*perv*—I
can see marks on his skin that look more organized than any scratch
would be. Almost like a tattoo, if a tattoo were raised and only slightly
darker than his skin tone. Like scar tissue. A brand maybe?

I'm not wearing shoes and carefully creep right to the edge of the
bed. I lean over him and inspect the nontattoo a little closer. What I
find puzzles me. A series of lines, organized into a shape that looks only
partially complete. It's like a subway map where the lines all lead off
into different directions before vanishing. There's a circular line winding
through the web . . . yeah. That's what it's like. A spiderweb. Both
organic and too organized at the same time. There are . . . I count . . .
eleven lines branching outward, a circular squiggle connecting them.
But regardless of where they lead, they all intersect within the circle. I
see my finger enter my vision like it doesn't belong to me. I tell it to stop
what it's doing, what it's intending, but it doesn't listen.

I press the tip of my pointer finger right into the center of the circle.
I barely touch him, only the feather of my skin across the smooth lines
of his . . . but that doesn't matter.

Hands grab my shoulders, rip me off my feet, and whirl me around.
My back lands on the bed, the mattress bouncing beneath me. I blink
and he's *there* looming over me, his stare angry before it morphs into
surprise. "Nessa, the fuck are you doing?"

"Peeping!" I blurt—*pervvvv*—and I don't give any more explanation
than that. Because all my awareness is currently zeroing in on the fact that

he hasn't let go of me. In fact, his hand has shifted its hold to my neck. He's not squeezing, but the position is menacing and intoxicating—I can feel every inch of his palm when I swallow nervously—and it's exacerbated by the fact that he's *naked*, and he's shifting his weight further on top of me, pressing me into the bed, hip to hip, putting us in a position that I've only been in with a man two other times. All he'd have to do is slip his knees to the insides of mine and . . .

I swallow hard. He hasn't said anything. His glare has released. His lips are parted, and somehow he doesn't smell like morning breath, despite the fact that he hasn't brushed his teeth, but rather still smells like smoke. Like the sun.

"We should have called you Ra," I say, brain firing in every direction. I should push him off. I *really* should push him off.

But I don't.

Humans crave touch from one another. I know this objectively, but *personally*, getting to the point where I can feel comfortable touching someone and being touched by them like this . . . well, let's just say that the last time it happened, I'd had to work up the courage over months. College boyfriend. He didn't last long after we . . . hooked up. I rebounded after him with the help of a lot of beer. The sex was better but not worth repeating. We fizzled after that.

But this? I've never felt tension like this. Need. Want. Pure and unbothered by stupid questions such as, Whose hands go where, and who does what to whom, and how do I know what you like if I'm too shy to ask you? There's just him dragging me underneath him and looking down at me like he's going to do whatever he wants . . .

And I'm going to let him.

"You smell like fucking candy." He drops his face to my hair and inhales deeply. His nose drags over my skin up to my temple and then back down to my neck. He breathes against the column of my throat and then nips the space under my ear with his teeth.

I gasp, the sound punching into my lungs. I swallow, and his fingers tighten just a fraction . . . just enough to make my eyelids flutter and my back arch. My legs squirm against each other restlessly, and my hands, my treacherous hands, reach up from their awkward positions at my sides to touch his ribs. And the instant my fingertips graze his hot skin, he hisses, shifts his hand, and fully bites the side of my neck.

I moan loudly in a way that can only be described as carnal. There's no doubt that it's a pleasure sound, and it deepens when Rollo slides his hands underneath my ass, dressed in jeans—because what other masochist but me would wear jeans in their own house—and down my thighs . . . and repositions his legs between mine.

The sounds I'm making are embarrassing. *Embarrassing.* Not because the sounds are . . . *sounding*, but because of how desperate they are. I've never been touched like this, but the strangest thing is the feeling in my chest telling me that even though I might not know this type of touch, I miss it. Badly.

My eyes burn. The blankets are tangled between us, and Rollo yanks them away. Something tears, but I don't care. Not when his hips leave the valley between mine and he sits back on his heels and reaches for the button on my pants.

"Not gonna fuck you," he says, and I don't know if he's talking to himself or me because, if he's talking to me, I'd tell him he's gonna make me weep. Need has bludgeoned me with a cudgel, and I can't articulate how big it is. It's too big to get past the barrier of my teeth.

His gaze flashes bright white as he looks at me. "But I need these off."

I nod feverishly, my head buried in the pillows behind me as I stare down the length of my T-shirt-covered body to his naked everything. His shoulders look enormous from this angle, like wings, tapering down to narrow hips between which a prominent erection stands stiff, reaching for me. His brown skin is flushed red, almost purple, over the massive domed head, which is fully visible with the foreskin drawn back, veins streaking down the sides making my mouth water like a sex-deprived succubus.

I reach down to help him with my jeans because he still hasn't moved, but he bats my hands out of his way. "Hands up. Over your head. Don't move them until I tell you you can."

I'm going to pass out. My throat is totally dry. My arms feel like they've been pricked with pins and needles from shoulder to fingertip as my hands fold neatly above my head in a bed of my hair. His eyes are blazing with questions I don't have answers to because I'm on a game of *Jeopardy!* right now; he's my opponent, but I can't reach for the buzzer because he told me I'm not allowed.

"Christ," he huffs. He rubs his hand through his hair, and that image, that picture of him all scratched and scarred, looking at me like I'm something soft he can fall into. The vision is searing and one I know will be burned into my memory until the day I die.

His fingers tug my button free, and the sound the zipper makes as it descends is salacious. "Hips up."

I comply, and he drags my jeans roughly down my legs until he reaches my ankles. He moves gently after that, freeing one foot and removing the sock I'm wearing before moving to my other foot and freeing my brace. He kisses the side of my ankle brace very gently, and I don't like the feeling that balloons in my stomach when he does that. The lust takes a new shape, a form that begs my surrender.

My hands twitch. He glares at them, and I move them back into position, holding my right wrist with my left hand as if I might keep it from doing anything crazy. Then Rollo gently lowers both of my legs and reaches for the simple black underwear I've got on. I can wish I'd chosen better looking panties till the cows come home, but I'm a psycho who buys her black, full-coverage underwear in bulk. Though . . . he doesn't seem to mind.

His eyes are unfocused, black pupils covering so much of the pink as he hooks his fingers between my skin and the upper band of elastic. He drops forward onto his other fist and tortures me, just a little bit, skimming the backs of his fingers over my skin as he settles my underwear back into place.

"Mhm," I whimper. It's a loud whimper too. Oh my gosh, shoot me now. I sound just as needy as I feel. There's no seduction here on my side. There's only obvious disbelief that this is happening and an even more blatant desire for him to continue. My hips lift.

"Nessa, don't," he snarls, sounding a little mean and making me flinch. "I'm hanging on by a hair here. You move when I say you can move." He pauses, leaning back on his heels, lifting away from me slowly and inhaling between his teeth. I didn't see him straining like this on TV when he was trying to move a mountain. "You okay with that?" His hands fit to my hips, his thumbs firm as they press into the soft skin just above my pubic bone.

I nod way too eagerly, enjoying, liking, craving this possibly a lot more than I should.

"Good. I'm not gonna fuck this up." His voice is low like he's speaking to himself, and his words astound me because I'd been having the exact same thought. And then he drops forward and moves to cover me once again.

I clench my fists as his hips come down to meet mine, the weight of them . . . the weight of what's *between* them . . . sinking right where I need it. The stiff shaft of his erection presses down onto my clit *hard,* and when he tips his hips forward, I forget my marching orders. I tilt my hips up to meet his and gasp. The friction is heavenly, and I moan even louder as he slides back.

He snakes one hand around the back of my neck and squeezes so tight, my head tips back and is stuck like this. "Jesus." His lips trail up the front of my throat, and then, gently, way too fucking gently, he kisses the tip of my chin, still covered in crusty scabs from my fall earlier this eternity, because that's how it feels—like an eternity has passed since then. A hundred lifetimes. A thousand.

And I fall in every single one.

It's too much, all of it is way too much. Too fast. And the sensations rocking me sideways are telling me that none of that matters because my body wants more. My hips tip up into his, and I shift them, working myself over the heavenly heat of his solid length because he's stopped moving. Sensation erupts in my clit, and Rollo's head drops forward onto the pillow above my head. I can feel his warm breath through my hair as he squeezes my neck a little harder. My mouth opens on a squeak that's part pain, part pleasure. I open my mouth to beg for . . . *something*, but he takes advantage of that and arches his back so that he can keep our hips together and still brush his lips over mine. Tentative. Seeking.

My eyes close. I lick my upper lip, savoring the charred taste of him, and bite his lower one. And then everything slams into motion. He starts making that sound that stems from a place deep within him that humans don't have, and as his head kicks back, his chest comes to cover my face and that sound moves through me everywhere. Everywhere. Ev-ery-where. His body is a vibrator, and my clit is not immune. I wail like a banshee, clinging to him for dear life, as desperate notes of a long-lost orgasm threaten to tear me into pieces.

Heat pricks the backs of my eyes with greater intensity. There's no way this is happening. No reason for this to happen. I touched him, and now my legs are spread and his hips are pumping into mine bruisingly, his erection rubbing angrily through the flimsy barrier of my panties, igniting my clit and the rest of me.

Dropping onto his elbows with one hand still around the back of my neck, his free hand comes down to the hem of my shirt, which he lifts, wasting no seconds in exploring the fact that I'm not wearing a bra.

"Nessa," he groans, breaking our kiss long enough to sweep my face with his gaze. He frowns. "You okay?"

"Yeah," I blurt on a wet laugh. "Yes. Sorry, this is embarrassing. It's just . . . been a long time . . . for me."

He nods, and his face relaxes. "Me too." He lifts my shirt up over my boobs, bunching the fabric along my collar. Then he looks down and bites his lower lip once before moving down, down, too far for us to maintain the friction of our lower halves. "And never like this."

He moves to suck on my left breast, pulling the nipple all the way into his mouth. He moans around it, and just when I think I'm not going to be able to keep my hands in place, I become sure of it when one of his hands moves to rub my clit over my panties. I grab his hair, but he shoves my hands aside and gives my clit a hard spank.

No one has ever done that to me before, and I gasp, partly in shock, partly in elation, and when he does it again, I whimper even louder. As my eyelids flutter, he slides his middle and ring fingers into my mouth.

"Suck." I suck. "Good girl." I'm such a good girl. "You want to come?" I moan and nod and squeeze my thighs together around his hips. I can't give any other answer. "Then you're going to need to learn to follow instructions, Nessa. Keep your hands still."

His fingers return to my clit, and somehow he manages to suck on my right breast, keep his fingers pumping in and out of my mouth, and keep rubbing my clit all simultaneously. At least, for a few minutes. Because as the heat in my body starts to build and I start to get closer, Rollo starts to lose tempo.

"Fuck." He grabs my hands above my head with one of his while the other squeezes my left breast hard enough to make me cry out. His mouth captures the sound, and he kisses me brutally as he prowls back up my body, lining our hips back up. I can't move at all. He's too heavy. He's holding me so close.

My clit throbs as he starts to thrust against me with more force this time. "You're going to come for me on the count of five, Nessa."

I nod, and it's at this point that I start to become aware that this male may be a problem for me. Because right now, if he told me to get on all fours and bark like a dog, I would throw myself to the ground, let him collar and leash me.

"Five." He kisses me hungrily, sucking the moans out of my throat, drinking my breath. "Four."

"I can't . . ." I gasp, breaking the kiss, my eyelids fluttering. "I'm coming . . ."

"No. You're going to wait." He speaks in a snarl, the rumbling of his chest so loud, it makes it hard to hear him. He lifts his hips off mine for a second, long enough to reach between us and slap my clit again, and then he does something dastardly. He hooks two fingers into the crotch of my panties and drags them to the side. He slides his cock in between the folds of my labia between my brown lips, without penetrating me, but teasing me mercilessly instead.

"Fuck, Nessa. You wet like this for me?"

"Yes, Rollo," I whisper, full of need.

His eyes blaze so bright a white, it catches me off guard. I moan as he slips his cock through my folds, up higher this time to rub directly against my swollen clit, and he grunts. "Three."

He pumps again, more forcefully. I'm barely hanging on. "Two."

He starts to thrust in earnest now, and I'm not going to make it . . . I'm not making it. My head is tossing side to side, my hands are reaching for him, but he keeps them locked. His hand on my tit squeezes so hard, I think I'll burst everywhere all at once . . . "One."

The pressure of my orgasm hurts, exacerbated by the fact that my core gapes, wanting his cock in me so desperately. As if he's heard my pleas, his fingers on my chest move down my body, and he slips two fingers inside of me.

"Christ, Nessa," he groans.

I cry out as my entire body clenches up, and he keeps thrusting against my clit while pumping his fingers in and out of me. His fingers speed up just as I start to come down, and I don't understand what happens in the next second because it's never happened to me before. My clit aches, pinching acutely in the afterglow, but that doesn't stop another orgasm from trampling right over the first. My back arches; my ass clenches. I can feel him everywhere. His heat is so much.

"Nessa." His eyes blaze white as he roars my name against my temple. The name *he* gave me.

I've always had a complicated relationship with my name, but from his lips, that single uttered word makes me feel like I truly belong to him, claiming me in a way that the first people who ever knew me had no desire to. No. This name is his name for his Nessa, and it makes me feel like I'm the first Vanessa who was ever born into existence. That no other Vanessa ever mattered before me.

At least not to him.

And it's a beautiful feeling.

His fingers slip out of me as he loses himself to his own pleasure, and my core clenches in the aftershocks. I feel electricity shoot through every nerve in my body as my clit takes me higher. I don't know if it's a third orgasm or if the second or even the first never ended, but I think I might black out, lost to whatever incantation he's thrown over me like a blanket. Distantly I hear him groan, speaking or cursing in a language I don't know as he reaches his own nirvana.

My eyes open seconds or minutes later; I'm not even sure. He's draped all over me, his still-erect penis wedged between us, a hot smattering of his cum warming my lower belly . . .

His face is contorted in an expression only the foolish would believe was pain, and he's slowing. His thrusts are gentling, the movements either a gentle rocking or an abrupt spasm. His muscles are easing, but only a little. He's cradling my head while his harsh breaths mingle with my desperate ones, and . . . I can't look at him. I need to get out of here.

He releases a final moan before stilling, spasming, and then stilling again. He leans in and bites my earlobe. I'm going to burst. It's too much. From the first moment he looked at me in the boardroom, I should have known that same brutal, punishing intensity would translate to everything he does. The way he makes love. Maybe even the way he loves.

"You okay?" His words are a whisper spoken into the darkness of my hair.

I nod, blinking manically up at the ceiling fan like a crazy person.

"I take it too far?" he says, thrusting against my soft belly.

I shake my head.

"I hurt you?" He stills on that, even after I shake my head again.

His lips push against my cheek, and he tracks kisses from my jaw below my ear up to my nose. My own lips are floundering, desperate to respond, but he doesn't return to them. Instead, he pulls back and looks into my eyes briefly, and then again for a little longer. His brows knit together, and I know what he's going to say before he says it, and I curl my fingers into his sides, and I remember finally that I do, in fact, have arms. I dent his skin with my nails in my determination for him to hear my words and not think what it is that he's thinking.

"I'm okay. I promise." I'm better than okay, but I don't think I can manage any more words than these. My throat is all gooey, and so are my legs. I can feel them trembling and spasming as he slowly peels himself off my body, his gaze on my face. He doesn't believe me. He's looking rejected . . . crushed. I can't bear it.

"You're a lot," I say, and my voice catches. My hands are shaking, and I rub my face, feeling like such a loser—that I'm about to lose something very precious to me. "For me." I hiccup.

I finish rubbing the heat out of my eyes, trying to stamp it like a runaway ember, sure that he's going to be disgusted this time when I meet his eyes. No guy wants a woman falling apart in his bed after dry humping. We didn't even fuck. What am I gonna do if we ever get to that point? I'll have to check myself into a mental hospital because my therapist doesn't get paid enough to handle the mess that I am, and I definitely can't take this to group.

But when I lower my hands and tuck them into my chest, my boobs still flying free, his cum still wet and smeared over my lower half, I see the strangest thing. He's smiling. His head is cocked to the side, and his expression is easy, bordering on sweet. "Baby, you've got no fucking clue what you do to me. No tears, okay?"

Sniffling, I nod anyway.

"I mean it. You start crying, and I'm gonna have to fuck you." My brain shorts. Should I . . . cry then? I feel my expression scrunch, and he laughs, and when his head tips back and his white teeth flash, he looks like an entirely different man—uh, male. "Don't tempt me, Nessa."

"Why not?"

He leans in close and kisses my T-shirt-covered shoulder before yanking the material back down to cover my chest. "I'm not ready." He groans and rolls off my body and onto his back. "Besides, you gotta buy me dinner first."

I smile, and just like that, the tension breaks. I feel the loss of his heat when he pulls away from me and performs a casual sweep of my body before running his own hand over his face. "Fuck." Panic licks at me. I wait for him to tell me something's wrong, that he's my client, he regrets it, he's out of my league, we're not the same species—but he says, "I made a mess of you."

He reaches for the hem of my underwear and strokes his pointer finger over my belly, gathering his own cum on his fingertip. His gaze drops to my mouth, and he whispers, "Open."

I open. He slides his finger into my mouth, and I taste his salty flavor, sucking his finger clean until he pops it out of my mouth. His pupils, big as they are, have dilated even further, and the light pink that they were fades even more to white. "Think I'm also gonna need a taste."

Before I can decipher what he means, he moves down the bed, hooks my knees over his shoulders, and buries his face between my thighs. Something tears. I think it's my underwear. But I don't give a shit about that as he makes me come again with the hard pressure of his tongue on my clit. I'm completely unprepared for it, and when he's finished with me, his beard is soaked. He's kneeling in a similar position to the one he started in, hand stroking up and down his cock. His foreskin is fully drawn back again, and he looks prepared to go back on what he told me earlier. That was ages ago anyway. I spread my legs just a little bit, and he slaps the inside of my thigh lightly, but hard enough for me to jump and laugh.

"What was that for?"

He ambles off the bed, his backside looking mighty fine as he steps into the bathroom and flips on the light. "I know what you're doing," he grumbles as he returns to me with a warm rag. I'm only half-coherent as he wipes his cum off my stomach and gently brings the rag up between my legs. My panties he takes with him when he returns to the bathroom, along with the dirty rag.

"Wh-what?"

"Don't play dumb. That shit may work on idiots, but I'm not that stupid. I know you're a hell of a lot smarter than me, and if you try to manipulate me, you might just do it, so don't."

His words are harsh but make me warm in the cobweb-ridden recesses of my soul. The places I haven't explored in a while, the drawers I've left shut for fear of what they hold.

"I have to buy you dinner first. Is that the rule?"

Rollo sticks his head out of the bathroom, a toothbrush half hanging out of his mouth. He's got a towel slung around his waist that does nothing to hide his still-prominent erection. "Since when did you become a sex maniac?"

My jaw nearly unhinges with how big my mouth gapes. I bust out a laugh and giggle into the ruined sheets underneath me. "I am not a sex maniac. Also . . . are you sure you're okay? The mark on your chest, it looks bigger . . . and is that another one on your ribs?"

"Fine. And yes, you are a sex maniac."

"Even if you are right, it's your fault." He grunts a laugh, but my smile slips. "And seriously, Rollo, what is that? It doesn't look good."

"It's nothing. Just some scratches. Must have gotten nicked worse than I thought when I went into that car."

"It didn't look like a cut when I was looking earlier."

"Peeping, you mean?"

I blush. "Well . . ."

"There are no rules to this, or if there are any, I don't know them. You might be inexperienced, but I guarantee you aren't as inexperienced as I am with this shit. Stuff." He spits, and the shower goes on. He speaks more muffled, like he's talking through the glass. "I want to take you on a date."

"A date? Really?"

"A real one. Not a fake anything." He sounds pissed off again, and I'm not sure why.

I feel a little insecure about this, wading into dark waters without a life jacket. "Like dinner?"

"Is that what women like for dates?"

"I don't know." I shrug honestly. "Like I said, I don't really date."

"Me either."

I snort. "You don't say?"

"You teasing me, Nessa?"

I can't help the lazy smile that sweeps my cheeks. I am teasing him, aren't I? That . . . might be a first for me. "No?"

"For that, I think you have to say yes."

"Are those the rules?"

"Told you there weren't any rules."

"You gave me rules earlier." My voice is soft, but I know he still hears me.

He goes quiet until, "You're tempting me again, Nessa."

"Sorry," I whisper.

He stays quiet. I roll off the bed and manage to find some clothes. I'll need to shower too—but my stomach chooses that moment to grumble. I think I might need some lunch first. What time is it? I glance around, looking for my phone at the same time that the water turns off. As I drag on black leggings and a black long-sleeve tee and take a seat on the edge of the bed, he makes his way out of the bathroom looking every bit a god of sun.

His eyes are pure fire as they watch me, and I stay seated, my hands relaxed on the tops of my thighs, as he steps up between my knees. He's still only wearing a towel, holding it up with one hand while his other grips my chin with his pointer finger and his thumb.

He says gruffly, "You're good with rules, aren't you, Nessa?"

I nod, feeling thirsty all of a sudden.

He's staring at me, an utterly indecipherable look in his eyes, and all but whispers, "My rules."

I nod again.

"Whose rules do you like obeying, Nessa? Use your words."

"Your rules," I whisper, lust tittering through me in a way that I should find scary. His voice, his commands, ignite a side of me I always knew existed but have never explored.

"The whole thing. Tell me."

"I like obeying your rules."

"Like a good girl."

"Your good girl," I whisper.

"Fuck." He looks me over and shakes his head. "Didn't stand a chance, did I?" He reaches up and scratches his chest—specifically the mark covering his left pec that looks like it's gotten darker in the past minutes.

My eyebrows pull together, and I remember that I have hands and know how to use them. I point at his chest with one finger. "Are you sure you're okay? That mark on your chest looks pretty gnarly . . ."

"Fine. Just . . ." He scratches it again and turns away from me, going to his phone, which he abandoned on the floor last night, and picking it up. "You like Italian food?"

I nod, but he doesn't even see. He's already out the door making a call. "I'll pick you up tonight. Seven p.m.?"

"Yeah, sure. Are you going somewhere in the meantime?"

"Got somewhere to be first. But I'll be back to pick you up. Sharp. Shit," I think I hear him mutter as he pounds down the stairs, making one hell of a racket. "Need a car."

"A car?" I shout after him, still sitting there where he left me. "You need pants!"

Chapter Sixteen

ROLAND

Dr. Larsen is being her usual self, and while I'd ordinarily find it unpleasant, I find it particularly unpleasant in this moment. I glare at Dr. Larsen, hating how chipper she's being about this.

"Fascinating stuff. You're saying the tattoo appeared first last week and that today it got darker?" She's prodding at the skin on my left pec, and when she's finished, she kicks off on her rolling stool, making her way to her computer in this office that's also a lab that's also an exam room.

"It's not a tattoo, but yes."

"And when it first appeared, did you feel it?"

"A little."

"What did it feel like?"

"Itching."

She shoves her glasses up onto her forehead. Her salt-and-pepper bangs flop back to brush her eyebrows as she shakes her head and gives me her best impersonation of a glare. It's not particularly threatening. "You're hiding something."

"I'm not." I am. I'm thinking about the fact that I spoke another language during sex. I'd said words I'd never heard before but knew what they meant. *I want to ravage you.* I'd have told her I loved her in that same tongue, but there's no word for *love* in that language.

"You are. Why won't you tell me?" She cocks her head and narrows her eyes, and this look feels much more sinister because she's thinking and she's smart.

I try to distract her. "I got two more today on either rib." Where Nessa held on to me. "They look identical."

"Really?" Successfully distracted, Dr. Larsen ducks her head and swivels back over to me, poking my left rib until I squirm. "Incredible. And you're sure that these markings appeared here *after* they appeared on your chest?"

"Yeah."

"And they don't cause you any pain?"

"No. Just itch sometimes." Like when Vanessa stares at me too long with that funny look she gets when she's deciding something—or anytime she does what I say. I don't think she realizes what she's doing to me when she does that. I couldn't give a shit about the sexual aspects of it—okay, that's a lie—but I don't think she realizes that every time she opens for me on my command, she's giving me her trust.

"What prompts it?"

"Random." I shrug, forcing casual with every fiber of my being. I think this time she buys it.

"Fascinating," she says, snapping on gloves. "I'm going to take some photos and a biopsy." She drags a big metal arm, which I thought was an X-ray machine, down from the ceiling, but she swivels it around my body, taking pictures.

"Have you seen this type of thing before?" I ask Dr. Larsen.

She shakes her head and shoves the camera back toward the ceiling when she's finished. "Nope."

"You seem to be taking it in stride."

She smiles, rounding her desk to return to her computer. Her teeth are a bit crooked in the front. She has freckles. She's also definitely . . .

weird. Whether because her surprising and borderline erratic behavior reminds me of Vanessa or not, she's been growing on me.

"I wouldn't have taken a posting at the COE if I'd thought I wouldn't see the strange and beautiful. You know when people say nothing surprises me, that expression?" She doesn't wait for me to answer. "Well, the truth is that here, things surprise me every damn day, and I love it." She sighs, staring almost lovingly at her computer screen, on which I can see my abs and the funky markings on them in a slightly darker shade of brown than my skin in the reflection of her glasses. "I have the coolest job in the world."

I snort.

"You really don't have any idea what precipitated the forming or disappearance of these markings?" she asks again.

"Nope."

She raises an eyebrow, making me wonder if this woman is twenty or seventy. She's got the confidence of one or the other. "You're lying again. That must mean it's something good. Did they appear the first time you pooped your pants?"

"What? No."

"The first time you had a wet dream?"

Sort of. "No."

"Does it have to do with your heroic acts?"

That . . . stalls me. I blink.

Dr. Larsen claps her hands. "It does? They appear when you do something heroic?"

"I . . ." I shake my head and then sigh, defeated. "Not . . . really."

Nessa's breath.

Nessa's touch.

Nessa's trust.

I wish I could say that I wasn't so obsessed with her, but that's a lie too. I crave my new obsession, fully committing to it like I've never committed to anything before in my life.

"Then what?"

I can feel my skin prickle, and I'm glad my skin tone doesn't reveal the depth of my blush. "Nessa. Vanessa," I correct. These changes happening to my body seem more pronounced anytime I get the urge to protect her. I'd never had the desire to protect or defend anything before her.

I felt it the first time she tripped, swooning when she saw me, and that strange and terrifying energy passed between us. My body moved before I had even registered what I was doing. Lunging forward. I had to catch her.

I shrug. "That's all I got."

I swear the look on her smug face is the reason I haven't said anything until now. She takes her glasses clear off, a practiced move, I'm guessing, and crosses one knee over the other. She rests her elbow on top of it and says in a singsong voice, "Diamond was right." And then she laughs. "Damn. I owe that woman fifty bucks."

I frown.

Dr. Larsen elaborates, "I thought your relationship was fake. My wife, Diamond, a hopeless romantic, was convinced it was real. She was ready to throw down over it. Well, throw me down anyway." She waggles her eyebrows at me in a way that I truly hate.

"Pervert."

She laughs hard and shakes her head, a pink tint in her cheeks when she looks back at me and says, "You're telling me that you get permanent tattoos when your girlfriend touches you, and *I'm* the one with the problem?"

I huff half a laugh myself as she tilts her head. She doesn't make any notes on her computer, and I really fucking like that. "Does she have anything to do with your dreams?"

The dreams were why I'd come to see Dr. Larsen in the first place. Vivid and terrible, they were dreams of darkness and of murder. I'd been so full of rage in the dreams, and I could see myself lashing out and attacking strange and terrible monsters that were also trying to attack me. And every time, I'd woken from those dreams angry and stayed angry until I saw her face. For whatever reason, she sparked the dreams, but she could also make the rage they brought go away.

"I didn't dream last night when I slept beside her. At least, I don't think I did."

"Hm." Dr. Larsen's mouth scrunches up.

"Hm? That's the best you got, Doc?"

"Call me Emily, and yeah, sort of. I can't say that there's a manual for this, and if there is, I'm sorry to tell you, but you and I are the ones writing it. The COE hasn't exactly been forthcoming with information either."

I grunt, frowning. "Don't you have all the files?"

"Most, but some are redacted, and Mr. Singkham won't explain why—though he might not even know. Those files were originally redacted by the SDD before the Champions Coalition got them. You also might remember we don't have the villains' records either; those were stolen in the VNA raid of the SDD twelve years ago along with all that equipment." The pods. I remember. The villains went back for some of the pods we'd landed in as little alien kids, lost in the cosmos. I've never given much thought to what they took but am suddenly struck by the feeling that they might be kind of important.

Fuck. Makes me wish I hadn't severed ties so irrevocably with the Marduk.

Emily continues, "I'll do a biopsy on the tissue, but I'm not expecting miracles. I'll also poke around in the Forty-Eight archives and see if I can't find anything to explain this or any evidence it might have happened to another Champion." Her graying hair is in a ponytail on top of her head, held together with a bright-green scrunchie that's fighting a losing battle against the mass as she works.

Not meeting my gaze as she takes a few notes, she adds, "I'd tell you that you're free to go if you weren't looking at me like you're debating whether or not you're going to gouge my eyes out or ask me a question. So." She spins fully around on her stool, something a little kid might do, and, on the upswing, smacks her clipboard down onto the counter, her bright brown eyes all but glowing with a curiosity she's trying her damnedest to suppress.

Go on. Throw her a bone.

"There's something else." I clear my throat and hold out my hands. She blinks. "You want a manicure? I'm very regretful to inform you, but I pay someone to do this." She holds up her own hands in a mirror of how I'm holding mine, and I see that her hands are, in fact, tipped in short bright-green fingernails that match the color of the scrunchie in her hair.

She waggles them at me, and I scowl. "I don't need my nails done." And then I pause. "Actually." I clear my throat. "I do. But every day. Every damn morning I wake up, and my nails are pointy." I swallow as she watches my face, expression unchanging. "And hard."

"Pointy and hard?"

I nod.

"And you're describing your fingernails, yeah?" She snorts, and it takes me a full breath to realize she's made a joke.

"Perv," I huff, trying to keep the smile from twisting my lips.

She rolls forward and takes my right hand between both of hers, without gloves on, and smooths the side of her thumb around the top curve of my fingers. "Well, well . . . ow!" She jolts on her first pass around my thumb and looks at the pad of her own. She shows it to me after a cursory glance, and I see that it's got blood on it. She's also grinning ear to ear.

"Jesus." I jerk my hand out of hers, fucking petrified, but she grabs my right hand and pulls it back. "They weren't sharp like that this morning, I swear." I swear . . . I hope. I had these fingers in-fucking-side Vanessa. What if . . . no. No, she'd have said something. I can barely get the lump down in my throat.

Emily's eyes sparkle with fascination. "My, my, my. You trim your nails every morning then?"

"After joining with the Champions, I noticed my nails getting darker in color. Tinting to almost black. Didn't bother me, but in the week leading up to Washington, I started having to file them every other day, maybe less. I didn't file them when I was out there saving those people, obviously, and when I got on the plane to come home, I noticed they were long—like half an inch. I cut them on the plane using a goddamn knife one of the security women had on her, and then I cut them again this morning." A couple hours before I touched Vanessa, I'd rifled through her bathroom and found a set of clippers; they weren't hard to find in a neatly marked container labeled **NAILS**. My little psycho.

"So this growth is, what—six hours?"

"Something like that."

"Your nails are already an eighth of an inch past the nail bed . . ."

"And I cut them to the quick this morning."

"And you say they get pointy if you let them?"

"They were on the plane."

"Pointy how?" It fills me with a strange relief how seriously she's taking this.

"I don't know, like wide and then to a short point."

"Almond shaped, maybe? Or diamond?"

"I don't know. Almond, maybe. Wider, though."

"Hm."

She looks at me as she grabs a tool from a drawer under her desk. They look like little pincers. "Come sit down here and put your hand on the exam table," she says, gesturing to a short stool the same height as hers and the metal table next to the exam bed.

"You gonna chop it off?" I say, taking a seat and swiveling over to the metal surface.

"Would you miss it?"

"Yes." I lay my hand down anyway, but it twitches.

She laughs. "I meant the nail." She shows me what's in her hand, and it looks like one of those things you use to take the calluses off your feet.

I give her my hand, and she takes a few shavings from my nails, whittling them each down back to the quick. "I'm gonna ask you to do something you aren't going to want to say yes to."

"Then I'll spare you the grief. No."

She rolls her eyes. "Let your nails grow out one week."

"One week? You kidding me? I'm not gonna wait a week to touch Vanessa."

She snaps her little plastic box of my nail shavings shut and points at me with her file. "You are going to get your girlfriend injured. I touched your thumb a few hours after you last filed it. If it cut me with only a slight amount of pressure, it could cut her, too, if you're engaged in more intimate activities." My face burns. "We need to figure out what your nails are made of, then we can devise a plan or even a coating to go over them, if needed, to make sure you can live your life and engage in all the benefits of a new relationship *safely*."

My face is hot as fire. And not in the way I find comforting. "Fine. A week."

"A week. And in the meantime, you'll engage in hands-free activities." She raises both eyebrows, and the smile on her lips is too large, even though I can tell she's trying not to tease me.

"Pervert."

She laughs again, even more boisterously this time. "Call me if anything changes with you. Have you told Vanessa yet?"

I shake my head and am surprised when Emily doesn't berate me for keeping secrets but says instead, "You can tell her I need to check her ankle, and I'll give you the results of your sample Friday. We can check your nail growth then too."

"Thanks, Emily."

"No problem, Roland." She swivels back to her laptop, and it's like she's forgotten I'm still in the room. I haven't left yet, my hand still on the doorknob as I turn to her. She finally registers I'm still here and cocks her head. "Can I help you?"

"You got a good recommendation for a restaurant?"

"What kind?"

I shrug. "Italian? Anything a smart, shy girl not used to dating might like?"

"And I'm assuming money is no object."

I give her a flat look.

She grins. "Just checking. After all, not even *you* might get in to some of these places looking like a grizzly."

"What?"

"You look like you haven't seen a comb in forty years."

"I'm not forty."

"You don't know how old you are. For all we know, you could be 340. Gravity could work very differently on your planet—not to mention all the time you spent in interspace travel . . ."

"Emily," I bark, hoping to derail what was sure to be an hours-long physics explanation.

"Right. Well, if you can procure a pair of normal nonsweatpants in the next hour or so, and possibly a haircut, I'd try these." She pulls out her notepad—the one for *prescriptions*, which feels decidedly appropriate—and starts scribbling. When she's finished, she tears my newest scrip from the pad and hands it up to me. "That should get you started."

I stare down at the list, but all I can think is that I've got no clue where to get a haircut, and when I had the COE send a car for me earlier, I had them bring me more sweatpants. I open my mouth, but Emily gets there first. "I'll call Shandra. She'll meet you in design in ten minutes to update your, uh . . . look."

Chapter Seventeen

ROLAND

I'm an hour late to pick her up, and I feel like a doofus in black dress pants, a navy-blue button-down, and no beard. Well, for me what feels like no beard. It's barely a shadow. The lineup Shandra gave me was good, though. I guess. But damn if I don't know how I feel about the hair. It's a big change. My hair was down to my neck, and now it's short. Shorter on the sides than on the top, but it still doesn't even brush the tops of my ears. She wasn't willing to budge either. The little blond waif of a woman didn't look equipped to cut my hair at all, but she handed me the aesthetic brief, handwritten in tiny, perfect writing I recognized. I had to smirk.

Superman's haircut—the way a Turkish barber would do it.

It's strange to me, remembering every so often that the woman who just about breaks down trying to speak in front of people she doesn't know is a hypercompetent entrepreneur running what is becoming a massive media company. Now, sitting across a tiny table covered in a red-and-white-checkered tablecloth from her, I'm more nervous than I can remember feeling before in my life. In fact, I'm not even sure I knew what nervousness was.

My childhood . . . the first memories I have, anyway . . . was riddled with emotions tinged in the residue of nervousness, but there was anger there too. I couldn't remember anything except that I had forgotten something very important and needed to remember it. And when time passed and I didn't, apathy set in instead.

I spent all my teenage years and through my twenties feeling a certain level of disappointment with these humans. As if I wanted them to be other than how they turned out, but I already knew this species wasn't capable of surprising me. They were new, different from what I'd known back wherever I came from—not that I could remember it in detail—but I remember the feeling that I'd *expected* them, and while I feared leaving behind whatever I'd left behind, I wasn't afraid of this new place. But how to explain all that to her? The first person I encountered who surprised me.

Surprised is too light a word. The strong, vulnerable, gorgeous, funny, witty, shy Vanessa Theriot shocked the bones free of my flesh and the sanity from my soul.

And she won't. Stop. Staring.

"Fu-freaking quit it, Nessa. You're freaking me out."

"Sorry." She jolts. Her cheeks get really pink, and I feel mine heat in response. "It's just . . . you know . . . you look . . ."

"Yeah, I know. You told me I look good," I say, leaning in toward her and dropping my tone. "But you're making it really hard to sit at this table with you with a raging hard-on."

She squeaks—*squeaks*—just like she did when she opened the front door to her town house looking like a dream with her hair piled on top of her head in a bun of some kind, a few dark- and light-brown curls styled to frame her face. She had makeup on and these chunky shoes that could have passed for either part of a school uniform or combat boots, and a black dress that hugged her from her collar to the hem of her obscenely short skirt. I had half a mind to make her change, and when I told her as much, she pouted, and then she tripped down the next step. I rushed forward, caught her against my chest, and held her there longer than a stranger would have considered normal. But I couldn't let her go. She was blinking up at me like I was the goddamn sun, and she didn't stop looking at me like that the entire drive and is still looking at me like that as we're seated at the restaurant by a stammering waiter.

"Sorry," she whispers a little more calmly before tearing her gaze away from me and back to the menu. And she just has to say it, doesn't she? "We could get out of here, though, you know."

I lean back in my seat, rake my hand over my face, and groan. "You're not being very nice, Nessa."

"And you're shaking the whole table," she says, laughing as she reaches to steady her wineglass. She brings it to her lips and watches me over the rim as she takes a swallow.

I'm not gonna survive this, am I?

"Hi there. My name's Manuel, but you can call me Mani for short. I'll be your, um . . . waiter tonight . . ." He must know that I'm glaring at him because his speech starts to devolve.

Vanessa takes pity on him, which I loathe, and smiles her shy little smile that makes me want to level cities for her and tear out Mani's throat. "Mani? My brother's name is Mani too. Emmanuel, so not quite the same."

"Oh really? Where's he from?"

"Our mom is Mexican."

"Oh, cool. I'm German. It's honestly really such an honor to wait on you tonight. Can I tell you the, um . . . the specials?" My glare has started to heat, and I know he sees the fire in my eyes.

"Of course," Vanessa chirps.

Marvin tells us the specials, which I don't hear at all but to which Nessa responds politely. She asks him a few questions, which he stutters through, and I fight the urge to melt the pen in his hand and the rubber soles of his shoes to the floor. He refills our wine and water glasses and then hastens to the back of the restaurant, where I can see four other staffers staring at us. I plan to shoot them my most searing look when Nessa kicks me under the table.

"The f—eff was that for?"

She's leaning toward me, her menu trapped between her breasts and the table, where I'd currently like to have my face. "Stop it," she says, and I'd think she was reprimanding me if she weren't also smiling. "You're being mean."

"Mean?"

"Yes, mean. You're supposed to be a hero, remember?" She gives me a playful look, and I get the sense she's teasing me. And I'm honored.

I sit back and match her teasing with a dry tone of my own. "I thought I was supposed to be a dragon?" I bring fire to my eyes, and her smile gets wider, and my heart damn near stops. She's not afraid of me anymore. At least, not like she was.

"That too."

"Why Wyvern, anyway?"

She huffs. "I thought we went over this."

"Yeah, but I could have just been Dragon-Man or something."

"Dragon-Man?"

I shrug, grin widening in response to hers. "I'm no branding expert."

"Clearly." She shakes her head. "Besides Dragon-Man being stupid, a wyvern is a mythical dragon, like from fantasy books, except a wyvern has a barbed tail and only two legs and is generally considered faster but lacks the magical powers that dragons sometimes have. So, in that way, it wasn't totally accurate. You basically *are* magic. But Wyvern tested better, and frankly, anything was better than Pyro," she says with one eyebrow raised, as if I'd been the one responsible for it.

I laugh and shake my head. "Pretty sure the leads in all those books you're talking about are white."

She just shrugs. "You could be the lead in that book if you'd just be nice. You could have little kids dressing up as you for Halloween. White kids and kids of any other color."

"You know kids dress up as villains all the time." I lean in toward her and reach for my wine. I don't care what it tastes like. It could taste like piss, and I'd still have drunk it just to get that look in her eye.

She's flustered. Breathless. Pupils all big. She blinks several times. "Yes." She drinks from her glass, too, more quickly this time. "They do. They dress up as villains. Darth Vader, Lex Luthor, Kylo Ren—all villains who died."

I don't answer right away. Just stare between her eyes.

When she looks nervous enough, I finally sigh. "You got a one-track mind, Nessa."

My gaze drops to her lips. I watch them as she whispers, "It seems you do too, Rollo."

"I do." I exhale deeply, and when I lean forward, she sucks in a breath. I say, "But I think I could try to be the hero for you."

"Hey there, it's me, um . . . Mani again. Have you all decided what you'd like to order?"

Nessa jumps, her wineglass teetering dangerously, but I reach across the table and stabilize it. She glances at me with pupils damn near fully blown. "Oh, sorry. I think we, um . . . we'll . . ."

"Give us a minute," I tell him.

When he leaves, she looks up at me, her hands stilling as they unfold the menu once again—a futile effort, but it's cute she tries. I've given up. "What?" she says. "Why are you glaring at him like that?"

"I don't like watching people drool all over you."

She blushes high in her cheeks and glances across the restaurant, a cozy space with a dozen or so tables like this one and only two booths in the very back—dark, away from the windows, and more private. They were going to take us to one of those first before I thought it too risky and made them move us directly up front. In the privacy of a booth, there's not a doubt in my mind that my hands would have wandered. And while most of the patrons of the restaurant are older and not paying us much attention, the rest are staring avidly. If we were in a booth, somebody would see something, and I'd have to burn their eyes out.

"I'm pretty sure he was drooling over *you*."

"Sure. Doesn't matter. I'm not gonna light him on fire or melt his glasses to his face, if that's what you're worried about."

Her water glass is halfway to her mouth. "I *wasn't* worried about that before. You . . . you're joking, right?"

"Sure."

Her little smile comes back, and she shakes her head, actually looking at the menu briefly before laying it down. "Not much of a hero then, huh?"

"I said I'd try. It's a process."

She clears her throat. "I, um . . . I'd like to try for you too."

I cock my head, confused. She exhales, and my pulse thrums with a zing. Something is happening.

"You read my file."

"Shit, Nessa—I mean . . ."

"No. Just . . . let me finish, because I need to, um . . . say this." So I wait. I wait like I've never waited before. It's unbearable. She exhales, her curls leaping up before fluttering back down to touch her cheek. "You read my file. You know already that I grew up in a not-so-nice family and that I was fortunate enough to find a new, amazing one. That file . . . you might have seen the pictures of the . . . what I looked like when I was rescued after all those days alone. The people who kept me homeschooled me because there's no regulation on homeschooling in most states, and they weren't . . . good." She exhales deeply, which is nice for her because I'm not fucking breathing at all.

"But what that file doesn't show is the other stuff they did. They . . ." She shakes her head, and I'm so shocked by the lack of rage in her features because that's all I feel right now. And then she looks up, directly into my soul. Her hand reaches in and takes hold of all my bones.

"If you want to know about me, you have to ask. You can't . . . surprise me. You can't call me names. You can't threaten me. You just can't. I can try, and I will try to be honest and not retreat from . . . this," she says, gesturing between us, "but you can't just try . . . You *have* to be the hero in this, for me."

I swallow razor blades. All I can do is nod. It takes me a while to be able to speak. I feel like I'm sweating even though my body doesn't really do that. The sweat just evaporates. It takes every ounce of my power to remain seated and not go to her, wrap her in my arms, and squeeze her until I absorb her entirely.

"I swear it, Nessa," I say. I choke. "I'll be the hero for you."

She nods down at the table and then takes another breath before meeting my gaze and nodding again. One corner of her mouth quirks, but it's shaky. "Thank you."

"You don't have to thank me. Jesus."

I card my fingers through my hair and drain my glass. She's still blushing at me when I put it down. "I also, um . . . I want you to know that . . ." She reaches for her glass, but her hand is shaking. She curls it into a fist and brings it to her lap in a way that makes my stomach melt. "You mentioned that you wanted this to be a real dinner . . . date. I'm okay if you want to drop the *fake* part of this thing that we're . . . doing here. I am . . . um . . . I'll resign from the Lois Lane contract. I'll just, um . . . be your girlfriend, I guess . . ."

I've tried as long as I can. I launch out of my seat so quickly, the chair topples back and lands on the floor with a hard slap. I round the table and hinge at the waist, and I grab her face, and I kiss her deeply, tongue down her throat, lips hard and beseeching.

I kiss her long enough to be satisfied, which means I'm there for a long fucking time. She's not the one to break the kiss, though, and that makes me happy. I pull back on a growl. My chest is making that sound that even Emily can't figure out, and it's loud.

Her eyes are still closed, her abused lips red and parted. I stroke my rough thumb down her cheek, careful not to accidentally scratch her. "Marry me," I growl.

"Rollo!" she squeaks. Her eyes fly open, and I stand up fully when she pushes me off with a smile. She shakes her head.

I begrudgingly move away from her only to see several people in the restaurant with their phones out now. I glare at them until they put them away and pretend to keep eating. The elderly couple seated a table away is grinning at us. The man has both of his thumbs and eyebrows up. I laugh at him and shake my head before picking up my chair and falling into it, unburdened.

"So is that a yes?"

"Rollo!" She smiles at me, and it's a magical thing. She's wrong. She got it all fucking wrong. I'm not the one who carries magic. "Can we at least get through dinner first?"

"How many dinners until I get to marry you?"

She balks. "That's not how it works."

"It's the deal we made for . . . other stuff."

She blushes darker, and it's the cutest fucking thing. And then, once again, my Nessa says the last thing I expect. "Twenty-two."

I grin like a maniac. "Then get a white dress, because twenty-three days from now, you're going to be mine for real. Forever."

She just rolls her eyes and orders from the waiter when he eventually stumbles back over. It's cute that she doesn't believe me. I reach for my wineglass and let the topic lie for now, instead changing the subject to her life, her family. I want to know more about her, and she's right. I don't want to have to root it out; I want her to tell me.

And she tries for me, just as she promised she would.

We talk about her brothers, the dicks who fought me. I like 'em, even though I've only met them once, because she tells me all the ways they've had her back over the years—ways I even had the privilege of witnessing when her youngest brother beat me upside the head with a lacrosse stick.

We talk about her parents—her real, adopted ones—about the movies she likes and hates, and then spend the next two hours talking about books. She rants about the underrepresentation of women— Black women, in particular—in sci-fi blockbusters over the past fifty years for a solid half hour, citing movies I've never heard of, but I pretend. And in return she gets to hear about my weird-ass childhood, my time in the SDD discovering my powers, the foods I hate, and how much I hate haircuts.

"How was it? Rescuing those people? Doing hero shit?" Vanessa's a little tipsy. Her tongue sticks out to wet her lower lip in a way I don't even know if she knows is dangerous. Course she doesn't. Nor does she know how desperately I'm hanging on.

"Not sure."

"What do you mean, not sure?" She scoffs.

"I did it because you pissed me off, and because I pissed me off. Wanted to prove to you that I could do it and maybe prove it to myself too. But when I was up there, it was all mechanical. Brute determination and grit. Just one thing after the next after the next. I don't think I even realized how exhausted I was until I saw some of those pictures Monika took."

"She's incredible, huh?"

"Crazy. The wildest part is that she was so discreet. I didn't even realize she was there most of the time."

Vanessa nods. "The best."

"And you want to know what made it all feel worth it in the end?"

Vanessa blushes, like she knows what I'm gonna say before I say it. "What?"

"The way you looked at me when I knocked on your door. Like I was the most impressive thing you'd ever seen."

"You kind of are."

My chest heats. I exhale smoke and shake my head, a lock of my already-disheveled hair drooping across my forehead, Shandra's whole aesthetic out the window. "*You* are."

"Me? I'm just a nervous wreck who can't talk to people."

"Who runs her own company. Who's fucking badass." I cock my head. "And what do I care if you can't talk to people? You can talk to me. In fact, it's better you can't talk to people, because anytime anybody talks to you, I wanna kill 'em."

"You're insane."

"Yeah."

"And also really sweet."

I laugh hard. "Shut up."

"You are," she insists, picking at her dessert. She hasn't offered to share, and even though I don't care about key lime pie, I still enjoy stealing bites from her plate and seeing the annoyed, almost involuntary way she flicks my fork away. "What you did for those kids was insane."

I shrug. "They deserve it. They didn't have to help you."

Her blush is deep, and she's nodding. "Still, I should have been the one to thank them."

"No."

"No? I was the one who fell . . ."

"And you were all right. I wasn't. When the COE called me and told me you were hurt, I lost my damn mind. I was expecting the worst. Wasn't expecting you to be smiling and a bunch of kids to have your back. Made me feel better. And definitely saved those reporters' lives."

Nessa snorts and polishes off her pie. "Seeing you skateboard with those kids was hot."

I laugh. "You drunk?"

She blushes and quickly blurts, "Tipsy! I promise I'm not gonna throw up."

I laugh even harder and order the bill. Vanessa insists on paying because I'm "poor now" after giving all my money away to those kids. I let her. Don't give a shit about money. She can have all mine so long as she buys me sweats every so often and maybe a couple new pairs of underwear.

Fat and happy, we take some pictures with the damn waiter, Moroney or whatever, and by the time we get home, I'm feeling more satisfied than I ever have in my life. Until I go to the bathroom and wash my hands and realize . . .

"What the . . ."

My nails grew half an inch and are sharp as goddamn razors.

"What the fuck?" I hiss.

"Rollo, you okay?" She calls me by the name she calls me when she's really happy. I'm not gonna fuck this night up with talk of the impossible, because what's going on with my hands is impossible. Forgetting what I told Emily, I grab the nail file from under Vanessa's bathroom sink and grunt, "Yeah, just taking a shit."

"Thanks for the info." She laughs.

Frantic, I take the file to my hand and start sawing away, except . . . the file breaks in half on the second pass. What the fuck is happening to me?

I need answers before I bring this to Vanessa. Solutions. Because what's not gonna fucking happen? I'm the hero now. I've got the girl, and I'm not gonna scare her away by telling her that I can't fucking touch her.

I angry text a picture to Emily, like this is her fault. And bless the damn woman, she texts me back right away. I open my messages and frown, hating her response enough to break my phone in half.

Either tell Vanessa or make up an excuse—either way, don't touch her!

If I hadn't just snapped my phone in two like Nessa's nail file, Fuck you, is what I'd have texted Emily back.

Chapter Eighteen

Vanessa

"He took the couch again," I whisper.

"Again? Hasn't it been four nights?"

"I know. And I thought . . . after our dinner . . . he sort of promised. But then, nothing."

"Has he kissed you?"

Oh yeah. Yes. Definitely. A lot. The memory of what he did to me yesterday in the kitchen definitely takes center stage in my thoughts. Up on the island, legs spread, his mouth and lips ravaging the space between them . . .

"I'll take that look on your face as a yes." Margerie squeals.

I sigh heavily, having just explained all this to Margerie at the tail end of our one-on-one in the COE offices, trying to get the photo shoot organized with Monika now that the Wyvern has his hair cut and his purple suit tailored to fit.

"Yes, but he won't sleep with me in the bed." Or sleep with me, period. He hasn't let me touch him for the last three days. I did go down on him . . . and I thought it had been great. But then after, he saw that he'd scratched my shoulder on accident, and since then, nothing. Kissing, sure. He wanted to touch me yesterday, but I evaded, feeling uncomfortable. Like . . . I'd done something wrong before. Maybe I was . . . bad? I wanted to ask . . . but was too ashamed. And I certainly wasn't going to tell Margerie any of that.

Margerie stands up, clutching her laptop to her chest. She claps her free hand down on my shoulder. "I'm not going to lie to you. This is all insane, and you are valid in your feelings of insanity." But then her hand falls down to my shoulder blade, and she rubs it soothingly, and she gets the strangest expression I've ever seen on her. She's giggly. Like she's fighting back hysterics. Her touch is comforting—consoling, even—but her face is about to erupt in shrieks.

"What? What is it? Did I do something wrong? Tell me, Margerie! I can do the taxes for a billion-dollar company in my sleep, but I don't get boys. You know I'm not good at this stuff."

She's shaking her head, all but wagging it. Then her lips split to reveal her grin. Her eyes are shining. "You *like* him."

I shake my head. "What?"

"You *like* him. And he clearly likes you back if he's proposing marriage twenty minutes into your first date."

I snort. "It's . . . he was kidding. It was a joke."

"Was it?"

"Of course."

"If you have questions, don't evade. Isn't that what you two talked about? Being open?"

"You think I should ask him what's with the bed?"

"Yes, of course. Don't let him make you feel bad. You said that he's gonna try harder for you, but baby girl, you've also got to help him. He's not a mind reader, and if he's making you feel bad sometimes, he might not know it. He's human too. Or, well. Sort of. And he's in love with you. He'll fix it if you tell him there's a problem."

"Love?" I shriek. "Are you insane?"

She holds up her hands in defense, her laptop a shield. "I'm not going to convince you. I'm here to go over the schedule for Forty-Eight Day and the photo shoot at the old airport. But you're not the only one who needs to see this. Shandra wants another go at the fabric. She thinks she can get the tigereye gradient in the purple color you were hoping for in time for Forty-Eight Day. It'll look really good against the airport museum backdrop.

"In the meantime, you are going to heed my words. You like him. He likes you. Try to poke holes in it, if you want, but don't sharpen your knife when you find that the fabric doesn't tear. Go talk to him." She gives my shoulder one final little squeeze, and I nod, my throat all clenched.

"I'll . . . try."

She rolls her eyes but still smiles and says, "And you'll succeed, because I've never seen you fail at anything. You got this."

"I got this."

"He's in design now. Go get him."

"I'll go get him." I stand up, and Margerie slaps my ass.

"That's my girl!"

I laugh, feeling strangely giddy at the prospect of confronting him about our lack of sex, and follow Margerie out of our temporary offices in one of the COE domes and into the larger COE tower. We split at the elevator. She goes up to the Wyvern's floor, and I continue across the atrium, planning to grab Rollo a coffee.

I cross toward the coffee shop in the center of the open space. The line isn't too long as the lunch crowd hasn't hit yet. I'm feeling optimistic and excited-nervous as I slip between men and women in power suits, some couriers, and delivery people.

One such delivery person in a generic brown uniform is walking toward me. I'm not focused on them but register their uniform coming closer and closer in my peripheries. I try to veer out of the way, but they counter, moving into my path until I'm forced to place all my attention on them. I trip. "Ooph." They're staring straight ahead, not looking at me at all, as they clip my arm with their shoulder.

"Sorry . . ." I start to shout, but the word is taken—the world is taken—smashed into a ball and shoved back down my throat as my body spins, colliding with nothing, and I free-fall.

My stomach lurches up into my mouth, and I swallow it into place, and when I blink next, I'm still. I open my eyes, and I know the smell of this place before my eyes even register it. I know where I am.

I can taste the age of the house on my tongue. I can feel the wind from the open window letting in a draft that claps greedily against open cabinet doors. They're all empty. I don't need to look again; I already know.

My whole body has been immolated. I can breathe, but I can't move. I'm not sure if I can't or if I don't, but the result is the same. Tears well in my eyes, ready to join the ghosts of tears already in this place.

How am I here? Am I really here? What if this is just . . . a dream? A nightmare . . . standing in a place I never want to remember and can never forget. In the kitchen of my childhood home, where I was left . . .

A rattling grabs my attention, like the hair on the back of my head when she used to shake me for being too slow. I choke. The sound of a flushing toilet echoes down the short hall that connects three small rooms. A tiny bedroom my . . . those people who birthed me used, a tinier bedroom that doubled as the place I slept and her closet, and this room. An empty kitchen with a view of a beat-up couch covered in trash and clothes positioned in front of a TV with a big crack down the middle.

The couch is bare, not covered in anything now, and the TV is gone, but it's still the same couch. The same green fabric worn gray in places. It can't be the same couch. It can't be the same room. It feels like . . . someone just emptied the place, ran out in a hurry, and never came back . . . *because they were sent to jail. The house was foreclosed on, and the bank took it, but nobody ever bought it, not even a developer to tear it down. Everyone who set foot near this place knew what it was: cursed.*

A door squeaks, and I jolt, recognizing the sound. The hinges of the bathroom door were all built in at wrong angles, so the door sweeps the floor, scraping it before it hits the wall. I look toward it, and where my mother once stood, eyes bleary, hair sticking straight up and out in a bleached-blond mop, appears a dark-haired person, androgynously dressed in a pair of black pants and a boxy black shirt, a heaping of layered gold necklaces weighing down their neck.

They remind me of a Greek neighbor Elena and William had when I first moved in to their house. Their neighbor had always been friendly. They'd never told Elena and William about the one time they caught me with all my worldly supplies, standing at a bus stop in town. I hadn't taken the bus, in the end, but seeing them drive by—in the direction of Elena and William's house—had been terror-inducing enough, I'd immediately given up on the idea of running. I'm glad I had.

This person has a small smile strung between their cheeks, but I don't feel soothed by that. Standing here in this house, looking at this person emerging from a bathroom that I've used before . . . nothing about this is friendly.

"Hi there, Vanessa. How are you feeling?" they say, smoothing a tanned white hand through their jet-black waves. Their sleeves are cropped short to reveal lean muscles that flex on each subtle motion. "I know you don't know me, so I thought, hey, what the heck? Why not bring you to a place you do know? I thought that might make you feel more comfortable."

They grin, ring-covered fingers rapping against the paper-thin wall devoid of pictures, not even stained by the outlines of pictures that once were, because there never were any. "No? It doesn't? You look a little distressed." They keep pausing between their words, dark eyes moving over me in a plain assessment. There's something they're trying to figure out. If only they'd ask, I'd tell them. I'd tell them anything they wanted to hear to get me out of here.

"You're a shy, skittish little thing, aren't you?" They lunge at me, arriving on the other side of the tiny, dinky kitchen island. The laminate cracks under their palms as they press their hands flat to the surface. I flinch back so hard, I hit my head against an open cabinet door. The feel of the hard particleboard covered in peeling plastic and the *exact* way it hurts as it digs into my skull drags me underneath an icy wave of memories where I drown, screaming.

My hand fumbles for my pocket, shock rendering all my movements clumsy. They don't try to stop me but watch as I reach into my pocket, pull out my phone, and immediately drop it. I'm too scared to pick it up. I don't want to let this person out of my sight.

They're leaning forward onto the island that separates us now, their bare forearms down on the cracking material. They're looking at me with amusement plain in their dark eyes. "I don't understand how you could be a key. And yet . . . here we are." They sigh, shake their head a little, stand up, and brush a hand through their hair.

"You know, you're the first key we've found. Do you even know who I am? No, I don't suppose you would. You might work for the *Champions*," they scoff, rings clanging again as they slap the counter, making me jump. "But they don't trust you enough to tell you anything real. Distract the world with cute photos of the darling couple and pictures of the *Wyvern* in tight pants, and the world won't realize they've been lied to."

I don't say anything. I don't know what they're talking about, don't know how I'm meant to respond, and frankly, don't care. I just want out of here.

"Well, I don't want to take up too much of your time. I have just a few questions that, if you answer honestly, will result in my transporting you back to your precious office space, and if you don't, will result in me locking you in here to starve, just like your parents did when they went on that weeklong bender, right? It'll be fitting. You'll die in here as you were always meant to as a child."

No.

No . . .

"Shall we begin?" They stalk around the island, coming to stand on its other side, right in front of me without a barrier to separate us. They smell like sugar and syrup and a splash of darkness that cuts through both. They step right into my space. Place both hands on my hips and pull me close.

"We know that he's begun his reversion. You've been helping with that, documenting his recent *heroics* and giving us clear evidence of his transition, but has he been recovering his purpose?" I stare at them blankly, feeling dumb, numb with terror. Their fingers squeeze into my hip bones with implied threat, painfully, with nails sharpened to a razor's edge. "I know you've perfected this doe-eyed stare that's clearly got his fiery hotness so enrapt, but it won't work for me. You see my eyes? They don't glow for you. You do nothing for me, darling.

"I haven't found my key yet. It's not supposed to be a person. A *human*," they sneer. "You see, I thought our keys would come to us with time. I thought they would be intangible, something encoded in our genetics. I was just . . . waiting . . . instead of scouring the fucking planet for a human to use to unlock my gate." Their hands squeeze me even more tightly, hard enough to cause pain, but being here, in this house, I don't feel it. Pain doesn't exist. Because it's like breathing. It's everywhere.

"You can't hurt me here," I whisper, because I'm a fool.

Their eyes round, and looking at them from this close, I feel like I can see a little bit of East Asian heritage, though I know it doesn't matter. They could be from anywhere but here. Because they aren't from Earth. And they hate me because they seem to know something about me. It makes me wonder about my first encounter with Roland. He hated me then too. Does he know something he hasn't told me? Does he know who this is? Are they in cahoots? Is he using me?

Fuck off, Vanessa. Nobody would ever want you . . .

"Who are you?" I whisper as their fingers dig in to my skin tighter and tighter.

"Tell me now, and I won't get angry . . . Has Sixty-Two spoken to you about his past?"

I shake my head, though I didn't mean to; the action came involuntarily, and that seems to make whoever this is even angrier. "He doesn't remember? Or he doesn't trust you to know?"

"I don't know." Probably the latter.

"You're telling me that you're the key to his reversion, the key to his gate, and he hasn't even bothered to tell you that his memories are coming back? Does anyone trust you with anything? Or are you fucking useless?" *You're so fucking useless, Vanessa.*

I don't respond. My breathing exercises are a fucking joke here. No amount of therapy could have ever prepared me for this. So I retreat, moving deeper and deeper into my mind; the cabinet that was reserved for things I never meant to relive or remember now hangs open, the lock broken, the door bent on its hinges. I lie curled within it, hands bound in the dark.

No . . .

No.

You're a fucking badass. I suck in stale air and jerk violently at the sudden invasion of Rollo's voice in my thoughts. *A good fucking girl. Who runs her own company.* He promised me he'd try for me. He could have manipulated me by doing and saying much less. He didn't need to lie to me about that. *Marry me.*

My chest shudders as I attempt a feat foreign to me. Bravery. I stutter, "If y-you th-think I'm use-useless, why did you bother asking me? Why don't you just ask him yourself?" I take in a deeper breath, and my words come out more evenly, acerbically. I spit, "Are you scared of him?"

The whack of their fist against my face doesn't come as a huge shock. I think if I were standing anywhere else, it might have. But not in here, where my face and body are already so used to it. I barely even feel the pain. It's a slight burn. My lip took one of their rings, and I taste blood. But I do something I've never done before in this wretched, damned place. I don't keep my gaze on the floor, even after the sting settles. I look back up.

Their eyes meet mine, and I don't break. I watch their jaw clench. A muscle stands out in their neck. They clench their back teeth. "His behavior is counter to the plan. But . . . if you're not lying and he really *hasn't* started to recover his memories, then that would explain it." They exhale, and I detect relief in their tone as they add, "He might not have even found his map." They tap my hip, contemplating while my mind fires in shock. *The map.* My mind instantly snags on the strange squiggles I saw on Rollo's skin, and I hate myself for being so obvious.

"Has he found the map?" Anger clouds their face. They give my hips a hard shake. "You have him too distracted. Tell Sixty-Two that he needs to get his head out of your pussy and find his weapon, open it, and complete his reversion. He should get his memories back then, and once he's fully reverted, he'll be ready."

"Ready?" I pant. "For what?"

Pain makes its presence known when they squeeze my hips one final time. I still don't crumble. Not yet. Not here in this kitchen where I've crumbled so many times before. At least, not in front of them.

"To lead," they whisper. I can't hold back my wince this time, and seeing it, they smile. "But only after he's finished getting what he needs from you. You can try to delay it, but it is inevitable. He's started to revert already. You'd best not stand in his path. Because if he finds out you kept this information from him, he's going to be angry, and then you'll burn first when he remembers his past. I'm sure of it."

No.

"No."

"No?" They smile at me, a condescending thing.

"You're wrong," I insist, even as I start to sweat.

They shrug. "Better to be the right hand of the devil than stand in his path, and maybe he'll let you exist in the new world. At least, for a short time."

"Or maybe he'll burn *you.*"

"You really want to bet on that once he remembers?"

I don't answer.

They grin even more maniacally. "Why don't you go help him get his memories back, be a good girl and help him find his map, and when he's ready to lead us, I'll remind him to go easy on you." They give my bruised right hip a condescending pat.

"Who are you?"

"Why don't you ask the COE?" They lean in abruptly, brushing their lips over my cheek. "I'm number Three."

They take a step back, and then they just . . . disappear.

There's no rush of wind or swirling smoke. They just are . . . and then they aren't. I sway forward, about to fall, but some strength I didn't know I possessed keeps me on my feet. I grab the edge of the kitchen island in front of me and clutch it with shaking arms until I'm certain my legs will hold me. Then I turn.

My chest is clenched so badly, each inhale tears at the seams. My face is hot, but when I rub it roughly, trying to get my shit together, I find that it's dry. I didn't cry here. Not often. Not until they left me alone like Three just did. But I'm stronger than I was back then because I have people . . . who love me . . . who care . . .

I can do this.

. . . fucking badass . . .

I'm making my way around the island, heading for my phone first and then the open front door, through which I can see the overgrown yard crawling with trash and weeds and memories. The press of ghosts all around me is palpable, and they're all me, all my childhood, and they each wound me *painfully* in turn. I make a loud choking sound and reach down, my foot kicking my phone once before I actually manage to bend over and grab hold of it. I catch myself on the floor, staggering wildly as I come back up to stand, and lunge for the front door.

A gust of strength fuels me as I stagger out of the shadows and into the sunlight. My hands are shaking as I hold my phone up to my face. I have a few people I could call, but I scroll past all of them. Number Three believes I have every right to fear him. But I don't believe people who hurt me. I believe people who look me in the eye and tell me they'll try for me, who issue me vows of hope.

Chapter Nineteen

ROLAND

The design meeting was derailed slightly when I refused to wear the gloves—not so much *wouldn't* as *couldn't* wear the gloves. "How have you kept this hidden?" Margerie is holding my hands. It's fucking weird, but I get why she's holding on to me like this. Like we're about to break out into a slow dance.

Dr. Larsen is looming over her shoulder, having just arrived. She gasps theatrically and then cackles like she's lost her marbles. "Oh my God! That's just since last Sunday?"

Even after I texted her a picture of my nails, she still wanted me to let them grow. Our official checkup is still scheduled for Friday, when Nessa has her checkup for her ankle. The little asshole hasn't been wearing her brace since our dinner. She feels fine—like the doc said she would—but I still catch her wincing every once in a while when she puts weight on it. If I deny her sex, I wonder if she'll put it back on.

Who am I kidding? I've been denying her sex all damn week.

I've been denying *me* sex all week because I know that if I let myself go with her, there's a high chance I'll grab her too hard, and right now I can't afford to do that. Not with my nails looking like . . . this.

That doesn't mean I haven't been enjoying her screams.

Her spread out across the kitchen island. All that brown marble underneath her body made her look a part of it. She glittered in sweat. She spread her legs on command, and she let me eat her pussy through two orgasms without giving her a break.

And it isn't like she hasn't noticed that I haven't taken things further yet. She's been needy, all but begging for my cock, but I don't want to show her my nails or my fresh marks. What if they freak her out? Hell. They freak *me* out.

I shiver and flex my hands. "Test failed. I need 'em cut."

"Are you sure?" Emily has the stones to ask.

"The fuck are you talking about? *Yes.*"

"We could wait just to see what happens, for scientific purposes."

"I will scratch your eyes out if you don't cut these nails off."

Emily sighs and gives me an annoyed look, her scrunchie and nails both pink today. "I don't know how to tell you this, Roland." She reaches out and grips my shoulder like she's about to give me six months to live.

"Fucking say it."

"I will if you'll stop interrupting."

I huff but manage to stay quiet as she comes even closer, too close, standing up on her tiptoes to get closer yet. Margerie leans in, too, not wanting to miss it. "You don't have nails, Roland. You have claws." Margerie's still holding my hands but drops them like hot stones the moment the words are out. She gasps.

I squint. "What?"

"You have claws. I suspected as much from the sample I took from your hand. It seems as if, unlike most mammals that have claws, you have six layers of a keratin-like substance coating a keratin nail bed. The COE scientists looking into the matter haven't been able to isolate each individual biological component that makes up your claws yet. We're not even sure all the types of matter exist within earthly human biology." Her voice rises at the end, finishing in a squeak.

"Glad you're fucking happy about this. What am I supposed to do with that information?" I say, stepping out of the mosh of women and shoving my fingers—claws—angrily back through my hair. I don't cut myself. I'm not sure how it's possible when I've chipped or torn so many other things while trying to let them grow—a wooden desk, a doorknob, one of Vanessa's fancy pillows—but I haven't cut myself yet. I've tried and found that I can't.

"Accept them. Besides, I'm not sure the polymers I've been experimenting with will even work. You use your hands too often, wash your hands too often, and when you cut your nails, they just grow back the same thickness and strength they were before. A regular nail file isn't going to cut it, Roland, if the photo you sent me was any clue. You're going to have to use gardening shears. And rather than that, I think you should consider that these may just be your new hands and learn to work with them."

"Work *with* them?" I'm about to fucking explode. I hold up my hands in front of my face and nearly topple the two women standing in front of me when flames shoot out of my ears. "How am I supposed to touch my wife with these?"

"Your wife?" Margerie all but screams. "You're married? And that little hussy didn't tell me?"

"I've got a few more dates, then yeah. She said she'd marry me," I grunt. Sort of.

My hands forgotten, Margerie backs away from me and reaches for her phone in hysterics. I know she's calling her friend; it was either that or beat me up, and she looked like she was a hair trigger away from it. I know there'll be repercussions from Nessa for putting that out there without her permission, but I honestly don't give a fuck. I want her to marry me, especially now that she's resigned her Lois Lane contract.

I've only got nineteen dates to go. We had dinner again Monday night after our Italian date night Sunday, and if she thinks I'm not including the coffee we had together yesterday morning as a date, she's gonna be disappointed. Food out equals date. Period. Nineteen dates to go . . . and you can bet your ass I'm counting.

"All right! Sheesh, don't blow a gasket," Emily says with a chuckle. "I'll cut them back this time, but we're not going to be able to keep this up indefinitely. How often do you realistically need them trimmed so you don't cut yourself?"

"I . . ." I clear my throat. "I'm healing fast, and my nails don't bother me. But I'm not gonna take that chance with Vanessa."

Emily frowns. Her eyes move over my chest. She can't see anything of me past my uniform, but she's a smart woman. She reads between the lines and asks, "How have your wounds healed from last week's heroics?"

It's scary. A little too scary to admit to. But the wounds I had last week are almost totally gone. "They're scarred over."

"Already?"

I nod.

"And the tattoos are unchanged?"

"No." I swallow hard, drop my tone, and say, "I got another one."

"Where?"

I don't know how to fucking answer her. Because the truth of it is awkward as fuck. I got a new tattoo after Vanessa gave me head on the couch. And the tattoo? I woke up with it wrapped around my cock. "Groin . . . area," I say quietly enough that the other members of the design team working in the back of the room on a new set of gloves— and Margerie smashing her finger down on her phone furiously—won't hear me.

Emily blinks at me, shocked. "Oh my."

I nod, feeling a little unnerved by my own body. And seeing Emily looking at me with such concern right now isn't bringing up my mood.

"I haven't found anything in the COE archives," she whispers. "But I'll keep looking."

"Thanks, Doc."

"I'd still like to take a look at Vanessa too." Her voice is casual. Too casual.

I narrow my gaze. "Her ankle, right?"

"Yes." She brought her tools with her—including an electric sander. The machine whirrs while she brings it to my hands. As she files my nails in the weirdest way I've ever seen, she continues to frown. And she should know better, because even over the sound of the machine, I can still hear her whisper, "Among other things."

"What other things?" I snarl.

Emily gives me a nervous look. She's not afraid of me, that's for damn sure, but she looks a little bit afraid, and I don't like that shit at all. She opens her mouth, but she never gets a chance to speak.

Margerie stomps back over, and when she whacks me on the shoulder, I've got no choice but to be distracted by her. "She's not answering, so I can't yell at her, so I guess I'll yell at you instead. How dare you get married to her without asking permission?!"

"Your permission?" I scoff. "I'm not asking you for permission."

"Not mine! Her parents', you big idiot. And her brothers are going to give you a hell of a time if you're serious."

"I am serious." I feel heat in my gaze, but Margerie doesn't back down from it. Stubborn woman.

"You haven't dated long enough, and you're pushy. You need to give her more time."

I don't like that she's right. I open my mouth to tell her off when the phone in my pocket starts to ring. I think about ignoring it, but a greater instinct has me reaching for it immediately. "You done?" I ask Emily.

"Just about . . ." Emily says, giving me back my right hand as she polishes off my left. I reach into my pocket and pull out my phone. I see Nessa's name flash on the screen—the name I want to call her. *Wife.*

Margerie sees the name pop up with Vanessa's face, and her cheeks get bright red. Her shoulders bunch under her ears, and I'm about to laugh at her ire when I answer the phone and hold it up. "Nessa, where are you? You threw me to the wolves down here in design."

"You're late," Margerie shouts, trying to be heard by the quiet breathing coming from the other end of the line. "And I need to have a talk with you, missy!"

But Vanessa doesn't answer. There's no breathless laughter; there's no quick apology. There's only quiet breathing. Something isn't right.

I jerk away from Emily, who almost drops her electric sander on the floor. "Roland? Everything okay?" Margerie asks while Emily turns her machine off and Shandra and the two minions working with her at one of the long wooden drafting tables in the rear of the room stop fussing with my gloves and turn my way.

I'm still wearing the old uniform, though there's something wrong with the color. I think it's all wrong. I feel like an ass and look like a grape. I drag the zipper down from the side of my collar to my shoulder, then underneath my armpit to my hip. Pulling my torso out of the uniform, I leave the top half bunched around my hips so I can fucking breathe . . . even though, right now, I can't.

"Vanessa?"

And then she releases a terrible sound. A sob. She may be tougher than old leather to have been through what she's been through and come out on the other side of it sweeter than sin, but she's still so fucking tender. Her tears tear straight through me. I'm standing, but when she sobs again, I stagger. I only miss that first step though, because in the next beat, I'm at the door.

"Where are you?" I somehow manage to say.

I can hear others talking to me, Margerie's worried warble, but I don't have time for that. I take the stairs. Too big to fly down the center column of the stairwell, I take each set of steps in a single leap. I try to keep my steps even and cool, not wanting to cause a panic without first knowing what the fuck is going on, but I *hate* that I'm forcing restraint when all I feel is untethered. I want to burn something to the ground.

I leave the small domed COE building through the first door I find and make my way out of the campus. On the street, the wind picks up. The sky is bright. I can't fucking speak, and she isn't fucking speaking. A headache sprouts behind my temples, and I feel achy from my crown all the way down to my teeth. My gums sear with an incredible pain that momentarily makes it hard to think.

"Nessa." I say her name three more times before she finally releases a shuddering gasp.

"Rollo?"

"Baby, I'm here. Where the fuck are you?" Outwardly I remain tense, hard—*fucking furious*—calm. She releases another cry, and I step into the alleyway between the COE campus and the next block of buildings. I punch the wall, and my fist chips away at the concrete. "Nessa, please . . ."

"They brought me to my old house, and they left me here . . . I can't be here."

The fire in my bones explodes through my shoulders. I have to marshal myself so I don't melt my new cell phone. "Address."

She rattles it off before whimpering. I take off into the sky. "Nessa, are you in the house?"

She makes a murmuring sound that I fucking hate.

"Get outside. Find a neighbor to take you in . . ."

"No . . ." I can barely hear her over the sound of the wind. "I don't want anybody else. Just you."

I can't speak, and it has nothing to do with the fact that my phone's cutting out. I just . . . can't. Because the headache that started when I first heard her sob is back, and my whole body feels strange, and none of that matters. I've never felt . . . like this before. Like I want to kill. Like I want to weep.

"Coming for you, baby," I say into the phone, no idea if she can hear me. "Get outside. I'm coming."

It takes me forty more fucking minutes to get to her. I must have flown over 150 miles. That's fast, even for me, but not fast enough for her. Because when I touch down, staggering with the force of my impact on the earth, she stands up from where she's been seated on the edge of a dusty road in the middle of fucking nowhere, hugging her knees. Her hair whips around her face, the sun turning the outer strands to gold. She pushes them back while I struggle to proceed.

She's crying, and . . . is that . . .

No.

There's blood.

She runs toward me, and I rush to meet her. It's dusty out here. The road is covered in a thin sheen of dirt. It's hotter than it was in Sundale proper, and it's a hell of a lot filthier than the place where I grew up.

The community I lived in might have been near here, but the grass was green in front of each house, the lots were manicured, and there were stores and little shops lining one primary strip. This place . . . out here . . . it looks like it's been abandoned for years . . . generations. And she'd been sitting on the edge of a road without a sidewalk, looking just as abandoned.

We meet in a desperate collision, the momentum of my flight pushing me down the street. The momentum of my shock making it hard to regulate anything other than my impulse to erupt into a bonfire. I'm falling all over myself, and when I reach her, I keep falling. I slam into her body, tackling her back to the ground and catching myself on one arm before I accidentally crush her. I wrap one arm around her neck while I try to find my limbs and control them. I'm shaking. Fucking shaking.

She starts to cry again, softer than she had been over the phone. She's wiping her face convulsively, tears mixed with red on her chin. "Sorry . . . I wasn't crying in . . . the house, b-b-but after I got outside, I haven't b-been able to st-st-stop."

"It's all right, baby," I try to say, but my voice comes out as a gash as I manage to get one knee under me as well as a foot and push myself up into a crouch, pulling her with me. Holding her up in a seat, I loom over her, blocking out the sun so that when she looks up, all she can see is me and all I can see are the bruises on her face and the blood on her mouth.

"What . . ." I have my hands on her face, and she's clutching my wrists as I tip her face to the left and then to the right.

Her cheeks glitter with tears. Her lips are swollen; her eyes are too. The blood on her chin is dribbling from a split in her lip, one deep enough that it might need stitching. Purple splotches decorate her face above the jaw on the right side of her face. She got hit. Somebody fucking hit her.

I blink longer than I need to, just to get my bearings, just to try not to fucking implode. Trying to cycle through every possible scenario I can come up with for how she ended up out here looking like this while I was stuck inside of the goddamn COE headquarters, one of the most secure buildings in the entire fucking world.

I'll slam my fist through the center of the earth and tear the whole thing apart from within. No one deserves to live while Nessa's sitting here broken like this.

But . . . that's not what heroes do, is it? And I told her once already that I wasn't gonna try. I was gonna do.

I cover my mouth with one hand and take a breath. My other hand cups the back of her head, her hair tangling between my fingers. She doesn't flinch from me as I thought she might, and the next breath I take comes a little easier. I drop my hand from my mouth, gather my senses and what tatters are left of my sanity, and I roar at the top of my lungs, *Who fucking touched you?*

No, I don't. I whisper gruffly, "Where else you hurt?"

Her lips part shakily. She shakes her head, and her hair falls around her face. Her hand flutters away from her knees, and it shakes as she gestures down her body. I'm distracted by what her other hand is doing, though. Like she owns me, she's placed her hand on my thigh.

"They, um . . . they grabbed my hips. I think I've got bruises. They . . . sting. Other than that, I'm fine."

They *what?* I'm frozen solid, made of ice instead of flame, as she reaches down and lifts the hem of her button-up. White today. There's blood on it. She shifts onto her knees, looking pained as she tries to show me what happened.

"Stop, baby. Hold up. Don't hurt yourself. Gonna take you to the doctor. I just need to make sure it's safe to move you."

"It's safe. It's not a big deal."

"The fuck it isn't," I grunt, covering my mouth again to keep myself from saying anything else stupid.

She sniffs and shivers down to her feet. "I just . . . really don't want to go to the doctor right now." A dry sob racks her chest, and I can't stand it. I pull her against me, worried I'm gonna hurt her, but when I pull an inch, she falls a mile. She slumps against me when I stand, forcing me to take her with me. It's no hardship.

"I'm not hurt bad," she says, nuzzling into my chest. Her eyelids look heavy. "I just need you to . . . do something for me. *Please.*"

"Anything." I'd tear my heart out of my chest if she needed it now.

She blinks and glances back toward the structure, the one I haven't even bothered to look at.

The smell insults me before the sight of it, because the empty house has been that way for a while. The wood holding it up is half-rotten. Even calling it a house is generous. It's a one-story rambler, maybe two or three rooms. The front door's ajar and is hanging off one hinge. There is no grass, only dirt and weeds. Some abandoned bottles litter the space meant to be a yard. But I recognize it from the photos I saw in her file. I know what this place is.

"What do you need, Nessa?" I whisper against her temple.

She's fully buried against my bare chest, holding me like she thinks there's even the slightest chance in hell I might set her down, leave her here, and fly away without her. I don't know how she got out here, but once I find out who brought her here against her will and how, I'm gonna find it and kill it dead just to ensure she never ends up this far away from me ever again.

She sniffs, but her breathing seems better, calmer than it was. She blinks, and the sky turns the bronze-and-brown color combination of her curls the same color as her skin. She looks like her whole body was dipped in gold and dragged through sunlight. She's too good for me. And I couldn't care any less.

"I need you to be the Pyro," she says. I give her a surprised look, horrified and touched in turn by the sudden surge of violence I hear in her voice. "Burn it down, baby. Be my hero."

I have to fight to stay on my feet. I nod at her silently, and without breaking her gaze, I push energy out and away from my body. I find the house's center, find the heart of this shithole and set it alight. The fire that starts in the center of the structure fans outward in a burst hot enough to feel from here. I take the structure down in less than three minutes. The fire swells and swells, forming the shape of a heart before I bring it back down in the center and, with it, the rest of the house.

I make sure the flame is doused, but I also make sure that not one single plank, one floorboard, one piece of shitty fucking plastic remains. The appliances I melt so they don't explode apart. I take the foundation out, the few cinder blocks that there were, and raze it down to the earth beneath it until only a blackened pit, a scar on the earth, remains. I take the weed-covered yard too.

She watches the fire burn, and I watch the reflection of the flames on her face all the way until the last ember is doused. She still doesn't look away. A truck rambles down the road. I can hear it coming though it's still far off. I stand there, letting her absorb this for a few moments more until I ask her, "You ready?"

She nods after a brief hesitation and then looks up and pulls on my neck, and it takes me a second to understand what she wants, but when it clicks, I don't hesitate after that. I kiss her with all of me.

Her mouth is swollen and tastes like tears and rain, and her kiss is wet and needy. She's pulling so hard on my neck that it's hard for my mind not to trip out of this plane and into another more illicit one. My cock doesn't know that this isn't the time or place, and I pull back too soon, before it's over.

"Shit. I forgot." I lick my lips, able to taste fresh blood. "Fuck. You're cut."

"Oh. I . . . it's . . ."

I slip my finger under her chin, forcing her gaze to mine. She blinks, this look on her face . . . this fucking look . . . and whispers, "You're right. I just . . . needed that." And then she does the damnedest thing.

She smiles.

"You ready?" My voice sounds like gravel. I'm gonna puke. I'm so in love with this woman, it's absolutely petrifying.

Because they took her, dragged her out here to torture her, and punched my woman in the fucking face.

Whoever they are, I'm going to find them and do terrible, terrible things . . .

"I'm ready. Now."

I'm ready.

Now.

It feels like she's saying so much more, but I don't have the strength to ask. I don't have the strength for much at the moment other than clutching her to me with every bit of hope that I have. I take off into the sky with her gaze still locked on my face, staring at me with rapture and wonder.

Chapter Twenty

VANESSA

My head hurts and my stomach hurts, but my chest feels lighter than smoke as I stand at the window and watch the scene below unfold. The unbelievable scene.

The Wyvern—*the* Wyvern—is playing basketball with my youngest three brothers. Him and Luca against David and Emmanuel. I'm in my childhood home, my fingers playing with the same pale-pink curtains that have been here ever since I moved from my previous short-term foster house. I moved between three of them before the caseworker assigned to me brought me here. It was only supposed to be temporary, too, so for the longest time I didn't let myself get my hopes up.

The place I lived in before all that—the one the Wyvern just burned to dust—was in the unincorporated township outside of Sundale. It's mostly abandoned now. I'd never been back. I'd never even Google Mapped it. But seeing it burn to the ground made me wonder why I hadn't done that already. I made okay money right out of college. I could have afforded a few boxes of lighter fluid . . .

But would it have been epic, though? Because being there with the Wyvern was surreal.

Not just because he burned it so efficiently, but because it was as if he took a branding rod to a wound that was raw and open and full of pus, and scarred it over instantly. The blackened earth looked incredible from the sky. Flying with him, feeling his arms smooth and steely around me, was . . . impossible. And just right.

And now, standing in my childhood bedroom—my real childhood bedroom—watching his insanely muscled body on the basketball court below, I can't help but feel like he loaned me a little bit of his strength out there on those abandoned country roads. Maybe more than that. He gifted it to me, if I was being honest with myself, and it felt happily given.

I've never liked asking people for things. I dislike the feeling that I'm forcing someone to do something they otherwise wouldn't want to do. But I don't get that feeling with Rollo. I never get the sense that he's doing a chore, being with me, doing things with me, taking me on dates, being here, playing basketball with my brothers—burning down my house. He seemed like he enjoyed that and like he's enjoying this too.

"This is fucked up!" Mani shouts. He curses a long string of Spanish words, half of which are muffled through the glass, but I still laugh as he gets all up in Rollo's face and Luca—Luca, of all people—shoves him off. Mani turns his ire on Luca then and takes off his backward baseball hat, throws it on the ground. It takes me to then to realize that he's dripping with sweat. All my brothers are. And Rollo doesn't seem to be sweating at all.

"They seem to be having fun, don't they?" Elena's voice is soft and doesn't make me jump. I don't know where she got the ability, but she can enter any room, even one she hasn't been invited into, and make everyone within it feel warm and welcome. I think that's what made me *first* realize that I could live here. Stay here. And be a part of this family that was already so much *family* without feeling totally like an outsider.

I half turn to face her, not willing to relinquish sight of the scene unfolding as David tries to cut between Mani and Luca. Meanwhile, Rollo doesn't seem to be helping matters. He seems to be instigating things, egging Luca on.

"He's just as bad as they are," I say, laughing a little.

Elena grunts. "A perfect addition." She moves to stand next to me and looks out the window until I turn my attention to her more fully. "You slept most of the day, niña."

I nod. "Yeah."

"Roland was worried." Elena gives me a look.

I give her a tight smile. "Thanks for letting him sleep in the bed with me last night."

Elena rolls her eyes. "I didn't. Your father couldn't pry him off with a crowbar. And he tried." She takes my hand. I notice she has a mug in the other. She slips it into my fingers, and it doesn't escape me that she's looking at my face with concern scrawled over hers.

"I don't remember that."

"You were out of it when he brought you in. I managed to get you changed and bandaged up the best I could, but I'd like to double-check my work."

I nod, and Elena tilts my face to the left and right. She reapplies some ointment and gives me a new butterfly suture, then lifts my shirt. Her eyes go round and red. She sniffs once and looks me in the eyes as she fights through whatever words are on her tongue.

"You're not bleeding anymore, Vanny." She makes a strangled sound and shakes her head. When the one called number Three grabbed me, either their rings or their nails punctured my skin in several places. The bruises were bad, but the scratches made them look—and feel—a thousand times worse.

"That's good."

Elena mutters something under her breath that sounds along the lines of *"Voy a matar al maldito que hizo esto"* . . . But before I can call her out for cursing, she sniffs once, straightens up, and pats me tenderly on the uninjured cheek. "I still think I should change the bandages. Let me get you cleaned up. Un segundo."

Of course Elena does nothing halfway and reapplies huge swatches of gauze to my hips, wrapping bandages all the way around my sides so only my lower back and the space above my groin is visible.

"Is this necessary?" I ask on a hiss. "It's cold, and as you said already, Mamá, I'm not bleeding anymore."

"And this isn't for bleeding. This is for bruising. The gauze is soaked in witch hazel, aloe vera, and a dash of frankincense and cypress essential oils. That's why you're getting a smaller one on your cheek," she says as she places tape over a swatch of gauze that covers my entire right cheek. "We'll put some ice on it downstairs." She takes my hand and starts pulling me behind her, and I comply, pulling my baggy sleep shirt down over my leggings to hide the bandages.

"Don't tell anyone about the hip ones, okay? They freaked out enough about my face."

"Hm?" she says as we make our way down the stairs. Dark wood, they creak on each step. Always have.

"I know you heard me," I grumble.

"Sorry, you know how hearing goes when you start to get old."

"Mamá!" I gasp and shake my head, nearly dropping my mug full of a special spiced tea she always served us whenever we were sick as children. I clutch it for strength now, really hoping she's bluffing. Rollo didn't get a full look at my hips, which look worse than they feel, given how focused he was on my face, which feels worse than it looks.

Her eyes are crinkled at the corners as we reach the bottom of the stairs. From here you can hear my brothers, my dad, and Rollo shouting at each other outside more clearly. "Drink your tea, mi amor."

I drink.

"And tell me the truth. You promise me, Vanny, it wasn't Rollo who hurt you?"

I choke, tea spraying from my lips. "No. God, no."

She frowns. "I'll let that slide, but next time, you owe me five. And good. I didn't think so, and don't worry—it didn't even cross your father's or your brothers' minds. I just know that sometimes men and women can be very different in public than they are in private. I just wanted to be sure."

"He . . . we . . . I . . ."

She gives me a dull look, rolling her eyes and sweeping her fingers back through her thick black hair. She's got freckles on her nose that I've always wished were mine. I don't know how she manages to look fifteen years younger than she should, but she glows with magical light.

"Por favor, you do not need to tell me everything, but you will not lie to me, Vanny. That boy is head over heels in love with you. No convincing me otherwise. What you tell yourself is one thing, but I know what I see with my own eyes."

I duck my head into my shoulders, feeling exposed but wanting . . . wanting to believe her. "I like him too."

Elena smiles at me, and this time I'm sure she's never smiled at me in quite this way. "I know."

"He would never hurt me."

She nods. "Then why have you not told him who did this to you yet?"

I wince, my hand going up to cradle my hurt cheek. I could tell her that Roland didn't push and so I just didn't offer, but that would only be a partial truth. Very partial. Because after the ashes literally settled and my mind fired all night long, I kept coming back to something. Something small.

Number Three didn't call Roland by his name, not once. Instead they called him number Sixty-Two.

Three. Sixty-Two . . . Forty-Eight?

The math wasn't mathing, unless Three was referring to something else, and I needed to decide how to wrap up my suspicions with words and then further decide who to share those words with.

They could be dangerous.

But only if I'm right.

I shake my head and shudder. "I . . . I'm . . . it's confidential." She looks so disappointed when I say that, even though she nods, that I tell her something I shouldn't at all. I lean in and whisper, "Mamá, I . . . met someone who shouldn't exist. I can't say more. I need to talk to Roland and the COE first."

Her faded eyebrows pull together; her voice mellows into a hush. "Mi amor, are you in danger?"

"I don't know. The person . . . something about them was wrong. I'll tell you when I can, I promise." If I can. "When it's safe."

My mamá nods and glances toward our front door, which hangs open, guarded by a magnetic screen through which I can see the boys in the driveway clearly. "You stay close to that boy then, princesita. At least until you know for sure."

"I will."

"You trust him?"

"I do." And then I huff, "You probably think I'm crazy, though, huh? Trusting one of the Forty-Eight?"

Elena smiles softly. She glances at the door again. "He told us what he did for you . . . to that place." She makes the sign of the cross over her chest, and for once, I know she's not making that sign because he's an alien.

I tense, but not for as long as I should. In fact, my initial hesitation at the mention of that wretched place feels more like a trained reaction. But when I think about that place? Really think? I don't feel anything about it at all. Just the shadow of a ghost of terror. When Elena mentions it, the words in my head are no longer in that terrible woman's voice; they're in mine.

"Roland may be special, pero es un buen hombre."

I beam at her, my lower lip pinching as the butterfly bandage stretches. I'm immediately annoyed when my eyes tear up *again*. I throw my arms around her shoulders and squeeze her shorter frame against my body with all the love I have in me. "This family is the best thing that ever happened to me, and I don't want anything bad to happen to you because of me. I love you, Mamá."

Elena's whole body softens like butter. She hugs me back ferociously. "No, honey. We didn't come into your life. You came into ours. *You* are the best thing that happened to *us*. We love you so much. I love you so much." She pulls back, and her eyes are glossy as they dart to the window, where the sound of the ball against the pavement lets me know that the game has restarted. "And maybe, just maybe, I might be willing to share a little of your love with the right person."

"Roland's not really a person, technically."

She swats my shoulder and points to the door, but she still doesn't make the sign of the cross. I take that as a good start and laugh as she says, "Now go. Go outside and break up the brawl before your brothers hurt your novio, or accidentally hurt themselves *on* your novio."

She flutters her hand toward me and heads toward the kitchen, leaving me to shuffle through the magnetic screen guarding the open front door. After admiring the doorknob, which is still misshapen from the very first time Roland met my parents, my attention pulls toward the sound of a basketball hitting pavement. I look up and *whoosh*.

Rollo is standing near the center of my parents' circular driveway, coming down from a jump shot that would count for a lot more than three points if this were a regulation-sized court because the hoop is all the way on the other side of the driveway. His bright-red sneakers hit the pavement, and I know they aren't his because he was wearing his uniform before with the shoes built in, and I feel some kinda warmth rise in my chest at the knowledge that one of my brothers must have loaned them to him.

He hits the ground. My dad's standing closest to the basket and nabs the ball as it drops cleanly through the hoop. It looks like it's all four of them against Rollo. I can't help the smile that envelops my face and soothes my soul. I feel the same way I did watching that blackened patch of earth from the sky, tucked inside the world's strongest arms.

My brothers are all waving Roland off. Luca is muttering under his breath. Mani, who's the most competitive among the bunch—after Luca—is shouting, "That's not fucking fair! We said no jump shots!"

"All his shots are jump shots. We said no *flight* shots." David might be defending him but sounds just as pissed. My dad passes him the basketball, and David tucks it under his arm. He points at me. "Your boyfriend cheats."

I try to suppress my grin but can't. I like the way my body heats when David says that. "I take it that means my boyfriend is winning?"

"Heaven help me." My dad shakes his head and punches the ball out of David's grip. It hits the ground, and he dribbles once, twice, turns, and shoots . . . The ball bounces off the rim. "He has a name. I'm sure he wouldn't mind if you all used it."

Mani runs for the ball while Luca and David turn toward me. David is closest. His hair is damp with sweat and brushes the tops of his shoulders. I glance at Rollo. He's smiling with one half of his mouth cocked up, his head tilted a little to the side. He looks almost wistful. Boyish, even.

Happy, most of all.

"Do you mind them calling you my boyfriend? Or me?" I ask him.

Rollo's expression shifts. His hand, which had been touching his naked chest, tantalizingly trailing over his abdomen, drops to the band of his basketball shorts. He swallows and shakes his head, then reconsiders on a nod. "Actually, yes. I do mind."

"You do?"

"Thank heavens," my dad mutters.

"Yeah." He takes a step toward me that raises the temperature of the air surrounding us. "Only because you won't let me call you *wife* yet."

"That ain't happening," my dad all but snarls. He passes his hand over his coiled curls.

I laugh *loudly*. I don't usually laugh like this, and I can see the surprise on my brothers' faces take root for a second before they start laughing too. "You all should mind! That's your baby sister. You're my baby girl, and you're too young to be dating."

I scoff—well, I would have if I weren't still laughing. Meanwhile, Luca's coming closer and closer to me. Reaching me, he picks me up and spins me around, making me laugh even harder. "This girl? You think this girl's too young to date? She's an old lady and gettin' older every day! It's about damn time she found an old man."

"*I'm* her old man. Now put that young girl down before her *boyfriend* lights your pants on fire."

Luca drops me, and I wince but still chuckle out, "He'd probably just melt your shoes to the ground."

"Shit, you can do that?" Luca says over his shoulder. He reaches into his pocket and steps back toward the driveway. He fishes out his phone. "Go on. Do it then, boyfriend."

"What?" I'm still chuckling, even as I bite through the pain. "Why?"

"So I can film it! I'll tell the world the Wyvern melted my shoes to the ground because I beat him in a game of ball."

"You little shit," Roland says from a crouched position on the ground, retying his shoelaces and shocking the hell out of me, making me smile so wide I can't control the muscles in my face. I can believe he'd cuss out my brothers, sure, but not that he'd do it in a joking way given how recently they were actually trying to well, you know . . . kill each other. "You know as well as I do, I beat you guys forty to two."

"Only because you cheat!" Emmanuel shouts.

"Is this still going on?" Elena comes out carrying a large tray covered in glasses of her famous lemonade that's actually lemongrass, sage, and agave and doesn't taste that bad if you ignore the earthy flavor—i.e., it tastes like grass. On the tray, she's got two ice packs for me. "What are you doing still standing up, corazóncita? Sit." She kicks the side of the rocking chair next to the front door intentionally and conspicuously.

"Mamá, I don't need it now. It can wait. Your wraps are doing enough."

She sets her tray down on the table between the two rocking chairs on her porch. She hands me the ice packs, trying to fight me to get them into the waistband of my sweats. "Mamá, quit it!" I shout on a laugh.

"What is this?" She curses in Spanish. "You already messed it up?"

"Sh . . . Luca picked me up." I see the flap of a bandage peeling away from my skin. Elena starts to pull it free while I fight with my shirt and her to push it back into place. "It's fine. See? Look."

"Did I hurt you, Vanny? Shit. I'm sorry, hermanita." Luca's voice makes me cringe. I give Elena my best glare.

"What?" she mouths back at me.

"It's fine. Elena just redid my bandages," I start, but when I turn, I crash into Roland, spinning directly into his grip. He grabs the edges of my T-shirt. Elena moves away as Roland lifts my shirt up and then higher. He reaches for one edge of a bandage, peels it back, has a look. He does the same to the other side. His nostrils flare both times, but his expression otherwise doesn't change.

He meets my gaze and lowers slowly into a crouch. With his height and my lack thereof, he ends up eye level with my hips. He kisses the one on the left, over the bandage, and then the one on the right, over the bandage through my T-shirt, while Luca makes gagging sounds. I don't care about that now, though. Not as Rollo tugs the bottom of my tee into place and looks up at me with eyes that flare orange as they flick to my lip. Not pink. Not white. Orange.

"Are you ready to leave soon?" His voice is hollow. I can't read the emotion behind it. His calm is frightening.

I nod. "Yeah."

"Drink your tea or . . . whatever that is," he says. Behind him my brothers chuckle and Elena scoffs. "Let me get cleaned up, and I'll meet you back here in five. You got all your stuff?" I nod, but he knows that. When he brought me here, I didn't have any stuff, and neither did he.

He takes my hand in his and rubs his thumb across the backs of my knuckles before quickly brushing a kiss across them. Caught in his shadow now as he stands, I watch him openly assess my face. I know he's looking at the bruises and the bandage Elena placed on my cheek and the much smaller one on my lip. The bleeding might have stopped, but the bruising is still there.

"They're better today. I'm better," I whisper. My lips quirk. "I'm actually feeling pretty good, not that I believe you'll believe that."

A muscle in his cheek ticks. He twists his neck only very slightly, but I still hear the crack. His hand reaches for me, passing over the back of my head and tangling in my curls. He leans in and breathes against my cheek, "You might be fine, but I'm not. We're gonna go home and get in our bed, and you're gonna fuck me, and I'm gonna be gentle, but first we're gonna have a talk about exactly what happened."

I squeak but don't want to give anything away in front of my family, so I let Roland go after kissing me on the forehead. My brothers stand around and watch me with eye rolls and frustrated stares. They haven't tried to ask me about what happened. Besides, Elena's the biggest gossip here. Elena will tell them what's okay to share.

"You sure you're gonna be okay, kiddo?" my dad says, taking a seat in the other rocking chair after I drop down into the first.

"Yeah. When I took this contract, I just didn't realize that . . ."

"That?" my dad prompts while my brothers pick up playing and arguing; I don't know which they enjoy more.

"That it'd be dangerous. I mean, I know I read all those waiver forms back to front and back again, but I just didn't really realize that this is real. There are *real* villains."

My dad is frowning at me, rocking in his chair. He takes a sip of his lemonade, makes a face, and says the last thing I expect. "You want this contract? You want to do this work?"

I nod. "Yeah." Without question.

"With him?"

"Yes."

"Then you stay close to that boy. Don't let him out of your sight."

"That's what Elena said. You really think so?" I smile sheepishly, not used to talking about boys with William.

"Yes."

"Why?"

"Because." The front door opens, and my dad raises a salt-and-pepper brow. "That boy made me a promise, and I believe him. You could do worse for a boyfriend, Vanny, but just so you know, if he even thinks of marrying you without asking me first for permission, I don't care who he is, I'm gonna sock him good."

He's speaking loudly enough for Roland to hear him as he reappears through the screen door. He snorts and shakes his head in my dad's direction but remains undaunted as he walks up to me wearing borrowed sweats that are too short and a T-shirt that's too tight. "You ready, Nessa?"

I nod and take his hand when he offers it.

Before I leave the porch, I plant a kiss on William's cheek. "Bye, Dad. Thanks for letting us crash."

"You know the rules, Vanny. No couples sleeping together who aren't married."

I'm about to respond, but Rollo wraps his arm around my shoulder and shouts over his, "Don't worry, William. I'm planning on fixing that!"

"You little shit."

My brothers laugh and wave us off as we pile into Vinny's car; he leaves one here for whenever he's in town. I haven't forgotten Rollo's promise, and I hate myself for what I'm going to say next.

"Rollo?"

"Yeah?" he says as he pulls onto the highway.

"As much as I want to take you up on your offer of gentle sex, there's somewhere we need to go first." I pull out my cell phone and dial Mr. Singkham's private line. He answers on the third ring, and I'm still looking at Roland as I say, "Mr. Singkham, I'm sure my team has told you that I was attacked. Yes . . . yes. And yes. We need a meeting . . . right now."

Chapter Twenty-One

ROLAND

Nessa sits forward in her seat, her left heel tapping out a pattern on the ground that spells agitation. She's being honest, and Mr. Singkham's trying to get his eyeballs melted. "They called themselves number Three. They were—are—a superbeing I've never heard of before."

"That's not possible."

"They were dressed as a delivery person walking through the COE lobby, and when I bumped into them, they transported me to my childhood—the place where I lived when I was small. They left me there." Nessa's voice gets more aggressive as Mr. Singkham's denial grows more adamant. "They are alien, but they aren't one of the Forty-Eight. I've never heard of them before, their presence wasn't disclosed in any of the briefs you provided my team, and their powers were extraordinary and terrible. Roland hasn't heard of them either."

"You think there are *unknown* ones?" Mr. Singkham scoffs, shuffling papers arbitrarily over his new desk; the old one was deemed ruined after the Marduk's attack. It's clear he's flustered. He already dismissed Mrs. Morales and all his guards with an order to turn the cameras in his office off, as if I didn't hear that. My hearing is sharper than any human's, and in the last days, my senses have all only gotten sharper. Like my claws. "As in, *more* than one?"

"Yes. I think there may be as many as sixty-two." Vanessa nods, and I squeeze her hand. "That's what Three called Roland."

She's seated in the chair next to mine, and I'm leaning forward so that our knees touch, and occasionally I reach out to pick her hand up off her lap. I need it. I'm fucking shaking. I don't know if she or Mr. Singkham can see it, but I can feel small tremors throughout every inch of my body. I attribute it to hearing Nessa's full story, down to the detail about how that fucker touched and intimidated her. I know what would make me feel better—this Three fucker dying today in epic violence—but since this is a being who seems to be able to move through space at will and is someone the COE claims doesn't exist, finding them is going to be my biggest hurdle.

"Ms. Theriot, it is of vital importance that you are honest with me," Mr. Singkham starts.

Vanessa cuts him off, and I'm fucking proud of her for it. "I *am* being honest with you, Mr. Singkham."

"We have the footage, Ms. Theriot. There were forty-eight pods that fell from the sky. Almost all of them shattered upon impact, and the few that were relatively intact are well within the safety of the SDD—those that weren't stolen in the VNA raid twelve years ago. And if you are sticking to your story, I will have no choice but to report you and have the SDD come here and launch a full investigation."

"And what of the footage of the COE lobby? Where's that? I requested it from your security, but according to them, the specific ten-minute block in which I was abducted has been wiped." She's leaning forward, rage tinting her cheeks pink.

Mr. Singkham flounders. "That's . . . a security failing. One that will be looked into—"

"That won't be necessary." I yank my hands away from Vanessa's skin just as my palms turn to flame and my claws tingle. "Vanessa is misremembering the event completely. Thank you for your time, Mr. Singkham. We'll be going."

Vanessa's surprise registers, but only for a second before resolve hardens her features. She grabs my hand with vigor, just as the flame in my fingers goes out. She hasn't commented on my claws yet, even though they're already pointy, having grown out at an alarming rate throughout last night. I'm gonna have to talk to Nessa about it—a conversation I'm dreading—though to be fair, any conversation is better than the one we're having now.

"Good day, Mr. Singkham." Vanessa grips my hand harder and tosses Mr. Singkham an angry glare that's frankly adorable. Still, it has the intended effect.

"Now, wait a minute. If you think you can simply walk right out of the door after having made such allegations, then you are grossly mistaken . . ."

Mr. Singkham is trying to die. I turn to face his desk and take a single step toward him without releasing Vanessa's hand. My eyes flare orange. I can feel the heat they generate, unlike when the white color periodically shines in my gaze, which feels blessedly cool.

"You mistake my participation in your little program for something else, Mr. Singkham." Our eyes have locked. He's holding firm, but I can see the displeased twitch of his mouth. "You threaten her again, and I won't play your little games anymore."

Mr. Singkham straightens and runs his hand down the front of his deep-blue suit. He was already in his office when we arrived, having caught up with a delegation from the COE's Germany branch. Mr. Singkham did not enjoy our interruption, or the adulation the German delegation gave me and Nessa. She didn't let them take her photo, though, and I didn't like the reason why. The bruises on her face are still visible.

"You either talk to her with the respect she deserves, or I will kill you." Vanessa squeaks and tries to pull her hand out of mine, but I don't let her. "I may be a hero, but I'm only a hero for her. For you, I can be a villain just fine."

Mr. Singkham gawks at me and is still gawking as I show him my back.

"Let's go. We'll see you next week. Vanessa is taking the rest of the week off after her ordeal, and I'm not coming in for any pretty pictures until she's healed."

"Monika's going to be pissed," Nessa hisses as I wheel her around and nudge her toward the door of Mr. Singkham's office.

We stop just before reaching it. "We know of six others," he says.

A feeling unfamiliar to me creeps up the back of my neck. Ice. My skin aches with a cold burn, and a wholly inhuman spasm shoots from my nape to my low back. I can feel my flesh shift, like there's something pressing at the underside of my skin. My skin is a cage not made for it.

"What?" Nessa whispers, moving to stand beside me, a little closer to Mr. Singkham than I'm comfortable with. "Six . . . You mean there weren't forty-eight? There were fifty-four?"

"I haven't been given full access to their files from the SDD, but yes. There were six additional carrier pods that fell from the sky . . ."

"You just said that the Forty-Eight were recorded falling at the same time," I bark, annoyed. Smoke wafts out on my breath.

Mr. Singkham has a harder time meeting my gaze now than he did. "They were. But the six arrived two weeks before."

"Two weeks?" Vanessa and I balk in the same breath. We share a glance, and it feels . . . conspiratorial. Like the way she looks at her siblings sometimes, so much depth passing through a look alone. I feel like smiling all of a sudden, even though it's not the time or place for that. I feel like kissing her until she's out of breath and passes the fuck out in my arms. Ain't the place for that either. Soon though . . .

"They arrived staggered but in groups. Six were recovered. Contact was made with some of the children who came from the pods, but it wasn't the same as with the Forty-Eight who arrived two weeks afterward. These children were . . . violent. They attacked.

"Defense forces in the countries where they were found were successful in containing them for a short time, but they were . . .

shocking in their abilities. Not only their gifts, which were impressive enough, but they could and were willing to fight. Children who looked as young as seven and eight fighting grown men and women with the intent to kill. And our forces had a harder time with that. Killing children wasn't . . . isn't . . ." He sighs, rubs his face, and shrugs.

"When I took over as president of the COE, the SDD only gave me so much information about the origins of the Forty-Eight—and the additional six, who haven't been seen since they landed and fought the ground forces of the nations they arrived in. We don't know where they went. So while I want to believe you, your account of what happened just doesn't make sense, Ms. Theriot. I'm sorry for my hostility. I mean no disrespect."

"Why doesn't it make sense?" she says.

"There were only six others. Their powers were never properly documented, but even from the transcripts from the soldiers who engaged with them all over the world, not one suggested that any of the children they came across could teleport. What you saw—experienced . . ." He shakes his head, his hair never falling out of its perfectly gelled coif even though his face looks like it's aged a decade or more in the past several minutes. "I don't know what to tell you, Ms. Theriot. It's just not possible."

I'm about to bite his head off—no, I can't do that. I don't have fangs. But I do have claws. I'm about to shove my fist through his chin and tear out his tongue—when Nessa intervenes. She takes my hand, holds it, squeezes it, needing me in a way that keeps Mr. Singkham's head where it is.

"Mr. Singkham, they called Roland Sixty-Two," she says softly.

"It's not possible."

"If six escaped detection so easily and if others have powers we don't even understand, it stands to reason there could have been more. Not just six, but eight more than that too. Maybe even more."

"Fourteen aliens is entirely unreasonable. Someone would have seen these fourteen by now. Or they themselves would have come forward. They were children—"

"Children who could fight. You just said so yourself."

"Weak—" Mr. Singkham says, trying to speak over her.

Vanessa stands up, lifts her sweatshirt, and peels away a bandage on her hip for Mr. Singkham to see. And he does see. "No. They aren't. And I know what I saw, what I felt."

Mr. Singkham's face goes pale. As the bruises have begun to heal, their finger-shaped silhouettes have only become darker and more distinct. As have the little pricks from nails or rings or *claws* that cover her in scratches.

I ball my hands into fists and go to Vanessa's side, where I carefully press the bandages back into place and yank down her sweatshirt. "When you come up with something, call us. I don't want this report filed with the SDD, though. So whatever you tell them, it doesn't come from Vanessa."

"I can't possibly . . ." Mr. Singkham starts.

"I should report it . . ." good girl Vanessa adds.

"Out of the question. If the SDD isn't sharing information with the COE, then we don't need to share ours. Besides, I'm not having them take you away and interrogate you, stick needles in you, put you in a hospital bed—any of that shit. You're mine, and if Mr. Singkham decides to obey protocol on this, then he's going to have serious problems because I will sink the SDD, the COE, and the VNA and any other subsidiary they ever create. And if you think about publishing any of this anywhere, I'm going to have to do bad things to you, Nessa."

I lift her chin, drag the dangerous shards of my claws down the delicate column of her neck. Watch her swallow hard before she says, "What . . . kinds of bad things?"

I tap her cheek with the tip of my claw, noting the pressure I apply doesn't seem to be enough to harm her. She doesn't cower away, and when she's very still, I can control just how hard I stroke her with them. "You'll see when we get home, all right?"

"Okay." She nods, pupils dilating. Such a good, good girl.

"Yes," I correct.

"Yes," she whispers back.

"Yes what?"

"Yes, Rollo?"

"No." I pinch her chin between my claws so, so lightly. Tenderly. Threateningly. I lean down and brush my lips over her ear, inhaling the decadent scent of her curls. "When you're naughty, you call me Wyvern."

She swallows, and when she opens her mouth, I watch her try to respond twice and fail. Finally her gaze drops, and I notice the tight way she holds herself. Not afraid, no. She's *excited*. And if that isn't fucking unfortunate. Because Mr. Singkham's still in the room, and I don't exactly feel like putting on a show for him.

"Goodbye, Mr. Singkham," I say to the red-faced man trying and failing not to watch my interaction with Vanessa. "Find out what you can about the missing six. Find me Three. Until then, don't expect to hear from me."

"That's not . . . part of our contract."

I give him a look. One he does a good job of not entirely withering beneath. But then I grin at him to show all of my teeth, and I feel active flames lick the tops of my cheeks and around my eyelashes. "It's cute you still think I give a shit about a contract. I'm not your fucking errand boy." I move to stand behind Vanessa, grab her throat around the front. Kiss her temple. "I'm Vanessa's. And if you can't guarantee her safety, then there's nothing left for us to talk about."

"We'll withhold your next payment."

"Don't need it. I got a sugar mama and everything else I need. Come on, baby," I say, dropping my pitch and speaking to Vanessa directly. I give her neck a little squeeze and push her through the door. "I've got a few days I need to make up for."

Chapter Twenty-Two

VANESSA

"Breathe, baby." The feel of his fingers scratching lightly down the outsides of my thighs has my hips pumping up again. "Keep your hips down," he says directly into my pussy, his lips brushing mine on every word. "Put your knees here, over my shoulders . . . Stay still. I don't want to nick you with my claws." Because yes, my boyfriend, the Wyvern, has started growing claws.

I should be more afraid of them . . . but I'm not. I'm just grateful that his claws, strange and alarming as they are, are the reason he hasn't wanted to touch me. And that he's promised to make up for the time we've lost.

"Yeah, just like that," he says as I exhale deeply and keep my torso from writhing as I want it to. "You're such a good girl."

Oh my God. The praise does terrible things to me. It brings tears to my eyes. It also reassures me that, no matter what comes out of his mouth next, I'll do whatever he asks of me.

"Relax for me, Nessa." Okay, maybe anything except that.

Another breath jerks into my lungs, and my head kicks back, my spine arching, my shoulder blades curling underneath my body. My mouth opening in desperation to try to remember the order he gave me before. The most important one. *Breathe.* I can't. Because he's lowered his shoulders fully between my thighs, his torso fully relaxed into the mattress. His jaw is all but unhinged, and he's got his entire mouth pressed to my entire pussy like he's trying to swallow it whole. And then he proceeds to tongue-fuck me, his lips sucking and pulling at all the shaved skin around my opening while his fingernails continue their ministrations, gently scraping up and down my thighs until it all gets to be too much.

His tongue retracts from my body, and I do the bravest thing I can imagine myself doing in the moment: I glance down. Seeing him watching me with eyes so bright it's like looking at an eclipse is too much. I'm panting; my thighs are shaking. I'm nervous about *this* because he all but promised me he'd take me . . . take it all the way this time, and I'm scared that he's going to stop.

"Rollo, please . . ."

He lifts his head and smirks at me, the jerk. Without breaking the line of my gaze, his arms curl around my thighs, holding them to his shoulders, fixing them in place so I can't move. I'm trying so hard not to anyway. His tongue snakes out of his mouth, looking so damn red, and flicks at my clit once, twice, swirling around it the third time. And by the fourth, I come.

His eyes widen and his brows arch, and I lose the strength in my stomach and flop back onto my bed while my orgasm sucks me in like a spell. It almost *hurts,* the force of it. My body curls up, trying to protect itself, but he spreads me out and lays me bare. He licks me slowly, gently, holding me that way too. He's so bloody warm, but in this moment, I think I might be hotter as my mind swirls and finally resettles.

I come to in time to feel the beast prowling up my body. He settles his weight onto me, still wearing sweats three sizes too small, though that hardly feels like it's making any difference. I'm not moving at all, not doing anything as he starts to kiss my neck, my collarbones.

I'm still in shock, smiling and laughing lightly, as he makes it to my breasts. He lavishes each one in turn, squeezing them gently in his palms. Pointy sharp, charcoal gray, and a quarter inch long, his claws look so dramatic against my human skin, but as I watch him worship my body, I feel no fear of them or of him.

Finally I find my hands. I touch the top of his head, almost afraid to at first; I don't want the spell to break. But he makes a satisfied sound, somewhere between a grunt and a moan, and I do it again, carding my fingers through his thick strands, surprised by the texture. His hair is so glossy and thick, like oil, softer than the finest sand. I've never felt a hair texture like it and massage all the way through it, down his neck, over his heavily muscled shoulders. I didn't realize how stacked they were until I watched the muscles bulge along his neck and upper arms.

Emotion makes my mouth feel thick with words unspoken and my chest light with breaths I don't take. "Thank you for coming for me, Rollo. And thank you for what you did. And for sticking up for me to Mr. Singkham . . . though you were kidding, right, about killing him?"

"Yeah." He's still lightly kissing my chest, and I don't know if he's listening to me at all.

I tug his hair and scoff. "Roland!"

He growls, grabs my hand, and presses it to the mattress. He grabs my other hand and does the same thing with it, anchoring both hands next to my ears. From there, he stares between my eyes. "You think I'm doing all this out of the kindness of my heart?" He makes a growling sound in the back of his throat and then rolls his hips down into mine. His cock is hot against my skin. I spread my legs a little wider. I just need him to line himself up and then . . . my God . . . why is he waiting?

"Because I am." He leans in and sucks hard on my throat. The pleasure shoots down the left side of my body and is so intense I almost miss it as he whispers, "I love you."

I gasp his name, and he pulls up, kisses me hard, then gives me a little more space to flower. Lost. The past two days' events have been insane, but this might be the most intense moment for me of them all. And the bastard doesn't go easy on me either. He doesn't wait. He chooses that moment to reach between our bodies. "You trust me?"

I nod.

"Use your words."

"I trust you, Rollo."

He kisses the tip of my chin and then my cheek, around my bruises and my butterfly bandage. "Good. Because I'm gonna fuck you now." He slides his hand beneath my lower back. From hip to hip, his hand is so massive, it almost covers me completely. "Christ. Wanted to feast all day, but I'm sorry, Nessa," he says, lining himself up with my opening without moving his other hand from my cheek. "Can't wait." His words have sobered me now. I'm feeling nervous. Overwhelmed. "You feel me shaking?"

I shake my head. "I thought it was just me."

Rollo's pinched features relax when I speak. He shoves the waistband of his pants down, and I feel him shift his legs, kicking his sweats free. I'm already completely naked—have been since we stumbled up and through the front door, making out in my hallway until Rollo swept my legs, carried me up the stairs, threw me on the bed, ate out my pussy, and now . . . here we are . . .

The Wyvern stares down at me with eyes that are white-hot, the ghost of a smile on his lips, the massive head of his cock prodding at my entrance. "You ready?"

I nod like a madwoman, sparing myself no embarrassment, but that's also . . . okay. He's seen it all—me at my best, worst, and then worse still—and he hasn't run away.

"I fucking love you," he says, and once again he moves before I can grab hold of the words, spread them out, and decipher their meaning. He pushes inside of me.

"Holy shit!" I cry out.

Rollo releases a short laugh and then a deeper moan as he thrusts, holding once the head of his cock is fully sheathed. My mouth opens on a gasp. It doesn't hurt, but the pressure surprises me. I've had sex before, but that was a really long time ago—not since college—and I've had vibrators . . . but I haven't used a dildo . . . so this is a lot for me. The physical pressure is only one part.

"Breathe."

I exhale shakily, my eyes blurring. His face is doing something stupid. He's smiling at me a little while his eyebrows are drawn together all concerned. "Nessa, quit it. If you make me emotional right now . . ." He clicks his tongue against the back of his teeth. "I need to concentrate." His claws alight onto my ribs threateningly yet carefully avoid the scratches on my outer hips.

"You're not being very nice," I say, squeezing the emotion down hard. His face drops forward against my left shoulder while his hand on my ribs travels up to squeeze my breast and then my neck.

He pushes inside of me a little farther and grunts, "No, I'm not." And as his hand hovers over the place where my heart so frantically beats, we both know he's not talking about the sex. "There's no retreat," he grunts and pushes another few inches inside of me.

"Roland, oh my God," I gasp, lifting my hips, circling my arms around his shoulders, and squeezing him everywhere with every piece of me. In his ear, I whisper, "Baby, fuck me."

He laughs into the shadow of my hair. "Thought that's what I was doing."

"Harder, Rollo. Please. I need . . ." My fingers dig into the skin of his shoulder blades. "Ohh!"

He bottoms out, and I lose control. I buck my hips, wanting harder, faster, more. I lift my head and find his temple with my lips. I kiss him softly, but it's enough for his neck to snap up and for him to wrap his hand around my throat and melt into my lips. He kisses me gently at first, moving delicately around my butterfly stitch, but as his urgency picks up, so does the rhythm of his hips.

"Fuck, Nessa. The feel of you . . . I could stay here forever."

And I know what he means. I'm flying away on a spaceship, going to faraway places I've never been. The pressure is there, but it's starting to transition from something scary to something incredible, and it changes with each position he puts me in. Sitting up on his heels, he drapes my calves over his shoulders.

"Touch yourself," he commands.

I obey without question, circling my clit with my fingers, the sensation entirely new, like I've never done this before in my life. The way it changes when he's inside of me, looking down at me like this. I don't last nearly as long as I should. I come around his cock, and his hips buck, and he curses.

"Gonna come on that pussy," he groans, but I squeeze his waist between my thighs.

"Come in me."

His hands are fitted around my waist, his claw tips just barely grazing my skin even though the pressure of his hands is firm, like he thinks if he lets go I'll fly away.

"You sure?" he says, his hips losing their rhythm, his forehead scrunching up, his lips twisting together.

"Yeah." I'm not on birth control, but I'm gonna get my period in a couple days, so I know that even if he were human, our chances of, like . . . baby stuff . . . are low. But the fact is, he's not human, so . . . I nod. "I'm sure."

"Fucking love you." He releases a gruff roar and collapses on top of me. He kisses me hard, and his hips slam up to meet mine, the sensations inside of me lighting so many different kinds of fires.

His eyes glow bright and then brighter to the point that I have to close mine. I hold on to his sides and crash up into his mouth and kiss him until his cock jerks inside of me. He fills my body in a rush. I can feel the temperature of his cum, and it's higher than it seems like it should be. Warm and wonderous. I gasp. He's panting, face twisting until he eventually stills and rolls off me onto his side.

"You're gonna be the death of me, kid," he says on a breathy laugh as he pulls me to him, yanks covers around us, and throws one leg over both of mine. He traps me to his chest. "You okay?" he says gently in this moment that hangs between us like a fallen star.

I nod. "Yes. Are you? You sounded like a demon was being excised."

A laugh belts out of him that makes me smile. "You're a knucklehead."

"A knucklehead?"

He kisses the top of my head and then just stays like that, his face pressed against my hair, his body fully curled around mine. "Nah, you're all right."

"Just all right?"

"Nah, you're the greatest thing that's happened to me. Probably to the whole world, but it fucking sucks for them," he says, sounding shaky. I've never heard him sound anything but sure before in my life. "Because you're mine." His arms firm around my shoulders. "You sure it's okay I came in you?"

I nod. "I liked it. I want your cum in me all the time."

"Fuck," he laughs. "I'm getting hard again. I want you drenched in me."

My whole body zings with electricity. My drowsy state is trampled by renewed alertness. "I wouldn't mind."

He kisses the side of my neck. "Don't know if it's even possible for me to get you pregnant, but even if I did, I wouldn't be pissed about it."

My arms around his body tighten. "You . . . wouldn't?"

"Not saying I want kids with you now, but one day, if possible."

"None of the Forty-Eight have had pregnancies with humans—or each other—yet. It might not be possible."

"If it's not, I'd be okay. We could always adopt. Or foster. You okay with that?"

He says the words so glibly, like he didn't just take a pickax to my heart and shatter the whole thing. I nod, overwhelmed, overcome. Tears prick my eyes, and all I can do is continue nodding.

He rolls me onto my back and hovers over me, looking at my face. "I'm here, and we don't need to talk about it now. Just know, I want you. All of you. All the time. I got nineteen more dates till you marry me. We can figure out how many more dates we want before we expand our family, if you even want that. For now, though, we can keep practicing."

"I . . . I've always wanted a big family, but I just assumed . . . I didn't think I'd find anybody I'd want to do that with." Who'd want to do that with me.

"You want me?"

I nod. "So much."

"Then I'm here." He kisses me and lines himself up with my body, already hard again. He pushes forward, and I moan, shattered heart blooming anew, twice as big and a hundred times more resilient.

"Roland, I . . ."

"Not yet," he says, cutting off the words I was about to tell him. Ones he must already know. "For now, just breathe, baby. And come for me when I tell you."

"Oh! Okay," I squeak as he gets to work.

His claws drag down the insides of my thighs. "Yes," he corrects me. "Yes, Rollo."

"No . . ."

My back arches. I fist the sheets. "Yes, Wyvern."

Chapter Twenty-Three

ROLAND

Admiring how well and thoroughly fucked Vanessa looks sprawled out across our bed is the greatest moment in my entire fucking existence. She's a wreck. There's cum absolutely fucking everywhere, and I chuckle at just how bad it looks. Sweet, composed Nessa with her library full of books all listed in alphabetical order by title and a spice rack that requires frequent visits from her label maker is now lying on her stomach, legs spread, one knee hiked up giving me torturously perfect access to her pretty pussy, that molten center dripping with the products of three of my orgasms and five of hers . . . She looks perfect. Too perfect.

And I can't help myself.

I'm barely awake, the urge to return to the bed and drop onto my knees right behind her too strong to ignore. From there I collapse forward onto my fists, my gaze trained on the snarl of her hair. I lower my weight onto her, feeling so damn . . . good. Yesterday's headache is gone, as is the subtle itching surrounding the cartography lines across my ribs and chest. My angry nail beds feel soothed. I am soothed as I surround her in the dark of her bedroom.

I kiss her shoulder. Her eyes are still closed, lips still slightly parted in sleep, and she releases a contented little moan.

"Gonna fuck you again, baby."

"Mhmm," she says, struggling to open her eyes.

"Keep 'em closed. I'll be quick."

She smiles. "Pervert," is what I think she mumbles, but the sound breaks up over her cry as I slide inside of her. She's hot as a brand, which doesn't seem right at all considering that I'm the one made of fire. The feeling of her velvet heat closing around my cock is heavenly.

"There is a God," I moan into the back of her neck. Laughter flutters from her lips, which I claim in a kiss.

"Mhm! Morning breath!" she squeaks. I laugh. I couldn't care less.

My hand moves around her body, sliding beneath her weight until my fingers find her clit. Careful with my claws, I pop her hips up just enough that I'm able to massage that little nerve bundle in gentle, gentle strokes. "Oh my gosh, Rollo, I . . . can't . . ." Her eyes are still shut, lids squeezing together, fists clutching the crumpled sheets in desperation.

"You come so fast in the mornings," I laugh into her ear as her whole body starts to clench up and her core squeezes around the length of me. I don't hold back but slam my hips forward, my hips meeting the lush curve of her ass. She's boneless beneath me, so fucking beautiful.

I come deep inside of her body, my cock twitching in absolute rapture. My back muscles are bunched, the backs of my thighs rigid. My balls jerk up against my body, feeling her heat brush against them in places. My cock jerks and jerks, and a pressure somewhere along the top of my erection makes me worried that I'm gonna come again. The sensation passes, with some coercion from my brain telling me to get up and get off her, otherwise I'll stay here forever.

My face tilts up toward the ceiling as I slide out of her, my cock tingling a little bit, feeling strange, but maybe that's because of this feeling in my chest. This lightness and wonder. This *desperation* to want to breed her again. My torso wavers as I kneel above her. Restabilizing myself, I look back down at her beautiful body—*mine*—and spread her cheeks apart with my hands just to watch my cum inside of her body. I smile, filled with a primal male satisfaction.

"What are you doing?" she breathes.

"Enjoying myself." I lean forward and bite her right ass cheek. She jerks, squealing a little, and when I pull up, I notice that my teeth have left indents in her skin. Strange. I didn't think I bit her that hard.

I massage the space I bit, and when I glance to her face, I see her smiling as she settles back into sleep, sunlight peeking from around the dark curtains and stroking her face in shades of holiness. Satisfied, so fucking satisfied, I manage to actually back away from the bed, successfully this time, and head to the bathroom.

There's a swagger in my step. Not sure if it's a swagger so much as it is a lurch. My fucking bones ache with how badly I've wanted and needed her, and having her has just about killed me. Wrecked? Is that what I thought of her? Wrecked doesn't come close to the male that she's made of me. And it feels so fucking . . .

. . . good . . .

I swing into the bathroom, flip on the lights, and look up to see the creature in the bathroom watching me. Red skin, horns, and fucking *huge*. The thing looks like a goddamn nightmare. What the fuck is it doing in Nessa's house? In our bathroom?

I jerk back, rage casting shadows over the pleasure still lingering in my chest. The fact that this massive thing has interrupted such a sacred moment of peace for me makes me burn even hotter.

"You dare . . ." I roar. My eyes fill with fire, and I attack, a fist of flame launching from my mouth toward the creature standing right in front of me. How dare it come this close to my fucking girl . . .

My fire hits the large mirror, which shatters in its entirety, shards raining over the vanity and skittering onto the white tiled floor.

My mind blanks, and I stagger backward into the bathroom door, the door handle punching clean through the drywall, loudly enough to wake a sleeping bear. In the bedroom, though, I don't so much as hear her breathing change. Which is a blessing. Because my thoughts have coalesced into one stunning, crystal realization, one that I don't want her here for.

The monster in the bathroom? That *thing* standing there so threateningly? It's *me*.

My legs move faster than my mind, carrying me back into the bedroom, where she still has yet to move. "Come back to bed . . ." I hear her murmur. She's asking me, and I'm so fucking moved by the soft trust in her tone and so fucking pissed to let her down. Fuck my claws, there's no way I can touch her—*again*—knowing what I do now. I look down at my own dick as I step into the walk-in closet to the small section where I've thrown my clothes. I choke. I put *that* inside of her?

I shove my legs through the extra-large sweatpants she bought for me and throw on the hoodie that matches it. I haven't worn either before; they're both too big for me, but not anymore. They *were* too big. Now they're tight around my ass and thighs, my shoulders and biceps.

I leave the bedroom, head into the bathroom, pad over the scattered glass with bare feet—bare feet, can I even call these things fucking feet? The glass doesn't bother these *things* hanging off my legs at all. I throw open the bathroom window and squeeze my body through it, lifting my phone to my ear as I take off into the sky.

It rings once . . . twice . . . "Roland, I'm surprised to hear from you. Talk of the town is that you cussed out the president and told everyone to fuck off until next week . . ."

"Doc, we've got a problem." My voice breaks. I don't know if she hears the urgency and the panic choking my throat over the sound of the wind because her voice is chipper in a way that makes me want to punch something.

"You wanna come in? I'm at the clinic now. It's actually great you called. I was looking at the sample I took from your claws the last time and noticed something strange . . ."

Strange? Strange! Did she just have the audacity to say *strange* to me right now? I'm fucking shaking. For the first time in my life, I'm a little terrified. Nessa may be cool with the claws, but this is something else entirely. Will she even want me after this? Who would? I'm a fucking menace.

I glance down at my hands. "The claws are not my problem . . ." And then I remember. "Wait. I don't have my badge. I can't get in."

"They'll recognize you."

No, they won't. "Meet me outside. The alley between the compound and the next building block. Street side."

"All right," she says, sounding confused. "Well, it'll take me a few minutes to get there."

"I'll be there in five."

I'm at the COE in three, standing in the dark alleyway, my hands shoved in my pockets, my hood pulled up so high, it stretches the material of the hoodie tight up and down the back of my neck. Because the top of my head doesn't touch the fabric of the hood anymore. Not with my brand-new fucking *horns* in the way.

I fiddle with my phone nervously in my pocket. It feels like a goddamn kid's toy now. I yank my fist out of my sweats and look at the shape of my claws—long and thick and dark and curved and bloody sharp and surrounded by red skin.

It's sunny today. It's always fucking sunny here. And when I lift my hand out of the sleeve of my hoodie and tilt it toward the light, I can see slightly darker runes carved all over, forming the same pattern as the marks on my ribs and collarbones. Now the repeating pattern is everywhere.

"If I'd known my patients would prefer meeting me in dingy alleyways, I could have saved a helluva lot of money on office space." Emily's voice is pleasant and light, and the stress that's consumed me is only exacerbated by it. I'm nervous . . . I was shit scared of Nessa seeing me like this, and though I don't care about Emily like that, I'm still nervous. "I brought the sander in case you need a top-up." She revs it. "It's electric. Why, uh . . . don't you turn around?"

I still don't move. She stops walking.

"Roland, you're making me nervous . . ."

I hear her take a step—probably backward, if she's smart—and I exhale heavily. I turn and glance up at the buildings, triple-checking that there's no one at any of the windows and no one walking on the sidewalk, and, relieved to know we're alone out here for now, I drop my hood back. Exhaling shakily, I carefully lower my gaze to Emily, who stands so much shorter than I now do. I must be a foot taller than I was when I went to bed last night and fifty—eighty—pounds heavier of solid muscle. I feel like a dense goddamn boulder.

Emily looks at me and sees me, and the sander tumbles from her grip. It hits the ground powered on, the sound grating as the sander revs against nothing. She doesn't reach for it. She just stares up at me, frozen.

"Well," she finally says, smacking her lips. Her gaze moves up and over my face, my hair . . . my horns.

"Well?"

"This is unexpected."

"No shit."

"Why don't you come inside, and we'll have a . . . Roland? Roland, are you okay?"

No. I'm not. I shake my head.

My vision starts to darken around the edges, and when I take another step toward her on feet that have elongated and flattened out at the front, thick pads like a dog's forming on their undersides, decorated by massive talons that scrape over the concrete, I fall.

Darkness wallops me, but it doesn't last long. Because in its stead come images, pictures, sounds . . . memories of a life that was once mine from a world far, far away from this one, and I remember . . . everything.

Who I am.

What I was.

Why I'm here and the horrors I'm meant to cause.

Chapter Twenty-Four

VANESSA

I'm sore *everywhere.* The bruises on my hips feel so minor now compared to everything else. I smile into my pillow. It's a good sore, though.

His warm breath on my cheek this morning, smelling of smoke and desire. *Gonna fuck you again, baby.* He didn't wait for my answer. I just arched into the fullness of him as he slipped inside of me. I was a mess, but that didn't seem to matter. He came so quickly, and so did I. I thought that, after last night, I'd have been well stretched, but when he slid into me, he felt even fuller than he had the last time. A twinge of pain was all I felt, though, before pleasure exploded through me, cutting with all its claws. I kept my eyes closed through all of it. I didn't want him smelling my morning breath, sure, but it also felt so fucking incredible, a dark fantasy I've never explored, an incubus coming for me in the darkness before dawn.

I stretch my limbs, reaching for the space on my right, then on my left. Disoriented, I lift my head from the bed and call out, "Rollo?"

But . . . he doesn't answer.

I pad to the bathroom, planning on grabbing an ibuprofen after I go pee and before I shower off, but the minute I flip on the lights, my heart slingshots up my throat. Broken glass litters the floor, shards of my own shocked reflection refracted back to me from a thousand angry angles. Did he . . . Did someone . . . My brain fires down different paths, but those paths wind and twist and merge together like a knot of hair without arriving at any conclusions.

Was it me? Did I do something to piss him off? And so he just . . . left?

Maybe, he's downstairs . . . Yeah. This must have been an accident. He's probably downstairs trying to find a broom . . . maybe.

What the fuck happened?

I close my eyes, recognizing that I'm being stupid, but the logic doesn't shake the heavy feeling weighing down my chest like an anvil. I make my way to the bedroom and find my phone. I find the guest bathroom downstairs and, while sitting on the toilet, shaking, scroll through my contacts and find Roland.

The phone rings once and then goes to voicemail. A generic bot taunts me. I scroll through my contacts again and again, calling Roland on every second pass. Finally, on the third try, the call goes straight to voicemail without ringing once.

And then a very, very dark thought comes to me. Number Three . . . *What if they took him?*

My doorbell rings, and I jump, startled. I glance at my phone app, fear striking me hard even though I know it's not Three. Three would never have knocked.

Instead, I find Luca and Charlie on my stoop, looking annoyed. They both glance down at my outfit as I throw open the front door wearing a fluffy bathrobe way too warm for the encroaching summer heat.

"What the fuck happened to you?" Charlie balks.

Luca makes a disgusted sound in the back of his throat. "What do you think happened to her? Smells like sex in here. Augh!"

"Cabrón," Charlie hisses, pushing past Luca and me and into my house. "Where is he? I'm gonna fucking kill him."

"We are two consenting adults, and wait—Charlie!" But Charlie's already up three steps. I have to practically leap to grab the back of his T-shirt and keep him from going upstairs to the scene of the crime—*crimes*, if you're counting both the bedroom *and* whatever happened in the bathroom. "What are you even doing here?"

Charlie stops and turns to look at me with his eyebrows drawn. "I was heading into town and Mamá wanted me to go check on you on my way, and see if you and Roland were coming to family brunch tomorrow. Luca was bored."

I wince at his words and Charlie's expression becomes even more severe as I confess, "I don't know where he is."

"He dined and dashed?" Luca guffaws.

I wrinkle my nose. "That is horrifying. And no. Yes. I don't know, maybe. But I think something's wrong. The mirror in the bathroom is totally shattered, like there was a fight. I think he might have been taken . . ."

"Taken? The god of fire was fucking taken?" Charlie says.

"Does that make you Liam Neeson?" Luca points at my chest.

I shake my head, pulling up my phone and dialing the COE offices—which go straight to static. "I need to find him, and I can't get through to anyone." I scroll through my contacts looking for Margerie while Luca gets on his own phone, dialing my other brothers, and Charlie steps back down the stairs, landing right in front of me.

"I think I can help. Where's your computer?"

I herd my brothers into my living room and unlock my laptop for Charles, who immediately proceeds to log in to some scary looking database. He enters Roland's phone number into a flashing green search bar.

"What are you doing?" I ask.

Charles angles the computer away from me and gives me a good glare. "Are you making your calls?"

"No one's picking up at the COE headquarters."

"Isn't it Saturday?"

"Mr. Singkham works most weekends. He should definitely be in."

Charlie's expression mirrors my unease. He glances past me toward the TV. I reach for the remote control, but in my scan of relevant news channels, I don't see anything alarming. Mostly just shots of the insanely gorgeous Olympian with her glowing dark-brown skin and waist-length black hair.

"The Olympian celebrates with the mayor of Sundale in advance of the Forty-Eight Hour Festival to commemorate the landing of the Forty-Eight superbeings who decided to make Earth their new home twenty-two years ago . . ."

There's a loud knock on my front door, followed by the doorbell ringing three times in quick succession. Luca and Charles share a look, and even though I'm first to turn toward the door, Luca beats me there. He reaches for the knob at the same time that it starts to open.

"I cannot believe . . . Oh, hi, Luca. Charles—you're here too. Why are you guys here? Anyway, never mind—the nerve!" Margerie bursts into my house wearing sneakers—*sneakers*—leggings, and an oversize shirt. Granted, all the labels I see are designer, but this is the first time, maybe the second, I've ever seen her in anything close to casual.

"I got a memo saying that the two of you weren't coming in to work next week? It's design week, and the Forty-Eight Hour Festival is two weeks away! Shandra is pissed, and so is Monika! She's been shouting at me in German all morning. Do you know how scary that is?

"The group photo with the other Champions of North America is scheduled for this Thursday! Pele is flying in for this! You can't snub her, no matter how much amazing alien sex you're getting!" Her gaze finally drops to me, and her head ticks to the side, her Louis Vuitton tote dropping from her shoulder to her elbow. "You really do look like you're getting good alien dick, don't you?"

"Margerie, you may be cute, but I will duct tape your mouth," Charlie mutters from the computer while Luca shouts, "Gross! Margerie! That's my sister!"

Margerie's face transforms slowly into a mask of shock as her gaze pans from Luca to me. "Did you really?"

I blush, my mouth working like a fish's.

"YOU FUCKED ROLAND?" Her voice could be heard through time with how loud she screams. And then she starts bouncing up and down on the balls of her feet. "You fucked the Wyvern! I knew you had it in you! How was it? Smoky? Fiery? Hotter than hell?" She winks at me, but when she finally stops jumping, she must register my expression because her own smile falls. "What is it? Did he hurt you?" She gasps and covers her mouth with both hands as her gaze moves over my face, finally taking in the bruises.

I shake my head and touch my mouth, my tongue sneaking out to taste the edge of my bandage. "No. This wasn't him. This is why he didn't want me to come in to work. It happened the day before yesterday, and yesterday we did . . . have sex. But he left. I think someone took him."

"Wait, wait, wait. Start over—no, start backward. He left like a sleazy one-night stand, or he was 'taken' like he's the daughter and you're Liam Neeson?"

"That's what I said!" Luca shouts from the front door, where he's talking on the phone to one of my other brothers.

I confirm. "The latter."

Her gasp gets even more theatrical. "Who?"

I suck in a breath, hesitate, and then confess *everything* that has happened in the past forty-eight hours. Well, not *everything*, but I tell Margerie and my brothers about Three, even though it scares the piss out of me. But with the COE not answering, I don't know what to do.

"He wasn't at the office?" I ask.

Margerie shakes her head. "I haven't been in today. I was at our old offices helping Dan and Jem. The folks holding our old lease agreement are being dicks—you know what? Never mind. I was going to head there, hopefully after grabbing you, so we could meet with design. Shandra wanted to do a final fitting for his new—you know what? This doesn't matter. Let me try Mrs. Morales's cell."

She holds her phone to her ear and, while it dials, says, "You're serious? You think there really are fourteen more aliens who landed here?"

I nod.

"Bad ones?"

I shrug, then nod again.

Margerie shakes her head. "I'm not getting anything." She heads to the dining room, where Charlie's moved with my laptop. Standing over his shoulder, she points at his screen. "Are you trying to track him?"

"Trying to get my buddy at the SDD to locate his phone. I used the cell number to get the sim number. Just need to wait on him to get back."

"Is that legal, Charlie?" Margerie sasses my brother in a way that makes me tense. Nobody sasses Charles.

But Charlie surprises me by quirking his lips, giving Margerie a heated look—one that I'd hazard to call *flirty*—and saying, "Nothing you wouldn't do, I'm sure."

"I am a law-abiding citizen, sir."

"And I'm a former marine, ma'am. Nothing but a dedicated servant to this country and the people in it." He leans back in his chair, his legs and arms both spread as he ogles Margerie in a plain and appreciative assessment from her sneakers to the neat bun on top of her head.

Margerie always has a witty retort. Always. Until now. She swallows and *blushes*, and when she lowers her forearm without breaking Charlie's gaze, her purse hits the ground on its side, a cluster of folders cascading out because, like me, she brings her work everywhere with her. As she makes a soft sound in the back of her throat, Luca and I share a look. Luca is *gawking*, and I'm about to bust out in hysterical laughter, despite the circumstances, when the doorbell rings.

"Good grief, who is it now?" I say as I turn toward the door.

Luca stops me. "You go stop . . . whatever that is. I'll get it." He heads to the door while I cross the living room and bend down to help Margerie shove her folders back into her purse.

"Please don't tell me you told Mom or Dad about this," I call over my shoulder.

"No, but it might be David and Mani."

There are some loose papers that take longer to arrange back into a pile. Margerie moves to help me. "Why don't you go shower and get cleaned up? Not that I don't love this look on you or anything, but you do smell like sex *a lot*."

My cheeks burn, and I shoot her a glare.

Her face softens. "I'm sorry about Roland. I'm sure that there's a reasonable explanation. I mean, how could a superhero get *taken*? He's seriously powerful. I'm sure he's handling himself, wherever he is. I mean, if Three can teleport, what's the worst they could do to him? Drop him off in Siberia? He can fly. Granted, it'll take him a little while to get back to you, but he will. Not a doubt in my mind."

I smile softly, my lips trembling a little even as her words soothe some of the razor blades in my belly and the thorns around my heart. "Thanks, Margerie."

She touches my forearm through the soft, puffy sleeve. "You know I'm not just your colleague. I'm your friend. Just so you know, I've gotten, like, twelve other job offers since we've been working together. I like the work, sure, but the reason I stay is for you." Her voice is soft. "I thought you knew that, but I want you to know for sure."

"I don't know what I did to deserve a friend like you."

"Friendship goes both ways, Vanessa, and you were there when I needed you most. I love ya." She winks, stands up, and offers me her hand.

"I love you too," I tell her, feeling shy as I say the words out loud. They're sticky on my tongue and accompanied by a spoonful of guilt because I didn't get a chance to say those words to Rollo before he left. I can't decide if I should be glad or sad about that.

I stand and offer her the pile of papers, but as I do, my gaze catches on the one on top. "Margerie, what is this?"

"This?" The paper on top is facing down, but thick, dark lines are still visible through it. As Margerie flips it over, I read the words printed on top at the same time she echoes them aloud. "Old Sundale Airport. For the photo shoot."

"Yes, but what is this? I've seen the blueprints, but this isn't that . . ." I snatch the paper out of her grip and turn it upside down. I tilt my head, my eyes bugging. "Oh my God. These lines. Are these the . . ."

"The runways, yeah. I outlined them in Sharpie so I could chart how far he'd be flying and how many cameras we'd need and how best to place them since the runways will be operational for the first time in years. Monika asked for it."

"This is the map," I squeak.

"The what?"

"The map!" I'm shouting now, racing for my phone on instinct, though I have no idea who I'd tell. No one is freaking answering! "This is the map! I have to get ahold of Mr. Singkham. Can you try the COE again?" I shout to everyone who can hear me.

"What's going on?" she says, rifling through her gigantic purse with one hand while the other clutches her phone to her face.

The phone at my ear goes straight to voicemail, and I shout up at the ceiling in frustration, "What is happening?!"

"This is important. I know you're her brother," comes shouting from the front door. And then more loudly, "Vanessa! Vanessa, are you here?"

"These guys wouldn't take no for an answer," Luca says, annoyed as he leads Dan and Jeremy into the room.

"Oh, thank God," Dan says, falling over Jeremy as Jeremy comes to a hard stop. "Have you turned on the TV today?" Rushing forward, Dan trips over the foot of the couch, falls onto the footstool stomach-first, grabs the remote from where it's fallen onto the floor, and just like that, starfishing on my velvet ottoman, he points it up at the TV.

"Uh . . . yes?"

"In the last few minutes?"

"No . . ." My voice fades out. The news comes on. The same news channel that had been broadcasting happy images of smiling superbeings waving and rocketing up into the sky and doing spins like the dolphins at SeaWorld is now covered in bright-red warning symbols.

" . . . COE headquarters in downtown Sundale is under attack. Local Champions Taranis and the Olympian have arrived on the scene and appear to be battling *three* suspected members of the VNA;

however, one of these beings appears to be causing a strange . . . collective hallucination to anyone who stares at the scene directly. As you can see, our camera footage only shows murky images . . ."

The footage shows smoke billowing out of the COE tower, not far from where the Marduk attacked Mr. Singkham's office on the thirtieth floor, only this time the smoke is pink and swirling, too thick to see through, and moving in unusual formations.

The reporter standing in the news studio pans back into focus. "Because of the display, we have yet to ID the villains who attacked the COE, but we stand confident that Taranis and the Olympian will be able to vanquish the villains . . .

"COE internal systems are down. Cell phone coverage appears disrupted—our camera crews are having difficulty transmitting—and no one within the building has been reached. We are unsure of the suspected reason for the attack, or if there are any injuries, or worse, but what we did witness only minutes before, recorded by a local coffee shop owner, were two bodies being carried across the street from the COE building into three black SUVs. The Sundale Police Department chief is calling in reinforcements from the Central American Champions' offices, as well as the US military.

"No demands have been made, and so far the VNA has yet to claim credit for the attack, but this is troubling given the clear signs of escalation from villains such as the Marduk, who attacked the COE offices early last month . . ."

My vision goes fuzzy as I watch the footage that flashes onto the screen, recorded from around the edge of a building by a shaky phone camera. I watch a woman in a white lab coat hovering off the ground, suspended by nothing. There's a figure in the haze of smoke standing by the SUV, but the camera only pans to them temporarily before shifting back to the mouth of the alley, where a second floating figure dressed in dark clothing bobs toward the SUV right after her.

I gasp. "That's him. That's Roland."

"His hood is up," Jeremy says. "You can't see his face. How can you tell?"

"I . . . bought him that sweatshirt."

Dan shouts, "We can't get through to anyone from the COE at all. We don't have contacts for any of the other Champions networks either. Should I call the police?"

"The police are clearly busy," Charlie shouts at the TV screen. He turns to me, meets my gaze, sucks in a breath, and says, "My SDD contact traced his phone to I-82, heading southbound near exit 38. The phone hasn't moved in a while, but since there's nothing near there, my guy suspects the phone was discarded. What do you want to do, Vanny?"

Margerie gasps, truly a candidate for Broadway. "There's not *nothing* near there." She points at the piece of paper still trapped in my grip. "That's two exits before the Old Sundale Airport."

"I have to go." I shoot up to my feet.

Everyone starts talking simultaneously before Charlie whistles *loudly*. "Everybody, calm the fuck down. You"—he points at me—"aren't going anywhere alone. And if he's been Liam Neeson's daughter 'taken,' and if it's by Three or any of these other unknown supers, this could be dangerous. I have a couple military contacts who could be here by tonight . . ."

I'm already shaking my head. "The police and the COE aren't going to be able to help. They're too busy *at* the COE now. And we can't get through to anyone to tell them where Roland is; I'm not even sure anybody else has identified that hooded figure as Roland yet. Also . . ." I love him. "I love him," I blurt.

Charlie's face hardens a little bit, but then he surprises me. "I know, hermanita. Which is why I was gonna suggest my military buddies back us up, and in the meantime, we'll go scope out the situation, and if there are any openings where we can get him out safely without engaging any of these supers directly, we take it. But *only* then. Hopefully the SDD will have handled the situation at your HQ by then and can help too."

"We're coming with you," Margerie says.

"The fuck you are," Charlie says. "Y'all are all civilians, and none of you are armed."

"Speak for yourself," Jeremy grunts.

"You carry?" Charlie sounds surprised.

"Don't you?"

"I'm former Marines. Course I carry. What's your excuse?"

"I'm a gay man from backcountry Georgia."

Charlie snorts. "All right, well I guess we got two guns. You can come."

"You guys can't come," I say, voice becoming shrill. "It's too dangerous. I can't let you."

"Can't *let* us come?"

"You think I'm letting my baby sister . . ."

"You're going, I'm going . . ."

"Who gives a shit how many of them there are . . ."

"You don't even have a gun . . ."

My people all start talking over each other, all at once. If I weren't so close to a panic attack, I might have found it endearing. Instead, I want to strangle all of them.

I try Charlie's whistle and fail, so I do the only thing I can think of: I get up on my pink ottoman and, in my bathrobe, shove my arms up to the sky. "Everybody, enough!"

The people filling my living room turn, most staring up at me like I've grown a fifth limb. I point around at them all. "Fine!" I shout at the top of my lungs. "If you insist on being stubborn, then so be it! But I am the leader of this here outfit, and I say that you are all adults and that anyone who wants to go or stay can decide for themself, but we need to leave ASAP."

"Well, I'm coming," Dan says.

"I've got the gun . . ." Jeremy says.

"We're all coming," Margerie asserts, hands on her hips.

Charlie rolls his eyes and gives us all a perfect imitation of our father's most unimpressed stare. "Fine. Let's go save your boy." He lifts his phone to his ear.

Luca snorts. "I think you mean, let's go save the world."

And then Margerie crosses her arms over her chest and juts out her hip. She looks me up and down. "I still think you should shower first."

Luca, Dan, and Jeremy lay the map of the airport flat on the dining room table and start shouting at each other about possible points where someone might be able to sneak in, but I'm more interested in what Charlie's saying to the person on the other end of the phone.

"Vinny, you still in town? Yeah . . . good." He meets my eye. "Vanny and I need a ride . . . Old Sundale Airport. Consider it a sightseeing mission. We're gonna circle the perimeter, but we're not going inside . . . Just in case, yeah." He swallows. "Bring the cavalry."

Chapter Twenty-Five

ROLAND

It's dark when I open my eyes. I don't know where I am. Can no longer remember where I'm supposed to be. *Or when.* The violent collision of my past with my present makes me feel like I was hit by a dump truck filled with sand, and every move I make to claw my way up and out of the pit only spills more sand into my face, into my eyes, so I try to burn my way out, but everything just turns to glass. I shatter.

Groaning, I roll from my back onto my side. Feels funny. My stomach pitches. I taste bile and, through sheer force of will, swallow it down. My head is on the ground, being propped up by something, and I'm reminded of my new look at the sound of clattering and the realization that my forehead and cheek aren't touching the cold concrete because there's something else there, between the side of my face and the floor. *Horns.* I have horns now. No—I have horns *again.*

I remember . . .

When I left my home world, my horns hadn't fully taken shape. They'd been nubs starting above my ears, sticking straight up and out. Now, if the vision I saw of myself in the mirror before I smashed it was correct, my fully developed horns still start above my ears but now curl down and forward in a backward C before moving past my temples and ending in stabby twin peaks a foot above the top of my head. They're thick, sharp, and big.

It takes a lot longer than it should for me to revolve entirely around, for my chest to hit the concrete. My chest is puffed out, twice as thick as it was, all roided out. My chin barely grazes the ground past it. I don't feel right, and I'd be shit scared about it if I weren't already shit scared about everything else.

Where is she?

I cough, clearing my lungs. It's like I'm waking up for the very first time. I didn't even feel like this when I was a child and my pod hit the ground. Disoriented, I crawled up and out of a hole in the ground half a mile long only to see beings who looked . . . strange to me. That had been my first thought. But then, later, I saw my own reflection and recognized that I looked a lot like they did. Now I understand my human appearance for what it was: a clever disguise imprinted into our genetics to help us blend in until we recovered our memories, our purpose, our weapons . . .

Then we'd revert to our original forms. Then we'd be ready.

I'm not fucking ready.

Slow clapping pulls my attention to the present. I reverberate a low, intimidating sound, but the clapping continues. "Sixty-Two, so glad you've returned," a female voice calls. "You honor us by returning to your true form. The first Tratharine among us who has."

I manage to get one knee underneath me, then the other, then both palms. My claws are thicker and longer than they were and clatter over the floor as I roll up to standing, feeling powerful in ways that I don't know I should enjoy as much as I do. But I do. I love it and fear it because I know why I am built like this, why I was chosen, and what I'm supposed to do next. I remember all my training, combat and otherwise, the vow I made to the Tratharine Elders standing on the pulpit, gazing up at the planets our armies would soon conquer.

But there was one thing the Elders didn't account for in all their planning.

They sent us as children, hiding our true purpose and our true forms until we'd successfully embedded ourselves into the societies we would later conquer. They encoded keys into our own biological strands; I remember the moment they did it. A creature built even more deadly than me told me my key. He told me I'd be awoken by a feeling of hatred so strong, I'd commit terrible acts of violence. He described it to me as a feeling, a single sensation sparked by a single act, a single moment . . .

How could the Elders have been so wrong?

Because I know now as I lie on the floor, tasting grit and rage on my tongue, that it wasn't anger that triggered me. It was her. I saw Vanessa, and for whatever reason, supernatural or of this earth, all I wanted was to protect her.

Protect and have her.

As a war child on Tratharine, the only thing I *never* had was one thing that was mine. Vanessa's mine now, and neither the past nor the present nor any of these fuckers can take her.

Where is she?

My hearing was always exceptional, and now it's beyond that. I immediately count the cadences of four different sets of hands clapping to their own beats. I shrug my shoulders back, flex my hands, and when I blink, I meet each of their gazes.

I'm looking for Three, the one who hurt her, and I find them instantly. The compulsion to rip their head off before any of them can speak is strong. My right foot jolts forward, but I manage restraint. There are four of them, and while I might be strongest, I don't remember what their powers are, and for me to get what I want, I need to survive this.

"You all work quickly," I say, surprised by the sound of my voice. It sounds exactly like it did this morning. "What time is it?"

"It's been half a day. We took you this morning," says the same female who spoke before. She's a white woman—she presents as a white *human* woman—with brown hair and freckles scattered across her nose. She's short for a female, but her eyes sparkle blue. "I am Thirty-Eight."

I scour my memory like a Rolodex, finally finding the correct entry. Meeting her gaze, I say, "You are a caster of spells, capable of creating powerful illusions in the mind." She gives me a bow, but it is not a customary Tratharine bow. I frown. "You are Thirty-Eight, but you are not reverted. You do not remember the Tratharine ways."

Her lips tighten. She is younger than I am by several years, but she was my senior in another life. In *our* other life. But she doesn't know that. She shakes her head, her gaze lowering.

"No. I have yet to revert. For some of us who fell, our neural implants were faulty. Either our memories were somewhat intact or we regained them over time. But only partially. And the . . ." Her lips twist as she fights an anger I can feel wafting from her as powerfully as a breeze. "The SDD was too difficult for us to crush without our true forms and without our weapons, and with our diminished numbers. We have not found our maps, and we don't know how to find them. We need you to lead us, show us how, so that we may regain our true forms and claim victory over this planet and the pitiful creatures who inhabit it."

"If that's still what you want," number Three interjects. Three . . . the most powerful being here, the third most powerful within our ranks on Tratharine. At least, they were . . . until I reverted before they did. I cannot let them revert. I don't know how to stop them from it, so killing them will have to do.

I look at Three and quickly rein back in the fire that threatens to explode from my eyes. It's easier to control as I remember all my training . . . years and years and years of pain. I thought so little of the humans when I first arrived and was taken into the SDD facilities. But where I am from, Tratharine, the beings are perhaps even more simplistic, for the Tratharine are only one thing: cruel.

"You think I would have changed my mind?"

"I don't know what to think, if I'm being honest," the impish, dark-haired number Three coos. "I didn't expect the Elders to make our keys so . . . supple."

I don't let them bait me. I refuse. "The Elders, in case you've forgotten, didn't make our keys at all. They expected us to find triggers on this planet that would manifest reactions in our physiologies so powerful, we would remember who we are."

"The term *key* was a poor one, wasn't it?" Three shakes their head, a dark wave falling to cover one of their eyes. They brush it back. "It led us to believe our keys would be *objects*. But yours isn't an object . . . Or is it?" They smirk. "She is absolutely delicious. I only had the pleasure of a taste. I can imagine that having a feast every day would weaken your desire to follow through on the plan to rip her home world out from under her."

I keep my tone calm. Cold. "The plan to enslave humankind? Combine our weapons into a gate and open it to the Elders so that they can take control of another planet? This one?"

There's a stir among the gathered four. Three and Thirty-Eight stand alongside numbers Sixty-Nine and Twenty. Those two have powers I do remember. Sixty-Nine, a very young male with light-brown skin and black hair, has power over sand. Twenty is an older male with dark skin and white hair now, one of the oldest who was sent as part of our mission. He is powerful, with an ability to cause bodily pain through mental projection. He watches me critically as I flit my gaze back and forth over them all. No, I won't be able to fight my way out of here like this.

I clear my throat. "Yes, I know their plans. I remember."

"*Their* plans?" Three asks. "Don't you mean our plans?"

I am already making mistakes. Because yes, I may know our plans. And I know that, as the first reverted Tratharine, my purpose is paramount. *I also know that plans change.*

I growl, "No. The Elders have their own plans. Our plan is to get them here. We can only do that with our weapons, which I don't seem to have."

I glance around stupidly but with the express purpose of cataloguing my surroundings. I'm in a large warehouse. Much larger than I initially thought, though I suppose, at my new size and with massive structures hanging from the ceiling, that tracks. Airplanes. There are planes up there and planes scattered all across the concrete floor of various shapes, models, ages, and origins. But this isn't an airport. It's clearly a hangar of some kind but, based on the ages of some of the planes, one that's very out of date.

"Where are we?"

"You don't know?" Three's voice makes me want to punch them. They're number Three and pissed off they didn't revert first. I remember their original form vaguely, from before. Like number Four, they had an ethereal body. It made them powerful and extremely difficult to kill. I will not want to deal with them once they've reverted and, for all of our sakes, hope they never do. "You never solved your map?"

My growl picks up again, and I take a step forward. "I don't answer to you, *human*. I had better things to do than solve riddles."

"Like burying your head in that woman's cunt? And it's Three to you, Sixty-Two."

They're baiting me; I know that. What's surprising is that it's working. They can throw hierarchy power bullshit at me all fucking night, but I'm not gonna last if they keep talking about my girl. My growl reverberates more loudly.

Three takes a step toward me. Bold. Too fucking bold. I glance at their hands, knowing that these were the hands that touched her body, and I struggle to hold when I see that they filed their nails to sharp points to resemble the claws they had in a previous life. How cute. My own claws clatter against each other as my fingers flex. I feel vindicated when Three glances down at them and their nose wrinkles.

"You will tell me where we are and where my weapon is, or I will leave and continue my mission without your assistance. With your *claws*, you have hardly more utility than a human as is."

Three's upper lip curls away from their straight white teeth. They are a handsome human, but they are much prettier in their original form. They want it back. I can feel their envy as tangibly as a touch. They take another step, hard shoes echoing over the concrete.

"Easy, Three. We're on the same team. Sixty-Two, we saw your map formed on your skin in the news coverage of your *heroics* on that mountain," Thirty-Eight says. "Don't worry. We know you hadn't recovered your memories or you wouldn't have engaged the humans like that. The point is that we solved your map, and it brought us here. The Old Sundale Airport. We believe your weapon might be in one of these planes, but we couldn't identify it. We were hoping you could."

I nod slowly, turning toward Thirty-Eight. "I can, but it won't be easy."

Three balks. Ironic, because I'm not lying. It's a thin blade, sharp but utterly unremarkable until it's in my hand. "It was attached to the back of my pod."

She nods. "We know. We have your pod. We have most of the pods already, but yours was sadly without weapon." Suggesting that some were *with* weapon.

"How?"

"Three." She points at the Tratharine I'm going to murder first. "They have extensive experience stealing from the COE." She gestures then to Sixty-Nine, and the young male lifts a hand toward a large metal supply cabinet. Sand billows from his palms, and the doors to the cabinet fall open. Mr. Singkham and Dr. Larsen tumble out onto the floor.

I glare, the pattering of my heart stopping, then resuming. Don't give a shit about Mr. Singkham, but Dr. Larsen? Emily? She's my friend. The Elders were fucking fools to think that taking away our memories would help ingratiate us within the society we were meant to kill without repercussions. Because now, I care.

My pulse picks back up when I see Emily roll onto her back, groaning loudly. Twenty approaches her, and she moans in pain. I hiss, trying to keep my rage under wraps, and speak loudly, hoping to pull their collective attention back to me. "Hm," I say, voice breaking slightly. I growl to try to mask it. "But you didn't bring my key with you?"

"Why would we have?" Three blurts.

"She has fulfilled her purpose," Twenty adds, voice low but filled with question, and I grin. They haven't realized that the key unlocks both the reversion and the weapon. And since it's clear our keys on this planet aren't wholly intangible, I imagine Nessa could help unlock my weapon—or even find it herself. Not that I plan to voice any of that to them.

I shake my head. "Let's search."

"He's right," Thirty-Eight adds. "Let's work on finding the weapon first, before we take it back to the others."

"The others?"

"The Marduk." Thirty-Eight grins. "You might remember him as number Four. He's among those of us who fell with most of his memories from Tratharine—a mistake, but one we now are grateful for. Clever male, he's been leading us. It was his idea to distract the world with this whole idea of *villains* and heroes. He created the first of them, the Meinad, shortly after watching so many of these *superhero* movies." She makes air quotes around the word, and the other three around her snicker. Even Three.

"The humans were so eager to jump on the idea of these cute, fantastical little kids. They formed two corporations within the decade that have so much control. The villains shield those of us Tratharine doing actual Tratharine work with little villainous theatrics to distract and appease the world. The heroes who formed to counter them are just a bunch of bumbling morons."

They all laugh openly at that, Thirty-Eight so hard she's wiping tears from her eyes as she speaks next. "They'll realize how dumb they were when it's all settled. Once we Tratharine have *all* returned to our true forms and positioned ourselves in our rightful places in this world with these pathetic humans enslaved beneath us. You'll lead us there.

And when we finally amass all our weapons and open the gate, you'll greet the Elders first."

Lovely. I swallow hard and force myself to nod and say, "Good. My weapon first. You're sure it's here?"

"This is where the map led."

"You don't feel it?" Twenty says.

"No." And I need it. I'm going to need a weapon to get out of this. Because if I escape and leave these beings alive, they'll keep coming and put Nessa at risk. So I'm going to have to find my weapon—any fucking weapon—and kill all of them with it.

"What *do* you feel, Sixty-Two?" Three hisses, taking a slow turn around me while the others at least have the decency to pretend to look around the hangar. "A solidarity with Tratharine and its people? With the Elders who trained us to be the most feared and savage warriors in the universe? Or do you think now of *her*? The little human with the soft skin and the soft heart."

"He's not thinking of a human," Thirty-Eight insists. "Stop trying to provoke him."

"He's *not* thinking of a human? Don't be blind, Thirty-Eight. He's not with us." Three seethes. "He's compromised."

"A key can't compromise one of us," Thirty-Eight says. "The keys are but tools to be used and discarded; you remember that part of our training, don't you? The Elders wouldn't have sent us somewhere where a key could derail their entire plan."

I shout, "Don't speak about me like I'm not even here. I want to find my weapon . . ."

"You want to get back to her!" Three roars.

"Maybe the Elders did not know," Twenty says, soft voice cutting through the rising tension. "Maybe this planet has its own defenses . . ." His bleak, soulless gaze searches mine, and I know that I've lost.

A short silence reigns. I can feel the four turning their attention toward me in a way that spells doom. I need to say something to get me out of this. Even Thirty-Eight's gifts are pushing at me. I can feel a softening of the air, but I fearlessly make direct eye contact. I am still stronger. Their powers may work on me, but we are Tratharine. Everything about our world is based on the strong overtaking the weak. Their powers will not work on me fully. Not yet.

"Are you with us, Sixty-Two?" Thirty-Eight asks me.

I don't even try to lie. I just say nothing and prepare for battle . . .

"Do you hear that?" Sixty-Nine says, interrupting my thoughts.

I think for a moment that he's attempting to distract me, but then I hear it. The wings of a helicopter.

"Fuck. Must be the COE. They must have tracked him already."

"But they were distracted. Fifty-Five and Sixty-Eight were there, and I left my illusion with them. How could they have failed? Two of ours should have easily leveled the whole block, the whole city!" Thirty-Eight snarls, curls swirling around her face, turning momentarily to snakes in my mind's eye.

"Open the roof. Take them quickly, and in the meantime, I'll restrain the *Wyvern*," Twenty says slowly. "Unless you've come to your senses and you remember your mission."

"You think I'm your commander ready to lead the army to vanquish the planet. This planet and the people on it think I'm their superhero sent to save them." I shake my head and laugh, brandishing my claws and funneling flame through my horns to illuminate the darkness. "Sometimes superheroes don't give a fuck about the world. Sometimes they just want the girl."

"I told you he was corrupted!" Three shouts.

Sixty-Nine throws open the metal roof in a burst of dust and sand. It clangs violently as it opens, and the sound only grows more deafening when three helicopters appear in sight and—bloody hell. It isn't the COE at all. Is this . . . a rescue?

With my improved hearing, I can hear Vanessa's idiot brothers shouting at one another over the chaos. "Fuck," I hiss at the same time that a sense of urgency pulls my attention across the room to an old model helicopter.

I start to run toward it, trying to outpace the weight of all four Tratharine warriors hurling their gifts at my back, because Vanessa is in one of the helicopters circling overhead, and I'm going to need that weapon to save her life.

And I've found it.

Chapter Twenty-Six

VANESSA

"Fucking hell, we're going down!" Vinny shouts over the intercom in our headsets. I make eyes at Margerie sitting across from me next to Charlie, who's already standing up, reaching for some scary-looking yellow pouch affixed to the roof of the helicopter. I have a suspicion, which I don't want confirmed, of exactly what's inside it.

I look at Margerie and see that her gaze has followed mine to Charlie. "Fuck," she mouths, though I can't hear her over the angry blast of the helicopter's propellers—wings? I should have paid more attention when Vinny explained this shit to me.

I'm strapped into my helicopter seat, clutching it with all the force in my arms, wondering what in the high heavens I was thinking when I bitched long and loudly enough that my brothers consented to let me onto Vinny's chopper. I'm even wearing his sweatshirt with a helicopter on the front and the slogan, "I'm a psycHOTic helicopter pilot."

Vinny's adrenaline junkie buddies Arnold and Meron are flying the other two helicopters. When they found out why Vinny needed to borrow a couple choppers for the day, they bulldozed their way into this plan, and the worst part is, it's not even a plan!

We agreed that we'd scope out the airport and only touch down on the empty tarmac if it was safe. Our plan didn't involve us staging a full siege of the damn Old Sundale Airport, but when the hangar opened roof-first and a dirt and sand tornado engulfed Meron's helicopter and our helicopter started to drop from the sky, Arnold, a gun nut in possession of a machine gun—because *Amurkah*—opened fire.

We regained altitude, but only for a second. "The main rotor is jammed!" Vinny yells. "Everybody grab a chute! And a gun!"

"A chute? You mean a *parachute*?" I screech.

But Vinny's abandoned his seat. My stomach is up in my throat. He's charging at me, pulling me out of my seat belt while the helicopter does a funny dance that I'm pretty sure is reserved for drunken prom dates and cowboys shooting at each other's feet.

"I've got my gun!" Margerie shouts, brandishing the tiniest gun I've ever seen as Charlie pushes her right up to the helicopter's dangerous edge and shoves her arms into the straps of a parachute before taking one for himself.

"Should I jump?" Margerie shouts.

Vinny grabs two parachutes for us, and as I pull my parachute over my shoulders and yank on the straps to tighten the apparatus to my back, I scream, "Where did you get that gun?"

But before I can hear her response, Vinny's grabbing me and throwing the group of us out of the side of the helicopter.

I scream. I scream my head off. I scream louder than I've ever screamed in my life. My body falls and then jerks as Vinny *kicks* me in the stomach and pulls down on the latch for my parachute at the same time. The brutality makes sense when I see the helicopter cut between us like the blade of a guillotine. The jerking in my back and shoulders is painful as I glance around, panic in my chest making my heart thud like a drum, only to find Charlie and Vinny and Margerie happily floating thirty feet away from me, Margerie wildly waiving her gun. Every time it passes in his direction, Charlie winces back and holds up his arms.

I shout across the empty space, the tarmac looking appallingly far away even though we must be only a hundred or so feet up at this point. "Margerie! Put that thing down! That's dangerous!"

Margerie scoffs. "*This* is dangerous? Have you seen the ground?"

She's waving her gun, gesturing wildly at the world below as we slowly float toward the airport. Through the open roof doors of the hangar, I see that the entire place is ablaze.

"Your boyfriend must be down there!" Vinny shouts. "Use your handholds to steer yourself away from the hangar, Vanny! Head toward the tarmac!"

I glance at the holds hovering by my shoulders, reach up, and grab them. I mimic the motions Vinny makes and wonkily manage to steer myself away from the flames. Roland's *here*. I can't believe it. The last functioning helicopter of the trio is still flying in slow circles above the open door to hell. There's something chaotic happening within the building because I can hear things catching on fire, loud banging, things exploding.

A huge piece of metal flies out of the building. I can't see what it is, only that it's sharp and headed straight toward me. I yank hard on my left handhold, and my parachute drops down. I avoid getting impaled, but my parachute does not. I open my mouth to scream, but wind rushes into my mouth as the ground plummets up to meet me.

I hit the asphalt hard, and I swear I break all my fucking teeth. My forearms hit the ground before I crash onto my side. I hear someone shouting my name, and I know it's Roland, even through the haze of voices clamoring for my attention.

I open my eyes.

I'm lying on my side coughing into my fists when my torso jerks over the hard ground as my parachute catches wind. I clutch desperately at the buckle between my breasts and slap it open. My shoulders release, and I can breathe again as my parachute takes off without me. I cough, choke, gag on smoke fumes wafting from the building, but as if commanded by the weight of my gaze, they clear.

"Nessa, get out of here!" Roland's voice sounds so far away—too far. Which doesn't at all make sense when Roland suddenly runs from the building, his beautiful brown skin glowing with sweat. His dark hair rippling in the breeze. His eyes the brightest, prettiest pink.

"Vanessa," his voice calls much louder this time. "I'm here. Don't worry. I'm not going to let anything bad happen to you. I love you, sweetheart." He's almost on me, and I register three wrong things at once.

He called me *Vanessa*, he called me *sweetheart*, and he's *sweating*. He fucked me for hours last night, and he didn't so much as glisten; meanwhile, I was drenched in every possible sense. I was so shocked that, somewhere in the melee, I had enough presence of mind to ask him about it. He told me he never sweats, something about his body burning it off. So unless he was lying and my eyes deceived me last night, my eyes are deceiving me now.

I haul my ass up off the ground, kicking with my feet, getting tangled up in the cords of my parachute and going back down again. "Vanessa—Vanessa, are you there?" Without my headset on, I can hear Margerie's shouted voice close by, but I can't see her. I can only see this fake Roland apparition stomping toward me, looking all wrong . . . and I can't even see the building past him. It's just a hazy blur. Occasionally a tuft of smoke wafts from it, but I can't grab ahold. I feel like I'm going *crazy*.

"I'm here, Margerie! Can you see?" I don't even bother asking if she can see *me* because that's already one step too far removed.

"I can't see you! I can see the building on fucking fire, but I can't find you! Are you in the fire?!"

"No, she's not there," I hear a more distant voice say. It sounds like Charlie. "But what the . . . holy fuck is that!" His voice devolves into Spanish slurs and curses. "We need to get clear . . . There's a . . . There's something coming. It looks like a goddamn sandstorm!"

"I'm not leaving without Vanessa!"

"I'm here," I shout, but the creature . . . person . . . mirage . . . is almost on me. I kick at it, but the fake Roland lunges at me, drops down onto my body, and wraps his fingers around my throat.

"Holy fuck, I can see Roland, and what is he—Roland's attacking Vanessa!"

"Don't worry," Margerie shouts back to Vinny. "I got it."

"Margerie, no!" A multitude of my brothers' overlapping voices call out, Charlie's loudest of all. "You can't shoot Roland!" But Margerie's smarter than that.

"That isn't Roland! He would never touch Nessa like that!" she says, and I adore her for it. A high-pitched *pop* goes off in the next second, and fake Roland's mouth opens on a scream—a female's scream.

Her fingers loosen from around my throat, and when I tilt my hips to the left, she falls off me and slumps onto the ground, fully disrobed of her terrifying Roland suit and back to being a brunette wearing jeans and a baggy sweatshirt. She looks like anybody as she lies beside me, her face scrunching in pain.

I reach out hesitantly but quickly snatch my hand away from her face when I realize I'd been about to touch her. "I'm so sorry. You're gonna be okay."

"You fucking bitch! That idiot shot me!"

I'd say that I don't know which one of my idiots she's talking about, but the first thing I see when I look up is Margerie pointing her gun in my direction. "Did I get him? Her? Whatever the shit it is?" she shouts.

"You got her!" I give her a thumbs-up and a smile, ambling back onto my feet. "Thanks, Margerie!"

"Anytime, boss!" She gives me a salute.

"You stupid bitch, you're ruining everything." Stupid, stupid . . . I grin. The voice in my head is mine. The voice out of my head is hers. And thanks to my peaking adrenaline, I may be losing my mind, but I know I'm not stupid.

"No, I'm not," I tell her pointedly, brushing off my jeans. "But you aren't a very nice person."

She rolls onto her back, her gray sweatshirt charred around the collar and the left sleeve. She barely looks older than me, and when her face twists in pain, she looks almost fragile. Like somebody I could have been friends with. And then the expression ebbs from pain to rage, and she screams, "I'm not a person, and what—what is wrong with you?"

What is wrong with you? I laugh, remembering that Roland once asked me the very same thing. "Nothing is wrong with me," I say, nearly giddy. "I'm a nice person! And you are very rude!"

"You tell her, Vanny!" Luca shouts, laughing.

"Yeah, after we get the fuck out of here!" David adds.

"Yippee-ki-yay, motherfuckers!" The voice is Arnold's, and it successfully snaps my focus back to what's happening across the rest of the tarmac. Because the front doors to the hangar have been thrown open, and a wall of sand barrels out of it.

"Arnold, what the fuck?" Vinny yells. "¡Cabrón! Everybody get the fuck down! David, get her!"

I look to my left only to see Arnold wielding a gun—I don't know guns, but it looks like a fucking cannon—and he's pointing it at the hangar as the sand is advancing on us, a single being striding out of the hangar just before it. A creature I recognize.

"Careful of that one! That's Three!"

"Don't worry! I've got more bullets!" Margerie starts firing.

"Margerie, put the goddamn gun down!" Charlie tackles Margerie at the same time that Three disappears and Arnold starts firing.

"Vanny, get down!" David launches himself toward the concrete.

"I have to go!" I yell, taking a wide arc as I try to run as fast as my wobbly ankle will carry me toward the hangar. I can't feel the residual pain in my ankle. My adrenaline is roaring as loud as the clanging going on inside the old airport. I have the most uncanny feeling that *that's* where I need to be. Right in the thick of the carnage.

"Vanny! Fuck!" David is shouting, but I'm on a mission. A suicide mission? Perhaps. But a mission nonetheless.

I am not a sporty person, and my lungs are on fire. The smoke is thick, and even though my brain reminds me that Rollo will be fine with smoke and heat, that doesn't assuage my panic when a pained roar echoes from within the historic airport. I run faster.

The sand wall moves out away from the entrance at the same time that a figure appears on the other side of the tarmac, right next to Arnold. "Arnold, look out!" I try, but Arnold is screaming bloody murder. I clap my hands on either side of my head, terrified . . .

Arnold is there one minute, gone the next. And then I hear a scream in the helicopter overhead. It's coming down. "Everybody, move!" I scream at the top of my lungs, but Charlie and Vinny, Margerie and Luca—who are closest to the falling helicopter—seem to have noticed it at the same time I did. They're running across the tarmac toward me, David hauling ass with them. I feel relief, and then I feel it again when I see four parachutes dotting the sky. And then panic moves to overshadow all that precious relief when I see Three standing near Arnold's abandoned gun. They're moving behind the cannon, preparing to do something terrible. I've got to do something first.

"Hey!" I shout. "Three!"

Three's head jerks as their gaze struggles to find me in the chaos, and when it does, they smile. "Oh fuck!" I take off at a sprint toward the hangar, only to realize it's being blocked by a sand wall.

"She needs cover!" Luca shouts. Suddenly a gun pops off, and then another, and then a higher-pitched sound that has to be Margerie's insane weapon, and then the sand wall surges forward toward one of my family members, and in the gap it leaves behind, I've got no other choice but to take the opening my people sacrificed to give me and try for it.

I sprint toward the hangar, but I've barely got a foot off the ground when hands close around my elbows, tightening them to my sides. "This time," a familiar voice hisses in my ear, "I'm not going to be nice. I'm going to drop you off the edge of this miserable fucking planet . . ."

I hear it . . . the growl. It's coming from inside the hangar, and it's a pained sound. "Rollo . . ." I gasp.

"In due time. Right now one of my friends is having some fun with your boyfriend. This might take a while."

Rage comes for me, and I jerk in Three's hold. It wouldn't have had any effect if, at the same time, I hadn't heard the loud pop of a gun going off, followed by Three's shocked grunt. Three buckles, their hold loosening from around my limbs. I turn around, and without any idea what I'm doing, I hurl a punch at them.

My fist cracks against their nose, blood pouring over their lips. "You're a dick!" I shout, and Three staggers back, collapsing onto their knees and shooting me the most bewildered look.

"Vanny, go!" Vinny shouts at the same time David says, "We got this!"

I look up and, for the briefest moment, allow myself to absorb the scene before me. One I will never forget. My five brothers, most of my C-suite, and my best friend standing on the tarmac in front of the gaping, blazing mouth of the hangar, squaring off against two wounded aliens and a wall made out of rock, debris, and sand, the Sundale skyline looking gloriously unaffected behind them.

Vinny and David are working to get Arnold's dropped gun propped back up. Margerie's waving her little pistol around at the brunette who's gotten back up and is doing *something* that seems to have Meron, Mani, Jeremy, and Dan wandering in circles and shouting like they're lost in a corn maze.

Luca wields a broken helicopter blade like a spear as he charges the sand wall. Charlie uses a shield made from broken helicopter hull and follows him. The smoke and fire from three destroyed helicopters make up the backdrop behind them, all framed by large banners that fall from the ruined hangar and say, WELCOME, FORTY-EIGHT! AND THANKS FOR YOUR SERVICE!

Three grabs for my leg when I take a step toward the hangar. A gun goes off, and Three turns back to face Vinny, vanishing without a trace. "Vanny, go!" And so I go, disappearing into the smoke to find my alien boyfriend.

Darkness washes over me the moment I step inside, despite the fact that the roof doors are still open. It's hotter than hell in here, too, and the smoke is thick but clearing as I move forward. "Rollo!" I shout at the top of my lungs, trying to beat the smoke out of my eyes. The farther I wade into the dark hangar, the more it clears, until I'm finally able to make shapes out of the carnage. I don't like what I see.

A youthful-looking male stands at the hangar's entrance with his hands up, sand swirling around him, lifting his black hair. He isn't looking at me but is focused on his task as wind and bits of helicopter crash through the air and then smash their way out of the hangar.

"You traitor!" a second male shouts. He's got white hair and dark skin and wild, angry eyes that are turned toward something I can't see behind a huge pile of wrecked airplane parts.

Rollo . . .

Panic and determination fueling me, I reach for the first thing I see lying on the ground: a long, thin helicopter part that has a huge flat blade with notches cut into one side and a terribly precise point. It weighs almost nothing. "Leave Rollo alone!" I shout, drawing the attention of the two males.

I lift the weapon like a baseball bat. As a kid, I played softball for six days before Elena took pity on me and pulled me from that team, and every other team my sports-loving family had signed me up for, so I know I'm not much of a threat. Yet the look the males give me now makes me think otherwise.

"She can lift it," the younger male says, shocked.

The older male roars, face pointed down. "How is that possible?"

"Because she's . . . the key," Rollo's low, gravelly voice says from somewhere behind the pile of wrecked planes. He must be lying at the white-haired male's feet. "And if you touch her . . . I will—augh!" He roars in pain.

"Leave my boyfriend alone!" I shout, storming forward, weapon raised. Only . . . I'm slowed by the pile of airplane bits blocking me from Rollo and the one hurting him. I try to climb, but the metal pieces cut into my skin and crumple beneath the balls of my feet.

"Oh shoot! I'm sorry, airplanes," I whisper to them.

The younger boy says loudly, "Is she serious? *She* is the key? She caused his reversion? How?"

"It doesn't matter. The effect has been undesirable. We'll need to get rid of him. Her, we'll keep. Perhaps she can activate other weapons. We'll have to try everything . . ."

"No, you won't!" I shout, and I topple over the other side of the pile, my weapon tumbling from my grip. I reach for it, and when I pick it up from the cold concrete ground this time, it turns to *flame*.

I scream, but the weapon doesn't fall out of my hand even though I try to release it. Instead it gleams with a vibrant orange light that floods the darkness and scares the ever-loving shit out of me. I stumble forward, tripping over something massive and red. It can't be an airplane part because it moves when my toes bump into it. I stumble forward, fiery helicopter piece leading the charge, though now that I think about it . . . it looks suspiciously like a sword. Or maybe it only looks that way because, as I fall, I meet the eyes of the white-haired male, and we share the same look of utter shock as my flame-laced épée slides cleanly into his belly button . . . and then out the other side.

Oops.

I open my mouth with every intent of apologizing, only to recognize that this dude was just talking about killing Roland and abducting me. So instead, as he and I fall together onto the floor, my sword impaling him straight through the stomach, I scream, "You are not a very nice alien, but I didn't mean to do this!"

I scrabble up onto my knees and try to staunch the blood flow unsuccessfully with my hands. "I WILL FIX IT!" Maybe. There's a lot of blood, and the alien looks like he's in a lot of pain. I try to use his shirt to soak up the blood, but as I press around the blade, a sudden, horrible pressure slices sideways through my temples.

I scream, dropping over the older male's crotch, which isn't exactly where I want to die—though, make no mistake, I do feel like dying. I cry out and distantly hear a low rumble before the pain I'd been feeling comes to an abrupt end. I open my eyes and look over my right shoulder. Spread over the floor is the body of the male I stabbed . . . but the space where his head once was is now a puddle.

I gag in the back of my throat and hurl myself away from his body up into a seat. My back hits broken bits of the airplane junk pile, and I cry out, rubbing a painful spot on my side. I need to find Rollo and get the hell out of here. "Rol—" I go very, very still and completely and utterly quiet, forgetting instantly about the headless corpse when, lying there right beside it, a huge monster rises from the ground, hand dipped in blood that's just as red as its flesh.

Crouched on one knee, the monster looks at me briefly before turning away and launching itself over the ground, over the barrier of broken airplanes. I move into a crouch, tracking it with my eyes, not wanting to let it out of my sight—a mistake. Because I see then in full clarity as the younger male turns, his hands raised. The wall of sand that had been keeping my not-so-official extraction team outside suddenly falls. Sand blasts into the space, and I duck, but not before I see the monster retaliate. The monster's horns catch fire. It lunges. Lifting one enormous arm to block the sand, it arrives within arm's distance of the smaller male, and then it removes the male's head with one swipe of its massive claws.

Familiar claws.

The sand falls, and in the quiet of its absence, my squeak is *loud*. I cover my mouth with both hands as the creature with red skin and massive horns who stands eight feet tall and has clawed feet and black . . . talons and . . . is wearing . . . the sweatpants I gave him . . . turns toward me. He moves so slowly that time bends away from me, and I have to use both hands to reel it back in. Because then he's facing me, and I drop to my ass behind the wall of airplane bits because I can't unsee what I just saw.

A whoosh sounds. The monster is in flight. I see it move over my head, landing on the finished concrete between me and the headless alien who'd been hurting me. My hands are clasped over my mouth, and I look up, admiring familiar inky-black hair feathering around fresh horns gracefully, a chunk falling across his forehead like a Highland cow. It's cute, if anything so terrifying could be.

His mouth and nose and eyes are the same shape, just bigger to match his new proportions. His skin is covered in runes that glow very subtly when he first sees me and then die down to a shade just darker than the rest of his skin. And it isn't red, by the way. It isn't red. It only looks that way in the light of all the flames glowing around the building. Flames that are slowly dying away. The smoke too.

He's pink.

Roland, the giant pink monster, takes a step toward me, his sweatpants tight around his massive thighs and slung low around his hips so that I can see all his fancy new muscles. I swallow hard.

He isn't looking into my eyes but at my feet or possibly the ground between us as he says, "Are you all right?"

I shake my head and then, realizing what I've done, nod rapidly. "Actually." My voice is trembling. I clear my throat. His head cocks to the side and flicks his light-pink gaze up to mine. "I'm having the time of my life."

His whole face busts out into a smile, and it's mesmerizing. Because it looks exactly the same as it did in his . . . well . . . before. His lips are full, a darker color than his skin, his tongue darker than both. He licks his lips and then bites the bottom one between teeth that are . . . sharper than they were. Does he have . . . fangs? "I . . ."

"You're really handsome," I whisper.

He shakes his head quickly, his hair swishing around massive dark-gray horns. "What?"

"I came to rescue you," I blurt out next. "With my brothers and Margerie and Dan and Jeremy. Vinny brought friends too."

"They brought you out here?" He looks furious.

"It was my idea."

"They're supposed to protect you . . ." He sounds furious too.

I shake my head and smile up at him like a crazy person. My shoulders are starting to shake. I feel cold even though I'm in jeans and

Vinny's hoodie. Underneath, I'm wearing a black T-shirt with holes in it. It's one of Rollo's. I don't know what compelled me to wear it. *Comfort. I'm comforted by him. And horns aren't going to change that.*

"And I'm supposed to protect you. I love you."

He blinks at me, looking shocked, looking . . . vulnerable. He shakes his head and scoffs, "Like . . . this?"

I nod. "Especially like this."

He closes the space between us and drops to his knees at my feet. "Christ, baby. You're gonna be the death of me. I love you more."

"It's not possible. You don't have any idea how strong you make me feel. You make me feel like a superhero . . ."

"You are. Always have been. I didn't have anything to do with it."

"I love you so fucking much."

"Stop . . . talking," he says, and he kisses me, really fucking kisses me. I kiss him back just as hard, just as biting. Well, not *quite.*

"You have fangs," I whisper, breaking the kiss to admire his sharpened canines, dazzling white.

He nods. "They bother you?"

"No."

"Are you sure this," he says, glancing up at the same time his horns catch fire for a split instant that makes me jump, "doesn't bother you?"

I grin, adrenaline and elation and shock warring in my chest, making my heart pound like a tempest against the sail of a ship.

"Nessa, look at me. Be serious. I'm no Prince Charming."

"No." I glance from his horns to his impossibly thick chest to his gem-colored skin to his clawed feet. "But you'll never be the villain to me."

His chest shudders on the exhale, and I watch something in the vicinity of pain flash across his features before it settles into a cool veneer of relief. "It's a lot."

"It's kinda hot." I barely get the words out before he crushes his lips to mine again, kissing me deeply enough that I swoon. He cups the back of my head with one massive hand and drags his thumb across my jaw, the claw tickling my cheek as he does.

"Thank you," he whispers when he's finished with me.

I'm so confused, so deliriously drunk on adrenaline and lust and love. "For what?" I blink.

"For being my hero too." He kisses my cheek briefly and then pulls me even tighter against him, a rumble picking up in his chest.

He laughs and takes my hand, and when he pulls, he brings us both to our feet. I only numbly take whatever it is that he puts into my hand as he kisses me one more time, very sweetly. "This was an incredible rescue. Let's grab Mr. Singkham and Emily, then we can help your crew."

I smile. We. He said *we*. I nod, and I'm still nodding like a dope as he heads to the far wall, where I finally notice for the first time a groaning body—Mr. Singkham—and then a woman emerging from behind an open cabinet door.

"Roland? Is that really you?" the friendly COE doctor asks.

"It's me, Emily."

"Holy shit. I don't think the electric sander is gonna cut it."

He laughs, and though I don't get the joke, I smile too. "Let me give you a hand."

An explosion outside turns our attention toward the hangar door, and feeling like a total badass, I lift my new sword. "No, no. You go. I'll see to Mr. Singkham," Emily says. She brushes the back of her wrist over her forehead, smearing soot across her face, before turning her attention back to the disheveled, sleeping man. "Good heavens."

"Is he gonna make it?" I ask.

"Yes. He's fine. Now go!"

Rollo's feet lift from the ground. He comes back to collect me, and as he gathers me in his arms and floats us over piles of airplane debris, I awkwardly try not to cut him on my new weapon. Smoke clears around us, and when we touch down outside of the hangar, I can see that my brothers have already claimed their victory. Three and the female are gone. Wounds are being nursed. Margerie is running around filming everything with her cell phone camera. Dan and Jeremy have their phones out, despite whatever pain they're in, and are hopefully calling the right people.

"They left!" Luca says with a shrug before turning around and seeing us and shrieking. "Jesus Christ! What the fuck is that! Get him, boys!"

"Don't fucking get him!" Charlie shouts, running forward from where he'd been kneeling at Dan's side and grabbing Luca's arm. "Can't you see? That's fucking *Roland*."

Luca's face has gone slack. He runs his hand through his curls and shakes his head. "Roland? No. No way. That can't be the goddamn *Wyvern*."

I twist in Roland's grip, letting my feet find the tarmac. All I want is to lay my head on his shoulder and burrow deep into his massive chest, but I need to make this clear first. I position my body in front of his and hold up my hands.

"Vanessa, put that shit down!" David shouts, coughing from his position on his knees near Jeremy's body. He's got blood all over his hands, but I can see Jeremy gaping at me and know that he's going to be all right despite the gash in his left leg and whatever is going on with his knee.

"It's hers," Rollo says from behind me. "She's the only one who can lift it."

I am?

"She is?" Margerie says.

"She unlocked it. Might be possible for me to carry now, but she can have it if she wants. She can have whatever she wants."

"Christ, it really is Roland," Mani mutters as he staggers up to his feet. He's covered in sand and dirt and has blood leaking down his face from a wound near his hairline.

I swallow, feeling my heart hammering hard in my chest. "Fam, I see how you might be confused given that a wyvern might not seem like such an apt descriptor anymore, but if it helps, I'd like to reintroduce you. This is Rollo." I place my free hand on his stomach and step back into the cage of his warmth. "My boyfriend, who I very much love."

"Gonna be her husband soon enough," Rollo says.

"You better get permission from William first. Puta madre," Mani curses.

"William? Elena's the one he's gotta please," Vinny hisses, just as pissed. "By the way, I got off the phone with Arnold. We're gonna need help. He's in Paraguay at a bar, and he doesn't have a passport."

"I'll make some calls," Charlie and Margerie say verbatim in the same instant. They share a glance, both of them softening. I hear the K-I-S-S-I-N-G song playing in my head on repeat and laugh.

"Ugh, I hate all of you. The two of you especially," Luca says, pointing at me and Rollo.

"Can't believe you let her fall in love with this sorry Charlie," David adds.

"Ain't nothing wrong with Charlies," Charlie mutters, never breaking eye contact with Margerie, even as he cocks his head toward Roland. "And this guy's okay too."

My brothers continue muttering at each other while I look up at Rollo, my nose scrunched. Rollo glances away first—first!—and sounds oddly *embarrassed* when he clears his throat. Embarrassed? That's my thing! "Everyone okay?"

"Everyone but Arnold," Vinny says, shaking his head down at his cell. "He's drunk on tequila and telling everybody he got teleported from Sundale to Asunción by an alien—so he'll probably be in jail soon."

"We'll fix it," Margerie says.

"I'm getting a dial tone at the COE. I think they might be okay," Dan adds.

Jeremy says, "I'm calling the police. They've got me on hold. For fuck's sake . . ."

Rollo clears his throat. "Before the cavalry arrives . . ."

"Hey, we are the cavalry!" Luca interrupts.

Rollo smiles to show a mouth full of extrasharp teeth and rolls his pretty pink eyes. "Before the *rest* of the cavalry arrives, I just wanted to thank y'all for the rescue."

Charlie just grunts. "Course, man. You might look like a gigantic roided-out bottle of Pepto-Bismol, but that's what you do for family."

"Though truth be told," Luca adds, "we were actually coming to kick your ass for doing . . . stuff to our baby sister."

"I'm older than you," I sigh.

Roland gives my waist a gentle tug, but with his newfound muscle mass, I topple against his side. "Sorry," he whispers to me quietly before pitching his voice louder to the others. "I turned into a monster overnight. I don't think kicking my ass is gonna go the way you hoped." He exhales fire through his nostrils and tries to run his hand back through is hair, only to hit horn first.

I elbow him in the gut, but he's not paying me any attention. Instead his gaze is trained on the horizon. "What the . . ."

I look up and see a distant point on the horizon start to get closer and closer. It's not a bird, it's not a plane, it's . . . I gulp hard and clutch my sword tighter. "That's not one of the bad guys, is it?"

"No . . . I think it's . . . the good guy."

"The good guy? Who?"

Roland huffs through his nostrils and squeezes me more tightly against his chest, and we both watch as, seconds later, a Forty-Eight Champion I've only seen one other time in person lands only twenty feet from us.

"What the fuck?" I blink in the sight of Taranis's surprised face, and I don't feel any of the nerves that I should. After all, why would I? He's now only the *second*-best-looking male on planet Earth. He glances between me and Rollo with eyes that aren't pink or sparkly but boring, even if they are purple.

"Wyvern?" he says, voice cracking. My brothers are filming him, Luca approaching way, way too close. Taranis's skin crackles with electricity that shoots out at Luca when he gets within touching distance of Taranis and knocks Luca onto his butt.

Rollo grunts. "Something like that."

Taranis scoffs again. "The fuck happened to you?"

"I found what I'd been looking for." He looks down at me, and I blush.

"Are you high? Is this some acid trip? What the fuck does that mean?" Taranis throws his arms out to the sides and runs a hand over his hair. His jaw clenches, and his uniform glistens. He looks incensed. I giggle.

Margerie crosses her arms over her chest. "It means he fell in love, you idiot."

Taranis turns toward her, his skin crackling dangerously, and Margerie lifts her gun, pointing it straight at one of the most popular and powerful people on the planet. Charlie, of all people, grabs Margerie's arm and tugs her to his side.

"What the hell does love have to do with it?" Taranis says.

"Everything," Rollo answers softly, looking down at my face as if I'm the only person in the world. "Only everything."

Epilogue

Roland

"You're sure about this?"

"Oh my gosh, for the last time, yes. Yes. It's been three weeks. I'm not waiting anymore. Plus, we've done it once like this already."

"But I didn't know then . . . and wasn't . . . paying attention . . . and things have happened since. I think there's, like . . . it's gotten bigger," I huff finally, gesturing down at my pants like an imbecile.

My threat seems to have the opposite effect. Her eyes get big and drop to my crotch. She swallows audibly. *Giddily.* "Really?"

"That's not supposed to be an incentive. I could hurt you . . ."

"And if you hurt me, we'll stop . . ." The way she's squirming in her leggings isn't helping. It isn't helping at all.

Since I reverted, I've noticed strange things about myself. Not strange because they're new; they're not. I remember them from my life on Tratharine, but I'm using them in entirely different ways now that I've reached full maturity and now that I'm here on Earth with the woman I traveled the cosmos to find.

For example, my enhanced sense of smell. My Tratharine leaders would have expected me to use this power to hunt down prominent humans and crush them . . . but I'd rather use it to breathe in the smell of her *there*. She smells fucking incredible. She squirms even more, standing behind the couch looking at me with too much hope and desire to let down either.

I give her a slow nod. "Come here."

She sucks in a breath, but her eyes sparkle damn near more brightly than mine. She twists her hands together and takes short steps until she's standing in front of me in front of the couch. Her hair is a billowy cloud around her face, so many different shades of brown. I learned recently that she dyes it to look like that, and I find the whole damn thing fascinating.

"You're really pretty," I whisper as I cup her face. I've gotten better at using my hands over these past three weeks. Three weeks of utter fucking chaos after my new makeover.

The SDD and the COE and even the VNA have all demanded interviews and tests—all of which I've declined. I don't need anyone knowing who doesn't need to know that it wasn't an accident, or an inevitability, but meeting Nessa that changed my life. Don't need that heat falling onto her shoulders.

Emily happily kept her data to herself, and Mr. Singkham exchanged his silence for a vow from Emily that she wouldn't inject him with a cocktail of infections at his next physical. The weapon remains in our possession too. Everyone thought it was a spare helicopter part that Nessa was keeping for sentimental value. No one knew that she could light it on fire with her touch, or that I could either. I could lift it after she unlocked it.

Nessa asked me plenty of questions about it and about my childhood. I shared all the answers with her that I could . . . except for the fact that my childhood actually spanned three times as many Earth years on Tratharine as it would have here, subject to this planet's gravity. But I wasn't about to tell Nessa that, in Earth years, I'm actually *not* twenty-nine but over forty. We have enough to work through as is. Including . . . how I am physically going to make this work.

Nessa starts to move past me toward the couch, but I stop her, hooking two fingers into the collar of her shirt. "You want to keep this, or should I tear it?"

Her pupils dilate and the smell intensifies, all perfection and salt and sweet, sweet rain. "I'll take it off."

"Good girl."

"Everything?" she whimpers as soon as she's pulled her T-shirt off over her head. It's a T-shirt with my monstrous face on it that's being sold at ridiculous prices by the COE merch shop and that Nessa thinks is hilarious. I'd much prefer it shredded on the floor. Or incinerated.

"Anything you wanna keep. Stop," I tell her when she's naked in front of me and turning toward the couch. Her skin is so damn smooth. I don't know how she got so smooth. Little scars, stretch marks, a little jiggle in her ass and below her belly button. Full tits. All of it so damn . . . smooth.

"What?" she says, sounding as vulnerable as she looks, so small now below me.

"Just admiring the angle."

"What angle?"

My gaze devours her. "All of them."

She bites her bottom lip, and blood flowers in her skin. Her brown cheeks glitter.

My voice cracks. "Turn to face me. Unbuckle my belt." The design team has been having a goddamn field day trying to come up with an entirely new uniform—not to mention new clothes—to fit me. These pants I hate less than some of their other ideas, as they are a simple black pant that leaves room for my cock and doesn't hug too tightly around my thighs and ass *and* has a slit up the back ankle to make space for the fact that my legs are now shaped like some unholy mix of a devil's and a werewolf's. Vanessa doesn't seem to mind. She's actually taking this so easily, I worry a little that there's something deranged about her, but I damn sure am not gonna suggest she fix it. She's mine. And she's perfect.

"Fuck," I hiss. Vanessa's fingers graze the space between my hip bones as she undoes the button and pulls the zipper down, my cock bulging at the seam.

"Do you want them off?" she asks, completely naked, vulnerable everywhere. For me. Only me.

"Yes," I growl. "Go slow."

So slowly I could cry, she drags my pants down my legs. I lift one foot and then the other and let her take them down past my talons until she's sitting on the edge of the couch right in front of my cock. She licks her lips, and I nearly abandon all restraint and shove my rising erection into the back of her throat until she gags. Nearly.

Half-choked, I grunt, "Kneel on the couch for me." My hand covering my cock, I exhale deeply. "Want you to see what you're working with, baby."

"Okay," she says, but I can barely hear her, her voice is so strained.

I hesitate to show her. Had myself checked over a dozen times by Dr. Larsen just to make sure everything would be okay. She gave her stamp of approval for Vanessa and I to engage in . . . activities, but it's a lot.

"Do you trust me?" she whispers.

I blink down at her, surprised by the question. "Of course."

"Then don't hide from me." Her hand strokes up my naked hip, palm fitting above the bulging muscle in my thigh. I'm too fucking bulky, too goddamn big for her human shape.

"Don't know what I did to deserve you. I love you. Remember that when you see it." I drop my hands.

Her pupils are fully blown as she watches my cock bob toward her face. For a moment, there's only silence between us, which I take as a win. At least she doesn't scream.

My cock, which once had brown skin covering a veiny shaft, is now the girth of a goddamn Coke bottle, as long as her forearm and dark red. Veins zigzag down my erection, leading to a purple head that flares at the base before sharpening to a curved tip. And if all that weren't terrifying enough, in the past three weeks since my reversion has settled, I've developed strange bumps all along the underside of my dick, smooth to the touch . . . and hard until I come and they . . . *elongate.*

"What are . . ." She swallows, her voice breaking as she drags a single finger up the ridges on the underside of my cock.

I stroke my claws back through her hair, wanting to pull her forward but wanting her to find her own way more. "They don't hurt. The width will . . . take some work if you really want me to try . . . but it's what happens after I come that I'm worried about."

"You've been jacking off?"

She sounds almost hurt. I scrape my claws along her scalp and watch as her eyelids flutter blissfully. "For medical reasons. You've been jacking off, too, if you haven't forgotten."

"Only because you wanted to watch me."

I grin, showing her a mouth studded in fangs that she doesn't cower from even a little. "I did. I do. Why don't you lie back and . . ."

"No. I want this." She licks her lips and strokes my length again with her full fist before I can stop her. Shit, that's a lie. I don't try to stop her at all. My head rolls on my neck, and I just fucking enjoy the slow ministrations of her fingertips across my erection, over the weird-as-shit head, back down the even weirder bumps below.

And then that rumbling picks up in my chest, like a mythological dragon's purr, and her scent grows stronger, and she slams her knees together, and she whimpers around the head of my cock as she feeds it into her mouth, sucking the tip.

"I want you so damn bad, Nessa." I grab her by the hair and pull her back so that her lips are only just grazing the curved head of my cock. Her eyes flutter, and I wait for her to look up at me. "But you have to know." My chest is heaving. "When I come, the beads on the bottom will expand and fill you all the way up."

She chokes, topples onto her hip on the couch, and looks up at me with wide eyes. "Like a *knot?*" she blurts.

"I don't know what that is."

Her blush could singe even me as she looks away and stutters, "I just . . . It's something . . . I read it in a romance . . . book . . . once. I just . . . I'm okay with it." She's squeaking again, her back buried between the pillows, her knees up by her chest but awkwardly splayed. She tries to pull them back together, but I reach forward and hold her legs apart. I inhale deep and hold it, the scent of her absolutely fucking mesmerizing. Standing above her, I lower to my knees on the couch between her parted legs and leave my dick bobbing between us. My claws trail lightly down the outsides of her thighs.

"You're sure?"

"Yes," she squeaks so high, it's not even a word, but I'll take it.

Chuckling, I wrap my dark pink hand around her thin, brown neck. I press up, forming a necklace that covers her throat. I come down on her hard after that, my lips to hers. I nip at first, slow and then faster, encouraged by the sounds she makes. Her back is flush to the couch seats. Her knees are cocked at ninety-degree angles, shoved up by her armpits. She's so damn flexible. I can bend her into any shape I want.

"Breathe, baby."

She gasps, but she's struggling. I drag my hand from her neck to her chest. "Breathe."

She smiles as she starts to get her breath under control and then starts to laugh. "I should be embarrassed . . ."

I shake my head. "What did I tell you about that?"

"I know. I just was going to say . . . I'm not."

"That's my girl." I kiss the tip of her nose.

"I'm just not used to this, Rollo."

"Getting fucked by a guy who looks like the devil who's about to fill you with his cum? Because, baby, I hate to break it to you, I know that too."

"Oh my God, yes. But it's not . . . not just that . . ." Her breathing's picked up again, and I have to shush her twice before she can continue.

When she does, I plant two small kisses on her lips, pleased that her injuries have fully healed and have only left behind the smallest scars.

"Then what is it?" I exhale against her lips.

"I'm just *so* in love with you."

My voice hitches. I can't wait. I place my massive erection at her entrance and push forward. I need no additional lubrication. She's a mess already, and the head of my cock slides into her easily. The rest, though, takes work.

We rock against each other for the better part of twenty minutes, groping and pawing at each other. Kissing until my jaw aches and panting until she runs out of breath and we have to stop once, and then again for a longer period.

"I've told you before, and I'll say it again. You're gonna be the death of me, Nessa," I breathe against her ear as my cock finally slides home inside of her body. Hip to hip, pubic bone to pubic bone.

Her eyes are fluttering; she's shaking all the way through. I hold her legs against me, trying to support their weight. She's simultaneously boneless and crazed. Her nails are scoring my back, heels kicking against my ass every time I thrust into her farther. Her fingers comb through my hair, finding my horns and holding on to them at the roots like if she doesn't, she'll fly away.

"Not if I die first."

"You're never going to die," I growl, anger causing the tips of my horns to blaze bright with flame. She releases their base on a giggle. I smile in return, watching the light from my horns as it turns the fan of her hair from medium brown to reddish hues. "I'd light the world ablaze first."

"Don't . . . do . . . that. Just fuck me."

"I can do that." I can definitely do that.

My hips pick up speed, and I start to make the swing of my thrusts a little longer. "Oh my God!" she screams, and without warning, her hand reaches above her head to stabilize herself on the arm of the couch, and she comes all over me.

The slick of her cunt feels so good, it's almost unbearable. "Oh fuck . . ."

She's writhing under me, shouting something about the angle of the ridges or the bumps inside of her and the width of my cock and how she fucking loves the way I feel inside her. And how much she loves me.

"I'm not gonna make it. I'm gonna . . ." I come like a goddamn amateur.

"I can feel . . . the bumps . . ." Her lips are parted in a drunken smile. There's a faint sheen of sweat covering every inch of her.

I make it my destiny in this moment to lick her body clean, starting with her jaw, her neck, her collar bones. On a feral growl, I pull back and try to slip out of her, but she winces.

"It's the knots . . . They're swelling. Just stay," she whispers, her chest shaking as she edges toward the crest of another orgasm, even though I've stayed as still as I can, just like she asked.

"You done research on this shit or something?" I bark into her throat, sounding every bit the demon that I feel, ravaging a virgin sacrifice on the altar.

"Or something," she exhales.

"It hurt?"

"There's pressure, but it feels amazing. I think if you touch . . . my clit . . . I might . . ."

I don't hesitate but pull up as much as I can to squeeze my fingers between us. I manage to get my thumb pressed lightly to her swollen, sensitive skin and flick it gently without cutting her. I watch her head toss and turn while my cock continues emptying into her. Last time I tested this, it took three minutes for my body to fully finish coming. But inside her, where my cock is at home, I could live here for hours. As long as she'll let me.

"Oh Rollo, fuck!" The squeeze of her cunt around my slowly softening erection is too much. I feel my balls clench up against my body and my thighs get rock hard as my cock paints her insides in a surprising rush.

"This is incredible," she whispers, her eyes half-mast.

"This is insane that you're okay with all this." Panting, I very carefully squeeze my giant ass on the tiny couch in front of her without separating our bodies. My muscles sag and I wait to be able to pull my cock out of her fully.

I've nearly got her smothered into the pillows, and she doesn't seem to mind. Not just that—she seems pleased to be here with me. And that pleasure is worth fighting for against anything. I kiss her softly.

"You're my hero," I whisper.

She smiles. "And you're my key. I feel like I was strong before I met you, but you unlocked the cage and threw the lid wide open. I might have made you you," she says, glancing up at my horns, "but you also made me me."

"I fucking love you."

"I love you too, Wyvern, though I'm pretty sure we'll need a rebrand to go with your new look. A new uniform that matches pink too."

I huff. "I'm not pink. I'm red."

"You are definitely pink. As pink as cotton candy."

I grin into her lips and kiss her again with every feeling I have for her bottled in my chest and launched like a rocket into the abyss. "Fine. I'm pink. And you can call me whatever you like."

She cups my jaw, strokes her fingers up my cheeks, over my forehead to my horns. She grips them hard and yanks my head down to hers savagely in a way that's all brand-new for her and that I fucking adore. When she pulls back, my hips buck, finally ready to slip free of her heat and perhaps—most definitely—begin again, but first . . .

I reach under the couch for a box that feels way too small in my massive fingers.

We both moan in unison, and she says on a fluttering breath, "You can call *me* whatever you like."

"I was hoping you'd say that." I press the box against her chest, waiting for her fingers to curl around it. "Because I'd like to call you *wife*."

She blinks at me, startled, and then looks at the box, disoriented. I open it for her, showing her the pink sapphire within, and she shrieks, "You did not!"

"We're twenty-two dates in, baby."

"No, we are not!" She swats me on the arm, but she takes the box from me regardless, removes the ring, slides it onto her finger, tosses the box over her shoulder, and then kisses me ferociously.

"Close enough," I laugh between kisses. "Is that a yes?"

"Yes. It's a yes. It's an absolutely fucking yes." Her eyes are damp. I kiss the space between them. She grabs my horns, maneuvers my mouth to meet hers, and kisses me so, so sweetly.

"I love you," she says.

I come unhinged.

"Good," I snarl into her neck, and to the whisper of each other's desperate breaths, we begin anew.

ABOUT THE AUTHOR

Elizabeth Stephens is the author of *Dark City Omega* and *Shadowlands Omega* in the Beasts of Gatamora series. She has been living in a fantasy world since she wrote her first sci-fi story when she was eleven, and she still often gets lost in places that don't exist. With a growing backlist of over fifteen titles, her work is best known for its diverse casts, tough heroines, wacky world-building, and villains—or beasts—who get the girl in guaranteed happily-ever-afters. When she isn't tip-tap-typing away, you might find her enjoying the outdoors of the Pacific Northwest or traveling and making adventures of her own with her husband, tiny humans, and doggo, King Louis. For more information, visit www.booksbyelizabeth.com.